P. B.

**Praise for *New York Times* bestselling author
Heather Graham**

"*Home in Time for Christmas* is one of th[...]
that really touches y[...]
immediately want t[...]
whole experience…[...]
miracles. Don't miss[...]
of holiday smiles an[...]
reread every Christmas season."

—*Bookreporter*

"One of the most heartwarming novels I have
read in a very long time."
—*Romance Readers Connection* on
Home in Time for Christmas

"It's hard not to believe in the magic of
Christmas, especially when Graham spins a tale
of healing, renewal, hope and light… You'll find
your first must-read holiday tale of the season
right here."
—*RT Reviews* on *An Angel for Christmas*

"There is an abundance of thrills and suspense
throughout the story with a very 'warm and
fuzzy' ending."
—*Fresh Fiction* on *An Angel for Christmas*

"An incredible storyteller."
—*Los Angeles Daily News*

"Heather Graham knows what readers want."
—*Publishers Weekly*

New York Times and *USA TODAY* bestselling author **Heather Graham** has written more than a hundred novels, many of which have been featured by the Doubleday Book Club and the Literary Guild. An avid scuba diver, ballroom dancer and mother of five, she still enjoys her South Florida home, but loves to travel as well, from locations such as Cairo, Egypt, to the Florida Keys. Reading, however, is the pastime she still loves best, and she is a member of many writing groups. She's a winner of the Romance Writers of America's Lifetime Achievement Award and the Thriller Writers' Silver Bullet. She is an active member of International Thriller Writers and Mystery Writers of America, and also the founder of The Slush Pile Players, an author band and theatrical group. Heather annually hosts the Writers for New Orleans conference to benefit both the city, which is near and dear to her heart, and various other causes, and she hosts a ball each year at the RT Booklover's Convention to benefit pediatric AIDS foundations.

For more information, check out her website, eheathergraham.com. You can also find Heather on Facebook.

New York Times Bestselling Author

HEATHER GRAHAM

Home in Time for Christmas
and
An Angel for Christmas

Recycling programs
for this product may
not exist in your area.

ISBN 13: 978-0-373-60665-8

Home in Time for Christmas and An Angel for Christmas

Copyright © 2014 Harlequin Books S.A.

The publisher acknowledges the copyright holder
of the individual works as follows:

Home in Time for Christmas
Copyright © 2009 by Heather Graham Pozzessere

An Angel for Christmas
Copyright © 2011 by Heather Graham Pozzessere

www.Harlequin.com

Printed in U.S.A.

CONTENTS

HOME IN TIME
FOR CHRISTMAS

For Aaron Priest, Lucy Childs,
Lisa Erbach Vance, Nicole Kennedy
and John Richmond,
with all the very best wishes for the season,
however it may be celebrated!

Prologue
A Winter's Day

Perhaps it was fitting that it should be such a cold and bitter, yet stunning, day.

Jake Mallory took a minute to appreciate the awesome glory of the morning. The heavens were an extravagant shade of blue. Light puffs of soft white clouds were slipping by. The sun, a golden orb, was en route to a high point in the sky as the early hours of the morning defied the darkness of the passing night.

It was, indeed, a beautiful day.

A fine day to die.

They had all known it, known they might be called upon to die, all of them who agreed that the colonies must break from Mother Britain. All those who had set pen to paper and signed the Declaration of Independence. All those who had led the armies. All those who had fought.

And spied.

Not that spying had actually been his intent. He was a soldier. Well, he hadn't exactly wanted to be a soldier, either. Such an enterprise had not been his intent in life. He was a newspaperman—or, at least, that was what he *had* intended to be. Writing was his passion. His home was the small town of Gloucester, but even there, as in all the surrounding towns, the talk had been about politics. About breaking away. Then, there had been the Boston Tea Party.

Blood had been spilled.

He believed deeply in the freedom and equality of man. That and, of course, the editorials he had written regarding the need for the colonies to break free, were what had brought him to stand here today. In the taverns of Boston he had gotten to know many a man handy with a pamphlet, such as John Adams, who in turn had introduced him to another John—Hancock. He had become involved with men to whom the written word was a weapon. And handling such a weapon…

Had led to his carrying a different kind of weapon. And—quite sadly, really—to getting caught.

Ah, there was the rub. Getting caught. Men far too old to be soldiers knew that they would hang if captured by the British, if their cause failed.

So here he was today.

Upon the scaffold.

Truly, such a deplorable state of affairs.

Ah, well. He had written well, and sewn rampant

seeds of rebellion. He had taken to the field, running missions; he had picked up a gun, as well. He was guilty of sedition, so they said. Words on paper could shout loudly, and his had been heard, far and wide.

There was a precedent for his death. He wouldn't be the first to die here, hanged for his loyalty to a fledgling nation. Nathan Hale had died just a few months back. Hale had died heroically. Jake could only hope now that he could do the same.

Looking at the sky, one could almost pray for a miracle. There was such awe and wonder in the beauty of the sky. But there weren't going to be any miracles. The British were firmly entrenched in the city. No sudden horde of rebels was suddenly going to break through the ranks of Lobsterbacks and save him. Nor was it likely that Hempton, the British major in charge of his fate, would find any way to suggest that they pardon their captive for the holiday.

The holiday…

It was almost Christmas.

Well, he was a God-fearing man, so maybe that was a good thing. He didn't blame God for his fate. Things were what they were. It was a war, perhaps an ill-advised one, considering the might and power of the British war machine and the truly pathetic manpower and munitions of the Patriots. It was being fought on dreams and ideals. This morning, *especially* this morning, he had to keep believing in the dream. He had been in over his head, cast into a desperate position, and he had chosen the high road.

Of course, he'd be a liar if he didn't admit that it was just a wee bit difficult not to regret that choice right now.

"Sorry!" Captain Tim Reginald said to him. The British officer charged with the duty of slipping the noose around his neck had chafed his cheek with the coarse rope. He swallowed hard, his Adam's apple bobbing. Tim was a good enough fellow; they'd played cards together and shared a few drinks during the last days. He was young enough himself, a true Brit, following the way of the British army as his family would have him do. He was a man willing enough to fight for king and country, strong, intelligent and brave.

But executions were not his forte.

"Quite all right, good friend," Jake said.

Poor Tim. A good man, yes. War was so strange. Men became enemies when they did not know one another. If he and Tim did not give their hearts, souls and loyalties to different drummers, they might have been good friends in truth.

It almost looked as if Tim would give way to tears. Ah, a good British officer could never do so. "Friend," he said kindly to Tim, "don't fear. I do not hold you responsible for my impending demise, nor does God above."

Tim swallowed hard, just appearing more ill.

He could hear the Anglican minister droning on in prayer, advising him to pray, as well.

Jake prayed.

Jake did not pray for a miracle.

He did not waste prayers on what could not be. *God helped those who helped themselves.*

Therefore, there was just one prayer to make.

Dear God, do not let me falter; let me be the best man I am able in this moment. May it be quick; may I

not dangle at the end of this rope. May I not cry out,
but die with dignity in thy Grace!

As if in answer to his prayer, Major Hempton strode
center on the scaffold. A hush fell over the crowd. Oh,
and there was a crowd. Church bells pealed because
it was almost Christmas, and folks should have been
home cooking and thanking the good Lord for their
loved ones, but hell, Christmas or no, a good hanging
was a good hanging.

And in the sea of faces before him, there were
those who cried—blessed, lovely women with their
tearstained faces, those who rued his fate. Those who
believed in the sovereign rights of America, and, of
course, there were also those who thought he deserved
his fate as a traitor against the mother country.

Hempton was a puffed-up peacock of a man. His
position in the army had been bought through family
ties. He did well enough making the occupied city of
New York bow to its knees; he could drink well and
lock his jaw in silence when he realized his gambling
losses, but he was not the kind of man that the British
military hierarchy wanted in the field.

"Good people of New York!" Hempton announced.
"You see before you a gift for this Christmas season. A
traitor! A man who would cast you into years of want
and death and hardship! You out there who might think
to make such a treacherous move against your mother
country and the goodness of King George, beware!
This is the fate that will meet all traitors!"

Really, it did help that Hempton was just a pomp-
ous ass. He was little, and therefore, wore very high
boots. He was balding, so he took elaborate care with
his wigs. He had a huge gut from overindulgence in

food and wine, and thus truly gave the impression of a lobster in his red uniform. At least his appearance made for a last amusement Jake could enjoy on earth.

Trying for dramatic effect, Hempton swung around. "Any last words of regret, traitor?" he demanded.

"I regret that I failed my country, the United States of America," he said. "I regret that I leave behind my family and good friends, and the future of freedom that *will be* in this great land!"

I leave behind family....

Suddenly, to his astonishment and dismay, his "family," his adopted sister, was there before him.

Serena.

Sweet Serena, the little girl he had protected so fiercely ever since she'd lost her parents when they were young, and even more fiercely now that he'd lost his own. Little girl grown up now, furious, and facing the enemy. Serena, with her beautiful, wide, iridescent blue eyes. Her hair, like a raven's wing.

But she couldn't be there. Home was far away. Far up the coast, in Gloucester.

Someone had to get her out of here before she infuriated the wrong person. Good God, the British couldn't hang a woman! Could they? This was war. Atrocities had occurred. No, no, no...

Stay silent, Serena, he begged in silence.

"Oaf! Traitor!" Hempton stuttered out. Apparently, he had no ready argument.

Oh, dear God, Jake thought, *I prayed for help to die well, and you have brought this woman who is the closest I have to kin left in the world to see the spectacle of my jerking limbs and dangling feet....*

But she couldn't be there, she couldn't; word

couldn't possibly have reached her in time for her to
make the journey to New York, it was impossible.

Not impossible. She was there.

"You are the oaf, sir!" she shouted to Hempton.
"You would kill a man as Christmas comes?" Dear
God, but that sweet voice of hers which could resound
with such charming laughter could also peal out with
the resounding sharp clarity of a bell.

He winced. She would get herself arrested. And
with such a man as Hempton, he sincerely feared even
a woman could ride a gallows and meet a hangman's
noose.

"Get it over with quickly, I beg of you!" he said
quietly to Tim.

But Tim, like the rest of the throng—including
Hempton—seemed to be caught up in the spell created by the ringing tones of Serena's mockery. Hempton's lips were puffing, but now he really seemed to
be at a loss for words.

"Let goodness be, blessed be, let crimes against the
heavens be not against man!" she cried out. She raised
her arms. And she dropped rose petals.

Rose petals. In the middle of winter. Against the
white of snow still upon the ground, and the crystal-
blue of the morning. Rose petals, like blood drops on
the snow.

"Let Christmas be!" she cried out. "Christmas, and
God's grace on man, and woe to the enemies of love
and peace. Shame on those who forget that we come
into a season of love and forgiveness. What fool of a
mortal fails to honor the likes of Christ, or those who
teach us how to live in kindness and charity with our
fellow men?"

The crowd was beginning to stir. There was something about the passion in her voice, and the sweetness. Those who wanted a spectacle of pain and death were shamed.

Hempton found his voice. "Hang him!" he shouted to Tim.

And Tim indeed looked as if he would cry.

"For the love of God, Timothy, now!" Jake agreed. "Please, my friend, I beg you. Now, before my sister meets the wrath of that wretched oaf, as well."

Tim understood. His eyes were filled with the agony of his duty.

The noose was tightened. Jake looked at Serena. "I love you, dearest sister, sweetest friend. Go home!" he whispered. She shouldn't have seen him; she never should have been here. When had she come to New York? It was impossible for her to be *here*.

But he could see her; she was there.

Crystal-blue eyes were upon his. "I love you," she mouthed in turn. "And we will both come home for Christmas."

There was a drumroll. Tim whispered with tears in his voice, "God forgive me!"

And he pulled the lever, and the trapdoor beneath Jake's feet was sprung.

He fell....

And fell and fell....

He felt no pain.

Only the rush of the wind.

He saw the blue sky.

Then, at first, it seemed that Serena disappeared. Disappeared into a fine mist with only her smile seeming to linger as a vision in his heart.

Then, he felt a rose petal against his cheek. The sky was filled with falling rose petals.

A bloodred caress in the midst of a beautiful and snow-white day.

Chapter 1
Another Winter's Day

Christmas.

Ho, ho, ho. Merry, merry.

Yeah, *Merry Christmas*.

The road was a slip and slide.

Peace on earth.

Even when she had left New York City that morning, Melody Tarleton thought, people were practically trampling one another to get into Macy's, make the next subway or beat everyone else out for one of the cabs slip-sliding all over the street. The stores were advertising that they were open Christmas Eve and some even on Christmas morning, just so that the jerks who couldn't remember to buy gifts all year long could rush out last minute and buy some stupid thing that no one would really want anyway. But they'd realize they were going to grandma's for dinner, and hadn't even thought to buy the woman who had loved them their whole lives so much as a bouquet of flowers. Got to keep stores open for that. And God forbid, someone should forget they had another little niece or nephew. The children of the world definitely needed more stupid plastic toys! And, surely, the forgotten infant needed another bib that was embroidered with Spit Happens! or some other inane sentiment.

The car started to spin. Melody gripped the wheel and took her foot off the gas. It righted itself.

She let out a sigh of relief, and then winced. What in God's name was the matter with her?

What had become of her usual joy of the holiday season? She wished that her mood would lighten, and that she would pay heed to a few of the Christmas carols resounding from her car-stereo system. She had a million things for which she should be thankful; healthy, living parents who loved her, a wonderful brother who was just about her best friend now—even though they had fought wretchedly growing up. She loved what she did for a living....

Ah, there was the problem!

Mark.

In a few days, he would be there. Her mother had asked him to come for Christmas. Which, of course, he had expected. He wasn't taking a thing that she said seriously.

I can't do it, Mark. I can't marry you, or be engaged to you. I can't even be your girlfriend. I thought I knew you, but then you began to talk about our future. You're a fine man, just not for me.

Well, she had known him. Most of her life. They'd

gone to middle school and high school together, gone off to different colleges, and then met again at a book fair. It had seemed perfect at first; they'd been old friends, reconnecting. She drew pictures, he wrote words. They both loved illustrated novels. They'd both hailed from Gloucester, and moved to New York. So much to talk about, so much of the past to relive!

And they were friends. She was so happy to be his friend.

Then they'd been more. She thought she could see a wonderful future with him until he shared what he saw for the two of them.

She was just amazed at his vision of the future. He would take care of her. She wouldn't work—oh, well, of course, she could draw little pictures for their children. They'd have ten.

It was so odd how things had changed. She'd found him charming and attractive.

And now...

She was afraid of mistletoe.

There was no way out. As it had become clear that they were each seeking a different future, and the harder she struggled to escape, the more he had set the tethers upon her, it had all happened too late to salvage Christmas.

Her mother had already given him the invitation to come up. So, for Christmas, he'd keep insisting that she loved him and didn't understand that he just loved her and wanted the world for her. She'd be avoiding him, and no one would understand.

Ho, ho, ho. It was going to be great.

Stop feeling sorry for yourself.

So, okay, Mark was the one with the publisher and

he would probably see that she was fired off the project she had been hired to work on with him.

No, she had a contract.

Contracts could be broken.

Good God, she wasn't going to lead a man on because of a contract!

She believed in herself. Even if he didn't. And that was the point.

She'd just start pounding the pavement all over again if need be.

Think positive.

Christmas had always been her favorite time of year, maybe because her folks had loved the holiday so very much. Her mom went all out. Massive, overstuffed stockings for the entire family and whatever friends happened to be with them. A tree that was so heavily decorated, it almost sank into the floor. House lights that might have been a cause of global warming—the only non-earth-friendly concession her mother ever made.

Be thankful for my family, she told herself.

And she was really.

Oh, Lord, she would have to face her father. He was such a good soul. He'd be confused at first when she tried to explain what had happened with Mark— that she didn't want a relationship in which she was basically *owned*. He wouldn't understand a man like Mark—actually, she wasn't sure many people would. Mark gave new meaning to old-fashioned.

Her parents had met in college. Her mom had become a nurse, and her dad had become a professor. They had shared child rearing. In this day and age, she thought, they were truly adorable. Somehow, through thick and thin, they had made marriage a two-way street.

There—she could blame it on her folks. She just wanted the same kind of love and respect in a relationship. Support and belief. It really wasn't a dream—she had seen it work.

Okay, so her mother often shook her head over her father, but she did it with affection. "He's tinkering in his office," she would say, and roll her eyes. Her dad had been a professor at Worcester Poly-Tech once, and he was still always trying to tweak an old invention— or master a new one. Puffs of smoke arose from the building out back upon occasion, but he'd never burned anything down. And despite her protests to the contrary, Melody knew that this was exactly the man her mother had fallen in love with all those years ago.

Oh, her mother would hate the news of her relationship with Mark. Mona would be all indignant when she tried to explain the truth. How dare he think he was better than she was, or more worthy of expressing creativity! Or, it could be worse. Her mother believed that she came from a long line of mystics, or healers. She could trace her family back to Saxon England, and she was convinced that she could grow herbs and create medicinal drinks that actually had magical strength. She just might decide that Mark could imbibe enough herbal tea laced with God-knew-exactly-what that he would see the error of his ways.

The thought made her groan aloud.

Mark! she thought, feeling ill, *don't you see, we can't make it. And trying to pretend that everything is all right just because it's Christmas is not going to work.*

And if all that wasn't enough stress for this trip

home, there was her brother. As much as she loved her brother, Keith…

God only knew who or *what* he'd have found to come home with him.

Though he'd never played football, Keith looked like a fullback. He was tall, charming, and very good-looking, but he was their father in all aspects of geek. He was attending his father's alma mater, learning electronics and physics and so on, and when he wasn't busy studying, he was finding someone or some creature who needed help.

One year, he'd brought home a stripper.

Another year, it had been a wounded raccoon.

He had a great heart. She loved him to death.

She just hoped that they wouldn't have to share Christmas with Mark and a stripper.

Hmm. Maybe that wouldn't be such a bad thing….

No, it would probably be another animal this year. Like the blind Persian cat he had found last year, the basset with the little roller now to replace the hind legs a driver had crushed the year before, or Jimmy, the big old sheepdog mix he had found three years ago, starved and left to die in a crate on a trash pile. If Keith hadn't found a wounded animal, he would decide that Melody *was* one. Maybe, she was. Human beings were, after all, animals. Usually, it was events like Christmas that lifted man above the beasts.

Christmas. How she had once loved it. How she dreaded it now. And this feeling of dread was wrong, so wrong! Because no matter how uncomfortable the festivities proved to be for her, she *had* to remember that it was Christmas.

She frowned suddenly, slowing the car. The day

had been bright and beautiful, despite the ice on the ground and roads. But out of the blue, there was suddenly darkness, as if a cloud had passed the sun. The darkest cloud ever known to man.

And in the midst of it…

Good God, there was a figure in the middle of the road, a dark form….

Melody slammed hard on the brakes, even though she knew better. There was just so much ice on the road. Before the car fishtailed, she saw the figure more fully in the glare of her headlights.

It was a man.

A man dressed as if he were a refugee from the past. He was hatless in the snow, and wearing a white muslin shirt and tight-fitting pants. Tall black boots. He wasn't in a wig, but his long dark hair was queued back. He was staring at her with pure amazement.

As if the idiot had never seen a car before.

Then, the car started to spin. She had hit black ice. She knew better than to try to stop the way she had. But hell, it had been that, or…

She felt a bump; she'd hit the figure.

Hopefully not as badly as she would have, had she not tried so hard to stop!

She came to a halt against a snowbank. Incredibly, her air bag did not go off. Her lights streamed against the gray color the day had become and the snow, coming down now in a fresh swirling round of flurries. Stunned, she sat still for long seconds, thanking God that she was alive.

Then she remembered the soft thumping sound against the car. She tried to open her door, but she was against the snowbank. She maneuvered across the car to the passenger side and managed to get out.

He was there, lying in the snow. He was clad only in eighteenth-century attire, often enough seen around Salem, but ridiculous in this weather. His shirt and pants were simple cotton, no barrier against the bitter cold, though, at the least, his knee-high boots would keep his feet warm. He must have been freezing.

Her initial reaction was panic. She had just struck down a man in the snow.

She flew to his side, saw his chest rise and fall.

Oh, thank God, he was alive!

He was young…her age, maybe a year or two older, but he was under thirty, she was certain. His hair, somewhat frayed from what had been a neat queue.

At a loss in those first few seconds, her own heart thundering, she felt her second reaction kick in.

Anger!

What the hell had the idiot been doing standing in the middle of the road in a snowstorm?

Concern quickly replaced the anger. He was breathing, and she didn't see blood spewing from any part of his body, but had she…broken him?

She needed to dial 911. Fast. Get help.

She fled from the man back to the car, found her purse and cell phone on the front seat, and dialed. Nothing happened.

The No Signal information screen flashed on.

Swearing, she called her phone service a zillion names in a single breath, and tossed the phone back on the seat. She scrambled back to the man on the ground. Should she move him? She suddenly wished she'd taken some kind of first-aid class. If she moved him and he did have a broken limb, she could make it worse. What if his neck was broken? Moving him, she could finish him off!

As she knelt by him, the snow on the ground seeping through her leggings, the flurries coming fast and furious, he suddenly groaned.

"Oh," she breathed, looking down at him. "Hey, please. Sir, can you hear me, sir? What hurts? Oh, Lord, speak to me, please!"

The snow fell on the contours of his face and turned his hair white.

She might hurt him if she moved him, but if she didn't, he was going to freeze to death. Second problem. If she did move him, could she get him to the car? Was she capable? He was tall, she was certain— despite the fact that he was prone, he seemed awfully long. Also, it looked as if he was composed of pure muscle. That meant he'd be heavy. She'd never been that thrilled with her own figure, because, basically, there wasn't enough of it. She wasn't exactly a weakling, but she was a probably-too-slim hundred and ten pounds stretched out on a five-seven frame.

"All right, if I'm hurting you, I'm sorry," she said. "I have to try to get you into the car."

She stood, trying to figure it out. She'd have to grab him by the feet.

As she did so, she noted his boots were like nothing she had ever seen before. They were reproductions, she was sure, but they must have cost a mint—they had been singularly crafted and were sewn, sole to body, with leather strips meticulously threaded by hand.

Quit with worrying about his state of dress! she warned herself in a puffing silence. He was heavy.

She was barely managing to drag him a quarter inch a second. She could hear herself grunting and puffing in the cold air, and yet she was straining so hard that it seemed her muscles and lungs were on fire.

Then, suddenly, words in a deep, masculine and explosive tone sounded loudly against the stark landscape.

"Good woman! What on God's own earth are you doing to me?"

She dropped his ankles and stared at him, speechless. He was still stretched out, but sitting up, legs out in the snow, staring at her as if she had lost her mind.

"Oh, you're alive!" she gasped.

To her dismay, he appeared both surprised and puzzled. "Yes, yes, I am. I believe. It is cold, so I must assume this feeling means alive." He offered her a rueful and very puzzled grimace. "Excuse me, but…who are you, and where are we?"

She frowned. She didn't much mind the *who are you* part of the question, but the *where are we* was more than a bit disturbing.

"My name is Melody Tarleton. We're in the middle of the road, heading toward Gloucester. You ran out in front of me. I struck you with my car."

"Your car?" he said, truly puzzled.

She pointed. He tried to rise, staring at the car— *gaping* at the car, actually. Inwardly, she groaned. What? Was he taking this *reenactor* thing far too seriously?

"Yeah, yeah, my car. I hit you. I'm responsible, I'm so sorry, except you did run right out into the road. And that's insane, you know. Totally insane. What, are you crazy? There's black ice all over, with the temperature going up and down all the time."

He stared at her, still frowning, blinking furiously. He looked her up and down, noting her sleek wool coat with its fur-lined hood—now completely soaked and covered in melting flurries. He looked at her face, and then around him. Of course, other than her car against the snowbank, there was nothing to see but snow-covered trees.

"Please," he said with quiet dignity, "I don't understand. I swear to you that I have never seen such a conveyance. Or anyone that looks quite like you."

Anyone that looks like me? He had to be kidding. She studied him in return. His face was lean, well sculpted, and yet, in a way, he actually resembled Mark.

But he wasn't Mark, and she knew Mark had no family. He was just a very strange stranger she had just hit on the road.

"Look, did I break any of your bones?" she demanded.

"I don't think so," he said.

So what the hell was she supposed to do now? He had to be bruised and in pain. She couldn't leave him on the snow-laden, icy road.

Mark would have told her to get in the car as quickly as possible. He might have picked the guy up, but only to drop him at the nearest police station. If he'd been with her, he'd never let her try to help the man. He'd be instantly convinced the guy was a serial killer.

Mark wasn't with her.

And she made her own choices. And that, to her, was

important. She wasn't against accepting advice, but as far as her life went, she had to make her own choices.

So here, she had a choice.

What to do?

He didn't look like a serial killer. Then again, was there an actual *look?* Was there a stereotype, were they blond like Swedes, dark and romantic like Italians or Spaniards. *Did they dress up in colonial costume?*

"Let's get out of the snow," she said. She started walking. He followed her.

"You have no horses," he said.

"It's a car," she said. "It has an engine, a battery... pistons. I don't know, I'm not a mechanic, I have the oil checked and leave it with the Ford people."

"The Ford people?" he asked.

She gritted her teeth. "Stop it! Enough. You look great. I don't own or manage any of the historical museums around here. You don't need to keep up the act."

He stopped short, looking at her with indignation again. He stood very straight, and he was handsome and imposing, like a hero out of an adventure book. "My dear young woman, I assure you, I am not performing in any manner. I don't know where I am, nor do I understand this fascinating mode of transportation you refer to as a car. I..." His voice trailed off. He staggered forward, his knees buckling. She caught him, and he regained some of his strength, coming back to a full stand, but still leaning upon her. "I'm so sorry," he said.

If he was acting, his work was worthy of an Academy Award. Melody was afraid she had managed to give him a good clip to the head with the front bumper, and that he was suffering some kind of dementia because of it.

"Let's get to the car, and hope that I can get us out of this snowbank. My cell phone isn't working."

"Your *cell phone?*" he said.

"Oh, God!" she groaned. "Never mind. Let me just get you home."

She managed to get him to the car, she climbed in across the passenger seat.

He jumped as she revved the engine.

"It's all right, that's the engine," she said. "Please, just get in, and fasten your seat belt." Before he could ask, she added, "The harness, right here. It saves lives, trust me."

He got in and, with her assistance, put on the seat belt.

She forced herself to move slowly, patiently, and she managed to back out of the snowbank. Cautiously, she began to drive on the road again.

"Unbelievable!" he murmured.

She shook her head. "Okay, you don't know where you are. But where were you before I hit you?"

He stared at her. His handsome features knit in thought, and then confusion.

"New York," he told her. "I was standing on the gallows, a rope around my neck."

Great! He was crazy. He was a homeless lunatic.

Either that, or he'd somehow hit his head really hard when she'd struck him.

She narrowed her eyes, staring very carefully at the road, wondering if *she* hadn't completely lost her mind. She had picked up a madman.

"I don't want to know what part you were playing," she said, trying to keep her tone even. "I need to know who you really are, and what you really do."

"Well, in actuality, I write," he said.

"Great. Very good. Who do you write for? Were you involved in a publicity stunt?" she inquired. Talking to him was like pulling teeth.

"A publicity stunt?" he inquired, confused. He had been staring out the window, perplexed. He turned and stared at her instead, handsome features furrowed.

She shook her head. "A publicity stunt. Something to draw the attention of the media. Something to get your name in the papers."

"My name is in the papers," he said.

"Okay. Good start. What is your name?"

"Jake Mallory," he said.

She shook her head. "I've never heard of you."

"No?" He looked resigned and a little saddened. "I've written for the Boston papers and the New York City papers."

"And I read the papers. I've never heard of you. So, what do you write?"

"Treason—according to the British. Well, actually, I haven't written in quite some time. I wound up being a soldier. I went to war, but I was being hanged for treason."

"What war?" she asked sharply.

"You should have read a few of my pieces. Some were considered brilliant. Rousing. I'm not a warmonger, not at all. But the colonies couldn't be used like a Royal Exchequer forever. If we're to pay taxes, then representation must be absolutely fair. I tried to explain what was happening to us, and why it's so important that we part ways with Great Britain. I wrote about a central government, and about the rights of each colony. Even General George Washington read what I was writing."

Lunatic.

"Okay," she said calmly. "So—you were a soldier in the Revolutionary War. Right before I found you on the road?"

"Right before you struck me down," he reminded her.

So that was it. In a sneaking and conniving way, he was going to bleed her for what she had done to him.

"Right before I struck you down, yes. You were a soldier. In the *Revolutionary War?*"

His eyes hadn't wavered from her face. She was making a point of keeping them on the road now, but her peripheral vision allowed her to be keenly aware of his steady assessment.

"Yes. *Where* am I?"

"Gloucester, Massachusetts," she snapped. "Almost at my house. But I can take a detour to the police station or the mental hospital."

"I'm very sorry. Truly. I didn't mean to offend you," he said.

"Fine. We'll start over. What were you doing in the twenty-first century?" she demanded.

"The twenty-*first?*" he asked her.

She let out a long sigh. "Yes, the twenty-*first.*"

"Who won?" he asked.

She was startled by the sudden intensity in him; she didn't just hear it in his voice, but felt it in the constriction of his body as he leaned closer to her.

"Who won?" he demanded again. He was even closer. Practically breathing down her neck.

Lunatic. Serial killer. A madman–serial killer. She needed to humor him.

"The United States of America. And the federal forces won the Civil War, too."

He hunched back into the passenger's seat. "Thank God… Civil War?"

"The American Civil War, or the War Between the States, or, as it was referred to in the South, the War of Northern Aggression. We are one country."

He stared out the window at the white world beyond the car. "How sad, how excruciatingly sad. We won the Revolution, and fought a civil war."

"All war is sad."

"And there is a war now?" he asked sharply.

She hazarded a glance at him. "The War on Terror," she said. "Oh, there have been lots of wars. Before the Civil War, the War of 1812—those pesky Brits again, though we're just like this now." She crossed her fingers for him with her right hand, keeping the left firmly on the wheel. "Spanish-American War, World War I, World War II, the Korean War, Vietnam, Desert Storm, and all kinds of actions. Actually, I don't think there has been a time when some part of the world hasn't been involved in an action of some kind."

"Amazing," he said.

"Right. War is amazing."

"Man's inability to refrain from it is amazing," he said softly.

She couldn't hate him. Okay, so he was seriously more than just daft. There was a dignity to the tone of his voice, and a certain sincerity in too many of his words. Maybe she had hit him on the head, and he believed everything that he was saying to her.

"And it's…Christmastide?" he asked.

"Nearly. At the end of the week."

He nodded. "Rose petals."

"What?"

He half smiled, glancing over at her. "Do you believe in magic?"

"No."

"Neither did I."

"Look, I really don't know what you're talking about. But… I don't want to have to take you to the police. You may be hurt. But my mom was a nurse. She retired recently but she can take a look at you. I mean, seriously, if I have injured you, I'd want to pay the bills. But…wow, I don't know. You should really go to a hospital—"

"Please, no. I'm not injured."

She should dump him by the side of the road then.

It occurred to her that while Mark would *order* her to do that kind of thing, her brother would never consider such an action.

Where did she stand herself?

"So, I'm going to take you home with me. I don't know who you are, if you're crazy, or whether you sustained a blow to the head. I'm going to have faith that you're not a dangerous maniac."

"I'm not a dangerous maniac, I swear."

"God help me, I'm going to believe you. But there are a couple of things you're going to have to get straight first," she said firmly.

"Honestly, I'm just trying to get home," he assured her.

"So where is home?"

"Gloucester," he said.

"Fine. I can just drop you off."

"I have to find out where," he told her. "And I'm not so sure I can get there by…car."

"Great. You can walk, skip or jump, once you've gotten it figured out," she said. "But until then, you're a friend of mine. We met at college."

"You went to college?" he asked her, fascinated.

"Yes, I went to college," she said flatly. "So—"

"Where?"

"Boston College. That's where we met."

"Boston College," he repeated.

"Will you listen, please? This is important."

"Yes, yes, of course. Whatever you wish."

"We'll make you a…an English lit major. And your tremendous interest in local history and lore made you go to work for one of the tour companies. That's why you're still dressed up à la General George."

"Dressed up?"

This was ridiculously difficult. "You are wearing old-fashioned clothing. It's no matter, I can rummage through my brother's things, and my brother is the type who would literally give anyone the shirt off his back, so we're fine on that. The traffic was horrendous, I was desperate to get headed north, so I wouldn't let you go back for your things."

He was staring straight ahead. She realized that she had come around the curve that led to her house. She was about to take the turn onto the driveway.

"Jake, are you listening to me?" she demanded, trying to slow the car without doing any more skidding.

"My God," he breathed.

"What?"

The lights.

Of course, it had to be the lights.

Her mother definitely got carried away with lights. The house looked like a giant birthday cake with candles in a multitude of colors. There were reindeer on the lawn—fashioned in wire and covered in lights as well—that burned brilliantly, as well.

Even the old oaks laden in their snow blankets seemed to be glistening. Ablaze.

It was a warm house, a welcoming house.

It....

"It's my home," Jake said. "It's my house. Where I live."

Chapter 2

Okay, that was all she needed.

The mental-man thought that her house was his.

She inhaled deeply. "Okay, okay, I hit you on the head really hard. But you can't go in there telling my folks that this is your house."

He was staring at the lights. It was as if he had never seen such a vision.

Well, to be truthful, not many people had. Her folks did get carried away.

"Jake."

"Um, yes! Sorry."

He looked at her again. His eyes gave the impression that he was entirely sane, completely honest, and giving her his steadfast attention. She felt a little start. Something that tightened and trembled within her.

Why did he have to be a madman?

They were striking eyes. They made him something other than just a handsome man. They made him real. Deep and hazel, and seeing her, really seeing her.

"Jake, whatever happened before in your fantasy world, trust me. My folks own this home. They paid off the mortgage several years ago. They worked hard, they love it—and they own it."

"Of course."

"You're not ready for this," she said worriedly.

He had turned to stare at all the lights again in pure wonder. "How do the lights work?" he marveled.

"Electricity. Your buddy, Ben Franklin, laid all the foundations. Hundreds of years later, I think Thomas Edison got it all really going, and hey, now we're in the age of real technology—*you cannot stare at everything like a kid in a candy store!*"

He looked at her. "I'm sorry. But it's just wonderful. The colors, the brilliance! So very, very beautiful. Ben always was a genius."

"Yes, of course. There have been a few improvements," she said dryly. *Oh, this was going to be a disaster.* She leaned her head on the steering wheel and groaned. "What am I going to do?"

He waited. "My dear young woman, it will be all right." He smiled.

She gave him a fierce stare. "Listen, we can't tell my family the truth or they will take you to the nearest hospital. Let's say we know each other for now—until I can figure out what to do. Soo… We met at college. You're an historian, okay? You dress up and give people tours."

"All right. Tours of what?" he inquired.

"Um—Boston. You work for Boston Tours, Incorporated. All right?"

"Boston Tours, Incorporated. Yes, I understand."

He still stared at her.

She shook her head. "Just follow my lead. And don't gape at anything that's—that's not familiar to you in your, um, current state of mind."

He smiled, but his eyes were grave, as was his tone. "You must understand. I *was* hanged during the Revolution."

"Sure."

He looked at the house with the Christmas lights blazing and then looked back at her, that odd and endearing smile teasing his lips once again. "You need to learn to believe in magic," he told her. "But, I do understand. We met at Boston College. I studied English literature. Now, I'm working for Boston Tours."

"You're a costumed interpreter," she said, nodding.

"The lights are beautiful," he said.

She shivered suddenly. Reality. It was getting cold in the car.

"Come on. Let's go in," she said.

She leaned over and opened his car door. He grimaced, thanked her and stepped out into the glittering snow. Then he waited.

She got out of the car, questioning her own sanity once again as she walked around and crooked a hand around his arm. They hurried up the walk and onto the porch together. As they neared it, the door burst open.

Her mother had been waiting for her.

Mona wasn't exactly a hippie. She was a strange combination of old-fashioned lady of the house with a bit of the wild child thrown in. She had tons of thick, curling blond hair that had only a few strands of gray. She loved yoga and Enya and anything that smacked of man's peaceful coexistence with his fellow man. She had grown her own food years before the word *organic* had begun to appear in supermarkets.

She'd been at the original Woodstock.

She always wore long, flowing shirts and dresses, like the flower grower's version of Stevie Nicks.

Her one great drawback was that even though she had passed that mark of having lived on the earth for over half a century, she saw no evil in anyone, and believed that all could always be made right with the world. She had no enemies. Strangers were always friends waiting to happen.

"Melody! Mark. Oh, Melody, I thought you said that Mark couldn't come with you—oh, goodness, I'm sorry, you're not Mark!" Mona said, a hand fluttering to her breast.

"No, ma'am, I'm Jake Mallory. How do you do? I'm sorry to be a strange and uninvited guest, but Melody assured me that you would not mind the intrusion." He spoke naturally, even if his accent was more than strange. *More England than New England,* Melody thought.

But he was doing well enough. He was natural and courteous. Her mom greatly appreciated common courtesy in anyone. Manners were a main grievance with her—Mona believed they cost nothing and made the world a better place.

Mona smiled, accepting his hand. "Well, of course, you're welcome here. Everyone is welcome here, young man." There was warmth in her tone, but confusion in her eyes. She looked at Melody, questioning.

Melody gave her mother a big hug. "Mom, I found out Jake was going to be at odds for Christmas and picked him up last minute in Boston. He was working, and didn't have time to change, and when we realized we'd forgotten his things, I was already on the road."

"Oh, and the weather is horrendous!" Mona agreed, hardly listening as she ushered them inside. "And here I am, chatting away on the porch. You young people come in and sit by the fire and I'll make some hot chocolate." She turned, heading into the house. Melody and Jake followed. She paused, telling Melody, "Take Jake to Keith's room, get him something comfortable to wear. Poor dear, working all day, and then that long drive."

Poor dear! Oh, yeah. Poor lunatic!

The house was old, very old, some parts of it were built sometime in the early 1600s. A small entryway led directly to a massive parlor. A curving staircase led to the second floor where there were five bedrooms. Behind the massive parlor were the kitchen and dining room on one side, and a family room on the other.

Behind the house itself—now covered in snow— was her mother's summer garden.

And her father's office. *Laboratory,* as she and her brother called it. Her father had a fascination with waves. Radio waves, microwaves—sound waves. Any kind of wave.

A happy baying that seemed to fill every inch of sound space came to their ears; Brutus, the basset with wheels for hind legs, came clip-clapping happily into the room, his tail wagging a mile a minute. He was followed by Jimmy, the sheepdog, who was now fat and healthy. Melody knelt down to pat both dogs and they wove around Jake.

"Ingenious," he said, hunkering down to meet Brutus.

"Yes, and he does quite well," Mona said happily. "He's a darling. That's Brutus. And the pile of fluff there is Jimmy. There's a cat running around, and that's Cleo. She's blind, but she has an excellent sense of smell and hearing. Just don't panic if she walks into something—she still does that upon occasion."

"Charming," Jake said.

"We do love our strays," Mona assured him happily.

Melody stood. "Okay, we've done the petting thing for the moment. Come on up, Jake, and I'll find some of Keith's things for you to wear."

"Poor young fellow!" Mona said, "You're soaked, you must be freezing. Hurry along now, get into something warmer."

"Yes, ma'am," Jake said.

Melody headed for the stairs. She stopped and looked back.

Jake Mallory was in the parlor, looking around. She started to snap at him again, but her words froze in her throat.

There was something about his expression that seemed so pained and nostalgic that it was almost... real. She wondered if he wasn't suffering some kind of tormented dementia. Maybe he really believed that he had been a Revolutionary War soldier. He had fallen out of a time warp in the sky and landed on an ice-covered road more than two and a half centuries later.

She let out a sigh. She honestly didn't think he was

homicidal, and she had been the one to strike him down on the road. She needed to practice patience.

"Jake," she said softly.

He looked at her, startled, then nodded and followed her. They walked up the stairs together, and turned. "This is your brother's room?" he asked, stopping at the door where Melody pointed.

"Yes."

They went in. She left him standing by Keith's bed, staring at the posters of her brother's favorites, Axl Rose and the Killers. There was also a large poster of Keira Knightley dressed up for her role in the *Pirates of the Caribbean* movies.

"Beautiful," Jake said.

"Keira Knightley? My brother thinks she's the most beautiful woman alive," Melody said.

"I mean—the art. Amazing."

"It's a poster from a photograph."

He started to repeat the word, but didn't. Melody smiled broadly. "Okay, photograph. It's from an invention that captures the image of…well, just about anything. Cameras capture the stars now, through telescopes. Oh, a telescope—"

"I've seen telescopes," he said. "Just not…a photograph. Or a camera. But it sounds like an exceedingly wonderful creation. To capture images without charcoal or paints."

"Right. There are movie cameras, too. They capture—movement. Anyway…"

"Does your brother still live here?" he asked.

"My brother is still in college. But he comes home often," she said.

She dug into Keith's wardrobe, grateful that her

brother was a lot like her mother—he never minded in the least if anyone else made use of his things.

She found a pair of jeans and an Armani Exchange sweater and handed them to Jake, then hesitated, found a pair of Keith's briefs, socks and sneakers. She had no idea how to judge foot size, but Jake and Keith were about the same height. Maybe Keith's feet would be a little bit bigger, but rather too big than too small.

As she produced the sneakers, she found him playing with the zipper. "Ingenious!" he told her.

"Yeah, yeah, it's a zipper. Figure it all out. You know the house. We'll be in the family room," she said dryly.

"The family room?"

"Now it's a family room, I don't know what it might have been before. You know, when you owned it. Whatever. It's just below us," she said. She paused. He'd been drenched. Covered in snow and mud. "The shower is just next door."

"The shower?"

"Oh, my God, did I pick up a parrot?" she demanded. *Okay, play the game.* She shook her head and sighed. "The bathroom."

"An indoor washroom?" he asked, seriously trying to understand.

She crooked a finger at him. He followed her.

Leave it to her mom. It wasn't all traditional New England decorating that she'd used—it was more New England meets Goth. Her folks loved pirates. The upstairs bathroom was done in early Blackbeard; the shower curtain boasted pirate flags, the decoration had ships—and the standing toilet paper holder was a silver-colored spyglass replica.

She pointed to the toilet. "Indoor…necessary, I believe. Sink. Water comes on and off when you twist the faucets. The shower works just the same. Be careful—they have a mega water heater and when you turn on the hot, it gets hot."

He still stared.

She pulled a towel from the rack.

"Shower. You turn on the water to your temperature liking. Stand beneath the spray. Use soap. Rinse off. Dry with towel—put on clothing. Okay?"

"Amazing," he said.

"Oh, God! It's a hot shower. Get in and get out. And come downstairs when you're done. No gaping. We have a stove and a television and—"

"Television?"

"Television. You see moving images on it. Fiction, and nonfiction. The news, the weather." She made a face. "Reality shows for entertainment."

"Reality as entertainment?" he inquired.

"Precisely."

"But a television…"

She let out an oath of absolute impatience and hurried on out, closing the door.

In the family room, she found her father. He had been seated in one of the wing-back chairs by the fire, but he stood when he saw her, a tall lean man with a cap of snow-white hair. Cleo had been happily curled just behind his neck and she mewed a protest at his movement. Her father absently patted the cat, then came to Melody. He folded her into his arms. "Melody! I was getting worried about you coming today, the news about all the accidents on the roads has been terrible."

She gave him a fierce hug in return, and they parted. "So, what's up, Dad? How's it all going?"

"Beautifully," he assured her. "I like being retired."

Her mother breezed into the room, carrying a tray laden with cups of cocoa and fresh-baked cookies. "He nearly blew up his study last week," Mona said.

Her father shrugged, a tolerant smile for his wife on his face. "I did nothing of the kind. I had a little spark and a tiny fire going, and that was it. I keep a fire extinguisher on hand at all times, and I was never in any danger of losing the study."

"Humph," Mona said, rolling her eyes. She sat. "So, my dear, I don't remember you mentioning this Jake fellow. Is he related to Mark? He resembles him quite a bit."

"No, no, they're not related at all."

"You're kidding," Mona said. "I thought he'd be a cousin or something…even a brother. Wait till you see him, George," she marveled to her husband.

"And when is the man of the hour coming up?" her father asked, a sparkle in his eyes. "I'm referring to Mark, of course."

"Mom, Dad, Mark isn't the man of the hour," she said seriously.

"But…you were dating him, and you seemed to like him so much!" Mona protested. "He's such a gentleman, always opening doors for you, trying to get you to sit and relax…he's a lovely man, really. What happened?"

"He's still a lovely man, Mom," she said. "Nothing happened."

"Oh, my Lord, he hasn't been mean or rude to you, has he?" Mona asked indignantly. "I've asked him here for the holidays!"

"He hasn't been mean or rude, and I hope he enjoys the holidays, and I hope we can remain friends," Melody said.

"Mark is such a nice young man," her mother said sorrowfully.

"Mom—"

"I see. You're not as fond of the fellow as he is of you," her father said, nodding as he sat back more deeply into his chair.

"Melody," her mother said sternly, "you haven't brought your other friend—this Jake—to…I don't know, to upset Mark, have you?"

"Mom, I brought him because…he really had nothing else to do," she said.

"Is there a romance there?" her father asked, laughter in his eyes again.

"Good God, no," Melody said. "Please, no matchmaking with Mark, Mom, Dad. And none with Jake. Got it?"

"I wouldn't dream of it," her mother said. "You've got to live your own life."

"Never," her father promised.

"So, I'm confused. Aren't you and Mark working together?" Mona asked.

"Yes."

"Well, you're not going to stop doing the book, are you?" her father asked.

"I hope not."

Jake came into the room then. Keith's clothes fit him well, and Melody had to blink, he suddenly looked so right. With his hazel eyes, sandy-brown hair and good bone structure.

"Well, there now, you look more relaxed and comfy," Mona said. "Jake Mallory, my husband,

George. George, this is Melody's friend from college, Jake Mallory."

"Pleased to meet you, and welcome. So, you're staying the week?" he asked politely.

Jake glanced at Melody. "If you'll have me, sir."

"With pleasure, with pleasure," George Tarleton said, indicating the sofa and returning to his rocking chair.

"Cocoa, dear," Mona said, handing him a cup.

"Thank you most kindly," Jake said.

Melody looked downward, wincing.

"You sound almost as if you're from ye old mother country," George said lightly, taking a sip of his own cocoa.

"No, sir. I was born and bred right here, in these parts."

"It's a charming accent," Mona said.

"Thank you," Jake said. "My folks were born on British soil."

"There you go," George said, knowingly looking at his wife. He wagged a finger in the air. "I am good at discerning the little things in accents, huh, dear?"

"Yes, dear, if you say so," Mona agreed.

"How strange, though. I'm sure I don't know your folks," George said. "We don't have any English friends—do we?"

"My parents have been gone many years," Jake said.

"I'm so sorry!" Mona said.

"Thank you," Jake told her.

"But where is your home now?" George asked, concerned.

"He's living in Boston, Dad!" Melody said, jumping in quickly with the information. She grabbed a cookie and munched it quickly. "Mom, these are delicious. Jake, have a cookie. My mom's a wonderful baker."

"Thank you," he said politely. "Wonderful," he agreed.

"Where in Boston are you?" George asked.

Melody couldn't reply quickly enough—not without spewing sugar cookie over them all.

"I'm right off the Common," Jake said.

"Lovely area, lovely!" George applauded.

She'd be a nervous, twitching wreck if this went on too much longer, Melody decided. She had to get him off alone again. She leaped up. "Would you two mind if we run out before dinner? Um, Jake hasn't been around here for a while. I was going to take him down to the pond."

"Lovely idea!" Mona said. "I'm not sure if you've seen all they've been up to by the pond. They have some charming shops, and a little bar—I'm sure you'll have a nice time. Oh, Keith should be home by supper. I'm planning it for around eight."

"That's great, Mom."

"Wait a minute. It was snowing so much—" George began.

"I think the snow has stopped," Melody said. *Even if there was a nor'easter pounding, she was leaving the house.*

She grabbed Jake's hand. "Jake, let's get going so you can see the pond before dinner. Come on, now, please?"

"Of course." He stood immediately, trying to replace his cup on the tray, a little awkward since she was tugging at his arm. "Thank you so much. This was a truly enjoyable repast."

"Let's go!" Melody persisted.

Her mother was laughing. "Oh, that's wonderful. You must be a fantastic guide. How absolutely charming. Children, do have fun."

"There's skating—weather permitting," her father called out.

"Okay, Dad, thanks!"

Melody managed to grab two parkas from the hooks by the entry and get Jake out the front door. A pale streak of winter's day touched the sky; the snow had come down to just a few flurries.

She thanked God for small favors.

As they stood on the porch and she surveyed the muted light of the late-afternoon December sun, Mona popped out on the porch. Melody hoped that she didn't physically cringe.

"Skates!" Mona said, holding up two pairs of skates. "Keith's shoes fit you all right, don't they, Jake? If so, I'm sure his skates will do."

"I am more than comfortable and quite grateful, ma'am," Jake said.

"Thanks, Mom." Melody snatched the skates from her mother and hurried to the car. Jake followed her. She was already in the driver's seat when Jake joined her.

Mona called something from the porch.

"We have to stop, she's speaking to us," Jake said, sliding in beside her.

"It's okay—she's just telling you that I'm a klutz," Melody said. Before he could ask her what a klutz was, she added, "I have no coordination. I'm horrible."

He smiled, looking ahead.

"You can skate. You've heard of skates, right?"

"Yes, I have."

She started to drive, glad then that her home was Massachusetts. They were darned good at snow. Plows were always out in a matter of minutes. The roads were decent.

"Your parents are exceptionally kind," Jake said.

"They're—yes, they're good people. A little crazy, but good people," she told him.

"How do you see them as crazy?" he asked.

She hazarded a glance his way. "Pirate-themed bathrooms? Sculpted ravens, skeleton art, fairies and ghosts and goblins all over—you'll see. It's so strange. I feel like I grew up with the Addams Family or as the normal child niece in the Munsters' home."

"Pardon?"

"Never mind." She looked at him again and groaned. "How on earth can I give you a crash course in pop culture? Don't—don't you dare copy me! Pop culture is…what's popular now. Too bad it wasn't my dad who ran into you. He was a professor. He'd have you up to speed in no time."

"Up to speed—"

"Oh, God!"

"No, no, I understand. I find it a charming expression."

"Of course you do," she murmured.

"Is that a problem?"

"No. It's just that…oh, never mind. No. Are you always so…agreeable?"

"You wish me to be disagreeable?"

"No. I wish you to—snap out of it. And don't repeat after me!"

"All right." He was smiling, studying the scenery as

they passed. "It's so remarkable. We won the Revolution, and there have been many more wars. So many inventions. Remarkable."

They had reached the pond. There were a few skaters out, and a few children running around the outskirts, laughing, throwing snowballs at one another. The bar—aptly name the Pond Bar—was just opening. Melody parked and stepped out of the car. She wasn't sure what to do. She had driven to the pond because she was afraid she was already lying so much she'd start to confuse even herself.

But now…

"You've forgotten the skates," Jake called.

"I suck."

"Pardon?"

"I wasn't lying, I'm awful."

"Well, I'm a decent skater. Let's give it a try, shall we?"

Skate. Maybe while she was falling on her ass she'd figure out how she'd gotten into this mess.

"All right, all right, bring them."

There were benches by the pond. They sat down. The skates might have been somewhat modern compared to what he'd *thought* he had in the 1700s, but they were still basically skates. When they had both laced up, he stood, testing the way they fit, testing his own ability to walk in them.

"Aren't you going to say *remarkable, marvelous, fantastic*—or something of the like?" she asked.

"They'll do. Come on." He stretched out a hand to her.

"You go. I'll sit for a minute. Please."

He watched her for a moment, then went out on the

ice. At first, he moved slowly, testing the skates and then the ice. He picked up speed.

She watched him, feeling blank.

Keith picked up strange creatures. She picked up crazy ones.

A moment's panic set in. What if he was really hurt? If his head had been badly bruised? Was she doing the wrong thing, keeping him away from the hospital?

She thanked God that Mark wasn't due until Friday. He'd have given Jake the third degree by now, and the police might have even been called in. Mark wouldn't have gone against her parents' wishes; he'd have done it on the sly, certain that he knew what was best for everyone else.

So, great. What was she going to do? This wasn't like Keith, bringing in strays when he was younger. *Can we keep him, Mom, can we keep him?*

She was going to have to figure something out.

A spray of ice brought her back to the moment. Jake was stretching a hand out to her again. "Will you join me?"

"I'll make you fall."

"No, you won't."

She was unsteady as she teetered out to him. "Look, I'm usually all right if I'm just going forward," she said.

"You will be fine, no matter what we do," he assured her.

And they were. If she hesitated, he was sure. He was so comfortable on the ice that his balance and support leant her a steady hand. He didn't try to do anything outrageous; he just kept moving, picking up a decent speed, one hand supportive on her back, as they glided along.

Gliding. She was gliding!

The icy coolness of the air rushed at her face, and felt delicious. The world danced by them. She could hear the sound of their skates upon the ice, and it was exhilarating.

"Backward?" he suggested.

"No!" she protested in panic.

"You were born here, and you grew up here?" he asked curiously.

"Yes, I actually did."

"It's all right, you don't even have to move your feet," he said.

"But—"

"Trust me."

"I do trust you—on the ice," she said.

And he did prove to be trustworthy.

She didn't have to move her feet.

He twisted and turned, they skated backward, forward and backward again.

"Want to try a spin?"

"No!"

He laughed. "All right. We're good for the day, I imagine."

He slid effortlessly to a halt. She was looking into the green-and-gold sparkle of his eyes and didn't realize at first that they had come back to the bench. He was still supporting her.

"Oh, yeah, well, yeah, you know, next time, maybe," she said. She tried to draw away, certain she could at least make the steps to the bench on her own.

Her legs started to split. She was about to go facedown—or butt-side down, if she overcompensated—on the ice.

But he caught her. Without making any kind of big deal out of it. She smiled. "I told you—no coordination on skates!"

"It will come. It's all in learning to trust your instincts."

She cleared her throat, made her way to the bench and took off her skates. As she did so, she saw the bar across the pond. "Time for a drink."

"Really?"

"Oh, yeah."

"You drink?"

"Right now? You bet. Anything wrong with that?"

"No. Pop culture, I assume."

She stood, shaking her head. "And look, keep your story straight. I know a lot of people around here."

"As you wish."

"Don't keep telling me that."

"As you—all right."

"When we're out, and you don't know, just let me answer—please."

"Of course."

As they walked toward the bar, he was thoughtful.

"What?" she asked, exasperated.

"Eventually, you will believe me," he said quietly. "Somehow, I have to get back to my own…place."

"At the end of a hangman's noose?" she asked sharply.

"No. Right here. But when I'm supposed to be here," he said quietly.

She studied him for a moment. "You need a drink worse than I do," she told him.

"If you don't believe in magic, couldn't you even stretch a bit and try to believe in a miracle?" he asked.

"What I'm telling you is the truth. Serena loves me, and she tried to save my life. Obviously, since I do seem to be flesh and blood, she did save my life. And maybe her magic worked because it was like a prayer for the innocent or the righteous, whichever way you want to see it."

"Serena?" she said. "Your—wife?"

He shook his head, smiling. "My sister. Adopted, as a child, by my parents, when hers were killed in an Indian attack. She was my only sibling, and we were close. She shouldn't have been in New York—she should have been here, in Gloucester. I was so afraid for her. Am so afraid for her. And I have to make sure that she did make it home, that… I mean, good God, you really can't imagine what it is—*was*—like. Some believed the Revolution was a deadly and tragic mistake. Others saw it as a right to freedom. There were fine British sympathizers and soldiers. But those capable of cruelty come in all uniforms. I'm very afraid for her. She is my family, you see. Somehow, I have to find a way…back."

Melody stared at him blankly, unable to believe for a moment that what she'd felt at first was actually *jealousy.* Of an unknown woman.

His sister…

Adopted sister.

Was she crazy herself? Was that jealousy again?

Insane. The whole thing was insane.

"Look, Jake, we do have the internet now, planes that fly at supersonic speeds—but as far as I know, there is no pathway that leads to years gone by. No time travel. We just haven't gotten to that yet."

"Maybe it's time to get to it," he said. "There has to be a way."

She hesitated. "We can go and try to check through some of the church records. And this area does live in the past sometimes. So many of the houses are really old—diaries and the like are always being found. Maybe we can research and find out what went on. My mom might have some old books that will help us." She hesitated. "My mom…she thinks her ancestors were pagan healers, or Wiccans. She's always researching the past for what was really going on when the British came over. She has the entire trial records from the Salem witchcraft mania."

"Really? They never did hang any more witches, did they?" he inquired.

"Not that I know about."

"I really need your help. I'm most grateful. We have to discover a way for me to get back."

She shook her head, exasperated. *He was crazy— and persistent.* "I really need a drink."

And with that, she headed for the bar.

Chapter 3

The Pond Bar was neighborhood friendly and pleasant. It was a quiet night so far—probably because it was fairly early and the day's weather had been so bad. More people would come out later, Melody was certain, glad to escape their houses or the harrowing drives they had made during the day. But at the moment, the little place was quiet.

She chose a small table next to the cast-iron potbellied stove, and pulled her gloves off as they sat. Jake Mallory was once again looking around—then he focused on one young woman in the place who was wearing stiletto boots and one of the miniest minidresses Melody had ever seen.

His shocked gaze moved to her and he lowered his head to whisper, "Is that… I mean, is that woman a… lady of the night?"

Melody moved closer in, as well. "College student, probably," she said.

"One goes to college for that occupation now?"

She laughed, shaking her head. "No, no. Her outfit is modern—daring, especially in winter. But I don't think she's a hooker. Sorry. I believe the term *hooker* came from the Civil War—Hooker's girls. Never mind. I don't believe she's a prostitute. That's called a mini-dress. She's got the youth and the body for it, looks pretty cute."

"Ah. I'm sorry—it wouldn't be considered decent at all in my…world," he said.

"Thank God you didn't fall to earth on Miami Beach," she said.

He gazed at her, refraining from asking her about Miami Beach. She was glad—a waitress warmly clad in corduroy jeans and a turtleneck sweater came to the table. Melody opted for a totally fattening Kalhúa and hot chocolate, and Jake said that he'd have the same.

The waitress had just moved away when Jake came to his feet, a frown on his face, his posture defensive. Melody felt fingers come over her eyes and a teasing voice said, "Guess who?"

She grabbed the hands and quickly drew her brother around to introduce him to Jake, ruing the fact that Keith had already made it home. She really needed more time to figure out something to do about Jake.

"Jake," she said quickly, "this is my brother, Keith. Keith, Jake Mallory."

Keith was a good soul. Sure, he'd been a pain-in-the-ass baby brother at times, playing the usual stupid pranks like leaving the saltshaker lid on loose and going off into gales of laughter when she wound up with a white mountain on her French fries. But he had matured into a good-looking young man with an open mind, an easy humor and not much in the way of a temper. She thought of him often as a little mini-me of her father, because they were so into science. He had finally learned the difference between a Monet and a Picasso for her sake, and for him—and her father—she had tried to understand the basic concepts of physics. As a brother, he was coming along nicely. They both loved a lot of the same music, and that had always helped them along.

"How do you do?" Jake asked politely.

"Good, thanks. Jake, nice to meet you." Keith drew up a chair and straddled it, grinning. He looked at Jake. "My mom and dad are all agog over you. Tearing their hair out. They don't think they've met your parents. They used to be sure they knew *everyone* around here. And they're still convinced that you're related to Melody's—er—friend Mark."

"I don't believe I'm related to Mark. Your parents are charming," Jake said simply.

Thank God. He was getting better.

"So, you two met at school?" Keith asked.

"College," Melody said. Soon enough, she'd get good at the lie.

"Did you order drinks?"

"Hot chocolate with Kahlúa," Melody said.

"I'll go order the same. You're not on one of your diets, I take it?" he asked Melody.

"No, I'm not on a diet," she said, glaring at him.

Keith grinned at Jake. "Oh, wait, that's right. Melody and my mom never go on diets. They go on *lifestyles*."

"Keith!" Melody said sharply.

He shrugged.

"I'll seek out the young woman who took our order," Jake said, standing and walking toward the bar.

Keith looked at Melody. "You are such a liar."

"What are you talking about?"

"You've obviously forgotten that I came and hung around your college dorm every chance I could get, falling in love with all the 'older' women around you. I would have met this guy. Who is he?"

She stared at her brother. "You didn't meet everyone."

"Who is he?" Keith repeated.

She hesitated. "I hit him."

"What?"

"I hit him on the road. Keith, he's…he's having some kind of mental block. He isn't hurt, unless I did do him some serious brain damage. I—"

"Wait, back up. You hit him. You socked him in the jaw?"

"No!" Melody said. "I was driving and I think I hit some black ice. I hit him."

"And you didn't get him to a hospital?"

"No, he didn't want to go. Hey, I didn't hit him hard. And I just didn't know what to do. I panicked."

"You hit someone, you get them to a hospital," Keith chastised.

"But—he was, he wasn't behaving normally."

"Great. All the more reason not to bring the guy to a hospital."

"But…he was in costume. Revolutionary-period clothing. He thinks he was a soldier. He—he says the last thing he remembers is that he was being executed, hanged, in New York City. He had a sister or half sister or stepsister or someone who was a witch and said some kind of curse—and he wound up on the road. Then I hit him."

Keith just stared at her for several seconds. He blinked. "Oh, great. You are making no sense. He thinks he fell to earth from the past, and still—you didn't take him to the hospital!"

"He didn't appear to be hurt."

"You obviously gave the fellow a concussion."

"I don't think so."

"He—he could be crazy."

"Well, that's obvious!"

"Right. So this is getting better and better."

"He needs our help. Somehow, he has to realize who he really is."

"Since when was your degree is psychology?"

"I brought him home. I—I think his real memory will come back."

Her brother arched a brow skeptically.

"Look, Keith, he must have a job as a costume interpreter or something."

"In costume, huh. You think?" he asked sarcastically.

She glared at him. "He believes his own role right now. Quit judging me."

"I'm not judging you."

"He needs our help."

"Our help?"

"My help. I always helped you!"

Keith stared at her amazed, then started to laugh. "Okay, I've brought home a trillion puppies and kittens. But not a crazy."

She stiffened. "What about the pole-dancing stripper?"

"Hey, she knew where she worked."

"Keith, look, he's nice, he's pleasant…I'm hoping that some normal time will help bring back his memory."

"And you think anyone is going to have 'normal time' at our house?" Keith asked dryly.

"That's not fair," she accused him.

"So. You hit him, he's in costume, thinks he's a soldier, and you bring him home to feed him and warm him up. This isn't the same as what I did."

She glared at her brother. "You are not at all amusing."

"No, but you are in some weird water here, sis."

"Keith, stop it. I've kind of got a problem going here."

"Maybe you do," he said. His eyes were bright with amusement as he moved closer to her. "What do you think he's saying to the bartender? She's pretty cute, too."

"Oh, God, I don't know!" Melody stood up. She sat down. "Keith, go check on him. I don't want to look like a jealous idiot. Go on, get him back over here."

Keith shrugged, grinned, and then did as she asked. He walked to the bar and set a hand on Jake's shoulder and said something to him. The pretty bartender laughed at whatever was exchanged, and added the last cup to a tray that their waitress came to take. She led the way back to the table and, much to Melody's relief, Jake and her brother followed.

Melody picked up her cup and drank, barely aware that the chocolate concoction was hot.

"Sweetie, if you want to swill something, it really shouldn't be hot chocolate. Beer is best for swilling, wouldn't you say, Jake?"

"I suppose it's a proper beverage for hefty consumption," Jake said.

"He knows who you think you are," Melody said.

"I know who I am. My name is Jake Mallory," Jake said.

"And you were at the end of a hangman's noose?" Keith said.

Jake seemed very tall and straight. "That is the absolute truth," he said quietly.

"And you know nothing that's happened since the American Revolution?" Keith asked.

"Only what your sister has been kind enough to tell me," he said sincerely.

Keith stared at Melody. "Huh." He grinned suddenly. "Well, I know what we should do after dinner."

"What?" Melody asked dubiously.

"A DVD glut."

She cast her head to the side and smiled slowly. "History and pop culture."

"Excuse me," Jake said. "A DVD glut?"

Melody groaned. Her brother began a scientific explanation.

"I see," Jake said.

Keith rose. "Time for dinner. I came to fetch the two of you. Can't be late for Mom's nouvelle cuisine."

"We're having stew, I believe," Melody said.

"Whatever," Keith said. Then, "Stew? Oh, no. God knows what she puts in those Crock-Pots." He grimaced. "She thinks she has powers."

"So Melody said. Maybe she does," Jake said.

"Forget it, forget it," Melody said, rising. "My mother does not have powers. Please, don't go encouraging her to think that she does! Come on, let's get home."

Keith had brought his car. He encouraged Jake to ride with him, telling him that he could explain the workings of the vehicle much better than Melody might ever manage. She decided to let the two of them go—there was nothing that Keith didn't know already, so whatever Jake said to him, it wouldn't matter.

She reached the house first and Keith and Jake pulled in right behind her. Other than the fact that his hair was long—easily understandable, if he made his living as an historic interpreter—Jake looked as if he belonged right where he was.

That was good.

Oh, Lord, she was beginning to fall for his fantasy!

She shook off the thought as she headed for the house. Before she reached the door, Brutus was howling out a welcome. She entered the house quickly. One good thing about Brutus—no one would ever come sneaking up on the house. Brutus was louder than the most obnoxious doorbell ever created.

Wheels for legs did not prevent the basset from having a tail that wagged so hard it was like being whacked when it hit ya.

"Lovely!" her mom called, coming from the kitchen. Now she looked like Stevie Nicks in an apron. "Dinner is on."

"Yeah? So what's in it? Eye of toad and leg of newt?" Keith teased.

"Oh, you!" Mona protested, giving him an affectionate tap on the shoulder. "Don't you dare go scaring our guest!"

"I'm not scared," Jake assured her.

"She does add all her own herbs," Keith warned.

"We're having stew. Beef stew. And I'm afraid, other than the herbs, the ingredients are store-bought," Mona said. She brightened. "But I do buy only organic."

Jake looked at Melody.

"She loathes the idea that food might have pesticides in it," Melody explained.

"She's quite right I guess," Jake said.

"And quite expensive," George Tarleton said, joining them in the living room.

"Dad, you might want to find a lint brush. You're wearing more of Cleo than Cleo wears of herself, I think," Melody pointed out.

"Oh, yes, well, excuse me, I'll find the lint brush," her father said.

"Come into the dining room, sit, sit," Mona encouraged.

The dining room was probably the most traditional room in the house—the large dining table and chairs were early American, as were the buffet and china closet. The back wall offered a bay window with a built-in bench seat that looked out over the lawn, and it was enhanced by warm, deep blue cushions and handsome throw pillows. There was a fireplace in here as well—the house boasted eight—and at Christmas, more than any other time, Mona kept the fires burning. She was also a huge fan of scented candles, so the room smelled deliciously of stew and spices.

Jake paused in the doorway, breathing in. His eyes scanned the room, and she thought once again that she

saw a look of pained nostalgia on his face that couldn't
be feigned.

She felt her heart going out to him, and then she was
irritated with herself. She just had to pick up a crazy
who was completely charming, dignified and capable
of somehow seducing her into his fantasy. He'd been
in costume—the man was an actor, in a way. She had
to keep remembering that.

"Sit, sit, Jake. I swear, there's nothing at all wrong
with my cooking, my children like to torment me,"
Mona said. "George, will you get the iced tea from
the refrigerator?"

Melody, Keith and Jake had taken their seats as they
had been told. When Mona moved, Jake rose. She set
her hands on his shoulders to stay seated when she rose
to help her husband get the drinks.

"What do you want to bet it's green tea?" Keith
asked, feigning a whisper.

"I heard that. Green tea is excellent for you. A bil-
lion Chinese who have far longer life spans than we
do cannot be wrong," Mona said.

"Green tea is lovely, Mom," Melody said, kick-
ing her brother's shin under the table. "Don't get her
going," she mouthed.

"I heard that, too!" Mona said, sweeping back
around the table with a large tureen of stew. She set it
down with a flourish while her husband got the glasses.
"And it's all right because I'm so happy just to have you
home for the holidays—and to have our new friend,
Mr. Mallory, here, as well." She sat. "Keith, dear, will
you say grace, please?"

"Grace," Keith said softly, and grinned.

"Oh, honestly, Keith, it's hard to imagine that you're

a student going for a Ph.D., darling, you can be so juvenile at times."

"May I?" Jake asked.

"Well, of course!" Mona said.

Jake folded his hands and closed his eyes. "Thank you, Lord, for the food you've provided, for the warmth of the hearth, and the love of family and friends. May we all be home in time for Christmas. Amen."

He opened his eyes and looked at Melody. Again, there was something in them that entreated with dignity.

People didn't drop from a hangman's noose to find themselves in a street almost three hundred years later.

"How very nice, Jake, thank you," Mona said. "So, now, how was the ice skating?"

"It was nice, Mom," Melody said. She stood to help her mother; Jake stood, as well. "I'm just passing the plates. Please, Jake, thank you."

He'd been taught to stand when a woman stood, and it was going to keep happening. Melody made a quick job of passing the food around.

"Mrs. Tarleton, I understand that you have some wonderful books on local history," Jake said.

"Oh, indeed." Mona flashed a smile. "I'm simply fascinated by the mind-set of those who came before us. When they had the tricentennial of the Salem witchcraft trials, they printed up complete volumes of the proceedings, the court records, everything. It's fascinating reading. So sad and horrible."

"What happens in the minds of men—and women—is always fascinating," George said. "With all the theories they've had regarding the hysteria, I still can't imagine sane adults allowing those girls who accused their neighbors of being witches—some only because they used herbs to help cure sicknesses—to cause such a tragedy."

"I quite agree," Jake said. "Many people were killed with no evidence that they had done anything wrong."

"Do you believe in witchcraft?" Melody asked.

"Whether I believe or not does not matter," Jake said. "Massachusetts was a British colony, and witchcraft was illegal. Could someone really curse his neighbor's cow with an evil eye? Most probably not. But mixing potions—even herbal potions—could be considered witchcraft and sadly, the punishment for witchcraft could be death. But I don't believe that any of those caught up in the hysteria at Salem were practicing real witchcraft of any kind. They were just caught up in a miasma of fear. There was so much of the world that was unknown and frightening."

"Indeed," George agreed.

Mona pounced on the words. "That's just it, people act out of fear or ignorance. The true Wiccans were not guilty of any evil—they were part of the pagan way that existed before Christianity began to spread. And those who brought Christianity across from Europe were willing to do what was necessary to convince others to follow them. I mean, seriously, we don't know what day Christ was born, we have settled on a day for it to be Christmas. The high holy day of All Hallow's Eve coincided with a pagan practice that had long been celebrated. And Easter! The holiday and celebration are even named for Eostre, the Anglo-Saxon goddess of spring. The old Anglo-Saxons celebrated spring and rebirth, and the Hebrews celebrated Passover, and Christians celebrate the fact that Christ rose from the dead. Here's my point, we are all one creation, however we choose to see our deities."

"Mom, that's not at all how the Puritans saw it," Melody said.

"No, I'm afraid they weren't at all accepting of others, and they certainly wouldn't appreciate anyone pointing out the fact that Easter came from Eostre," Jake said. "Mrs. Tarleton, this stew is absolutely delicious. Thank you very kindly."

"Oh," Mona said, enrapt with her guest. "That's so kind of you. It's just a Crock-Pot stew. I'm so glad you're enjoying it! And I'm fascinated with what you're saying, of course, because it's just terrible to think of the wonderful and kind people who practiced old forms of medicine just to wind up burned at the stake in Europe and Scotland and hanged in England for witchcraft. They were often midwives, or people working with herbs, and as we all know now, many of the natural ingredients cured people."

"Mom," Melody pointed out, "just because something is natural, doesn't always mean that it's good for you. Hemlock is natural."

Mona waved a hand in the air. "My dear, you're missing the point."

"What *is* the point?" Keith asked, grinning.

Melody kicked him beneath the table again.

"Ouch! Stop that," he told her.

"What is going on there?" George demanded.

"She kicked me," Keith said.

"Mother, he's being obnoxious," Melody said.

"Children! We have a guest," Mona said, shaking her head. "Honestly, George, how old are they now? How can this still be going on?"

"Mom, I know the point, and our college genius keeps missing it," Melody said. "What matters is not always the truth, but rather, peoples' perception of the truth. And fear is something that often sways our perceptions. When you're afraid, you may see something that is entirely innocent as something evil. And in the old days, *science* was often seen as evil, as well."

"Was that a dig at me?" Keith asked.

"Never. Science is something wonderful," Melody said.

Melody stood. Jake jumped to his feet. "Please, Jake, sit, you're a guest. I'm just clearing the table so we can bring out the dessert," Melody said.

Keith stood, too. "Mom, Melody and I will handle this. You sit for a change."

"All right, thank you," Mona agreed.

Melody glared at Keith. He frowned, cocking his head. She hurried to the kitchen, carrying the used plates. When he had entered behind her and the connecting door had swung shut, she turned on him. "What's the matter with you? You just left Jake in there alone with Mom and Dad!"

"Jake's doing just fine. Hey, he's a cool crazy, Mel. I like him," Keith said.

"Get back out there, Keith!" Melody said, piling the plates in the sink to rinse for the dishwasher. "Please, come on, please? Hey, I'm the one who fought for you to keep Cleo, remember?"

"He's not a cat, Mel," Keith said.

"Get out there!"

"Going, going—I'll grab the pie and plates. You bring the coffee."

"All right, go. Oh, Keith?"

"Yeah?"

"Thanks."

He grinned. Her brother left with the fresh-baked blueberry pie Mona had made for dessert and a stack of plates. She quickly rinsed the dinner plates and put them in the dishwasher, then unplugged the coffeepot and headed into the dining room.

To her dismay, her brother was having some kind of exchange with her father; Jake's head was lowered and he was listening, fascinated, to her mother.

They all looked up when she arrived.

"The cups are in the cabinet, dear. Do you want your old Disney mug? Forgive us, Mr. Mallory," Mona said. "We all have our favorite cup. What would you like? Traditional, a mug—or a Princess cup?"

"Any cup will do, thank you," Jake said.

Mona passed out mugs and poured the coffee while Melody served the pie.

"Seen any good movies lately?" George asked.

A piece of pie nearly slipped onto the table. Melody's gaze flew to Jake.

"I'm afraid I've not seen anything I could recommend, sir," he said.

"I've got some DVDs up in my room I'm going to show him," Keith said. "Hey, I brought a documentary for you, too, Dad. It's on radio frequencies. You're going to love it."

"Wonderful," George told him.

Mona rose. Jake rose. She hesitated, and smiled. "It's really all right, Jake. Please, I'm just going to go get that diary that I found in the attic. I swear that that author's last name was Mallory—and that her brother's first name was Jake. What a coincidence that would be if you were related! Of course, to be honest, throughout the centuries, who knows who is really related to whom? You know, people didn't always steer the course of the higher road."

"What?" Keith asked.

"She means that women fooled around, so your father may not have been your father," Melody said.

"Oh, dear, that's putting it so crassly," Mona protested, waving a hand in the air as she went to one of the bookcases.

"This diary is amazing. I probably could sell it for a mint on eBay. It's authentic. And sad, really—it doesn't have an ending. I've been meaning to go to the hall of records, though, I believe, a lot was probably lost during the Revolution. And young men died in different places, so..."

Melody sank into her chair. Mona produced an old leather-bound book from a bookshelf.

Melody started to reach for it. Mona held back. "It's extremely delicate," she said.

"I'd be honored to handle it quite gently," Jake said.

Mona opened the book. "Serena Mallory wrote most of the diary here, in Gloucester. And it ends with her heading to New York City, aware that her brother had been captured and was about to be executed. The diary is absolutely charming. There's so much of the day-to-day in it—and so much about the feelings of the general public during the Stamp Act, and then the Boston Tea Party. She has all kinds of wonderful herbal recipes in there—and reference to the fact that she intends to use all her powers to save her brother's life." She paused, glancing up from the pages. "Oh look, I remembered correctly. Serena's brother's name is Jake, too. Jake Mallory. What a pity there isn't an ending to the story!"

Jake took the book, his fingers trembling. He handled it as tenderly as if it were a living being. He quickly flipped to the end to read for himself.

He looked at her across the table. "There is no ending," he said. "Her last words are here. 'May God grant that he be home in time for Christmas.'"

Melody stood quickly, unnerved.

It had to be a hoax. Someone knew that her mother had found the diary. Jake wasn't real. He was a hired actor—maybe Mark had even hired the guy to see what she would do. It was all a cruel hoax. Perhaps someone was trying to prove that Mona was a kook.

But how did anyone manage for her car to spin at precisely the time he was in the road.

"Is everyone finished with dessert?" she asked, her voice ringing coldly.

Keith said, "Come on upstairs, Jake. I'm going to show you my new computer—and dig out some DVDs."

Melody flew into the kitchen with the dessert dishes. Everyone followed, carrying in something from the dinner table. She curtly thanked them all, and shooed her mother out as well, cleaning up after dinner with a vengeance.

When she was done, she tiptoed to the door to the family room. George was in his chair. Her mother was going through more bookshelves.

She flew up the stairs to Keith's room. Jake was sitting in front of her brother's desk, he was still holding the diary and looking dazed.

Keith turned to her. "Civil War. We'll start with the Civil War."

"What?" Melody said.

"What's the best Civil War movie?"

"Gone with the Wind," Melody said.

"Gettysburg. That's the best. It's based on the Shaara novel."

"Yes, but...*Gone with the Wind* is a classic."

"Gettysburg is more of a guy's movie," Keith insisted.

"But *Gone with the Wind* has the manners and mores of the time."

"Gettysburg is better," Keith said stubbornly.

Jake turned, swiveling in the desk chair. "Perhaps, if you'd be so kind, I could see them both. It does seem that, at the moment, time is all I have."

Chapter 4

Melody started dozing off before Scarlett married Rhett.

Keith told her to go to her own room and go to bed; he'd see that Jake saw the end of both movies—they'd move on to the twentieth century after—and that he was settled in the guest room.

She left them uneasily, wondering just what her brother would tell their new friend about the current world, but her drive had been long that day. At first, she stared at the ceiling, thinking that now that she'd actually come to bed, she'd lie awake all night.

But she didn't. She was out cold in a matter of minutes, and if she dreamed, she remembered nothing of it when she woke the next morning.

She felt the morning light come through her drapes, and for a few minutes, she just lay there, appreciating the slow, lazy coming-to-grips with day when she didn't have to rush up for any reason.

Then she remembered Jake and she shot out of bed as if she had been catapulted.

She started immediately out the door, raced back into her bedroom to splash water on her face, give her teeth a furious lick and a promise, and grab a robe and slippers. Then she went tearing down the stairs, afraid of what he might be saying to her parents if he had woken up first.

The house was quiet. She burst into the kitchen, expecting to find her mother.

Her father was there instead.

"Morning, kitten," he said. "Coffee?"

"Um, sure, Dad, thanks. Where's Mom—and Jake? Is he still sleeping?"

"One might have thought—he and your brother watched movies most of the night. But, no, Jake is up and about."

"Where?"

"He went out with your mother."

"What?"

"He's out with your mom. She wanted to pick a few things up at the store, and she was going to take him by the old Anglican church down the way. They were going to look up some records."

"They—they can't just do that. Can they?" she asked, staring at him blankly.

"Are you all right?" he asked her.

"Me? I'm fine. Just fine. Dad—you can't just walk into a church and get to the parish records, can you?"

"If anyone can, it's your mother," George said, smiling and shaking his head. "Well, excuse me, kitten. I'm heading back out to work on my converter."

"Your converter?" she asked.

"Has to do with sound waves and radio frequencies," he told her cheerfully. "It's all so fascinating, if you think about it. Come on, my love, I know you think I'm often crazy, but…I did invent the Dust To End Dust sweeper."

She walked over and hugged him. "And you sent me to college on it, Dad, I'm grateful. I'm just always afraid you're going to hurt yourself. Electronics and chemicals are scary stuff, you know."

"I'm careful," he said.

She nodded.

"Is Keith up?" she asked him.

"I think I hear the shower going. Run in and use the one in the master bedroom, if you want, kiddo. I thought I heard singing a while back, too. That could mean that he's going to take a while."

She sipped the coffee he had prepared for her while she headed back upstairs. She found some warm stockings, a pair of jeans, a long-sleeved knit top and a sweater to wear over it, then padded her way down the hall to her parents' bedroom.

She showered quickly, wanting to be out when her mother returned with Jake.

But they were still gone when she came back down the stairs. Keith, however, was in the kitchen munching on toast and reading the morning paper.

"Where's Dad?" she asked.

"Out back." He grinned. "I'll let you in on a little secret."

"Oh?"

"He's trying to find out if he can contact anyone in outer space."

"Ouch!"

Keith shrugged. "There's more in this universe than you or I will ever know," he told her.

"Let's hope he's not trying to transport down any little green men," Melody said.

Keith reflected on that. "Surely—they won't really be *green*," he said.

"You're as bad as he is," she said.

"I hope I invent something as popular as the Dust To End Dust sweeper," Keith said with a shrug. "No, it hasn't changed the world. But, I'll tell you, it sure keeps my place clean."

"I have a couple in my apartment, too," Melody admitted. "He made good money with it—and I'll bet many a family gets to keep their cat or dog because it really picks up animal hair."

"So, Dad has provided a real service to the world."

"I never suggested he didn't. I'm just always afraid for him and Mom."

Melody heard a clacking sound and then a happy baying. Brutus half ran and half dragged himself into the kitchen, his tail wagging away. She bent to pet him. He was followed by a vivacious Jimmy. Their coats were icy cold.

"They were outside?" Melody said. "How'd they just get back in?"

Her question to her brother was answered by a merry "Hello!" from her mother.

They were back. And her mother had taken the dogs for the ride.

Melody raced out of the kitchen and down the hall to the entry.

Mona was taking off her scarf, giving off a little shiver as she did so. Jake was right behind her, ready to help her with her coat with one hand while he held a shopping bag in the other. Melody raced forward to rescue the bag.

Jake smiled at her. She felt a little pitter-patter in her heart and brushed the feeling away. She still wasn't sure he hadn't been hired by some nefarious and unknown enemy to make her and her family look ridiculous.

And then, of course, there was the possibility of a man who was totally insane.

Because she'd hit him.

Given him a severe concussion, and declined to take him to a hospital.

"Thank you, dear, just drop the groceries in the kitchen—there are a few more bags, boys, if you'll come on out again," Mona said.

Jake and Keith obligingly followed her out. Melody ran the bag into the kitchen, nearly tripped over Brutus, set the bag down and raced back to the door. It was a little late to panic over what might be said in front of her mother when she wasn't there, but she couldn't help feeling ridiculously anxious.

"Did you two have a nice time out?" she asked.

"Oh, it was lovely," Mona said. "We met that nice young Anglican priest, Father Dawson. He hasn't been here all that long, and he was delighted to go through the records with us. Then, we went to the café just down the street from the church, and had a lovely time. Jake is *so* knowledgeable about Colonial days and the

American Revolution. It was just a wonderful and enlightening chat. Father Dawson thinks that Jake must write a book. He says Jake speaks just as if he really understands events—he could do a bang-up job on a first-person historical fiction type of thing."

"I'm sure he could," Keith said, coming in the door with two more grocery bags. Jake was behind him.

"Well, certainly, one day, I'd like to maybe work on a book," he said. "Most of the writing that I've done has been for pamphlets and such other materials."

"Oh, have you written guidebooks?" Mona asked.

"Oh, some of my own rhetoric, that's all," Jake said. He arched a brow to Melody, as if awaiting her approval on his reply.

"Well, I'm glad you had a good morning," she said. "What did you find out?" she asked carefully.

"Nothing. And it's quite strange! The records are there—and, of course these must be Jake's family. I mean, it's just so obvious. There is a record of the other Jake—the revolutionary Jake's ancestors coming to the parish, of Jake's birth, Serena's birth and then adoption into the family," Mona said. "Then, there are records regarding his, the other Jake's parents' deaths—we even found the headstones, and they're legible, they have a very active women's club at the parish. They keep up the graveyard. Oh, the church is lovely. Father Dawson asked us if we'd come by for services sometime on Christmas or Christmas Eve, and I thought it would be a wonderful idea. It's so beautiful, really. The baptismal font there is from England, it was carved in the 1500s. And they have truly magnificent stained-glass windows. Now, mind you, it's not that a church's appearance makes it any more a place of worship. Or a temple, a mosque, what have you. That's all in the spirit of a place, and Father Dawson gives the church such a lovely spirit!"

"What about this other Jake?" Melody asked. Her mother was heading for the kitchen, following her brother and Jake with the grocery bags.

"Only the meat and dairy need go in the refrigerator, Jake," Mona said. He was holding tomatoes, and watching Keith set deli-wrapped cheese in the refrigerator. "Actually, children, get on out of here and let me manage. Take Jake down and show him the tree that's set up outside the courthouse. It's really just beautiful. All lit up!"

"Mom, you do realize that nothing is more lit up than this house, right?" Melody asked her.

Mona shrugged. "I love Christmas."

"And it's truly lovely, the way you love it, Mrs. Tarleton," Jake said.

"You two go on," Keith said with a yawn. "I'll go see what Dad is up to out there. See if he needs any of my help."

"Be careful, dear," Mona said.

"What—is he trying to transport aliens?" Melody whispered to her brother.

He shrugged.

"Come on, Keith!" she said. "Look, I'm actually afraid. I have visions of *The Fly* going through my mind here, Dad winding up half in one place, half in another."

"The Fly?" Mona said.

"I don't even know if she's referring to the Vincent Price original or the Jeff Goldblum remake. What do think, Mom?" Keith asked.

"Melody!" her mother remonstrated.

"It's a legitimate fear," Melody said.

"Have faith in your father."

"I do," Melody said.

Mona came to the door, waving her hands. "Melody, go on out. Jake has only seen the church and the grocery store. He's living in Boston now and hasn't been around here in ages. Go show him the town."

Jake was still wearing a coat, one of Keith's old ones. God knew, they owned enough coats. He wore Keith's clothing well. He had the shoulders, and the height. He really was a good-looking man. But it had nothing to do with his stature, his build or even the well-sculpted lines of his features that made him attractive. It was something in his eyes, in his slow smile, and the way he looked at the world around him. With appreciation—with awe.

It was the way he looked at her, always, with sincerity and appreciation.

"All right," she said briskly, "let's go. But you still haven't told me what happened. You found records regarding eighteenth-century Mallorys. But—"

"There was nothing more. Birth records, and baptismal records, for me and Serena. There's a mention that I went to war. But then…we disappear into history, so it seems."

"There was no death record—for either?" Melody asked.

Jake shook his head. "And it has to mean something," he said.

"Yes, it means you had ancestors. And that maybe neither Jake nor Serena stayed on in Gloucester after the war," Melody said.

He turned to look at her, offering a rueful half smile, shaking his head. "You're never going to believe me, are you?"

"Jake, this is what I think, or what I want to think. You do work for an historic company somewhere. I hit you. You thought you were all right, but you've really got a concussion."

"You want to think that?" he asked.

"It's better than thinking that you're an actor, taking advantage of us in some way," she said, keeping her eye on the car as they walked out.

He stopped moving. She turned around. He stood in the snow, tall and straight.

"Perhaps I should leave," he said.

"Oh, good God, what would you think?" she demanded. "Your story is preposterous."

"I'm not a liar," he said, his jaw rigid.

"You're not a liar. Look, try to understand my position," she said. "I'm sorry. Please, let's just go downtown. You'll love the tree."

"I'm not a liar, and I'm not a child," he said. She was startled when he came to her and set his hands on her shoulders. "I'm telling you the truth. I swear, before God, that I'm telling you the truth. And I must get back. This world—this is a wonderful world. And I'm sure I'd be happy here. But I have to see that my sister is safe. Her name has disappeared from all the records. By God, don't you understand? I'm afraid that she saved me somehow, and wound up dead herself at the hands of the British. Maybe I need to go back and die. But I can't leave her fate hanging…on my life. Can't you understand? Please, I'm begging you."

She stared at him. Truth or not, she was convinced

he wasn't an actor. Or he wasn't acting when he spoke to her now. She let out a deep breath.

"Let's go into town. There's an internet café. We'll start trying to find New York records regarding the Revolution," she said.

She waited for him to ask her what an internet café was.

He didn't.

"Do you know what that is?" she asked him.

"Of course." He was still stiff. Still touching her, and still close. And she suddenly thought it was all too bad; she really liked him. Liked his touch on her. Liked the way his eyes met hers.

"Your brother showed me his computer and explained what he could about the electronics of it last night." He shook his head. "You communicate at the speed of light. All over the world. You don't question that words suddenly appear in your email. You send pictures—moving pictures. You can connect to one another live, see one another's faces from across the globe. That, you must understand, is to me no different than the fact that I am suddenly here."

He was earnest; he was passionate. She was tempted to touch his cheek, and tell him that it was going to be all right.

But it wasn't going to be all right. He was flesh and blood, certainly. He was no ghost.

And living beings did not transport through time.

She stepped back. "Let's head to town. We'll go to the internet café, and we'll look in some shop windows. You can be treated to a bit more culture shock."

"Thank you," he said.

As they headed for the car, he suddenly stopped

again. Melody heard a droning noise, and she looked up. A plane was moving overhead.

"My God," he breathed. He looked at her. "A plane."

"You know what a plane is?"

He smiled. "Your brother told me about aeronautics. Men have gone into space. Man has come so far—you'd have thought he would have found a way to stop war by now."

"Technology has come forward," she said. "Man—not so much. Come on."

He opened the driver's door for her and walked around to the passenger side. When he was seated, she reached over to show him where his seat belt was. He had already found it. "I am understanding this," he told her. "Perhaps you would be willing to teach me how to drive this type of vehicle," he said.

"Um, sure," she said.

She eased out of the driveway. "Winter, however, isn't a great time to learn to drive. You can skid on the black ice. And I think we're going to have some kind of ice storm either tonight or tomorrow. I heard about it on the radio, coming in."

He smiled.

"What?"

"Well, I now know a lot about your life," he said. "Your mother told me a great deal about you."

"She did?"

"Yes, she said that she had thought you were happy. She's glad I'm here, as long as I'm not here as a buffer. She thought you were in love with a young man named Mark, who will be here tomorrow night or Christmas Eve, and she doesn't really understand what went wrong."

"My mother should not be talking about me."

"She loves you."

"She still shouldn't have been giving you my personal history."

He shrugged, looking out the window, still rapt at anything they passed. "I believe she assumed I knew about your life. And you're very lucky, you know."

"Oh?" she asked carefully.

He looked at her. "Your parents are both living. They love you, and they love your brother very much. You have a wonderful home, a beautiful place to come home to, and that's something very special, something to be appreciated."

She felt a flush rise to her cheeks, and she winced inwardly.

He was right.

She spent way too much time dreading what they might do, and not appreciating them for all that they were.

Not even realizing that she needed to appreciate the fact that she had them both, they were still young and vital, and would one day make wonderful, crazy, eccentric grandparents.

"You're right," she said quietly. "I am very lucky." She chanced a quick glance at him. "So, tell me more about your life."

"Why? So you can call me a liar?" he asked. His voice didn't rise with the question; he spoke with dignity.

"You know, it's rather cruel and unchristian not to forgive," she said.

"How can I forgive you when you do think I'm a liar?" he asked.

She let out a groan of frustration. "I don't think you're a liar. I think you're...hurt. But tell me more about your life. Apparently, you wowed Father Dawson."

"Have you met him? He's a charming man."

"Um—no. Actually, we did grow up going to church. I go in New York. Sometimes."

"Ah."

"Okay, please, I like church. But sometimes, if you grew up with my mom, it's a little weird. She's seriously friends with a community of Wiccans. They come and go saying 'blessed be,' all the time. One of her best friends is Muslim, and my dad takes me to parties thrown by a lot of his Jewish contemporaries all the time."

He was smiling. "There's nothing wrong with 'blessed be.' Belief is in the spirit, it creates the soul, and I think it's beyond wonderful that this country has come to a place where people are truly free to worship how they please."

"Don't go thinking the world is all hunky-dory," she warned. "People out there still have prejudices. They practice cruelty. As you've learned—there's always a war to be found somewhere."

"But there's always hope, too, isn't there?" he asked.

She shook her head, unable to prevent a smile. "Okay, there's the tree my mom was talking about. I'll park, and we can walk around."

She parked. The day was cold, but the sun was out. The snow glistened in beautiful shades of dazzling silver. Kids raced around the little gate that kept the tree safe, throwing snowballs and laughing.

Melody found herself suddenly whacked in the head.

She turned around to see a boy of about eleven looking horrified. But even as he stared at her—an adult—in trepidation, a small smile started to curve on his face.

"Hey!" she protested. But she found he made her laugh, and she reached down and formed a snowball quickly.

He realized her intent too late, and she got him good on the shoulder. One of his friends cried out, "She's in, she's in—get her!"

"Hey!" A rain of snowballs was suddenly coming at her.

But she wasn't fighting alone. Jake was laughing behind her, dishing up and throwing as fast as he could.

One caught her in the chin. "Devils!" she accused.

Jake grabbed her by the shoulder, leading her behind an embankment. To her astonishment, other adults started joining in, which made other children join in. From somewhere, a stereo was sending "Joy to the World" out among the crowd, and though she was getting wetter by the minute, the snowball fight was like a return to her own childhood and a simpler time of life.

She suddenly stepped out to get a really good throw in.

"Get down!" Jake warned. He'd come behind her, and he pressed her shoulder, getting her out of the way as a mammoth white flurry came soaring by. He was armed and ready to return fire, but she slipped down beneath the pressure of his touch.

Another hail of snowballs fell upon Jake, and he slipped into the snow beside her, almost on top of her. The next thing she knew, there were five or six children standing around them, pelting them. She was laughing so hard she couldn't fight back. Jake reached out, though, and brought one of the kids down, and suddenly they were all slipping and falling and lying together in the snow. Jake rolled, and he was on top of her; he lifted his weight and stared down into her eyes, smiling.

"It's true that some things never change," he said softly.

Some things never changed. Moments like this. When he stared down into her face, that smile on his lips, and she wanted to touch his face because some things never changed. There would always be that spark that could exist between a man and woman, and whatever it was, chemistry, pheromones, a tone of voice, a scent, whatever the sex researchers came up with, it suddenly wrapped her in a warmth that took away the slightest feel of the chill of the snow.

His expression grew oddly taut and grave, and he smiled again, and eased himself up, extending a hand to draw her up with him. She was stunned when she heard the kids around them applauding. A little girl said, "Wow. Cool grown-ups. Don't see that often."

"Good fight, kids!" Jake said. He looked at her. "You're trembling. Let's get in out of the cold."

"The internet café is right over there."

He slipped an arm around her as they walked. It was a natural gesture. It wasn't a pickup. It was a courteous way of keeping her warm.

They stepped into the café. There was an empty table by the hearth where a warm fire was burning. The fireplace didn't offer the only heat in the room, but it was cozy-looking and extremely inviting.

"Sit, and hold our place. I'll get coffee and pay for the time," Melody told Jake.

He caught her hand as she was leaving. "I'll repay you for this. I swear. I am not accustomed to allowing anyone to pay my way."

She smiled. "Of course."

At the counter, she bought coffee, paid for a half hour of time on the computer and returned. She logged on with the code given to her by the café clerk. A list of recent news choices flashed onto the screen, along with a picture of President Obama.

Jake stared at the screen, entranced. "That man is the president—of the Unites States?" he asked.

"Yes."

"Well, of course," he said. "I watched the movies… of course. It's incredible. I love this new world of yours. We have come so far. I had never imagined."

"Yes, it's amazing. But as I told you before, there are still people out there who hate each other for being of a certain color, religion, nationality or sexual persuasion. Laws have come a long way. But there are people out there who would change them again. It's still a fight to see that we are all treated fairly."

"But the laws…my God, I am proud."

She smiled. Then her smile faded. She was playing his game, and he was so easy to believe—but what he kept telling her was impossible.

"All right, I'm looking up New York in the Revolution on Google," she said.

He sat there quietly in amazement. Thousands of pages popped up so Melody did a search with Jake's name and the Revolution.

To her surprise, pages popped up. "Jake Mallory, Patriot hero," were key words in many of them.

"You were a hero?"

He shrugged. "I was the same as many a man. I happened to get caught. What does it say about me?"

She went on. There were references to the many pamphlets and essays he had put out in various papers of the time. Thus, when his company was captured during one of the many battles and skirmishes that took place before the British solidified their hold on the city, he was selected to be executed as an example to others. Nathan Hale had already gone to the noose.

"Is there any reference to my sister?" he asked anxiously. They were trying to read together, which wasn't easy.

"I'm not seeing anything yet. Oh, look—here!" Melody said.

"Where are you? Where, where?"

Melody read out loud. "'Jake Mallory's execution took place at 10:00 a.m. on the morning of December 22. Though Christmas was quickly approaching, the commander in charge, Major Hempton, wanted the people to be given a severe warning regarding rebellion against the mother country. He believed that Mallory's execution would warn citizens away from speaking or writing against the Crown, or harboring any individuals involved in any covert or open subversive activities. Historical references to the day are sketchy, one witness wrote of a snowstorm that obscured the execution. Another wrote of a bizarre storm of roses. There are no eyewitness accounts to be found that say whether the execution was carried out, and there are no death records for Jake Mallory. It's possible that the execution was carried out, and that Mallory's body was quickly buried in an obscure plot since the execution caused something of a Christmas riot, or a mass hallucination.'"

She stopped reading and stared at Jake.

"There's no reference to Serena," he said.

She exhaled. "There are more pages, more references to be read."

She looked away quickly. *Why did so much seem to be true?*

Perhaps his job had been portraying Jake Mallory at a theater. Or at a park. Through the park service, national or state. Maybe he put on a one-man show, and now believed, with his whole heart, that he was this man.

"May we keep reading?" he asked.

She nodded.

One of the references read, "Jake Mallory disappears from the end of a hangman's noose. Witchcraft suspected in New York execution."

The article wasn't really that bizarre. The author this time suggested that Mallory's friends had devised a way to spirit him away when the noose was tightened. Perhaps his British captors, fond of the man, had even helped in his escape.

Another article finally mentioned that Mallory's sister had come to the execution, and created a scene, thus allowing for his escape.

Jake read aloud. "'Mallory was hanged from an open gallows. His body should have been visible to all witnesses. That they speak of sudden snowstorms and rose petals suggests that the escape was cunningly and meticulously planned.'"

"So you escaped," Melody said.

"I wish there was another reference to Serena," he said.

"Well, here's the good news—we can't find anything that suggests that she was captured, held or killed by the British. I'm imaging that whatever happened that day, chaos probably broke loose and she simply went home. I'm sure she was all right," Melody said.

The screen suddenly warned them that their time was up. She realized that despite the fire, she was still shivering.

"Let's get home," she said huskily.

"Home," he said.

Melody couldn't help but grin then. "You did say that it was your home, once. So…"

"Home," he said again, and he smiled. "But it's your home now. So thank you, thank you for taking me there."

Her heart fluttered again.

Why couldn't she feel this way about someone sane?

They left the café and walked to the car. He was thoughtful, staring out the window as they headed to her house.

Just as they pulled into the driveway, there was the sound of an explosion.

And a huge puff of smoke erupted from the laboratory at the back of the house.

Chapter 5

"Dad!"

Melody was out of the car so quickly that she nearly slid facedown in the ice. She caught herself and went racing for the back, barely aware that Jake was behind her.

As she came around the corner, Keith was leading her father out the door of the laboratory; both men had blackened faces.

"Dad, Dad, are you all right?" Melody demanded, running to him.

"I did it!" he cried, grabbing her and swinging her around.

"Dad!" She strained against his shoulders, forcing him to put her down. Keith stood wryly at his side, wiping at his face. "Dad!" she scolded. "That was an explosion. Is the fire out? Are you all right?"

Keith answered. "All out—much more smoke than fire. What you saw was bright light—alpha light, as Dad is terming it."

"What are you trying to accomplish?" Melody demanded.

"A frequency for physical movement," George told her.

"What?"

"It's complicated," Keith said.

She threw her brother a furious glance. "I majored in art, not stupidity. Dad, please, I'm so afraid that what you're doing is dangerous. And I do think you're brilliant, and I'm grateful, but I love you and I just think that you should be working on...things that will be useful in life."

"The Clapper is useful if you're elderly and it's difficult to get up and turn out the lights," Keith said.

"You're telling me that Dad is trying to improve on the 'Clapper'?" Melody demanded.

"No, no, that's not what I'm doing," George said. "Think about the many things people don't really understand. You hit a button on a remote control and the TV channel changes. You hit buttons on your phone, and you can speak to someone on the other side of the globe."

"Not with my service," Keith said dryly.

Everyone stared at Keith. "Lighten up, guys, lighten up," he said.

Jake, who had been standing silently, watching them all, spoke, "It's really true, you know. Discoveries are exactly that. Once upon a time, remember, the learned believed that the world was flat. And trust me, during the Revolution, even the lights you take for granted would be the most amazing creation ever. Men lived by candlelight, by lamps, and none could imagine that a whole city could seem to be ablaze with light. And then—an automobile. And vehicles that fly through the air. Men on the moon. Modern warfare in which an entire city can be destroyed with the push of a button. Melody, think about it, really. There's no reason to believe that your father can't invent anything."

"But he's going to blow himself up!" Melody protested.

"Daughter! I'm the man who put you through school, kept clothes on your back—believed that you could make a living at being an artist and that you *shouldn't* have to major in physics, English or something entirely practical and guaranteed," George said indignantly.

Melody was at a loss. Keith always sided with their father—they were two of a kind. And Jake was obviously not going to help her.

She was about to throw her arms up and walk away.

She didn't get the chance.

Mona stuck her head out the back door. "Supper is just about ready, all. Come on in. George, dear, oh! And Keith! I think you two really need to go on up and wash your faces. You've got about ten minutes."

"Yes, dear, right away. Thank you," George said.

He pinched Melody's cheek and headed on in. Keith did the same. She glared at him.

Jake, grinning, walked by her, too. "Mrs. Tarleton, please, will you allow me to help you set up for the meal?"

"How charming, well, of course, Jake. Thank you so much. There's really nothing to it these days, just throw a few things out on the table," Mona said.

The back door closed. None of them seemed to realize they'd even left her out there.

She started to follow, but changed her mind. She went to the door of her father's laboratory and opened it carefully.

Whatever had occurred had taken place on one of his lab tables. The fire extinguisher was still next to the table. Keith, however, had wiped up the chemicals. Despite the fact it had sounded as if a bomb had gone off, the place looked clean. Well, other than the layer of soot on the windows, but she knew that when the meal was over, George would come right out and finish the cleanup.

She walked over to her father's desk. Looking at the many scattered papers, she did suddenly rue the fact that she had been totally enamored of the arts in school. She'd had basic courses in math and science, but not much more. She just wished that she could begin to understand the initials and squiggle lines drawn on the spreadsheet her father had out on his desk.

Curious, she hit the mouse for her father's computer, bringing it back to life. She had expected to see squiggles and chemical initials, as well. But there was an article open in the corner that spoke about black holes and magnetic fields. There was another article on the Bermuda Triangle, and it's counterpart across the globe. There were many suggested theories regarding the Triangle—one, aliens were controlling the space; two, there was a different kind of black hole to be discovered there; and three, it all had to do with the magnets of the earth's poles.

She tended to think the last might be the most logical, herself.

There was also an email on the page that was open beneath the articles. Oddly enough, it was from her mother.

George, I've been reading a book written by a scout working for the French before the French and Indian wars. A Massasoit chief had brought him to what they called "the place of the waters and five trees." The scout swore that the chief showed him how a rabbit could disappear—and an owl could fly out when the rabbit was gone. It had to do with the shaman's magic, he said, but it could only take place at that one spot. I'll show it to you later. This may have something to do with your waves and frequencies that cause movement.

Melody backed away from the computer, dismayed. Now her mother was in on it all. She wasn't just being tolerant—she was trying to turn some of her Wiccan or pagan beliefs into something scientific.

The door to the laboratory opened. She stepped back from the computer.

She flushed, aware that she had been reading a private message.

It wasn't her father, or her mother. It was Jake.

"They're crazy," she said, shaking her head. "Oh, my God, they're both crazy."

Jake stared at her, smiling very slowly, shaking his head. "They thirst for knowledge—that doesn't make them crazy. Melody, they are very dear people. You are blessed."

"I know they're dear people. Don't you understand

how much I love them? That's why I worry so much. And Keith is certainly no help."

"Your brother is a good man, as well," Jake said. "And you love them—you're not giving them your faith. You want everything solid, in black-and-white all the time. But love isn't solid, and you love your family. Give them your belief, as well. Belief isn't tangible, you'll never hold it in your hands. But it's a beautiful gift to give someone."

Well, of course, Jake would speak so well on belief. He had the craziest story in history, and he wanted her to believe him.

"Sure," she said, turning away. There was bottle of glass cleaner and a roll of paper towels near the lab table. She picked up both and started working on her father's windows. Jake helped her. He was good, and he was quick. He seemed awed by the glass cleaner. "This is so much easier," he said. "So…and the paper towels. Amazing."

"Jake, I'm really glad that anyone can get that excited by Windex. We don't use paper towels that often. My mother is trying to save the trees," she said.

"Save the trees?"

"Yes, that's one problem with all the technology we've created. The air is going bad because we cut down the rain forests. Fish are tainted because industry has caused the mercury levels in the seas to rise. Industrial waste is incredibly high, and even when we— Americans, the biggest group of users—pass laws to protect the environment, we can't force other countries to do the same. You've seen all that's wonderful, but it all comes at a price, too."

He nodded gravely. "So it is better to use cloth with which to clean, and vinegar, and other old sources."

"Natural sources."

He nodded again. "As you pointed out, I believe, hemlock is natural."

"All right, so there is a neutral ground. Sadly, we haven't found it yet."

"Even back where I came from, one person could not solve all the problems. Working together is the only way," Jake said.

"Yeah, and that sure works out just great all the time," Melody said.

Jake shook his head. "Melody, I do believe that you need a good slap—which, of course, I will never deliver. Don't cry about what you see that you don't like, work at it."

"I can't send my father to his room for bad behavior," she said.

"Your father hasn't behaved badly. You have," he said. There wasn't accusation in his words; it was just something that he was pointing out.

"I love my father!"

He answered slowly and carefully. "I know I'm an outsider, looking in. But your mother has shown me pictures you drew in kindergarten. She's told me that friends and neighbors thought it was actually silly that you went to school for art—artists didn't make it, not often, anyway. But she and your father knew that you were good. They loved you, and they had faith in you."

"You really don't understand. My father is a brilliant man, and I know that. I don't want to see him go brilliantly crazy," she said firmly.

"Are dreams all crazy?"

"You know, you're just being aggravating," she said. "You're right—you are an outsider. You don't understand."

"All right. But I think he's an amazing man. He's fearless, and he's proven he's talented. I confess, you're right—I don't understand. I don't know why you won't let him have a dream."

He turned around and headed for the house. She looked after him, feeling chastised and resentful.

And wondering if she did fail to believe in others when she so craved that they believe in her.

"I should have dropped him at a hospital!" she muttered to herself.

She could still do so, of course. Walk into the dining room and announce that she had struck him while driving, been certain that he would come to his senses if she just brought him home to be fixed, but it wasn't working.

She wondered vaguely if she could be arrested now for striking the man and *not* filing a police report immediately. She could just imagine herself in the lockup for Christmas with her family gathered around her.

No. She wasn't going to do anything. And it wasn't because she was afraid of being arrested.

She wasn't ready to let him go.

Resolutely, she walked toward the house. What bothered her, she knew, was that he got beneath her skin.

Everything was on the table when she went in, and her father was pouring lemonade into glasses to go around the table.

"Mom, I'm sorry, I should have been in helping," she said.

"Oh, your dad and I have this down pat—we're all fine here. You can do the cleanup if you wish, dear," her mother said.

"That will be perfect," her father said. "Your mom and I like to snuggle and watch that new game show that comes on at eight."

Keith, across the table from her, made a face. "They're too cute, aren't they?" he asked. "So, what are we going to do tonight?" he asked.

"I was thinking that there are a zillion more DVDs that Jake really needs to see," Melody said.

"I was thinking that we should take him clubbing," Keith said.

"There will be a designated driver," her father said sternly.

"See, there's one of the great aspects of living in New York City," Melody said. "Your entire group can pass out and you're okay because you take taxis everywhere."

"Melody," her mother said worriedly.

"Mom, I'm just saying in the city we don't think about designated drivers. I don't actually go out and pass out. Of course we'll be responsible," Melody said.

"Wherever did we get such a sarcastic child?" Mona said, shaking her head.

"Hey—Keith's the one who spends his life torturously teasing everyone," Melody protested.

"Torturously teasing?" Keith said. "There's a mouthful."

"We do have a guest," George said. "Let's all behave."

Mona turned to Jake. "I'll bet you know wonderful little tidbits about the Founding Fathers from your job at the tour company. Have you any great stories that the general public may not know?" she asked.

He finished chewing—meat loaf—and mulled over the question for a moment. "What I don't think people realize today, perhaps, is what a losing proposition going to war against Britain really was. Every single man who signed the Declaration of Independence was, in essence, signing his own death certificate. The United States was a group of separate colonies, all with different problems, and different beliefs. Even—among the Thirteen Colonies, there were terrible arguments about how a new government should be formed. All these men who were the Founding Fathers were individuals. They all had their strange habits, some drove the others crazy—they were people. Somehow they got it together to form a nation."

Great, he just managed to sound better every time he opened his mouth.

"You must be a wonderful guide!" Mona said enthusiastically.

"You speak as if you've seen the past and the present," George told him. "My God, what a wonderful way you have of putting everything into perspective. We spend so much time these days just bitching and moaning!"

"Dad, we're supposed to bitch and moan. It's our God-given right," Keith said.

"If we don't bitch and moan, how do we change things?" Melody asked. She turned to Jake. "Isn't that half the point of the Constitution, too? It was written to be amended. Dad, if people didn't bitch and moan, women wouldn't have the vote. Slavery would still exist. We have to speak up to change things, right?"

"Absolutely," Jake said. "Hopefully, though," he said sorrowfully, "most changes will not require a civil war. But then, I suppose that was inevitable. I mean, even when they were writing the Constitution, it was an issue. Many people wanted antislavery laws written in, but many of the men going to war were slave owners. Some made a point of saying that upon their deaths their slaves were to be given their freedom, but then again, I took umbrage with that myself! I mean, if that's your belief, make it a point during your own lifetime."

Keith flashed his sister a smile. There was an indignation in Jake's voice that rang sincerely.

Just as if he'd really been there at the time.

"I wrote about it, of course," Jake continued. "I made a few enemies, and certainly rhetoric spun around and around, and you must remember, certain of those men did despise one another. Of course, I was never in that inner circle, but my realm surrounded it, and it's important to remember that we forced ourselves to make compromises, to rise above our own personalities. It doesn't mean that it was perfect, little in life is ever perfect. But we made it work, despite ourselves."

George and Mona were staring at Jake, dumbstruck.

"He's gone into guide mode," Melody said hastily.

Jake stared at her. His eyes widened with alarm, and he quickly turned to George. "Sorry, I suppose I did go into…*guide* mode. Mrs. Tarleton, the meat loaf, as all else, is wonderfully palatable, quite delicious, really. Thank you so much for the kindness of this meal."

"Um—you're welcome," Mona said quickly.

"All right, looks like we're all done here!" Melody said, rising. She snatched her brother's plate and her own. She started to reach across the table for Jake's.

"Melody," her mother protested, "Jake is still eating!"

"He just has that last bite and he's all done!" she said cheerfully. "Right, Jake? Scoop it on in."

He chewed his last bite; the fork was barely off the plate before Melody had it in her hands. She breezed through the swinging kitchen door, then returned in seconds flat for the rest of the plates. Jake, who had risen after his last mouthful, was collecting more of the dinnerware.

"Lemonade back in the refrigerator, please!" she said.

"My goodness, they're in a hurry," Mona said.

"Clubbing," George told her knowingly.

"Responsibly!" Mona added.

"No, Mom," Melody said. "We're all going to get completely wasted, do a few drugs, maybe go park somewhere in the woods where we know that slashers in masks come to attack the foolish young people. It will be great."

"Where did we go wrong?" George groaned.

"Well, we didn't actually go wrong," Mona said. "They're just very mouthy children. Come on, old fellow, let's go get comfy in the family room and leave this all to them!"

With her brother and Jake, it was quick and easy for Melody to get everything picked up and done; Keith was a twenty-first-century guy, much like her father, ready to pitch in with housework, babies, whatever might come his way. Jake seemed ready to fall right in, too.

His fascination with the dishwasher was endless. He

seemed to have gotten the concept of the indoor plumbing down all right, but the dishwasher still amazed him.

"He might go crazy vacuuming," Keith whispered. "We need to show him how!"

She jabbed her brother in the elbow.

"We should be watching DVDs," she said. "He has a lot more history to go through—we could show him *Defiance,* or *All's Quiet on the Western Front,* or *Pale Rider,* or *The Unforgiven,* or—"

"We can start a moviefest in the morning," Keith said. "Come on, let's go clubbing. Cut a rug, all that stuff."

"Cut a rug? What, now you fell out of the last decades, too?" Melody demanded.

"Hustle and shout, baby," Keith teased.

"Hustle and shout? Is that like a rebel yell?" Jake asked.

"Kind of. My brother insists that you want to see the current pickup mode. Bar hopping, or clubbing. A bunch of drunk people sit around in ridiculous outfits. Sometimes they dance. The music is loud enough to blast your ears. Sometimes, they ask each other questions like, 'What sign are you?' Sometimes they're honest, and just try to buy each other drinks—or get right down to it and find out if they want to sleep with one another," Melody said.

"Shocking," Jake said.

"See? He doesn't want to go," Melody said.

"On the contrary, I'm quite fascinated," Jake said.

Keith started to laugh. "It's time to hit the nightlife! No, wait—it's almost time to hit the nightlife. I mean, we have some good stuff right here, but…children!" He set an arm around Melody's shoulder and then one around Jake's. "Go spiff up. No, sorry, Melody, you go spiff up. I'll have to give Jake the right stuff to spiff up with. Thirty minutes, we meet on the porch. I'll play tour guide for the evening."

"What are you up to?" Melody asked her brother suspiciously.

"Trust me."

"That's a slightly frightening concept," she said.

"Oh, ye of little faith!"

She glanced at Jake. He was smiling, watching her.

"Oh, what the hell. Sure, I'm going to trust the guy who used to like to exchange my shampoo with cooking oil. The one who put frogs in my bed. Yeah, right. I will. I'll just go on blind faith!"

She took off up the stairs, shaking her head. "See you guys in thirty."

Thirty minutes later, they were on the porch.

And Keith had done an extraordinary job with Jake.

He was strikingly handsome. While Keith hadn't given him a short cut, he had cleaned up a bit of the rough edges. Jake was clean shaven. He was wearing black dress jeans, a black turtleneck sweater with a jagged red Z down it, and a clean-cut dinner jacket beneath Keith's black wool coat.

He could have posed for *GQ* in a flash.

Her brother was equally impressive in shades of black and amber.

She was glad that she had taken Keith's warning to heart and dressed up a bit. She had never been able to understand the desire to wear something sleeveless beneath a coat, even if most places did heat up the insides to a toasty warmth. She had chosen a long-sleeved black velvet dress with a wicked side slit and a sweetheart neckline. She didn't actually own a pair of stilettos, but she did break down and wear stockings and heels, a pair her mother had bought her at a sale at Filene's Basement. They were actually beautiful shoes, with rhinestones down the back of the shoe and the heel. She'd only worn them a few times.

Keith whistled when he saw her come out on the porch.

Jake asked Keith if whistling was all right because he was her brother, or if it was offensive to whistle, or perhaps expected these days.

"Good question, my man," Keith told him. "If a pretty girl is just walking down the street minding her own business, I never whistle. If I'm seeing a friend, my sister, my mom, or the new light of my life, I whistle. Because they know I mean it as a compliment. Whistling. Hmm. That's one you have to play by ear."

"May I?" Jake asked Melody.

She laughed. "Go for it," she said.

He whistled.

"Great whistle. Okay, whose doing the driving, you or me?" she asked Keith.

"Neither of us."

"We're clubbing it on the front porch?" she asked.

"Keith has arranged for a livery," Jake said.

"What?"

"Sis, I hired a car. For some reason, I don't see Jake here really getting blitzed, but who knows? And he doesn't any ID anyway, and he doesn't know how to drive a car. Personally, I'd pay to see you a little snookered. And I didn't feel like making any promises. So—voilà. There he is—our hired town car. Right on time."

Melody arched a brow. She was thinking that she should protest.

But she didn't want to. The idea of the three of them out on the town with Christmas on the way was a pretty nice one.

"Where are we going?" Melody asked.

"I thought Jake should see Boston. What do you think?"

"Boston sounds fun," she agreed.

"As I told Jake, I would dearly love to see Boston as it is today," Jake said.

"Let's go," Melody said.

"George," Mona called to her husband from the laundry room.

"Wait, just a second, Mona," George said. "I'm just waiting to see if the construction worker from Des Moines gets the Big Money!"

"Oh, George! He gets the money. He's a very smart fellow."

"How do you know, Mona?"

"It's a repeat!"

"Oh." George was deflated.

"I'm so sorry, dear."

"It's all right."

Mona heard him rising and walking back to the laundry room.

"What is it?" George asked.

"I picked up Jake's clothing in Keith's room. Will you look at this? Hand-darned socks. His clothing is all made by hand, look at the stitching. It's amazing work."

"Well, he must work at one of those places where they do everything exactly like they did in Colonial times," George said, shrugging.

"It's amazing. Everything about that young man is amazing, really. I mean, his name. His association with that book I have…"

"Mona, this is New England. Every town has a Main Street. Everyone is named after everyone else. What's so amazing?"

"George, you have no imagination."

"Mona, you're always accusing me of having too much imagination."

"There's something up here," she said firmly.

"What? You think he plopped down on us from Colonial times?" George said dryly.

"Maybe."

"Oh, Mona. *CSI* is on. I've got to watch."

She sighed. "Yes, dear, so you can complain about what they're doing wrong?"

"I don't complain."

"You do."

"Well, come join me anyway."

"I'll just get the laundry started and…hmm, let's have some warm wine!"

"Whatever you like, dear."

He headed on back to the family room. Mona studied the fine hand stitching in Jake Mallory's clothing once again.

They started off at a place called Trinity. The music tended toward trance, and the dance floor was hopping. There was no conversation because it was impossible to speak over the music. But they had a drink, and Jake managed to insist that Keith and Melody dance on the dance floor with it's huge strobe lights.

After one number, Keith told Jake that he needed to dance.

"I don't know these dances," he said.

"You don't have to know anything. Just gyrate," Melody told him.

"I think I'll observe a bit longer."

"That's okay, we're moving on. How about some kind of heavy-metal rock next?" Keith asked Melody.

"I'm along for the ride," she said.

And it was a ride well worth being on. Jake was entranced by the skyscrapers dotting the landscape, and more fascinated to see that Faneuil Hall was still standing. They asked their driver to let them off and circle the block a few times so that Jake could see the changes. Through his eyes, the world seemed new. He pointed out where incidents had taken place, where a printing shop had stood, where he had first met John Adams.

Jake walked away, staring at the shops that now surrounded so much that was historical. "We'll come back in the daytime," Keith called to him, "and you can see the Old North Church."

"I'd like that," Jake said.

The car came back around for them. They opted for their next spot, down near the Boston Common. This one played hard rock. Jake was fascinated by the amps.

"Do you play anything?" Melody shouted to Jake.

"Some fiddle, a bit on the flute, a few other instruments…" he told her. He pointed. "That's like a harpsichord, or a piano."

"Right—it's called a keyboard now!" Melody shouted.

"Do the players go deaf after a while?" Jake shouted back.

"Yes!" Keith assured him.

They ordered chicken wings and beer, and listened while the band played.

"This is good music. Good dancing music," Keith said.

"The couples do seem to be dancing together," Jake pointed out.

"That's a hustle, super easy," Keith said. "Melody, show him how."

"I—I—I can't lead," Melody said.

"Jake, one, two, back step, one, two, back step. Follow Melody."

"Well?" Jake offered her a hand.

"I'm not that good."

"I won't know, will I?" Jake asked.

They went out on the dance floor together. Jake was awkward at first, but he was willing to be back-led. And it was a simple step, and after a moment, he had it. And as he followed her, she found her confidence growing. "Okay, you're swinging me," she told him.

"Swinging you where?" he asked.

"Just go with it," she said.

She took a chance, got him to raise his arm, and she went out in a spin, then led him into a counterspin. When the number finished, she was flushed and excited. They met Keith back at the table, and he looked like the cat who had eaten the canary, very proud of himself.

"Time to move on!" Keith told them.

Apparently, her brother had done some planning. The next place they went, the band played oldies and the decibel level was a bit lower. Jake seemed very happy there, listening to renditions of Elvis Presley, the Beatles, Journey, Boston, Styx and a number of other bands.

This venue offered jalapeño poppers, and Keith thought Jake should certainly try them as a tasty treat. And Jake seemed to enjoy them.

"Heading on to a pub now. Mahoney's," Keith advised.

The band at Mahoney's was actually Irish. Jake grinned as they took seats at a booth and ordered Guinness stout.

"I know that ditty!" he told them.

"I'm familiar with it," Melody said.

"I can dance to this," Jake told her, grinning. "I can even lead."

"Well, I can't dance to it," Melody said.

"I was willing to take a chance," Jake said. "Have some faith—in me? Please?"

She nodded. He spoke quietly as they headed for the dance floor. "Basic steps," he said. "Very easy, I swear. Point your right toe, straight out from your knee. Step, and bring your left foot together behind it—one, two. Then, right toe to your left knee and do a wee hop. Right leg back, and hop on your left foot."

"This isn't easy—it's complicated!" Melody protested.

"Easy, you'll get it. Just doing it, you'll get it. Now, right foot on the floor behind your left foot, three small steps behind you, starting with your left, repeat it two times, all with your right foot in front."

"Jake, this is a lot harder than step, step, back step!" Melody told him.

"But you've got it."

And more or less, she did. The band was encouraging them, the place was clapping. She was hopping, spinning and laughing, and having the time of her life.

"Hey, buddy!" the fiddler player asked. "You play, too?"

Jake looked at Melody.

"*Buddy* is an expression. He doesn't know your name," Melody advised.

"Should I play with them?"

"If you know a tune."

"Several."

"Go on up!" Melody prodded.

He hesitated, then accepted a fiddle. He spoke with the band members for a minute, and then they began to play.

Keith came to stand behind Melody.

"There's the coolest guy I've met since I don't know when," Keith said.

"Too bad he's crazy."

"Maybe he's not."

"Keith, please! What he's saying is impossible."

Keith swung her around. "Melody! How do we know that for sure? A man on the moon—that's crazy. Space travel, laser surgery, microchips—they're all crazy. Maybe, just maybe, he's telling the truth."

Melody watched Jake.

And Jake seemed to be in his element.

"He wants to go home," Keith said. "He's worried sick about his sister."

"And that's…commendable, I guess. Whether it's real—or in his head," she said firmly.

"Pity," Keith said.

"What's a pity?"

"He will figure out a way to go back. With or without your help. He'll figure it out somehow."

"Why is it a pity, if it's what he wants?" she asked.

Keith looked at her. "Because I wish that he would stay. And if you decided to get honest with yourself for just a minute, you wish it, too."

He started to walk away from her.

"Hey!"

"What?"

"Where are you going?"

"I'm going to get another Guinness and watch the music. Don't want to waste that limo, eh?"

"Yeah, wait a minute, how are you affording that limo?"

"Building websites, sis, building websites. If you were smart, you'd let me build one for you—and you could start selling your art. Then you'll quit worrying about breaking up with Mark, 'cause, ya see, though it's none of my business, that's not going to make it."

She opened her mouth to protest that she hadn't been hanging on for gain—in any way or form. It wasn't true.

She had been having a hard time trying not to hurt Mark.

But maybe, just maybe, she had been hanging on too long.

Because she did lack faith.

In herself, as well as in others.

Chapter 6

"Eye of newt and toe of frog?" George teased, slipping into bed beside his wife. She had barely noticed him coming to bed, she was so engrossed in her reading. He recognized the book; it was one of the old diaries from the attic.

"You know, you could offer that diary to the Peabody Essex Museum and make a mint, maybe," George said.

"Lovely, dear," she replied.

"The moon fell into the Atlantic tonight," George said.

"Hmm. Great."

"The sun is due to drop into the Pacific at 3:00 p.m. eastern time tomorrow."

"Yes, of course."

"Mona!"

"What? What!" The old diary nearly went flying as she jumped.

"Why on earth are you so spellbound?" he demanded.

"It's this journal—by Serena Mallory," Mona said.

George groaned. "I know—*you* are related to her somehow, and her talents for witchcraft have come through the genes through the centuries!"

"Don't be silly, George. We're not related. You and I bought this house when I graduated from nursing school. No, I'm just reading what this woman wrote, and it's fascinating. George, it's all relating."

He plumped his pillow. "What's all relating?"

"You and I, dear."

"We have been married since time began," he said with a sigh.

She was no longer completely concentrating. She gave him a good jab in the ribs.

"Ouch!"

"Speak for yourself, my love. *I* am not that old."

"Hmm."

"And, my dear husband, you do recall that *you* might be considered an alchemist."

"Right. Just like Merlin. Where's the sword? I can pull it out of a stone."

"George, Merlin couldn't pull the sword from the stone. Only King Arthur could do that. No, what I'm saying is this. Serena Mallory speaks—sorry, writes—with a lot of metaphors, but she had tremendous faith. Beautiful faith, really. Magic existed in her world to protect the good. Those who did not practice goodness and love pretty much deserved what evils the earth might cast their way, but those who were fighting for their poorer neighbors or for justice—"

"Truth! And the American way," George put in.

She rewarded him with a warning glare.

"We're not talking Superman here, George."

"Just superpowers, eh?"

"My darling, you must take me seriously here. I do that for you. Have I ever protested at the rise of our bill for fire extinguishers?"

"No," he said, giving her a peck on the forehead. "No, you have not."

"Well, we all know that you folks teased me for years about my belief in tea—especially green tea. And now, of course, the health benefits of tea are touted all over the place," Mona said.

He nodded. "Um, Mona, I don't think that the health benefits of tea align with magic."

"Hear me out. I told you about the reference to a sort of black hole by the scout who knew the Massasoit chief?"

"What?"

"Research, George, research."

"Sorry."

"Well, Serena Mallory believed that such places existed, and when they didn't exist, certain herbs could be combined to create a fissure in time and place, bringing the black hole where it needed to be."

"That's impossible. A black hole is—a black hole."

"A black hole in space, perhaps. We don't really know what a black hole is yet, do we? But, perhaps, as well as in space, there are black holes in time. And a black hole in time must be found. And perhaps other elements are needed for a black hole to be at the time that the black hole is needed in time. Maybe Serena even knew how to move a black hole in time."

"That's impossible, Mona."

"George! How dare you—you know that things exist beyond what we see."

"Well, of course, but—"

"But, but, but! Is it science, George, or is it magic? Or maybe a bit of both exist."

"All right, dear, go on."

She smiled and told him, "Guess where the black hole is?"

"I thought that you thought that it could be moved?"

"Maybe—but it has to be somewhere to be moved from that place."

George groaned. "Okay, where is the black hole?"

"Out in our backyard."

George stared at her, then shook his head. "Mona— how long have we owned this place? A quarter of a century? How many dogs and cats have those kids brought home? We've never lost a single animal. No, once they get here, we seem to keep them."

"The black hole isn't just open. I believe that either herbs and magic or sound waves and frequencies— your line—can create the black hole."

"Mona, could we turn out the light now?"

"Almost, George. Just think about it, okay?"

"I have been playing around back there with sound waves, microwaves and frequencies for almost as long as we've been married, Mona."

"Right place, right time, right circumstances and a bit of magic."

"So, you're trying to tell me that this fellow, Jake, isn't really a friend of Melody's. He dropped into her car magically when she was on her way home. If that's so, he didn't come through the black hole."

"Roses!" Mona said.

"What?" George demanded. He fell back on the bed, groaning as he covered his face with his pillow.

"Roses, coated with a mixture of herbs. Perhaps it's only illusion. Perhaps they cause a mist in the air, and what happens is all real and tangible, but not seen."

"Mona, can we watch Jay Leno?"

"George! The last passage here was written just before Christmas, 1776. Serena Mallory is about to head to New York City because she's gotten word that her brother is to be executed as a warning to other Patriots. Listen, George!" She began to read aloud. "'Through the Great God Our Father and all the blessings on earth of ancient gods and goddesses, through all that has been put at human disposal, and mostly, through all He has granted through our hearts and the power of love and the human spirit, I swear that I shall prevent such a cruelty. And at this time of the year when we have chosen to celebrate the birth of His Only Son, our Christ, He will not allow injustice, so I believe, and in my belief, I will travel. I am armed with my faith, and with the knowledge He has granted, and with the wisdom of my mothers, and the goodness of the earth. So much is put here for us; so much lives in our hearts. I know that He will travel with me, and that love and the spirit will prevail.'"

"Is that it?"

She knuckle punched him gently in the shoulder.

"What do you mean, is that it?"

George yawned. "You have an hypothesis. It must

be proven, my love." He chuckled and turned around, punching his pillow. "Whatever makes you happy, my dear."

"Is there a castle in Gloucester?" Jake suddenly asked.

"Yes, actually there is," Melody said.

"A castle?" Jake said again, perplexed.

"We've got a few of them in the United States these days. Some are called castles—because they were built as castles, they're as grand as some castles—and some are castles because really rich dudes had them brought over from Europe, brick by brick, stone by stone, or whatever," Keith explained. He'd had his share of Guinness. He was leaned back happily in the limo, arms across his chest, a semipermanent smile plastered to his face.

"Why?" Melody asked Jake. She was smiling, too. She didn't know why.

Yes, she did.

Guinness stout.

Their last stop had been the most fun of the evening. Jake had done more playing. A violinist—a very pretty one—who sat in with the band on a few numbers was also a good Irish dancer. She'd managed to get Keith out on the floor.

He'd done pretty well, too. In spite of the Guinness—or because of it.

"I've been asked to play at the castle. They will pay me. Their usual fiddler has a family commitment, and if I fill in for him, he can make his mother and wife happy."

"Oh," Melody said. "When?" she asked worriedly.

"Tomorrow night. If I'm here."

"Dude, where else will you be?" Keith asked.

"Home."

"But you are home," Melody said. "You told me, my parents' house was your home. So you've come home."

She realized that Jake had not imbibed quite as much Guinness as she and Keith had. He'd had a few drinks, but he'd been busy playing and dancing, as well.

He was looking out the window—they were still in Boston proper, and he was studying it with that gaze of amazement and wonder with which he looked at so much. He was a kook, but he was still someone with whom she did find herself more taken on an hourly basis. He was surreal; he was, in a way, an intangible, though he was flesh and blood. And despite all that, something about him seemed rock solid; there was a moral fiber running through him that was steady and sure.

She wished that she was that steady herself.

"I'm home, but not home. And I know that you understand. I've watched you—the two of you—together. You know what it is to be a sister and a brother. I could take anything, I believe, if I just knew that Serena was safe, that she was happy," he said.

Melody looked out the window.

He was damn stubborn, too.

Of course, with her luck, when his memory returned, she'd find out that he was a married banker from Orlando who had been taking part in some kind of theatrical recreation.

She felt a sudden punch in her arm.

"You are pretty cool now. Well, you've grown into

being cool," Keith told her. "You used to be a real bitch, but now you're pretty cool."

"And you used to be a pain-in-the-ass dork, but you're coming around, too," Melody told him.

Keith laughed. "You're only saying that because I finally got muscles, and now your friends think I'm a hottie. And a younger man. Seductive. Hot."

"No, no, I don't think that's it," Melody told him.

"See?" Jake interrupted quietly. "I have to get back. If my being here, being alive, caused Serena any hardship, I couldn't bear it." He cleared his throat. "Actually, I'm not at all certain that I would have called my sister a bitch, and I'm quite certain that she's unfamiliar with the word *dork*."

"She is a bitch," Keith said sagely. "But I'm not a dork," Keith said, waving a hand in the air.

Melody gave him a push and he fell back against the seat, grinning. "How will you ever know?" Melody asked him. "I mean, you are here. You are flesh and blood. How will know about your—your sister?"

"I got here somehow. That means I can get back. Somehow," Jake said.

"Well, meantime, are you going to play with the band tomorrow?" Keith asked, leaning forward again.

"I certainly believe that I should," Jake said. "I have been accepting your kind charity long enough. I must repay you somehow."

Melody didn't tell him that one night of a paying music gig was not going to give him much. She smiled and nodded. "Hey, if it's a private party, will we be able to come?"

"I can tap on a tambourine—or Irish drum," Keith suggested hopefully.

"And I can…I don't know what I can do. Sketches or caricatures for folks," Melody suggested.

"I will call my new friend Donald on that marvelous creation, the telephone, tomorrow, and find out what is possible," Jake said.

When they reached the house, Keith stumbled a bit as he tried to exit the limo. Thankfully, he'd taken care of the driver when he had called for the limo, Melody discovered, dreading the thought of going through her brother's wallet for his credit card.

Jake, trying to get Keith's arm around him, was unaware of the quick discussion she carried on with their amused driver. She was glad. She had just realized how it must have been hurting his pride to accept all that they had done for him.

"Whoa…whoa, Nellie! Slipping on the ice here," Keith said.

"Keith, there is no ice tonight. Come on, let's get you up to your room. And shush! You don't want to wake Mom and Dad. You're the good kid, remember?" Melody said.

"Shh! Shh!" Keith told Jake.

Melody caught his other arm. Together, they led him to the porch and up the steps. At the door, he suddenly decided that he needed to start singing one of the slightly off-color Irish ditties they had learned that night.

"'My wild Irish lady lass, sweetest lips and biggest ass—'"

Melody clamped a hand down hard over his mouth.

"Sorry," Keith muffled out.

They made it into the house and up the stairs. In

Keith's room, Melody had barely drawn his covers down before he plopped face-first into his bed.

"Go on, Melody. I'll take care of him," Jake said.

"His shoes, just his shoes."

"I can take care of him. He's taken wonderful care of me. I will take care of him," Jake insisted.

Melody nodded. "Okay."

She slipped out of the room and down to her own. She lay in her bed, and she stared at the ceiling.

It was impossible.

Why did he seem so much like the real thing?

She lay awake, still. She listened, but she didn't think that her parents woke up.

There was a soft tap at her door. "Yes?" she whispered.

The door opened a crack. Jake stood there, a dark silhouette against the hallway night-light.

"I just wanted to let you know, your brother is all set, and fine."

"Thank you, Jake."

He hovered for a moment. It was her parents' house—even if he were someone with whom she'd been having a wild and turbulent affair, she wouldn't have asked him in her room.

And yet…

She wished that he would come in. She'd like to be held by him. She just wanted to touch him.

"Good night, Melody. Thank you for a lovely evening."

"Good night, Jake," she said. "Thank you."

"The thanks is mine, Melody. You have done so much for me."

"I hit you on an icy road."

"No, you gave me a brand-new world. And more. The kindness of this family. Well, good night."

She didn't have a chance to say more. He stepped out, closing her door behind him.

Mona was humming. She was in the kitchen preparing pancakes. Bacon sizzled on one griddle, while pancakes were fluffing up. Her mother loved to cook, and the kitchen had been outfitted for that love bit by bit over the years.

"Smells wonderful, Mom," Melody said.

Mona cast a shrewd gaze in her direction. "You took your baby brother out last night, eh?"

Melody snatched a piece of bacon. "Mom, I have news for you. My baby brother took me out last night. Well, he took Jake out, too, of course."

"I heard you all clattering up the stairs," Mona said.

"He hired a car, Mom, so none of us would have a single drink and get behind the wheel," Melody said.

"Yes, I know. That was good. But still…"

"It was Guinness, Mom. Guinness stout. We must have Irish in us somewhere along the way."

"Really? I love Italian wines. And I'm not Italian."

"Oh, Mom, we don't know what we are. We're a bunch of mutts."

Melody grinned. Her mother wasn't angry; she was glad that her children had the sense to hire a car, and she didn't know that Keith had gotten a wee bit more than carried away.

"Mutts, hmm? Speaking of mutts, will you feed the dogs for me, please?"

"Of course. Jimmy, Brutus? Where are you, you monsters?"

The little clacking sound that always accompanied Brutus could be heard coming down the hallway. In a minute, both dogs were in the kitchen. Melody gave them affection along with their dog bowls. As she did so, she was aware that her mother was still watching her.

"What's wrong, Mom?" she asked.

"Why, nothing is wrong. Is something wrong with you, dear? Something you care to share with me?"

"No. Oh, guess what? Jake played with an Irish band last night. He's taken a job with them tonight, out at the castle."

"Really?" Mona said. She smiled.

"What?"

"Your father and I are invited to that party."

"Oh?" Startled, Melody almost dropped Kibbles 'n Bits all over the kitchen.

Mona smiled serenely. "Do you know whose having the party?" she asked.

"No," Melody said. The way her mother was smiling, she didn't think that she wanted to know. "Who?" There was no choice but to ask.

"Friends of mine," Mona said.

"Which friends?" Melody asked.

"Yes," Mona said serenely.

Melody frowned, hesitated, and waited, then carefully asked her question again. "Mom, I asked which friends."

"Oh. I thought you said *witch* friends, and yes, actually, it's the Wicked Wiccan Christmas Ball that's being held there. You know those folks—they do love Irish music. Well, I suppose because a lot of the current Wiccan beliefs date back to pagan times and Druids and all that. Back in Ireland. Well, other places as well, I suppose, but mainly Ireland. So, I had assumed they'd be hiring an Irish band. I didn't realize that Jake was Irish. I thought he said that he was English."

"He's probably a real American mutt, Mom, no matter where his family hailed from. He…he knows a lot of Irish tunes, that's all."

"Well, how lovely. I hadn't decided yet whether to go or not—you know how your father can be around some of my friends."

"Oh, come on, Mom, Dad is never rude."

"No, he's just a bit…well, you can tell he doesn't believe in them, or worse. He doesn't believe that they believe in themselves, that it's all kind of a commercial thing. I mean, let's face it, down in Salem, the witch shops there do flourish."

If her mother and father were going, she certainly had to find a way to be there.

She closed the bag of dog food thoughtfully. "Mom, what exactly do you believe?"

"Well, I still go to the Anglican church," Mona said.

"I didn't ask you that. I asked you what *you* believe."

Mona flipped a pancake, and then took it off the griddle. She turned to Melody. "Me? I'm an eternal optimist. I believe all things are possible. I believe that there is a God, and that he does show himself to different people in different ways. Christ was the son of God, and the son of man, but to a child living in the center of Asia or Africa or China, perhaps he has himself seen in another way. I believe, more than anything, in the power of love. I think we'll be judged on how we behaved to our fellow citizens here on earth, and not on how we sat in a church, a temple, a synagogue, mosque or any other place of worship. I believe…I believe that we do have the power to find love and happiness, and perhaps finding that within us is the greatest gift that we're given, but we must work to achieve it. I believe that everyone out there has the absolute right to believe what they choose to believe, and that I have no right to ridicule them. The worst thing we can do is persecute others for being different from ourselves. I…"

Mona ran out of steam and stared at Melody.

She hadn't heard her brother come into the kitchen.

His wry comment startled her.

"Bravo, Mom! But then, you are from Massachusetts, and we are one liberal state."

"Thank you, son. I pour my heart out, and that's the comment I get!" Mona said.

Keith grinned and went to his mother and hugged her. "I think you're wonderful. I'm proud of you, maternal figure."

Mona pushed him away. "Breakfast is almost ready. And I adore you, son, and you know it."

"Mom has an invitation to the castle tonight, Keith."

"Really? Great. What is it?"

"It's the Wicked Wiccan Christmas Ball," Melody said.

"Oh? Cool! Hey, we won't need Jake to finagle us invitations then, will we?" he asked his mother, frowning.

"Of course, you children may come along," Mona said. Keith went to steal a piece of bacon. Mona slapped his hand. "I'm ready to put this all out on the table. Get the maple syrup, please, and milk, coffeepot, and someone grab the orange juice."

Mona went on out carrying the platters of pancakes and bacon.

Melody went to the refrigerator, staring at her brother.

"Headache?" she asked him.

He grinned. "Sorry, none at all."

"No hangover at all?"

"Nope."

"You deserve the worst, you know!"

"Hey, I was a good guy. I thought we had a great time."

"We did," Melody admitted. "But I'm worried about tonight."

"Kids?" Mona called.

"Why?" Keith asked quickly.

"It's all her Wiccan friends. What if…"

"Don't live life on what-ifs, sis. It's not good. And, hey, let's go have a good time. Lover boy Mark will be here tomorrow!"

She grated her teeth. "He's not my lover boy."

"Ah. He thinks he is!"

"Where's Jake?"

"On his way down. I see a love triangle a-comin'."

"Keith, will you give me a break? Stop it."

"Gonna tell on me?" he teased. "Think they'll send me to my room?"

"Careful, little brother, I can still make you pay."

Wiggling his brows, Keith went out with the maple syrup and coffeepot. Shaking her head, Melody took the orange juice and milk from the refrigerator and followed him.

As she went through the swinging door to the dining room, she saw Jake coming in from the hallway. He caught her eyes and smiled. It was just a smile. Juice trembled in her hand.

Got to stop this, she warned herself.

And, of course, she didn't want to be worried about Mark, but she was.

It wasn't so much a matter of losing her determination that they weren't meant to work together as a couple, it was that she was worried about hurting him, about her family, the combination of her family and Mark—and now, Jake.

Mona asked Melody to bring an extra bottle of syrup from the kitchen. Finally about to sit with the others, Melody discovered that her father, Jake and Keith had gotten into a discussion on waves and the speed of sound.

"There were a number of studies going on at the university regarding the speed of sound," George said, helping himself to the bacon. "Any of it is quite fascinating. Sound traveling, light traveling. To reach certain points in the heavens, we're talking hundreds and thousands of years. How far will sound travel before it fades completely? What frequencies will be heard by others? Is there life on other planets?"

"Dad," Melody said, aware that Jake was watching him intently.

"So what is your work now?" Jake asked George.

"Telepathy," Keith suggested with a smile.

George frowned at Keith.

"Hey, I've seen telepathy at work," Keith assured him.

"Telepathy. What am I thinking?" Melody demanded, shaking her head.

"I didn't say that I was capable of telepathy," Keith

said. "But—once again, at a prestigious university, mind you—they are doing many experiments and it's amazing what can be accomplished. I saw a fellow guess every card on a deck of fifty different symbols."

"Maybe he memorized them. Maybe the cards were marked," Melody said.

"Ouch. Poor baby—your glass is half-empty, isn't it?" Keith teased.

"Nothing that I'm working on right now has to do with mental capabilities," George said. "It all has to do with frequencies and waves. But just think about the things we've been able to do. Or how remarkable, unbelievable—some things we take for granted today would appear to someone who, say, just popped in from a couple of hundred years ago."

Melody nearly spit coffee across the table. She choked, and coughed.

Her mother patted her on the back.

"Are you all right, dear?" Mona asked.

"Fine," she said.

George wagged a finger at her. "And another thing I'm interested in is—black holes! Amazing. Magnetic properties of the earth combined with the technology of man."

"Help me, help me!" Keith teased.

"All right, when you see me walking around with a giant fly head, I'll quit, okay?" George asked.

"Dear, speaking of flies, I think we will go to the Wicked Wiccan Christmas Ball tonight. Jake has a job playing there with the band, and the kids want to go," Mona said.

"Mom, what does that have to do with flies?" Melody asked.

"Flies—fly. The concept of witches is that they can fly on broomsticks. Of course, we all know that's not at all true, but…fly. And fly," Mona explained.

"Great logic, Mom," Keith assured her.

George groaned. "Really?"

"Dad, it will be great," Melody said.

"Honestly, sir. I met the fellows last night with whom I'll be playing. Quite fine. I think it will be tremendously enjoyable," Jake said.

"And what do you think of all this Wiccan malarkey?" George asked.

"I think it's amazing that we've come so far in American history that any man can practice any form of life or worship," Jake said sincerely.

George looked at Mona helplessly. "I suppose it is better, much better, than…well, than the old way." He frowned. "Yes, we've come far. Yes, we've a long way to go." His frown became a grin as he looked at his wife. "Yes, I think most of your Wiccan friends just really love dressing up in black, and looking like the real thing for their commercial stores," George told her.

"You're going to have to behave," Mona said primly.

"I intend to behave. I'm never rude, Mona."

"Not purposely, but you can't laugh when someone says that they're a medium, George," Mona said.

"There will be mediums there? Fortune-tellers, crystal-ball readers?" Jake asked.

"All of the above," George said wryly.

"If waves can go anywhere, then so can the human mind, perhaps," Jake said.

"Dad, Mom is right, you know—and so is Jake," Keith said. He winced. "The last time one of Mom's friends said she was a *medium,* you said that she looked as if she were a small. Not a good joke at a Wiccan party, Dad."

"Oh, come on, don't Wiccans have senses of humor?" he asked.

"Not when you push it, Dad," Melody reminded. "You asked another of her medium friends if she was ever rare or well done," Melody said.

George groaned. "Okay, okay, I'll just have my palm read. But if they tell me I'm going to have four children, I'm leaving!"

Mona rose, rolling her eyes. "You will behave, or I'll start working on some kind of waves myself out there in that lab of yours, and I promise you'll be sorry!"

She carried her plate into the kitchen. They all rose to do the same.

"What will you kids do today?" George asked. "The snow is soft up on the hill. You could take Jake snowboarding or tubing."

"That sounds great," Melody said.

"I really must continue with research," Jake said.

"Research?" George said, frowning. "But you're here for Christmas vacation, young man."

"Ah, but Christmas comes quickly," Jake said. "And I'm afraid that—"

"He's such a hard worker!" Melody said, grabbing Jake's arm. "Come on, Jake, I'm sure we can play in the snow and get in some research, too. Right, Keith?"

"Oh, yeah, sure, certainly," Keith said. He added in a whisper, "You owe me!"

"Hey, I feed your broken-down pet parade all the time!" Melody whispered back heatedly.

"Oh, right, like this is anywhere near the same thing!"

"What are you two squabbling on and on about?" George demanded.

"Nothing," Melody said.

"She's whining about feeding the dogs," Keith said, grinning.

"I am really going to strangle you!" she hissed to him.

Keith was having way too much fun with this. She dragged both him and Jake down the hall to the parlor, and away from her parents.

"One more! One more crack, and I'm going to tell that the girl you brought home that year was a stripper," Melody warned.

"A stripper?" Jake asked.

"I'll take you to see a few soon enough, my friend," Keith promised. "Melody, okay, okay, I'm sorry. I'll lay off."

"Lay off—and perhaps tell me the truth?" Mona's voice demanded.

They all swung around, even Jake, surprise and guilt on their faces.

Mona stared at them one by one, stern accusation in her eyes. "Well?" she demanded.

"What—um—truth?" Melody asked.

"Child, you have actually sucked as a liar all your life," Mona informed her. "Not a bad thing, not really." She gave Keith a parental swat on the shoulder. "And you! The lies come a bit glibly to your lips. And it's not nice to torture your sister."

"I wasn't torturing her—"

"Just shut it," Mona said firmly. "Shut it!"

She stared at Melody. "You didn't know Jake before, did you?"

"What?"

"You didn't know him before the day you came here."

"Well, I met him…"

"We met in the middle of an icy road, Mrs. Tarleton," Jake said. "I never meant for anyone to lie to you. Melody simply assured me that no one would believe the truth."

"And what is the truth?" Mona persisted.

"I hit him in the road, Mom. Jake has—amnesia."

"I do not have amnesia," Jake protested.

"Then?" Mona demanded.

"Mom—"

"From him, young lady," Mona said.

"Where's Dad?" Keith asked.

"He's gone out back. Let me hear this, then I'll decide what he'll believe and what he won't," Mona told them.

Melody inhaled on a deep breath, trying to still think of some way to hedge.

But Jake took a step forward. "I was being hanged, Mrs. Tarleton. It was a beautiful morning, crisp and clear, in New York, New York, but I had been captured by the British, and a certain commander had determined that Christmas season or no, I should be hanged. Serena Mallory is my adopted sister. She came to the city and I was terrified that she would do something to stop the execution, and that they would find some way to…hurt her. She said a few words and threw rose petals into the sky, and the next thing I knew, I was on the road, and lights were coming at me. Extraordinary lights. From an *automobile*. And the thing is, I have to get back. I have to find my sister, and I have to make sure that she's all right, that she made it home from New York."

Mona stared at him as Jake finished speaking.

Melody thought that her mother would burst into laughter.

Or that she would shake her head in disgust and demand to know the real truth.

She did neither. She looked at Melody.

"Why didn't you just tell me the truth from the beginning?" Mona demanded.

"Mom...I don't think, honestly—I mean, it's not possible. It's just not possible. I believe that Jake does work for a reenactment company, or the park service, or some such entity. I think that he went down in the snow and hit his head. I believe that Jake believes what he's saying—sorry!" she added quickly, looking at Jake. "But that what he's saying is just not possible."

"Honestly, daughter, where's the magic in you?" Mona asked her, shaking her head.

"Um, you believe all this, Mom?" Keith asked.

"I certainly think we've seen a few unusual *coincidences* regarding this young man and our own home, and he certainly knows a great deal...and his clothing and boots are amazingly authentic. I think it's sad that you thought you had to lie to me. And I think it's wonderful that you're here for Christmas, Jake, because whatever time period you came from, and from wherever in all the frequencies of life, you are a fine young man, and it's a delight to have you in my house. Now, the three of you—get out. Go snowboarding or something. Give me a bit of time to try to get a few ideas going, and get some research done! Shoo—shoo!"

"Um...." Melody said.

"Go!" Mona told her.

"Mom, are you—really all right?" Keith asked.

"I'm fine, just fine. And, by the way, I knew perfectly well that the young lady you brought home that year was a stripper. Though it may not be the most family-friendly activity, she was, at the least, honestly employed. So, excuse me—I have a few things to do. Go on. Get out of here. All of you."

But they didn't leave. They were all still stunned, and they stood there.

Finally, Jake took a step forward. He reached for Mona's hand, and held it. "Thank you. Before God, what I'm telling you is the truth. And your kindness and charity toward me have been amazing. If there is ever any way for me to repay you, I would most humbly beg the chance."

Mona grinned. "You've done quite enough, young man. You've brought a lot of…magic into our house. Now, get out of here. All of you. And trust me, by the way." She stared at Melody. "And your father. He's a little slow at the gate sometimes, but he's an amazing and brilliant man."

"You're not going to tell Dad any of this—" Melody began.

"Not yet, not yet, don't worry. I know how to handle your father. So, please, right now—go!"

Melody was too surprised to do anything other than what her mother had ordered. She headed for the closet and reached in for their coats.

"Go up the old hill, they have tubes to rent. You'll have a great time," Mona called over her shoulder.

"Let's go up the hill, like Mom told us," Melody said, still stunned and uneasy.

"Sure, sure, let's just get out of here for now," Keith agreed.

They stepped outside. It was a beautiful day. The snow appeared brilliantly white in the dazzle of the sun. The sky was blue, with just a few powder-puff clouds rolling slowly by.

Jake stepped down to the walk, looking around, seeing the sky and the snow.

"Tubing," Keith said numbly. "We really should just go tubing."

"I don't think I really have all that much time," Jake said. "I keep feeling that…I'm supposed to be home for Christmas."

"But—this is your home. Or was your home," Melody reminded him.

He didn't answer. He was just staring at the day again.

"Jake?" she said quietly.

He turned to her; she had his full attention.

"I'm sorry, I was just thinking."

"Thinking what?" she asked.

"How happy I am just to be alive."

Chapter 7

It was cold, but they were in the right shoes, right parkas, and, if that wasn't enough, Melody had bought a bunch of hot packets. They were really quite incredible; you broke the packet—almost like a glow-in-the-dark necklace—and it released heat. They could go in boots, down your back, your front, or anywhere you thought you might need a little extra heat.

Right at the beginning, after their first wild ride down the hill, Keith decided that his rump was freezing and he used two. Then his rump was too hot and he jumped around trying to shift the packets. A group of teenage girls laughed gleefully, and that started a snowball fight.

The second run, Melody hopped on with Jake when he didn't seem to know how to get the tube going. They flew down the hill, her arms locked around his chest.

At the bottom, the tube tossed them out and over, and they lay locked in the snow together, laughing.

When she looked into his eyes, she knew that she was suddenly praying again that he had merely lost his memory, that he would turn out to be a guide in Boston, Salem or Concord, perhaps, that he would prove to be unmarried and unattached, and she could spend her life with him....

Ridiculous thought. She didn't know him that well.

She did know that she wanted to get to know him. She knew that she could have stayed there in the snow with him forever, no matter how cold it was, that she was warm enough with him above her, that his closeness promised everything in the world that she could ever want.

"Here! I'll help you up!" Keith said, running over with their lost tube.

Jake was quickly up, of course, and they both reached a hand to her, bringing her to her feet.

"Great. Wow. Thanks so much, Keith!"

He didn't seem to catch a bit of her muted sarcasm.

Yes, he did.

He was grinning as he looked away.

They did several more runs down the hill—Jake and Melody together every time. And every time they landed entangled and laughing, and she wanted the day to go on forever.

Even with Keith there to make sure they moved every time before the next tubers could come crashing down.

They broke in the early afternoon, heading to a hill's little coffee shop, and warmed up by ordering rich clam chowder served in bread bowls.

"I should have been doing…something," Jake said. "But, I must admit, that was tremendous fun."

"I wouldn't worry, my mom will be doing something," Keith told him.

"There's the afternoon," Melody said.

He shook his head. "I have to get to the castle and practice with the band."

"Of course, wow, I forgot that," Keith said. "But, as I said, don't worry, my mom will be up to something."

"Don't tell him that," Melody said.

"Why? Your mother is extraordinary," Jake said.

"My mother is ever so slightly crazy!" Melody protested.

She saw Jake's hand tighten around his coffee mug. But his voice was level when he looked at her. "You don't believe me, but she does."

Melody shook her head. "Jake, you can't travel through time. I'm so sorry, but…no. And if your memory doesn't return soon—"

"My memory is in perfect working order," he said.

She let out a breath. "Okay, say everything that you're saying is true. That doesn't mean that there is an answer. It doesn't mean that you can go back. Maybe this was the only way that you could be saved and your sister knew it. Would it be so terrible if you had to stay here?"

She felt the tension ease out of her. Once again, he was staring at her with his crystal eyes, hazel eyes that held green and brown and, more than the color, something that oddly spoke of honor and humor, and his fascination with life. Maybe even with her.

"Oh, come on. That would hold impossible logistics," Keith said. "He wouldn't have a birth certificate. Or a social security number."

She didn't really hear her brother.

"It wouldn't be terrible at all to be here," Jake said softly. His hand covered hers. "I don't know about the rest of this world. But I do know that you have created a beautiful place in time and history here, you and your family. But what if…what if I was supposed to be in my own time? What if…I don't know. Christmas comes, and the noose tightens? More than that, I must try. You have to understand. Serena was willing to die for me. I have to make sure she is all right, that she made it home. I have to know that she made it alive and well. Truly. I could not live with myself if I did not do everything in my power for her."

"But what if you just can't get back?" Melody asked.

"There is a way. I know there is a way," he said. He almost reached out and touched her. He seemed to remember that her brother was there, that they were in a crowded room, and he did not. He offered her a rueful smile, and gave his attention to his food.

"We'll get you to the castle so you can rehearse. We'll be there with my folks when the party starts," Keith told him.

"That will make the evening complete. I'll be able to pay you back for some of what you've given me," he said.

"You really don't owe us anything, you know. Heck, you could have sued Melody for a small fortune," Keith said.

"What?" Melody protested.

"Pardon?" Jake said.

"Oh, you really don't understand our day, do you?"

Keith inquired. "We've done some good things. We've also become a sadly litigious society. A car accident like that? Melody running you down in the snow? You could sue her to smithereens."

"But I wasn't hurt," Jake said.

"A good lawyer could get you a bundle," Keith told him.

"Why would I want a good lawyer to get me a bundle when I wasn't hurt? That would be horrible. A frivolous lawsuit would be a terrible event in which to engage," Jake said seriously.

Keith looked at Melody and shrugged. "He means it."

She rose. "Let's go. We have to get Jake to the castle."

Melody was worried when she left Jake with the Irish band. God alone knew what he might say or do. The band members greeted him with claps on the back and welcoming words; they liked him. They had played with him. Music was a universal language, so they said, and it was constantly proven true.

It must be a timeless language, as well.

One of the fellows, a tall blond man, raised a hand to Melody and Keith as they drove away. "Will be seein' you later?" he asked politely.

"Oh, yes, thanks!" Melody returned.

Keith backed along the drive to make a U-turn. Melody sat in brooding silence.

She felt her brother looking at her.

"Really, Melody, what if this is all true?" Keith asked.

"It's not."

"It could be."

"No."

"Then pretend he is telling the truth. What if something goes terribly wrong if he isn't returned to his own time?"

"Keith, stop it. I don't care how…how good he makes it all sound. It's simply impossible."

"Hey—Christmas is impossible. It's faith, and faith is impossible. Is it tangible? Can we touch it? No. Does that make us all a bunch of fools or liars? Melody, what I'm saying is—"

"Keith! The truth of it all is this—he's either an actor having a hell of a time, or he should sue me because he has really whacked his head. And I'll find out he's married. And he has four children, or something of the like."

Keith was quiet a minute. "Maybe you should just go ahead and think that way. Because you really can't keep him. He isn't a stray."

She flashed her brother an angry glance. "I don't know what you're talking about. Of course I know I can't keep a man!"

She winced. "I mean—"

He laughed. "That didn't come out quite right, did it? You can keep a man—evidently. You just wound up keeping one that you didn't want, and now you want to keep the one that you can't have."

She shook her head. "Give it up!"

"No," he said, his tone quiet and serious. "No, because…I believe him more every day. And I understand how he feels. And I intend to help him."

"Abracadabra! Magic. We'll send him back," she said. "Honestly, Keith—"

"Honestly. You wait. Our mother will have thought of something."

"Great, yeah, wonderful, she can contrive with Dad, and between her potions and Dad's experiments, we'll just—heck, we could blow him up. Great. Then he'll be in bits and pieces and we'll all be in jail. It will be wonderful."

"You don't want him to go back, do you?" Keith asked.

"Keith, you're missing my point. I just don't believe that there is a past he can go back to. And it's almost Christmas. We need to have a nice time for Christmas."

"What happens after Christmas? When it's time to get back to the real world? Then we take him to a hospital, the police, a psychiatric ward?"

"I just keep praying that he'll figure out who he really is, and then…Keith, please, really. It would be easy. We could all fall for it, you, me and Mom. Because he is so believable. But, yes, I guess, if we don't figure something out in the next few days…"

To her surprise, her brother laughed. He reached over and tousled her hair.

"Until then, I'll just let you live the little dream."

"I'm not living any dream."

"You're made for each other."

Melody swung on him. "I have to accept one thing. If we can't get him to remember something by Christmas, I'll have to bite the bullet. We'll have to find out who he really is. I suppose I should have taken him to the hospital right off, but…I don't know. I didn't. It was cold, it was snowy…I was trying to get home."

They had reached their parents' house. Keith turned off the car engine and turned to her.

"Bizzare, preposterous, absurd. There's still just something about him I believe. Maybe he's doing the same thing. He's really just trying to get home in time for Christmas."

"All right. Sure," she said.

"Smile."

"I am smiling."

Inside, they found Mona busy in the kitchen. She was working over a big spaghetti pot, but it didn't smell like spaghetti sauce.

"What's cooking, Mom?" Melody asked.

"Something weird," Keith said. "Hey, Mom, you don't need to cook dinner. The event is being catered. We saw all the trucks at the castle when we dropped Jake off."

"Never you mind, children. I'm working on something for the future," Mona said.

"What?" Melody asked her.

"It's a new recipe. I don't want to be distracted."

Neither Melody nor Keith moved.

Mona looked up at them. "Didn't you hear me? Shoo—go away."

"Weird smell, Mom," Melody said.

"Herbs," she said. "Some are very pungent."

"That's not really something that we're going to eat or drink, is it?" Keith asked worriedly.

"Two seconds more, and I'll find the frying pan and give you a whack," Mona warned.

"Mom, it is a bit—no, it's *very* pungent."

"Not one of those aromas that lures you to the kitchen, for sure," Keith agreed.

"Go away," Mona commanded. "I need to finish

this, and then get ready for tonight. Oh, and remember, dress accordingly."

She pushed the two of them out of the kitchen. Heading down the hall, Keith looked at Melody. "What the heck is she steaming up in there? I don't want to hurt her feelings—"

"Too late, I think."

"Oh, please! You'd let that stuff touch your lips?" Keith demanded.

"Maybe it's for the dogs."

"Don't wish it on the poor dogs."

"She'll tell us when she's ready, I guess."

"Wow, you can smell it down the hall. I think all the pets are hiding. Even a blind cat is too smart to hang in close."

"Forget it—let's get dressed. I want to get back to the castle as soon as possible," Melody said. "Come on, we have to dress 'accordingly.'"

"What's accordingly? I have a feeling people will show up in all kinds of apparel."

"Probably. As far as Mom goes? I think we're supposed to avoid red and green and Santa hats. I don't know. The Wiccan stores I've been in around Christmas carry everything. I'm going to wear a long black velvet dress and that cape Mom bought for me in Salem years ago."

"Got a dress for me?" he teased.

"Black. Basic black. You'll be fine," she said.

Upstairs, they parted ways. Melody laid out her clothing, showered, and washed her hair. She realized she was giving particular attention to her hair and dress. Jake.

She walked over to a snow globe music box her parents had bought for her, years ago in Orlando. Beauty and the Beast danced, standing in a field of snow.

And red roses. The red roses were tiny hearts that fell with the snow when the globe was shaken.

She watched the snow and the roses fall, and she thought about Jake, and then she realized that she did little else but think about Jake lately.

She heard a noise in the hallway and stuck her head out, certain that Keith would be about to ask her if his apparel was appropriate and if he had dressed "accordingly." But Keith wasn't in the hall; it was her mother, and Mona was headed up the stairs to the attic.

Melody started to call out to her, but waited. When Mona had gone up the draw-down steps, she followed.

The attic was the type that might be found, certainly, in the Addams Family house. It was an absolute mishmash of old trunks and wardrobes, dressmaker's dummies, modern-day cardboard, Christmas ornaments that didn't make the yearly cut, a giant Easter bunny, dressers her father intended to fix one day, and toys. They'd never parted with anything; Mona loved it all too much. Many of the things were decades—even centuries old.

There were spaces that resembled ragged paths that led between much of the chaos. Mona had made her way to the far back; Melody followed her, nearly tripping over a huge elk head—the prize of some hunter who had lived in the house long ago.

"Mom! What are you doing?"

Mona had been intent on her task, whatever it was. At the sound of Melody's voice, she let out a shriek. She had just opened one of the old trunks; it fell shut with a slam.

"What? What's going on? Why are following me?" Mona demanded indignantly.

"I'm not following you," Melody protested.

"Yes, you are, you're following me—that's exactly what you're doing!" Mona said.

"I…well, I thought you might need help. It's time we should be heading on out, so I just thought you might need help with something up here," Melody said.

Mona shook her head. "You don't need to follow me around like a puppy."

"Mom—"

"It is time to go. Let's just go," Mona said.

"But what were you looking for?" Melody asked.

"Nothing."

"Mom, you had to have been—"

"You know, Melody, it is my attic. My house, and my attic."

"Well, of course, but—"

"Let's just get going. I can dig around in here tomorrow. I was just looking for some old books. Honestly, time flies. Years ago, I meant to seriously dig into all the treasures that came with this attic, and time goes by, and you haven't done half the things you planned. Anyway, let's not be the last to arrive. I hate to be the first, but I do like to arrive in a kind of socially timely manner."

Mona moved to get around Melody, balancing with her hands on her daughter's waist, since the paths were hardly wide. It was also a crafty way to keep a hand on Melody and steer her back out of the attic.

"Mom, seriously, what are you up to?" Melody asked her.

"When I'm ready, I'll tell you—and not before,"

Mona said stubbornly. "Come on, let's get going. You don't want any of those Wiccans getting their hands on Jake when the band takes a break, eh?" Mona asked.

"Will there be anyone there besides Wiccans?" Melody asked worriedly.

"Oh, yes. Christians. And our Jewish neighbors, and new Muslim folk in the area, Hindus, Confucians—I don't know! Everyone is invited. Invited to buy tickets. This is America! Land of the free—and the capitalists!"

Melody smiled. "Good. Maybe we're safe."

She let her mother breathe a sigh of relief as she gave in and headed down the attic stairs ahead of her. Mona followed quickly. "Are you wearing your cape? How beautiful, darling."

"Yes, I'm wearing it. I truly love my cape, Mom. Thanks. I don't get the chance to wear it that often." She smiled suddenly, giving her mother a hug.

"Keith, George!" Mona called.

Neither replied.

From the rear window of Keith's room—which they could see from the upstairs hallway—they saw a giant flash of light appear across the backyard.

"Oh, God!" Melody gasped with horror. "Was Dad out in the lab?"

They looked at one another and tore for the stairs, racing down quickly and knocking into each in their hurry to make it out the back door.

George was there, outside his laboratory, in the yard. Keith stood across the grass from him. There was nothing burning at all.

"What was that?" Mona demanded.

"Dad?" Melody said.

"It was a wave. Or a frequency. A frequency combined with a wave," Keith said.

"And what did it do?" Melody asked.

"It…flashed," her father said.

"It flashed in only one place," Keith reminded him.

George looked over at Mona and flushed. "Yes, only one place. Right around the old well."

It looked as if her father thought that the explanation might just mean something to her mother. What, she had no idea. The old well had been covered up for years before they had moved into the place. It was rather charming; the stonewall base could still be seen, and every owner had kept up the old arborlike structure that curved above it, where, in spring and summer, ivy crawled and flowers bloomed.

She wondered how her father had created the waves and frequencies that he had somehow mated, then saw that there was some kind of machine that resembled a fog machine near Keith's feet and another just behind her father.

It looked as if they were playing at being Ghostbusters; they were only missing the outfits.

Indeed, they had both opted for black, and looked rather handsome, she thought. Her father had on a long cape, much like Melody's own and purchased in Salem as well, while Keith was wearing something that looked more like a Georgian frock coat.

She was suddenly grateful that Mark wasn't due until tomorrow.

She could just imagine what he would have to say about her crazy family.

"Do you need to…zap it again?" Mona asked.

George shook his head. "No, no…we need a bit more experimentation. That's all."

"And how? What kind of experimentation?" Mona asked.

"There are many different theories that can be tested," Keith said.

Melody suddenly felt as if they were all speaking a foreign language, and she was not in any way in on the secret.

"What's going on here?" she demanded.

"I'm experimenting—I'm always experimenting," George said, looking at her quizzically.

Maybe she was wrong.

"We should get going. Really," Keith said, clearing his throat.

"Yes, yes, of course. Girls, get your coats," George said.

Melody was still suspicious, but she was anxious to get back to the castle. The concept of Jake with one Wiccan was scary, much less the dozens that would be there.

Then again, what could be weirder than her own household?

As they arrived at the castle grounds and were directed to park, Melody saw the huge tree that stood on the snow-covered lawn just before the cliffs that rose in back.

"The Christmas tree is actually an old German tradition, right?" she murmured to her father.

"Yes," George said. "The first ones apparently showed up in several towns at the same time, in front of guildhalls, I believe. There's a German church record of one being erected in the mid-1500s."

"Ah, but there was big trouble regarding trees for many years and in many places," Mona said. "Some of the stricter church folk back then saw them as a pagan symbol. The time of our Christian holidays revolves around the ancient dates of the Roman Saturnalia and winter solstice of the Druids," Mona said.

"There are angels on the tree," Melody noted.

"Ah, because we all pray there are really angels watching over us, don't we?" Her mother said. "The tree goes with the castle. The folks who run the castle had the tree decorated. Let's head on in."

They found themselves entering in a throng of people. As they walked, Mona and George responded to friends and neighbors who hailed them. Melody and Keith knew most of them, but not all, and so they were introduced. As they neared the entry, they could hear the band playing within, an Irish ballad at the moment.

"Mona!" The Wiccan hostess at the door—dressed similarly to Melody, but in a fuller black skirt beneath her sweeping cape—greeted her mother affectionately.

"Peggy!" Mona said, hugging her fiercely. "How's the shop going? Well, I hope. You know my husband, George, right?"

"Oh, yes," Peggy said, studying George. He must have given her his "medium—what about rare and well done" joke at some time.

"And my children are home for the holidays," Mona said. "My daughter, Melody, and my son, Keith. Please meet Peggy Winston, our official hostess for the evening. And high priestess, of course."

"Of course," George said solemnly. Apparently, he meant to keep his good-behavior promise for the evening.

"A pleasure," Keith said.

"Nice to meet you, Peggy," Melody assured her.

"Well, come in, come in, it's all going beautifully. Wonderful band, eh? Oh, you have a family friend playing in it tonight, right? The very handsome young man who is new to the group said that he's a guest staying with you," Peggy said.

"Yes, yes," Melody replied for her mother. "Oh, no, I believe we're blocking the path. Jake is a doll, a good friend, an old friend. From Boston. He didn't always live there though. We really should let you greet your other guests. He's a historian. Amazing fellow. We should move—"

Keith sent an elbow into her rib cage, catching her hand and leading her on in.

"Boy, are you slick!" he whispered to her.

"They've already been talking to him," Melody said, alarmed. "We'd better get in front of the band."

"You go get in front of the band. Now that we're out of the house and I can no longer smell Mom's herbal concoction, I'm starving. I'm off to find the food."

"Traitor!" she told him.

"Yes, but a hungry traitor."

He waved a hand and left her. She made her way downstairs to the open area where the band was playing.

The castle was real, having been brought to the States from Europe by a millionaire. It was Gothic in appearance with a treasure trove of antiques, though many had been taken to safety for the evening. The paintings and statues were gone, so nothing could detract from the beige stone walls and marble of the architecture. The band set up on a level just two steps above the main floor, while flanking staircases brought the guests up to the level above, where drinks were being served, and the balcony, open to the night, could be ambled. Melody noted that there were signs advising guests that there were mediums present, those who read cards and palms, tea leaves and crystal balls. They were advisers, so the signs claimed—and their services were an extra charge.

There were already lines leading to the rooms where the various readings were taking place.

She knew, of course, that Jake couldn't be seeking any Wiccan counsel at the moment—he was onstage playing.

She wove her way through the crowd of people, dressed mostly in Gothic capes, but some in Christmas finery as well, and made it to the stage.

Jake was playing violin at the moment. His eyes were closed, as if he was feeling the music. She marveled at his talent, and was startled when she discovered that her brother was behind her. "Hey, they were holed up all winter with no television, no Wii, no Movies On Demand. Kind of cool to think about, in a way. Folks learned instruments, read and probably even talked to one another," Keith said.

"He's really good, huh?" she said a little wistfully.

Keith smiled at her. "Yeah. Mozzarella stick?" She remembered he had gone for food; he carried a plate.

She shook her head, her eyes still on the band.

Jake's eyes opened then. And they were on her.

She smiled, and he smiled in return.

The band leader announced a break at the end of the tune. Jake set his instrument down and hopped to her level. He greeted her setting his hands on her shoulders and pulling her close a moment for a kiss on her cheek. He shook her brother's hand.

"So, you folks have made it," he said, sounding happy.

"Yes, it's not always easy actually getting my entire family out of the house," Melody told him.

He nodded, and glanced at her brother. "Mind if I take Melody for a walk?" he asked.

"No, dude, go for it," Keith said.

It was evident that Jake was learning. He didn't question the word *dude*.

"Where are we going?" Melody asked him.

"Just out beyond the balcony. It's so beautiful. If you're warm enough. We'll stop for mead."

"They have mead?" Melody asked wryly.

"Yes, of course, and it's very good. And I'm quite in awe of the whole place. There are so many people here. People in all colors. And they are so varied in their nationalities, or origins. They all get along with one another so pleasantly."

"It's not always sugar and roses, I promise you," she said, but then she grinned. "You should see New York City. You can hear dozens of languages in a one-block walk."

"Fascinating."

His hand on the base of her spine, he led her up the stairs to a table covered in black and decorated with black roses—tied with little ribbons of red and green. There were several women working behind the table, passing out plastic glasses of warmed mead. They accepted two, and Melody found herself proud to hear Jake complimented for his playing, and prouder still to hear his humble thanks to all.

Then they moved through those hovering around the bar and headed to a door that led them out to something that was a mixture of a balcony and a rampart.

The night was beautiful. Stars were abundant above them, and though it was cold, the breeze was gentle. The castle sat upon cliffs that looked out over the water, and they were bathed in the colorful lights from within and soft glow of natural light from above. Jake looked out with a joy and wonder at the night that seemed to touch Melody all over again. The world itself seemed to be new through his eyes. So many things she took for granted were miracles to him.

Perhaps it wasn't so odd that he should expect another miracle.

Real, or created in the magic of the mind.

"This wasn't here, you know," he said. "I see places, and they have changed, and yet they are the same. Some of the old houses…your house. My house."

He looked at her. The breeze was just lightly moving his hair. Apparently, the band had brought their own forms of Gothic uniform for the night, for he was in snug-fitting black jeans and a black poet's shirt.

He was compelling. Striking in the sculpture of his face, and in coloring, and yet far more seductive because of the light and laughter in his eyes, and the warmth that seemed to emanate from him.

He set his mead down on the edge of the brick wall, then did the same with hers. He took her hands suddenly, drawing both to his lips. He kissed them fervently and gently, then met her eyes again. "Thank you."

She flushed, wanting to draw her hands away, loving the feel of lavalike warmth that seemed to spill over her and seep through her. She winced. She barely knew him. A few days ago, he'd yet to *appear* in her life. And yet she knew that she wanted to spend so much time with him. Chemistry, pheromones, whatever drove the human race, leaped within her in abundance. He stirred her imagination, and she felt extremely young again, holding tight to just the moments in which they had tumbled in the snow, bodies touching.

Through an awful lot of clothing, yes...but!

She smiled. Her heart was thundering too quickly, as well.

"Thank you. Thank you for being here. For making us all laugh and stop and think and see everything that's around us. Thank you...for being you."

She was leaning into him, she realized. But it was all right. He was leaning into her.

She was going to lean closer; he was going to lean closer. He was going to kiss her, and it was what she had been waiting for.

His lips touched hers, warmth and magic. A gentle touch, nothing forced to it, and there was something of the wonder he saw in all the world that seemed to come with that kiss.

And yet it was brief.

"I shouldn't have, I had no right," he told her as he pulled away.

"Pardon?"

"I think you are the finest of women. I did not mean to take liberties."

He was barely an inch from her. He was earnest and intense. She smiled slowly and told him, "Jake, twenty-first century. A kiss is not a liberty. You did nothing wrong at all. The world has changed. You don't need anyone's permission but mine for a kiss, and that is freely given."

"Oh? You're quite certain?" he asked. But there was a teasing smile on his face now. "I would never harm you in any way, take any advantage."

Melody laid her palms against his cheeks and reveled in touching him, feeling the warmth and texture of his face. Then she drew herself closer to him until their lips touched again. This kiss wasn't just warmth. Their lips melded together, and then parted, and a spiraling edge of passion began with a sweet slow simmer. His arms came around her, and she was against him, feeling his heart, his every breath, and the heat of his body, as if it infused her with warmth against any hint of winter chill.

Then, from somewhere, she dimly heard a throat being cleared. And then a whisper. "Hmm, is it him?"

That they were being interrupted didn't enter Melody's mind for a moment. She was oblivious to people and conversations taking place near them.

She had waited, and she had wanted.

She felt as if she had fallen into a moment of pure sensation and bliss.

But it wasn't to be.

"There you are!" chimed an excited feminine voice.

Melody and Jake started and broke apart. She turned to see one of her mom's friends, Infinity MacDonald.

Infinity had been born Mary MacDonald. When she had joined her coven, she had legally changed her name to Infinity.

Some people were energetic, but Infinity *bubbled*. She didn't just speak with her hands, but with her whole body. She was a tiny woman, about five foot even and maybe a hundred pounds, but she seemed to have a much greater presence since she—bubbled.

"Hi, Infinity, how are you?" Melody asked.

She realized then that Infinity had not been referring to her when she had spoken. She glanced at Melody again, seemed to realize who she was, and greeted her cordially. "Melody! Lovely to see you, child. I've been looking for this young man!"

Jake smiled at Infinity. "Can I help you with something?"

"I want you to meet my friend Sherry. She's a wonderful medium. I told her how I had felt you such a very old soul when I met you while the band was setting up. She's so anxious now to meet you."

Great. Jake and a medium. He wouldn't be rude; he'd start telling his story, and it would all turn into real chaos and disaster. Potions would fly!

"Jake has to be back with the band," Melody said. "Break is just about over. Maybe he can meet her a bit later."

Maybe she'd find a way not to let it happen.

"Nonsense, dear, nonsense!" Infinity said. She slipped an arm through Jake's, drawing him from the balcony. "Sherry is just inside. It'll take two shakes of a dog's tail."

Jake offered her a grimace and followed along with Infinity.

Melody followed hot on their heels.

Sherry—as big a woman as Infinity was petite—was standing just inside the arched doorway to the main house.

She didn't need an introduction. She stepped forward, smiling broadly, and took Jake's hands. "So this is the young fellow who so impressed you, Infinity. Handsome young man. I'm so sorry. Sherry Simmons. And you're Jake Mallory. That's rather a famous name in these parts."

"Oh?" Jake said.

"Mallory, yes. I believe there was a Revolutionary War hero with your name. His body was spirited back from New York City after he was executed. I believe. There are all kinds of rumors. No one really knows."

Jake stared at the woman, betraying no emotion.

A dead war hero...it was the story he gave. Maybe he knew the real story and the legends, and was somehow playing into both.

But, despite his efforts at stoicism, he did look a bit as if he'd taken a sucker punch.

"Thank you. I'd love to see where he's buried," Jake said.

Sherry still had his hands. "You are an old soul, my friend. A very old soul. I'm having a difficult time seeing your future, but it seems that your past was fraught with violence and passion."

"He's an historian," Melody put in nervously. "Not much violence in that!" she said lightly.

Sherry didn't look at her. She was still studying Jake. "Not in this life," she told him softly. "You're struggling to make everything right in worlds you can no longer touch. And I can't see the future because, of course, too much is left in our own hands. We are creatures of free will, and I don't know what will happen."

"Oh, look—the band is setting up again," Melody said, staring through the doorway. "Jake, you do have to get back onstage!"

She managed to get him through the archway, but

Sherry's hand fell on her arm before she could follow him.

"Melody, just where did you meet this young man?" Sherry demanded.

Chapter 8

The band played.

People danced, ate, drank—and were merry.

Melody spent a great deal of the night worrying.

Everywhere she looked, it seemed she saw her mother with a new group of Wiccan friends. And they were whispering. They had grave and thoughtful expressions, and they were whispering.

What could be worse?

She quickly found out.

She felt a hand on her back and a warm presence behind her. "Surprise! Guess who?"

Her heart sank. She spun around.

"Mark."

He bent to kiss her lips. She didn't turn quickly enough. He was a strong man, and not expecting a refusal. His kiss was a big and obvious smack.

To his credit and her own humiliation, he really had no reason to expect anything other than enthusiasm from her. He'd been invited to family Christmas. By her mother, yes, but it had been quite safe for him to assume that her mother had invited him because she had wanted him. He knew that she was hemming and hawing about marriage, but he didn't know that it was over, completely over, in her heart.

She glanced quickly toward the stage.

And, of course, Jake was staring at her.

"Mark…I thought you couldn't possibly make it until tomorrow," she said, and then prayed that dismay wasn't evident in her voice. He didn't deserve cruelty from her.

"I know. I managed to get that meeting changed, and I took off out of the city as quickly as I could. And it wasn't all that bad getting here." He grimaced. He had dressed for a party. He was a handsome man, dressed stiffly in a suit coat and tie. His clothing was designer label, but belonged in a New York club, not at a Wiccan ball.

"I'm glad you traveled safely," she told him.

"Yeah, I just didn't know I was coming to a crazy house," he said.

She frowned. "It's a Wiccan ball."

"Your crazy mom's crazy friends, right?" He didn't say the words with malice, and still, though she might say it herself, she didn't want her mother called crazy.

"It's a free country, we're all entitled to our beliefs," she said.

He slipped his arms around her, hugging her to him. "Well, I know, but we're going to have to spend a little time figuring out just which way we're going. Our children must be raised in faith—and not a Wiccan faith!"

She opened her mouth to tell him that her *crazy* mother wasn't a Wiccan; she had friends everywhere. She just shook her head and realized he was talking about the two of them having children.

"Mark, it's definitely not something we need to worry about now," she told him.

"Right, but we should be giving it some thought."

"Mark, it's not just that I don't want to get married immediately," she began.

He didn't seem to hear her. "Can we get out of here? Have you done your daughterly duty long enough? I mean, there's got to be somewhere else we can go."

"I can't leave, Mark. And actually—"

She didn't get to finish. She felt a presence behind her, and she realized with horror that the band had stopped playing.

Jake had joined them. "Hello, how do you do? I'm Jake Mallory."

Mark looked at him. "Sure. Nice to meet you. I'm Mark Hathaway, Melody's fiancé."

Jake started, but kept his composure. "Congratulations."

"We are not engaged!" Melody announced.

"Not officially. Not yet," Mark said. "So, Jake, do you live around here?"

"He's from Boston," Melody supplied.

"Oh?" Mark said.

"I'm a very old friend," Jake said, glancing at Melody. "I was at loose ends, and she was kind enough to bring me home for the holidays."

"Well, uh, great," Mark said, looking at Melody.

She wished she could crawl into the floor. She wondered why, in all their conversations, she had never explained about Mark and the relationship that had almost been but wasn't. Jake's eyes were so intent on her, and she knew, no matter what the time period, it was wrong to lead someone on, wrong to make two people think that you longed to be with them.

She suddenly felt like the worst harlot in history, even though she wasn't actually sleeping with anyone. Was there such a thing as a semiclean Jezebel?

"Jake is an amazing musician," Melody said. "He agreed to sit in for a fellow who works with the group normally."

"Nice," Mark said. He was stiff, but being polite. He was merely suspicious. Jake, on the other hand, seemed to have been struck with the truth, and he was handling himself politely anyway. But the way that he looked at her! It caused a physical pain within her.

She was saved from the awkwardness of the situation when her mother came breezing in upon them. "Why, Mark! You've made it. How nice. We didn't expect you until tomorrow," Mona said, as if she was completely oblivious to the tension in the group.

"Mrs. Tarleton, hello, I came in early," Mark said. He gave Mona a kiss on the cheek and a hug. With her usual enthusiasm, Mona hugged him in return. "Have you met Jake, then, Mark? Or had you two met already? Anyway, it's lovely that you're here. The party is really in full swing. There's food and drink just up the stairs, and the band is just…just…just perfect. You all are just playing everything!" she said, addressing Jake.

"They're great fellows to work with," Jake said.

"How long does the party go on?" Mark asked.

"Oh, till the wee hours!" Mona said with a wink.

"Well, hello there!" Melody saw that her father had woven his way through the crowd. Keith was with her father.

"Mr. Tarleton, great to see you!" Mark reached out to shake her father's hand as if it were a lifeline.

He thought her father was the normal one in the group.

"Good drive down?" George asked Mark. "Or up, however you choose to see it."

"Yes, sir, the drive was fine, thank you," Mark said.

"Hi there, Mark," Keith said.

"Keith, great to see you. Great to be here," Mark responded.

There was real warmth to his voice. He was being polite but he did seem to care about her family.

He wasn't a bad guy, he wasn't a villain. She just wasn't in love with him, she wasn't the one he was looking for.

"Oh," Mona said. "Lora Richards, your third-grade Sunday-school teacher, is here, Mark. She'll be delighted to see you. Come along, let me steal you for just a sec!"

Mona linked arms with Mark.

Mark looked back with a panicked "Help me!" look on his face.

"My Sunday-school teacher is at a Wiccan ball?" Mark asked Mona helplessly.

"We all enjoy a good party, Mark," Mona said seriously.

"This isn't good," Melody's father commented gravely, shaking his head.

Melody flushed, thinking that her father was referring to the fact that she seemed to have two young men with whom she was involved staying at the house.

"Dad, I've been trying to explain to everyone—"

Jake interrupted her. "Melody, I wish that you had mentioned you were engaged."

"No, no, no," George said. "Mark has just arrived way too early."

"I have to get back in with the group," Jake said. "They are paying me. But you mustn't feel obliged in any way, Melody, to stay the night if your fiancé is here."

"He's not my fiancé," Melody said.

"He thinks he is," Keith said flatly, "that's the problem."

"Look, I've told him but he won't listen. He's not a bad guy, Keith. He just thinks that I'll change my mind," Melody said.

"None of this is important. The only thing that matters is getting Jake back to his own time," George said.

All three of them, Melody, Jake and Keith, went dead silent, with three jaws dropping simultaneously.

"What? Did you think I was stupid?" George demanded.

Then, of course, they all talked at once.

"Of course you're not stupid, Dad," Keith said.

"Mr. Tarleton, never in a century of centuries would I presume you were anything but an extremely intelligent man," Jake said.

"Dad, wait a minute, I mean, what are you talking about?" Melody demanded.

"But, sir, with your knowledge of so many things, your involvement would be greatly appreciated," Jake said.

"Dad, you can't mean that you believe—" Melody began.

"Cool, Dad, really cool, except, for real, we're not going to blow Jake up, right?" Keith asked.

George backed away from the three of them, raising his hands. "I am a scientist—when enough evidence is presented to me to make me believe some experimentation is necessary, I pay heed. Now, I have read through all these diaries your mother has found. I have seen Jake—hell, I even studied his shoes and clothing. Yes, there are historical tailors and boot makers who can reproduce these items, but I am convinced that Jake's belongings are authentic. And I don't believe in coincidence, so…do I believe what Jake believes to be true regarding himself as something possible? Back to basics—once, the greatest minds in the world believed that the world was flat. So…."

"Mom told you about Jake?" Melody said with a squeak.

"Cool," Keith said.

Jake was staring at her father with a crooked smile. "You two give a great deal of faith to one another, sir. It's quite beautiful," he said.

"Yes, but…Mark is here now. That's going to make our efforts more difficult."

"Clandestine!" Keith said, laughing. "Spies run around their own house, trying to avoid detection by the ordinary guest. Have to say—I rather love it."

"You're all crazy!" Melody said, punching her brother in the arm.

"Ouch, stop it!" Keith said.

"The sooner I am away, Melody, the sooner you'll be able to straighten out your own situation. Your kindness has truly been magnanimous. And I have sadly and rudely failed to realize that you do have another life that doesn't include strangers snatched from the snow," Jake told her.

"Jake, please believe me," she began earnestly. And then, she didn't know what to say. She lowered her voice, but that didn't matter, her father and her brother were standing there, watching them. "Jake," she said. "I believe that at least my mother will stand up for me here." She glared at her father and brother as if they were the worst kind of traitors. "I am not engaged to Mark. Nor did I intend to be. I had been seeing him, he is not a horrible human being. I will never be his wife, but I did not intend to hurt him. You are not a stranger snatched from the snow to me. You have become…you have become close to all of us. We care deeply about you."

"Even if I am mad, and this is all a delusion?" he asked her.

"Even if."

"Jake! You're needed up here!" one of the band members cried.

"Excuse me," Jake said. "Have to earn my keep."

He left them.

She realized that her brother was smirking at her. "The plot thickens!" he teased.

"Wretch!" she said.

"Melody, now," George said firmly. "Will you two children ever stop bickering?"

"But, Dad!"

"No, but dads," George said. "This is a serious situation we have here."

"Maybe we could put Mark at a hotel, or in a bed-and-breakfast," Keith suggested.

"Mom would never do that and you know it. She asked him, he's an invited guest," Melody said. "But, Dad—"

"What now?" George demanded.

"You—you believe this? And you honestly believe that there's some way to get Jake back where he thinks he belongs?"

Her father looked at her. "What do you understand about physics, Melody?"

"Newton's law," she said. "What goes up must go down, and I may be paraphrasing. Dad, there are no physics to bring a man back in time."

"What is time, exactly?" George asked her. "And for that matter, how many dimensions are there? Do more exist then we've seen so far?"

"And if you put it all together, maybe you could tell me what time it is right now on Jupiter," Keith said.

"What?" Melody demanded.

"My point, exactly," George said, nodding at Keith as if they shared some secret knowledge. All right, maybe, in a way, they did.

"Dad, if this means another explosion, though—" Melody said.

"No explosions," he promised her. "And I think your mom is a bit on the daft side with this, thinking that we need to follow all of Serena's herbal potions. Science isn't magic. Or maybe it is. Maybe magic is science. But your mom and I have been working on things, only now…well, now we've added another element."

"Mark," Keith said thoughtfully. "Melody can just take him somewhere."

"What?" she said again.

"We'll take care of Jake, and you get Mark out of the way," Keith said.

"Oh, no, no, no, no," Melody said. "I brought Jake home. You are not experimenting on him without me being present."

Her brother leaned down to whisper to her, "Melody, I told you before—you can't keep him, you know. He really isn't a stray."

She was startled by the feel of a sting in her eyes; she'd be fighting tears in a minute. Mark was here. She didn't want to hurt Mark. Jake probably held the lowest possible opinion he could regarding her, and she was falling into lust or love or like with him, and everyone around her—including her father!—seemed to think that they could get him back to a different time.

She turned around to look at the band. Jake was looking at her. He was playing the violin, intent on the music, and the song was a sad ballad.

She suddenly turned on both of them and made her way through the crowd blindly. She found the drinks station and ordered whatever a Wicked Wiccan Willy might be.

Suddenly she felt hands on her shoulders again. She winced.

Mark.

"Seriously, can't we get out of here, please?" he asked her, spinning her around. He grimaced. "A little alone time? Away from the craziness. Honestly, even my old Sunday-school teacher has gone nuts. She took my hands and held them and then read my palm. She went on and on about how I was such a new soul, and needed to look to the past. She called me a fuddy-duddy!"

Mark was indignant. His expression actually drew a smile from Melody, and the Wicked Wiccan Willy was already warming through her system. "Mark, you are an old fuddy-duddy."

"Pardon me? What on earth does that mean, Melody?" He was hurt; she hadn't meant to hurt him.

"Mark, you're living...or you want to live...in the past. You think everything has a time and place. Women should be barefoot, pregnant and in the kitchen."

"That's not true at all."

"Oh?" she asked, wondering if he had changed his thought pattern at all.

But no. Mark was simply a realist.

"Don't be ridiculous. It's freezing or cold a good third of the year. No one should be running around barefoot," he said.

"Mark, colleges are filled with women these days. Mothers work outside the home. Fathers stay with the kids at times. And guess what—they love their kids, and don't mind changing diapers."

He shook his head, slipping an arm around her. "Kids. That's the whole point, don't you see, Melody? Kids are the future. They need to be shaped and molded, supervised. I don't want my kids growing up with strangers."

"No one wants that, Mark."

"And the thing is, I can provide for a family."

"Mark, everyone needs a sense of accomplishment and worth."

"Yeah? Is that how you feel—or does it have something to do with this new guy from Boston you've suddenly brought home?" he asked her.

She opened her mouth, startled by the bitterness in his tone. "Mark, it has to do with me. Do I want children? Yes. Do I think that you can have something of a career and children, too? Yes. Both my folks worked. I couldn't love anyone more."

"Oh, please, Melody! Your mother is half-crazy—just look where she's brought us all tonight!"

She stared at him, stunned by the depth of fury that suddenly seemed to be burning throughout her.

"My mother is not crazy!" she said, enunciating every syllable.

"Melody, Melody, I'm so sorry," he said. "I didn't mean that the way it sounded. I am so sorry. She's a dear and kind person. But I don't want our children growing up with all…with all this weirdness surrounding them."

"When I have children," Melody said, "she will be their grandmother. And I will want her in their lives. I will want them touched by the love and *craziness* that she has within her. That's just it, Mark, don't you see? We cannot be engaged to one another. Now. Or ever."

"You don't mean that, Melody. We're perfect together. I can't help but believe this all has something to do with your friend from Boston," Mark said.

She took another long swallow of her Wicked Wiccan Willy. As she did so, Peggy Winston—apparently relieved of her duty as hostess at the door—swept down upon them. "Jake, dear, I wanted to ask you about—oh! You're not Jake, are you?"

"No, Mrs. Winston, this is another of my friends,

Mark Hathaway. Mark, please meet Peggy Winston, our official hostess," Melody said.

"Lovely to meet you," Peggy said, taking Mark's hands and studying him curiously. "You must have slipped in when I turned over door duty to one of the other women. But goodness! You certainly do resemble Jake. Are you two related?"

"No!" Mark said firmly.

"Genetics are so strange, aren't they?" Melody said. She looked at Mark. It was true that he and Jake had a similar look. Same hazel eyes, green and tawny. Dusty-brown hair. And yes, strong handsome features. Mark was a very nice-looking man. She was just aggravated with him. She wanted to be his friend. She cared about him.

She just didn't want to be engaged to him, and now, the very thought of marrying him made her twitch.

"You're quite sure?" Peggy asked.

She still had Mark's hands. He looked as if he wanted to rip them away from her. He somehow refrained.

Because he was a decent human being. He just had different beliefs and desires.

"I'm quite sure," Mark said.

"Well, this is New England," Peggy said. "So many of us had ancestors long ago, and every once in a while—just as you said, Melody—genetics pop up here and there. Absolutely intriguing."

"Yes, of course." Mark cleared his throat, indicating his hands.

But Peggy didn't give up easily. "There's a strength in you," she said somberly.

"Thank you," Mark said stiffly.

"An old strength," she said.

"Great. I was just told I'm a new soul." Maybe he didn't intend to sound so sarcastic.

But Peggy wasn't put off. "A new soul...with a strange old-time strength. Ah, that's it. Old-fashioned to the core!" Peggy said.

Mark was very straight. "And there's something wrong with that?" he asked.

"Only when it hampers the present, and brings out the pain of the past," she told him. She released his hands. "Pleasure to meet you, Mark. Blessed be."

Mark was silent. Melody responded by rote. "Blessed be."

When Peggy had turned and disappeared through the crowd, he swung on her. "What the hell was that? You belong to a normal religion!"

"Oh, Mark! What is wrong with anyone saying 'blessed be'? It's like 'God be with you,' or 'through the grace of Allah,' or 'Jehovah.'"

"No, it's not. That's it. You've given up your faith. I don't know why. There's no reason for you to have turned against Christmas and all that it stands for," he said earnestly.

"I haven't turned against Christmas! Oh, Mark, please, I'm Christian because of my world, because of what I was taught, because I even love my church. But others have learned differently, or they've come to believe differently, and I'm really sorry, but my *Christian* teachings have made me try to understand and be tolerant of others, especially when they're trying to do good!"

She was growing so angry and aggravated with him. Maybe that was good. Maybe she could say right then and there that there was no hope for them, even as friends.

And then he could go away and stay in a hotel!

She winced. No. Her mother had invited him. Honor code of Mona—he had to stay, and she had to start being more patient.

But Mark looked at her and exploded. "They're *witches,* for God's sake."

"What? And you want to hang them, or go back to medieval Europe and burn them at the stake?" she demanded. "Mark, the Wiccans—those I know today, certainly!—believe in doing nothing but good to and for others. Evil deeds come back on you threefold. Mark, open your eyes, please. We may be New Englanders, but we're not single-minded Puritans anymore. Oh, Mark. Please. Enjoy the party. These are nice people. It ends at one, we'll pack up and go home then."

She spun around and left him there, standing by the drinks table.

Rude. Terribly rude. Her mother would be appalled.

Her mother was welcome to deal with him.

Melody wasn't sure where she was going then, what she wanted to do, or how on earth they were going to handle the situation.

It had all gone mad.

Now, her mother had talked to her father, and as unbelievable as it might be, her father seemed to believe that Jake had fallen in from an alternate universe, as well.

She made her way back to stand in front of the band. Jake was now on guitar. She marveled at his love for instruments, and his ability to pick up one after another, and play so easily with a group he had just met.

He looked up and saw her. She smiled weakly.

He looked away.

Melody looked at her watch. It was almost time for the evening to end. She prayed that in this instance, time would go quickly.

The castle was emptying.

There was no more music, and the food and drinks stands were closed. Servers cleaned up, quickly and efficiently, eager to get home.

Melody saw her folks at the door, chatting with Peggy. Her brother was helping the band pack up along with Jake.

She stood alone, watching as the last of couples, singles and groups exited the castle.

She didn't see Mark.

Anxiously, she scanned all the rooms she could see, and then hurried over to her parents.

"Mom, I can't find Mark."

"He came in his own car, right?" Mona asked.

"Um, I think. Or maybe he went to the house, and then took a cab. I don't know, Mom, I never asked him."

"I'll take a look out on the balcony," her father said.

"I'll go on down to the basement area," Mona offered.

"Mom, I'll go," she said. "You just stay here."

But Mark wasn't on the lower level. Melody came back upstairs to find that the band had packed up completely, and Jake and Keith were with her parents and Peggy Winston and the castle representative.

They were ready to lock up for the night.

"I can't find him anywhere," she said worriedly.

"All right, well, he might have gone on to the house," her father said.

"He might have, but…I don't know," Melody said. She was trying not to look at Jake, but he was studying her seriously.

"Were you two arguing?" Mona asked.

"No, no, of course not. Um, maybe we were exchanging a difference of opinion," Melody said.

"Why don't you go home, and I'll stay here," Jake suggested. "Donald Ferguson is still packing up. He can bring me back when he's ready to leave."

"Jake, dear, we wouldn't leave you. You're our guest, and…well, frankly, you know the area the least," Mona said.

Jake laughed pleasantly, giving Mona a squeeze on the shoulders with a deep and appreciative affection. "I do know my way, if need be. Not that much has changed, honestly. But Donald is still here, so I'm fine. And you'll probably find that your friend is at the house."

"I'll stay, too," Keith said.

"I'm the one who should stay," Melody said.

"Except that he might be at the house, out front, waiting to get in," her father said.

"Shall we look for his car first?" Keith suggested sensibly.

They all stared at Keith and nodded.

But Mark's car wasn't parked in the lot. "Go on home, please," Jake said. "All of you. I'll be on the lookout for Mark."

"Just remember that sunrise comes early," Mona said.

"Of course," Jake said. He looked at Melody. "We'll find him, don't worry."

Melody winced. She wanted to make him understand.

She didn't want to do so with an audience.

Keith said, "I'll stay."

"But three of us won't fit in the van," Jake said.

Keith tossed Jake his cell phone. "You've learned how to use it, right?" he asked.

"I hit the word *answer* to answer. I hit the word *end* to end. I think I've got it," Jake said.

"Right," Keith agreed. He flipped open his phone. "And if you want to call us, hit my sister's name right here, and then *talk*."

"I understand," Jake assured them.

He waved to them. Melody's mother slipped an arm through hers and firmly started toward the car. "Come on, dear, don't be worried. We'll find Mark."

"Thanks, Mom," she murmured.

She looked back. Keith and her father were following behind them. Jake had started out in the cold of the night, circling around the castle and the cliffs and lawns that surrounded it.

"I'm sure we're going to find him parked in front of the house, or maybe on the porch," Mona said. "He really didn't enjoy the ball at all, you know."

"He doesn't believe in witches—or Wiccans," Melody said.

"Well, dear, every man and every woman out there has a different way of thinking," Mona said gently. "Some people just come with tolerance, and for others, well, with any luck, they get to learn it. Here we are, at the car."

Melody slid into the back. She was surprised when

her brother, seated beside her, set a supporting arm around her shoulders.

"We're going to find him, and he's going to be okay, and everything is going to get straightened out," he told her.

"How do you know?" she asked bleakly.

"Well, it's Christmas. I think it's a time when we just may be able to make little miracles happen, when the right will and love are in our hearts, don't you think?" Keith asked.

He gave her such a grin, she didn't know if he was serious or not. The scientist, who seemed to believe in the absurd, as well.

"Sure," she said.

The castle wasn't far from their house. As they approached it, she found that she stared at the lights, and she was surprised that the colorful glow seemed to touch her heart, even over her fear for Mark. Lights, angels, crosses, beauty and belief, all shimmering against the snow.

What if something terrible had happened to Mark? It would be all her fault.

His car was in the driveway. Melody leaped out of her father's car and went racing along to look in the driver's-side door of Mark's car.

Empty.

Mark didn't drink and drive. Maybe he thought he might be drinking at the party and had called a cab to pick him up at the house.

So where was he now?

The castle sat on cliffs that fell dozens of feet to the sea.

No, no, no. Nothing had happened to him.

"Oh, God," she said, feeling ill.

"I'll check out the porch, the lab, the backyard," her father said.

"Give me your phone, sis. I'll give Jake a call and let him know that we haven't found him here," Keith told her.

Melody sank down on the porch steps, trembling.

She looked up to the sky, at the North Star, burning brightly in the night.

"Please, please, let him be okay!" she prayed.

"Hello!"

Jake Mallory found Mark Hathaway sitting on the arched buttress that was part of the outer castle wall. By day, it would have afforded an unbelievable view.

At night, it was cold.

And all that could be seen was the darkness of the water below.

It took Mark a minute to turn around and look at him. When he did, he offered a rueful and crooked smile, lifting his large plastic glass. "Wicked Wiccan Willy, or some such thing. I had a few. I think it might be poison. I can't get up."

Jake came around and sat next to him on the stone wall.

"It's all right, my friend," he said gravely. "It isn't poison. It's just alcohol. In certain quantities, it can be the same thing. Are you sure that you're all right?"

"Oh, yeah," Mark said, staring at the sea again.

"It's quite cold up here, you know," Jake said.

"Can't feel it. But then, I am a New Englander. We are tough, you know."

"Yes, I know. But, there's a warm bed waiting for you. Hot chocolate. A place of comfort."

Mark shook his head. "She doesn't want me," he said. He turned to Jake. His eyes focused for a minute. "Nope, she doesn't want me. And you know what? I don't get it. She wants you. And they're right. You look like me. Or I look like you. So—what's the difference? I give to charity. I love kids. By God, I played football for U-Mass once!"

"Mark, I have a ride back to the house for the two of us," Jake said. He hesitated. "And I'm not going to be around long, so don't worry about me, huh?"

Mark shook his head, not ready to get up. "Haven't you ever seen the way she looks at you?"

Yes, and I know that I look at her that way, but you don't understand that we're not really existing on the same plane, and I could never stay, be what I wish I could be, touch her again. What a fool, I can never touch her again....

"Mark, these are very good people who care about you and they're worried sick," Jake said. "We've got to get back there."

"Friends," Mark said glumly.

"Pardon?"

"She wants to be friends, I'm sure. Friends. That's the kiss of death!"

"Look, Mark, there's a lot to be talked out and figured out. But freezing up here all night isn't going to help anything. Come on, let me get you back," Jake said.

"Witches—swear to God, they were trying to kill me," Mark slurred.

Jake had to laugh. "I swear to God, I don't think so."

Mark, with Jake's help, managed to stumble to his feet. He held on to Jake, shaking his head. "I just don't understand. Whatever happened to family values? I mean, what I'm looking for isn't something bad, or negative. Just a home. A wife who cooks. A family. I want to work hard and provide for them. That's not bad, is it?"

"No, it's not bad, Mark. I think it's what many men want," Jake said.

"So, what am I missing?" Mark asked.

"Belief?" Jake suggested.

The breeze moved through the cold night air as they stood there, Jake supporting Mark, and Mark honestly lost.

Far more lost than I am, Jake thought.

"Belief?" Mark asked. "Like in—Wiccans?"

Jake shook his head. "Belief in the one you love," he said.

But Mark wasn't in a state of mind to comprehend. "I do believe, I do believe. I believe she can be the world's most wonderful wife."

Jake thought that he could explain that yes, indeed, Melody was beautiful and kind, and she loved her home, pets, kids and family. She was a ball of energy and didn't mind work in the least.

But she was more.

Maybe tomorrow he could try to explain. Not right now.

"My friend Donald is waiting with the van. Come on. Let's get back."

They started down the slope of the lawn together. Jake was good with snow, and he was decently strong, but carrying most of Mark's weight down the slippery slope wasn't easy. He moved down carefully.

"Ah, there y'are!" Donald called. "Friend had a few too many of those Wicked Willy things, eh?"

"A few," Jake agreed.

Donald met him as he reached the pavement and slipped an arm around Mark, as well. Between them, they got him into the van.

"Brother? Cousin?" Donald asked.

"No, just a friend."

"Y' don't need to be embarrassed. I'm Irish. We've had a few in m' family known to take one or two too many," Donald said.

Jake laughed. "No, he's a friend. Just a friend," he said.

As he settled into the van himself, he heard the melodic chimes of Keith's cell phone ringing. He answered it.

"Hey!" It was Keith, calling from Melody's phone.

And answering the incredible piece of technology was quite easy.

"I've been trying to reach you," Keith said. "Mark isn't here—"

"It's all right. He's with me. Donald is giving us a ride home now," Jake said.

"Thank God," Keith breathed. "We were worried sick."

"We'll be there soon," Jake said, and hung up.

He thought that Mark might have passed out. He hadn't. His eyes were still blurry, and he wasn't doing an exceptional job of trying to sit up straight.

There was a gravity in his eyes—despite the shimmer in them.

He wasn't a bad fellow at all, not really.

Maybe, when he had made his way back home...

Jake was startled by the pain that seemed to sear through him.

Going home meant leaving Melody. It meant never seeing her again. And it seemed that the sound of her voice was engraved in his memory, the scent of her perfume, the joy of her laughter. He could forever close his eyes and see her face. And now, he could remember the taste and the feel of her lips, and the fact that touching her skin felt like a brush with silk.

He looked away.

Serena could very well die because of him.

George and Mona seemed to have figured something out—or so they had told him excitedly. Yes, even George. Potions—and waves. Sound waves? Had that been it? He didn't know, but he knew that he had suddenly appeared, and that they believed in him, and before too long, he'd be gone.

Mark's eyes were closing now. Jake winced, and he leaned close to him.

"Just believe," he said softly. "Just learn to believe in those you love."

They pulled up in front of the house.

Donald helped Jake get Mark out of the van without destroying any equipment. By the time he had done so, Keith and Melody had raced down to help him.

They all thanked Donald.

"Hey, Jake, it was grand, working with ya," Donald said. "We'll be giving you a call again, somewhere along the line."

"Thanks. I'm honored. I'm afraid I won't be here much longer," Jake said.

"We'll give you a try, anyway!" Donald said, then waved as he got in the van.

Melody looked at Jake anxiously, trying to balance Mark's weight between herself and her brother.

"Thank you," she told him.

He smiled. She was so beautiful, and her heart was where it should have been. Beautiful and full of life. She was energy and motion, dreams and magic, even if she didn't know just what magic the very fact of her being created for him.

"My pleasure," he said. "Let me get him up the stairs with Keith, you'll never manage."

She nodded again, realizing the sense of his words.

As they walked up the stairs, Mark mumbled, "Witches!"

"Wiccans," Melody said.

"Witches— Wiccans. Wicked witches—what did they put in those drinks?" Mark asked mournfully.

"A whole lot of booze, buddy," Keith said.

They got Mark up the stairs, and into the guest room. "I got this one," Keith said. "You took care of me already, Jake. I'm just getting his coat and shoes. He can sleep in his clothing. Sadly, it's not something most of us haven't done at least once."

Jake nodded. "Where are your folks? Did they get to bed?"

"Yes. Mom and Dad were both concerned about getting enough sleep," Keith said.

"Well, then, good night," Jake said, heading down the hall for Keith's room.

But Melody came after him. She touched his arm, and he turned around.

"It's not what you think," she said. "Please…I was

never engaged to Mark. We—dated. We're working on a project together. But when he grew serious, I knew that we couldn't make a life together. Our dreams are different. I...I should have been far more clear with him, but..."

"He's a good fellow. He cares for you deeply," Jake said.

"And he is my friend. I want to be his friend. Just not his wife or his lover," she said.

"Melody, you don't owe me explanations," Jake said. *Don't!* he warned himself. *Don't touch her.*

But he did. He had to. He reached out, and his fingers brushed over a length of her hair that was like a stray strand of gossamer silk, trailing along her cheek.

And he smiled and stepped back.

"Good night, Melody."

Goodbye.

No. That would be unbearable.

"Good night," she said.

She turned to leave him, but she spun back around.

"No! Not good night. I have done nothing wrong. I haven't been firm with Mark because I didn't want to hurt him. But I care about you so much. It's all quite insane, but it's all there, and—"

Her arms were suddenly around him, drawing him to her. He didn't know if he kissed her or if she kissed him, but he knew the infusion of electricity and heat that filled his body, and the warmth of her mouth, the passion of her movement.

He kissed her, and he held her close. And he memorized the way that she felt in his arms, and the way it seemed that her scent was more than just part of the air he breathed. He held her closer and closer, and he felt as if he etched every curve and subtle crevice of her form into his mind and his being, and he cherished the seconds that seemed forever and far too short, and at last, breathless, his heart thundering, he stepped back.

"Good night, Melody," he said.

"Good night." She smoothed her hair and touched her lips. And whispered, "Do you believe me?"

"I believe you, *and* I believe in you," he told her.

One more. Just one more.

And so he stepped forward, taking her into his arms.

They were both dimly aware that a door closed in the hallway.

"Ah, come on, break it up, kids!" Keith said. "It's late, you know."

They broke apart. Melody gave her brother a quick hug, then escaped to her own room.

Keith looked at Jake. "Sunrise will come early," he said.

"Right."

Chapter 9

Sunrise.

Melody's eyes flew open. The word was hovering in her mind.

Why?

She had woken up with the pleasant feel of the warmth of her bed and the comfort of her pillow. Then the word had popped to mind. Then the memory of a single Wicked Wiccan Willy, and the worry about Mark, and then...

Sunrise.

They had been talking about sunrise. Both of her parents. And Keith.

And Jake.

Had they all conjured up something, and had they chosen not to tell her?

The nerve of them!

Melody leaped out of bed and raced to her curtains, her heart thundering. What were they up to? Oh, thank God! The sky was still dark, though the first pink and pastel lights of morning were beginning to fight their way through the shadows of the night.

She turned, so anxious she was ready to run straight for the door. At the door, she realized she was barefoot and in a cotton flannel gown. She found her fuzzy slippers and reached for the first cover she could find— her Wiccan cape from the night before. Throwing it around herself, she tore down the stairs.

The downstairs was empty. Okay, she was crazy and suspicious.

But she could smell coffee. Yes, there was coffee brewed in the coffeepot. She hesitated, poured herself a cup, then let out a little gasp.

Outside.

Melody hurried out the back and down the back steps.

There they were. All of them. Jake, Keith, her mom and dad.

George was busy walking a circle around the area of the old well. Mona was holding a steaming cup. Coffee?

Melody doubted it.

"What in hell is going on here?" Melody demanded.

They all jumped—like kids who'd been raiding the candy shop.

They stared at her with guilty faces.

All except for Jake. He stared at her with a level gaze and sadness in his eyes that threatened to break her heart.

"I have to go, Melody."

"Oh, no, please! What is this? What's going on here?

What kind of a pack of traitors are you?" Melody demanded, staring around at her family. "Dad, Mom—you could hurt Jake, don't you see? You could kill him. We can't do this, maybe he's even right, but we can't do this!"

"I found more of Serena's diaries, Melody. I know what herbs she used. We know where we believe the magnetic fields are," Mona said.

"It will be all right. I'm not dealing with chemicals, radiation or anything harmful," George said. "I swear!"

"Keith! You talk some sense into them," Melody said.

Keith lifted his shoulders and offered a helpless grimace. "He's worried sick about his sister, Mel. I can't help it. I understand that."

"Jake?" she pleaded.

He was dead center in front of the well. The two strange machines her father had been working with for the last months were arranged on opposite sides of the well.

Jake was standing in the middle.

"Melody, I have to go," he said. "My God, Melody," he began. But he didn't speak. They weren't alone.

"We'll lose the sunrise. Jake, the potion," Mona said.

"Potion!" Melody yelled. "Mom, this is crazy. You're talking about black holes, and frequencies and waves—and *potions*. Please, please—"

She nearly jumped sky high when the door to the back slammed shut.

She turned around.

Mark had joined them.

Of all of them, he certainly looked the sanest at the moment. He had showered and dressed in dark jeans, a sweater and a warm wool coat. He was clean shaven, and his hair was neatly trimmed, and he almost looked as if he belonged in a *Men in Black* movie.

He was distressed; he was also strong and sure.

"Please! What in God's name is going on in this asylum?" he demanded.

"Mark, this doesn't concern you," Melody said uneasily.

"Well, well, I'm afraid I came in early, and I'm sorry, I like Jake a lot, and you're not going to play any kind of dangerous abracadabra on him," Mark said firmly. "Whatever you're doing, stop it. I'll call the police."

"Mark, please, you're no part of this, and it's true—you don't understand," Jake said.

"Clue me in," Mark insisted.

"I'm not from this time, Mark," Jake told him. "I told you last night—I'm not intended to be here. They're just trying to get me back home."

"He was a Revolutionary soldier. Taken as a spy, about to be hanged," Melody heard herself explaining. "He's just trying to get home."

Mark looked at George. "You are kidding me?" he demanded.

George looked at Mona.

"The sunrise is coming," Keith warned softly.

Mark started from the porch.

"Hit the switch, Dad!" Keith warned.

Both men hit the switches and a humming sound touched the air. Melody wasn't sure, but it seemed as if she could *see* waves in the air.

"Jake, here!" Mona said.

"Mona, for the love of God!" Mark exclaimed.

And then, before anyone could stop him, Mark snatched the cup from Mona's hands.

"No!" she cried.

"Mark, please, no!" Melody begged.

"This is nonsense, just nonsense, and I'll prove it!" Mark said. "Hey, buddy, nothing ill intended. You did prove to be a damn good friend last night, though I had just met you," Mark said to Jake.

"Mark, give me the cup and get back, please!" Jake begged.

But Mark pushed Jake aside.

And swallowed the contents of the cup.

Just as he did so, the sun burst across the pale pink horizon.

The home between the two machines became a sizzle.

And Mark Hathaway disappeared cleanly into thin air.

They all sat around the dining room table as if shell-shocked.

A thorough search of the yard, the house and all nearby premises had shown no sign at all of Mark Hathaway.

He was gone. Vanished.

"What do we do now?" Mona finally asked bleakly. "Oh, this is terrible, just terrible. We haven't helped Jake, and we don't know what we've done to poor Mark."

"And it's Christmas Eve," Keith said worriedly.

"You believe that we need the sunrise, Mona?" Jake asked. "Is that what my sister wrote in her journal?"

"I can show you the page," Mona said. She shook her

head. "Imagine, that book of hers has been up in that attic all these years. So much information, and still... no ending. Oh, dear."

"This is crazy. All crazy," Melody murmured.

"Crazy?" Jake came over to her and hunkered down by her chair, taking her hands. "And you're so indignant when someone suggests that you shouldn't follow a dream."

"This isn't a dream anymore, Jake. It's a nightmare," she told him.

"Instead of whining and tossing about disparaging remarks, how about helping?" he suggested.

"I am not a scientist, nor do I know anything about potions," she reminded him.

"But you can read," he said with a smile.

"Yes, I can read."

"I can't quite decipher all of the old lettering," Mona said.

Jake lifted a brow to Melody and helped her to her feet. "Your mother said that you'd studied a lot of the old funerary art in school and that you could probably read my sister's writing easily. *I* can't even figure out all of her script," he said.

"You know that I didn't want you to leave," she said, alarmed at the huskiness in her tone.

"But you do want Mark back in this world where he belongs, right?" Jake asked.

Guilt surged through her. "Yes," she said simply. She walked over to the book. Serena's thoughts on the war and the world in which she lived were certainly fascinating, but Melody skimmed quickly to the part of the book that had to do with what Serena had called the "black doorway" and how certain potions and events could be combined to open the door—and close it.

She shook her head after a moment, aware that they were all watching her anxiously.

"Sunrise—and sunset," she said. "According to this, both times of the day lay open the possibilities of taking a person through time and space, or through different dimensions, or alternate worlds." She couldn't believe that she had said it aloud, explained it aloud.

Except that she had seen Mark disappear. After he had told Jake that he'd been a good friend to him, after he had proven himself, trying to make sure that nothing bad happened to Jake.

It wasn't that she had suddenly discovered that she was wrong, that she was in love with Mark. It was just wrong. He didn't deserve whatever had happened to him. At heart, he was a good man. And she understood as well—what Jake was feeling for Serena. He loved her; she had grown up with him, and so, they were brother and sister. And he feared for her.

As she feared for Mark.

"So, sunset, Mona," George said. "Sunset, we set up, and try again."

"Try again? How will Mark be able to take a potion and stand in the right place at the right time?" Melody demanded.

They were quiet around her.

Then Jake said, "I'll have to go back. And when I'm back, I'll get Mark set up to return here. It's fairly simple. And my sister will—hopefully, oh, God, hopefully!—be there. To help him, and guide him. Maybe I'll wind up back at the right time, and so will Mark."

"At the right time? What are you talking about?"

Melody demanded. "This is simple? There's a doorway. A doorway, a black hole, something that is there, in time and space. You're calling that simple?"

"Maybe," Keith said.

"And maybe not," Mona told her with a sigh.

"But can we take a chance and send Jake back in time?" Keith asked her.

"Do you see Mark anywhere?" George asked.

Silence followed.

"So, what are you all saying?" Melody asked.

"We try again at sunset," Jake said.

"I have more potion," Mona said. "I mixed a fairly large batch. Then, of course, who knows? Maybe we only need your father's machines. Maybe the 'black hole' or the 'black door' opens of its own accord upon occasion, and maybe it can be manipulated. After all, Jake was being hanged in New York, and he fell through time onto a roadway far north up into Gloucester."

She looked terribly depressed.

"It's all right, Mom." To her own surprise, Melody came to stand behind her mother and hug her shoulders. "It's all right. We will be able to fix everything. Everything will work out."

Mona nodded. "I'm going to take a shower," she said. "And…and make breakfast."

"No, dear, we'll go out to breakfast," George said.

"No, dear, you will stay with me. And the kids will get out of here. We'll stay here—just in case time decides to spit Mark out in the backyard," Mona said.

"Mrs. Tarleton," Jake said. "This is my dilemma, it has been from the start. You must go out, and I will remain behind, watching."

"No," Mona said. "George and I will stay. And you children will get out of here because you are driving me right out of my mind."

Mark Hathaway lay on his back.

On something hard. A floor. A rug on a floor, he realized. And there was warmth, coming from somewhere. The light was muted, but...

Wincing, he sat up. He was back in the parlor of the Tarleton house, but it looked different. It was dim—there were no lights on and the morning rays were just beginning to creep through the drapes.

Different drapes.

Different furniture.

He blinked furiously. For a moment, he thought he was still caught in a wretched hangover from last night's Wicked Wiccan Willy.

Then he began to wonder just what mushroom Mona had put in that potion he had swallowed.

But as he blinked furiously, thinking that he must have taken something very, very wild, he was startled by a sudden cry and he swung around.

The fireplace was just where it was supposed to be, of course.

But the mantel was different. And a fire burned in the hearth.

A giant cooking pot simmered with something in it over the fire.

Cooking pot?

Or witches' brew?

Immaterial at the moment. Because the woman who had let out the cry was standing next to the pot, staring at him.

"Jake!" she cried out, her voice a trembling sob.

She started to rush to his side.

"Jake? I'm not Jake," Mark protested. He struggled to his feet and met the woman's gaze.

She stopped dead.

And he stared.

She was beautiful. Stunningly beautiful. Her eyes were the blue of the sky on a perfect spring day. Her hair was the color of a raven's wing.

"Dear God!" she breathed. "You're not Jake. But—oh, my God. You must be some relation! Someone I didn't know...and, oh, God, dear God! Where is my brother? What happened to him?" She stared at him, his eyes searching his out with desperation.

Then, she jumped back. She took in the length of him, the clean-cut Armani coat and his Kenneth Cole boots. His hair cut, and everything about him.

"Where are you from? Who are you? Speak to me!" She backed away from him farther, and before he knew it, she had the fire poker in her hands. "Speak and speak quickly, and if you're part of the British army, sir, you had best explain, and you had best know that my brother lives somewhere, or your own life will be considerably shortened!"

"Hey, hey—please, wait! I'm not British, I swear it, although, to be honest, I have a lot of British friends. Wait, wait, wait, sorry, wrong thing to say at the moment," Mark gasped out. "Your brother is fine, though I met him last night for the first time. We were at a party. In Gloucester...hey, wait. Where are we now?"

"Gloucester. Gloucester, Massachusetts," the woman said.

"What—what year is it?"

"You jest," she accused him.

"Oh, I so wish that I did!" Mark told her. "Please… no, no, no, wait. I have it now. I did take a hallucinatory drug. It was last night. Then again, maybe they were trying to play a trick on me. They gave me more this morning. I'm being…it's a practical joke. Okay, I've got it. You work with Jake Mallory, you're an historian somewhere, or whatever they call it now—historical interpreter. And you all are just trying to make me think I'm crazy."

She stared at him blankly. All that she seemed to take from his entire exposition was the fact that he really knew Jake Mallory.

She stepped closer, the fire poker tightly in her hands. "I want my brother back here. Now. What have you done with him?"

"Nothing. Nothing—I swear, I haven't done a thing with your brother!" Mark told her. He swallowed. Oddly enough, in his confusion and fear, he became aware that whatever was cooking in the pot did not smell like any strange potion.

It held a wonderful aroma. Like a stew flavored to perfection.

It was morning. Who cooked stew in the morning?

"What is the year?" he asked again.

"You seriously don't know?" she asked.

"Please?"

"Who are you?" she demanded.

"I'm Mark. My name is Mark Hathaway."

"And where are you from?"

"Gloucester, Massachusetts. Originally. I've been working in New York the last few years. My family— my immediate family has passed away, I'm afraid. I came to see—to see friends living back in my hometown. Last night, I went to a party. It was a Wiccan party. I drank—"

"A Wiccan party? Near Christmas? Oh, you are a dastardly liar!" she cried.

Dastardly?

She wasn't that big. Surely—and with no harm done the woman—he could wrest the fire poker from her. Then he could step outside, and see exactly what was going on. Why in God's name had Melody never been able to see that her parents were certifiably crazy?

"I'm telling you, I came to see my friends, but they were out. The neighbors told me where they were, and so I went to the party. Thank God I took a cab, because the drinks were killer. I'm telling you the absolute truth. This morning, they were playing around with some black hole or something of the like. They're— they're a little on the odd side. The dad is a scientist, an inventor—he came up with a real great broom or mop or something of the like, and I guess he thinks he's Edison or something." She stared at him blankly and he continued. "The mom is…well, I don't know what she is. A hippie, I guess. New Age, in a way. A Catholic New Age. Like a Catholic Wiccan. If you can be such a thing. Anyway, she made this potion thing and…"

His voice trailed away. She had stepped back.

"What?"

"Go on. Go on with your story."

Mark shook his head. If this was a prank being played on him, the girl was wasting her time on small stuff. Her expression was one of pure amazement and question. "Oh, come on, please," he said. "Is this a prank? Why are you dressed that way?"

"This is my customary house apparel," she said, her tone aggravated. "And believe me, I am in no disposition for pranks of any kind."

"Right. Right!" He ignored the poker and turned around, striding to the door. He threw it open.

Snow covered the ground.

Snow and more snow.

And that was all that he could see. There was no house across the street.

There was a picket fence around a side yard, and a furry horse was nuzzling through the snow.

He closed the door.

Hallucinogenic!

Had to be, oh, God, had to be.

"Get in here! You're letting the heat out."

Mark turned to face her. He shook his head. He blinked. He slapped himself.

He still stood exactly where he had been, facing the beautiful girl.

"What year is it? Please, just tell me that. What time is it, what year is it?"

"Seventeen seventy-six. It's Christmas Eve, Seventeen seventy-six."

"What on earth are we going to do? This is enough to make you crazy," Melody said.

She stood on the porch steps with Keith and Jake.

They had been thrown out of the house.

"Get in the car," Keith said.

"What? Why? Where are we going?" Melody demanded.

"Just get in," Keith said.

Jake shrugged and started to agree. He followed Keith.

"Jake!" Melody said. "What are you doing? He won't tell us his plan?"

"Well, he's getting in the car, and I don't have a plan, so I thought I should get in, as well," Jake said. He was quiet and thoughtful, and had been for the last hour.

In contrast, Melody felt as if she were a mouse in a field of traps.

And Keith...

"Melody?" Jake asked, turning back.

She threw up her hands. "You two are too much. And Mom! We don't know where Mark is. We don't know what will happen. And we have to wait for sunset on Christmas Eve to even try a crazy stunt to find Mark. And if we find Mark, then Jake is lost somewhere in time, and we'll never know if—"

"Melody!" Jake interrupted.

"What?"

"Chill!" Keith said.

She hadn't paid any attention to the direction in which Keith had headed when they'd left the house. Now, biting her lip and trying to remain silent, she realized that they were heading away from town.

"Where are you going?" she demanded.

"You'll see," Keith said, and turned up the radio.

Bing Crosby was singing "White Christmas."

"Beautiful," Jake murmured.

A few minutes later, they turned off the road, and Melody knew where they were going. Her father had an old hunting lodge back on property in the woods.

He'd never hunted anything.

It had just been a place where he went with his old

cronies now and then. And where they had all gone sometimes, just to be away. It was two rooms. Made of wood, with a bedroom, and an all-purpose room. The refrigerator was small and hadn't worked in years. The plumbing was iffy.

"Get out," Keith said to Melody, pulling to a stop.

"What?" she asked incredulously.

"Get out. You're driving everyone crazy," Keith said.

"You can't throw me out at this old lodge!" Melody said. "It's freezing. There's no heat. There's no—there's nothing out here."

"Actually, there is," Keith said. "Mom and Dad have been using the place now and then for a getaway. There's a new little refrigerator, and they have one of those automatic fireplaces in there now. You just turn it on. So—get out."

"Keith!"

Jake got out of the car.

"Hey, I didn't mean that you had to get out. I mean, she's driving you as crazy as me, right?" Keith asked.

"I'm not leaving your sister alone in the woods," Jake said.

Keith shrugged. He turned to Melody, next to him in the front passenger's seat. "Get out," he said quietly. "It's going to work out all right. I know it. We'll find Mark, and we'll get Jake back where he needs to be. But you're never going to be in love with Mark, and you are in love with Jake."

"I can't be in love with him," she whispered. "I barely know him."

"Get to know him then. I'll be back at three. We can't miss the sunset, and God knows, it will come early tonight, we've got to be back at the house, ready. Melody, this is your last chance. Spend some time with him. I'll see you at three."

She saw the gentle mischief in her brother's eyes—and also the love he bore for her.

She smiled, kissed his cheek and hopped out of the car.

She stared at the house, aware that Jake was by her.

She spun back around to stop Keith before he could drive away.

"Keys!" she told him, but he was already tossing them to her.

She walked to the house, Jake behind her, as the car drove away. She opened the door, shivering. "We'll build a fire," Jake said.

"We don't need to; we just have to turn one on," she told him. And, walking to the stone-enclosed fireplace, she flicked the switch. A fire leaped to life.

"Incredible. Quite incredible. I will miss all these things," Jake said, staring at the flames. Then he looked at her. "More than anything, I will miss you," he said softly.

"Will you really?" she asked him. "I didn't believe a word you said—not really—until this morning. I haven't been at all charitable. Okay, frankly, I suppose I have been something of a bitch. And I don't begin to understand what it is that you could be seeing in me...."

Her voice trailed away. He had taken a step toward her, and he was smiling. "You took me home. From what I've seen of your world, most people would have driven away. Or dropped me at the nearest facility for the insane. You brought me home, and you wanted to make things right. Home is a special place, and you have made me feel special in yours."

She thought that he was going to take her into his arms, but he didn't. He walked past her, taking a framed picture from the mantel.

She had all but forgotten the picture. It was a charcoal sketch. She had done it when she was about seventeen; it had once been part of her portfolio.

It was a sketch of her parents. Her mother was reading a book, and her father was a foot away at the end of the sofa.

But, somehow, she had caught her father's expression perfectly as he looked at her mother. And her mother had just looked up to see, and give him the same smile of absolute love and affection in return.

Actually, at the time, she hadn't known how good it was.

"This is yours," he said.

"Yes."

"It's very, very good."

"Thank you."

"You should never stop with your art," he told her.

"No...never," she said. "Mark—he never understood. I want the same things as most human beings—in anytime in history and beyond. We all want to be loved. Need to be loved, perhaps. I just like the world we live in, where we're allowed to love and be loved and have children and still pursue our interests. I mean, I don't want my children raised by strangers, either, but—" She broke off and suddenly turned away from him, hurrying over to the kitchen area. She hoped that she still had what had always been "Melody's drawer."

She did. There was a sketch pad, her pencils and her chalk.

She didn't want a chalk drawing, she decided. She wanted a pencil sketch.

"What are you doing?" he asked.

"I—I want to remember you," she told him.

"I will never forget you," he told her.

She lowered her head, surprised at the way she was blushing. "Please? Will you…just sit?"

"Of course, as you wish."

But he didn't just sit. He talked, and that didn't matter. "I tried to think last night about all the wonders I've seen, and weigh them against my world, my time. First, the lights amazed me. And being able to talk to someone miles away in a second on a telephone—and a cell phone. And then there is television, radio and computers…and, from what I have learned, wonders that can come from medical breakthroughs. And, of course, I've thought, too, about some of what has been lost. We have no computers, no video games, and so we talk when we are home at night, and we learn to whittle, and to play instruments. We have our books, of course. They are precious and not so easily obtained, and so we treat them tenderly."

As he spoke, musing, she sketched. He came to life beautifully on the page. All the animation of his features was apparent in the sketch, and she was good, she believed in herself, and was usually determined to work with a drawing until she was proud of it.

This drawing…

The subject. He made the drawing amazing.

"May I?" he asked when she looked up.

She knew that she was blushing again as she showed it to him. He stared at it a long while, and looked at her.

They both sat upon the sofa then, facing the warmth of the fire, and she found that she trembled when his eyes touched hers. *His wasn't a showy strength,* she thought. He wasn't the kind of man who needed to raise his voice to be heard. He had fought for his country; he had faced a hangman's noose, and she believed that he had done so with dignity. Despite the fact that she hadn't believed him, he had steadfastly set his course, and she had been forced to believe in him at last.

Because others had done so, she realized. She wasn't unlike Mark herself.

There was so much magic in her world. But Jake had shown her real magic. The beauty of lights at night. The love that came so freely to her that she had forgotten to appreciate it.

He set the sketch down and turned to her, taking her hands.

"Okay, well, we are alone here at last, and now time is the enemy. So. Tell me, what about your friend Mark? Is it…perhaps you've just had an argument. Perhaps you'll make up once he's back," Jake said.

Melody shook her head. "I like Mark. I care about Mark. I'm not in love with Mark, and I never will be. But I would never hurt him, and I pray that I haven't done so."

"We'll bring him home," he assured her. "But…I do feel that we—you and I—have formed something. Something of a bond. And I believe you care for me, and if time and the world were not what they were, I would fall deeply in love with you, and you with me. And yet, I'm so much like Mark."

Something of a bond. Obsession, she thought. *I want to hear you speak forever. I want to see the way your mind works. I love the sound of your laughter, and even your forehead when you frown. I don't remember my life before I picked you up out on that snowy road.*

Yes, he looked a lot like Mark.

But there was something different.

She often thought that she would die, or explode or implode if she didn't touch him. And she knew that the world was going to be empty when he was gone.

"Melody?"

"You are like him in appearance, but not him. You are…you. And that's what it is with all of us, I suppose. There's truly chemistry, or perhaps it's in the mind, or…both. I…I don't know," she told him.

"But you do care about me?" he asked her. He had moved a little closer.

She sat very still, afraid to move herself. This was the twenty-first century, but…

"It breaks my heart that you will leave," she admitted.

"Truthfully, it breaks my heart, as well. But…there are other things in the heart and soul. It would kill me to leave my sister alone," he said. "I would hate myself."

"And in time, hate me," she whispered.

"I could never hate you. Just myself."

Keith was coming at three. There just wasn't that much time.

"I wouldn't want that for you," she told him, and the words were painful. "When we ask someone to be what they can't, or expect something out of them that they can't give…it's just wrong. And I…care for you all the more because I know how much you care about your sister. And you've made me see that my brother is as fantastic a gift as my parents. I understand. It's just…not fair, I suppose, but if there were such things as wishes, I would wish that we could find a way."

"To be together?"

"Forever. Or a lifetime, at the very least," she said.

It seemed that her blood and limbs were screaming. As if she were reaching out to an astral being, begging him to come closer, to touch her, take her into his arms.

"Forever and ever," he whispered.

And then, he did.

He held her, and the world was warm. He kissed her, and the world was a strange heaven of simple existence. When he might have drawn away, she whispered that it was the twenty-first century, and she knew that she had to let him go.

But not then.

She wanted to know him. And remember him.

She wanted to know him very well, and remember all of him.

They laughed. There were pillows and blankets, and a place to bury themselves beneath them.

They didn't have forever.

Only a few hours.

Outside, the day was beautiful. Cold, but beautiful. Snow on the ground, and the evergreens blanketing the forest. The world was far away, and in the little hunting lodge, it might have been anytime, any place, where two souls met, where a man and a woman fell in love.

Time still ticked away.

Chapter 10

Mark Hathaway sat in a wing-back chair, staring at the flames in the hearth.

He was still, he believed, in shock.

But he was feeling better.

Serena had ladled out some of the stew cooking over the fire and it had more than met up to the promise of the aroma. He was sated, and warm.

He'd pinched himself a dozen times. He'd set his hands near the fire, and felt the heat.

It was all real. It wasn't a dream or an alcohol-induced nightmare.

Serena was real. And she was handling the shock of this situation with far more aplomb than he.

Then again, she was the witch who had caused it all, wasn't she?

But she was so beautiful. And matter-of-fact. And

she'd had a talent for making him feel as if he were at home here. It did ease it all somewhat.

"That was one of the finest meals I have ever eaten. Thank you," Mark told her.

She glanced up. She was seated across the room from him, a cloth-bound journal in her hands.

"Thank you," she said, blushing prettily. "I have my own herb garden, and we preserve our vegetables, you know. The meat is fresh. Hank Janey from just down the road brings me deer meat and fowl. There was a skirmish in the war in which Hank's boy was almost killed, and Jake leaped on him just in time, bringing him down before the ball whizzed by. So Hank looks after me now. I love to cook. And sometimes we go out ourselves for fish. Fishing I enjoy, and the fresh fish is so good. And I'm prattling on and on, and I need to find a solution to this dilemma." She turned her attention back to the book. But she looked up at him again. "It hasn't been that long, but it does seem that the hostilities have been going on forever. Before the war, life here was beautifully pleasant. My brother has an office just upstairs with a wonderful writing desk. It looks out over the fields and the forests. Of course, Jake was often in Boston on business, but I know the neighbors so well. I have gone into Boston myself, but I prefer to stay home and I don't believe there will be any more fighting here—though, God knows, the British have the might and the power. We just have our lives and our freedom to be thinking about and…oh, dear Lord, I'm doing it again."

She looked so distressed that Mark stood up and walked over to her and then hunkered down by her side. "The Americans are going to win the war. And, believe it or not, in the decades that lie ahead, the Brits and the Americans will become allies against much more horrible forces in the world."

Serena studied his face, then smiled at him. "Do people change?" she asked.

"Yes, and no. Social customs change. What's right and wrong changes. But do we still need to survive, do we seek out love and family, good friends and warmth? Oh, yes."

She stood up, walking away from him. "I'm not really a witch, you know. Well, not that anyone around here would admit to being a witch. It's nearly a hundred years that have gone by, but the horror of the Salem witchcraft trials remains. No one can begin to understand what happened, and I have never understood myself how a people who came to the colonies to escape persecution could be so intolerant of everyone else. There was a young woman living in Salem at the time who was named Aislinn Mallory. She minded her own business, and stayed far away from controversy. Her mother had been a healer in Wales, but King James had been terrified of witches, and so, all those who practiced the arts of healing with herbs, of studying alchemy, astrology and other such sciences, went mute, helping only those closest to themselves. Aislinn knew the power of many herbs, and she also knew a great deal about physics—far more than I will ever understand."

Serena looked at Mark. He really had no idea what she was talking about, but he loved to watch her talk. Her soft accent, so slightly different, was beautiful.

"I came to live with the Mallorys when I was a young child. My parents were killed in an Indian raid.

The Mallorys loved children, and had just Jake. Jake was always the finest brother. He taught me how to get around in the woods when we were children, and he was the one who taught me to read, how to play the spinet and the flute, and even how to understand what was going on around us. He writes so stirringly!"

"Really? I'm a writer," Mark said. "Commercial fiction—thrilling and fun, one hopes, but not exactly… stirring."

"Jake's essays before the war brought many a man to the Colonial side," she said proudly.

"A lot will be needed throughout the years of the war—and beyond," Mark said. "But…I'm sorry. Aislinn Mallory lived in Salem during the trials. You grew up here…I'm losing the threads."

"Aislinn left Salem and came here when it seemed that everyone was being arrested. The thing is, of course, the practice of witchcraft was known to be a capital offense, but those who went to the gallows were certainly not practicing any form of witchcraft. Aislinn actually was, at times. At least, in burning certain herbs, in making healing potions, it could be considered that she was practicing witchcraft. When Aislinn's husband perished during a wretched winter, she and her children moved here and bought this house. All of Aislinn's books and journals were here, and so I started reading them. I didn't understand much of the science, and so I assumed that all I was reading was more fantasy than anything else.

"But then I heard that Jake had been captured in New York City, and because of his rousing essays, he was going to be hanged as a spy, though he had been a soldier at the time. Jake has always, always taken care of me. I couldn't let him be hanged. I certainly didn't have the power to stop the British. All I had was the possibility of magic and illusion. And it was all so complicated. Aislinn believed that there was a black door in the yard here, which I believe there must be, but Jake was being hanged in New York City. Then, according to Aislinn's texts, the way that the stars, moon and planets were aligned, the door would open at sunrise on Christmas Eve and close at sunset on Christmas Day. That seemed to give me time, at least, and she had a ritual of chants and rose petals that would bring the black door to another place. I didn't know if it would work or not—but I went to New York. And Jake disappeared from the noose. I was afraid—of course. But there was such chaos when he simply disappeared that I was able to escape, and friends got me out of the city and home. I thought that Jake would be here, but he was not." She paused, huge blue eyes on him. "Then you appeared."

"Your brother was trying to return. In the future, this house will be owned by a family named Tarleton. Mrs. Tarleton also finds books and diaries in the attic, apparently. I admit to thinking that they were all crazy. I was afraid that…that one of the nutty potions would hurt your brother. And though I just met him, he was very kind to me. So…Jake should have been back here."

She nodded. "I must think of something. So, are you related to the Tarletons?"

"No. I wanted to be. I was in love with the daughter, Melody."

"You were? No more? Did you intend to marry? I'm so sorry, did something tragic happen?"

"No, thank God, nothing tragic." He shrugged. "She isn't in love with me. We are simply looking for different things in the world. I don't know where it all really began, but she's been trying to help your brother."

"Hmm," Serena said thoughtfully. "Sunrise and sunset. At sunset, I can send you back. We'll go to the well, to the door itself. I pray that I can return you safely, and bring my brother home."

He took her hand. "We will make it happen," he vowed. "May I say that your brother is a very lucky man, to have such a woman for his sister."

She flushed. Her eyes so blue, her hair so dark, and all her coloring combining to make an extraordinary picture.

He found himself thinking then that Melody should do a sketch of this woman. Her talent lay in finding the life in someone, even though she drew a flat image.

He had never really appreciated that fact, he realized, until he had looked at Serena.

"Well, you see, he would die for me, and I know it. Could I do anything less than try to make sure that he lives in happiness, as well?" she asked.

"Of course not. What do I do? How can I help?"

"You'll need some of Jake's clothing," she said. "God knows, we don't wish to start anything among those who may be superstitious. I'm going to start with the potion. I would love some help, and I'd be delighted to show you about the basement, where we keep our stores. And the old cradles and basinets...the Mallorys always dreamed of a big family."

"And what about you?" he asked.

"Of course, I have my dreams," she said.

* * *

Keith arrived at the house in the woods at exactly three o'clock.

Melody stepped into the car, trying to behave completely normally, and resisting the temptation to cry and cling to Jake.

She could not hang on to him.

She understood. And the fact that he felt he had to go back was part of the man's personality, the very reason she admired him so much.

She was determined to be rational.

"Do you think that Mark is really all right?" she asked anxiously.

"I'm assuming Mark wound up where I was supposed to wind up," Jake said. "And if he's with Serena, he's all right. Of course, she probably accosted him upon arrival demanding to know what he had done with me, but Mark is an intelligent fellow, and I'm sure he'll have been able to explain. Well, at least, as best as anyone can possibly explain."

It didn't take long for them to reach the house. When they arrived, Brutus and Jimmy greeted them with madly wagging tails. Mona called out from the kitchen.

"Lunch is on. Or supper. Or whatever. It is Christmas Eve, and we're having ham and turkey and all the trimmings. Come along, children. George is about to carve," she said.

They trooped back to the dining room. Melody walked over to her mother and gave her a huge hug. The table was set beautifully. The turkey had been prepared perfectly, and was golden and gleaming in the center of the table.

"Mom, this is a fabulous spread. Thank you so very much."

"Well, it is Christmas Eve, come what may," Mona said. She hugged Melody in return. "And we've just got to get Mark back here, and then Jake...."

Melody could have sworn that her mother sniffed. That she was holding back tears. No one wanted Jake to go.

"Hey, please, folks, this isn't like an—execution," Jake said. "It's Christmas Eve, just as you said. And somehow, by the grace of God, I'm here with you, and you all are the embodiment of Christmas spirit, so... let's eat!"

He took his place at the table. The others did, as well.

"The winter sunset comes quickly," George murmured.

"Let's say grace," Mona suggested. "And no, Keith, you don't just get to say grace and have that be the end of it!"

"I'll go," Melody said. "Heavenly Father, thank you for this meal. Thank you for my brother and my parents. Thank you for bringing Jake into our lives, for the time that we had with him. It makes us realize that every minute we have with one another is precious. Please help us bring him home in time for Christmas, and please, make everything right with Mark. Amen."

She looked up. Her whole family was staring at her. Her mother suddenly burst into tears.

"No, no, Mom!" she said.

Mona shook her head. "I'm all right. I'm all right! I promise. Okay, George, carve, please. Keith, pass the sweet potatoes."

"I'll take the peas, please," Jake said. "Mrs. Tarleton, thank you. What a delicious meal."

"Hey, would you be having turkey at home?" Keith asked him.

"Some kind of fowl, probably," Jake said. "Of course, it would depend. The last months, I was with the army. Army food is not good at all."

"Well, that never improved," George said. "I spent time in 'Nam. Oh—does he know about Vietnam?" George asked, looking at his children.

"Full Metal Jacket," Jake said. "Keith tried to catch me up on history. Sad thing is, we more or less went war by war."

"But good things happened, too," Melody said. "We had amazing characters rise up during the course of history. Mother Teresa, Mahatma Gandhi, Martin Luther King—

"And you saw *The Defiance,*" Melody continued. "Just plain old people—living off the land and not known for their heroics—turn around and save the lives of hundreds through sheer will. Human nature is what it is, but there's so much good in it! This isn't a bad age in which to live. Okay, so maybe we're all afraid now and then that someone is going to go mad and touch a nuclear button and the whole thing will blow up. But it's an exciting time, too, the world is still trying to solve the differences in peoples, and the world seems so small now that it must happen."

"I like the world," Jake said. "That's never been in question."

The meal went on. Turkey and all the fixings. Pumpkin and blueberry pie. The sun began to fall in the western sky.

It was day, but George turned on all the Christmas lights.

Hand in hand, Melody stood with Jake in front of the house as he stared at the colors of the twinkling lights, and admired them.

They were still there, standing in silence, when Mona said it was time.

They all retired to back of the house, near the well.

She could aim! Good God, could the woman aim!

Mark felt the snowball crack him dead center in the chest.

"Minx!" he accused Serena. He reached down to form a snowball. The snow was beautiful, soft and new. It hadn't been rendered to pure slush by the tires of a zillion cars.

Another snowball hit him before he could even form his own. This one off his left shoulder.

"Hey!" he protested. He had snow in his hands, at least. He ducked his head and went running for his enemy, knocking Serena down into the snow and dropping his small snowball upon her.

"Not fair at all!" she sputtered, laughing up at him. Eyes so blue.

So much laughter in them as they touched his.

But her smile faded. "The sun. Look at the sun. We've got to go and get ready."

Melody watched as her father and brother set up the wave machines on either side of the well.

Mona had prepared more of her potion.

They watched as the sun continue its slow fall down the western horizon.

She gripped Jake's hand suddenly. "Jake, what if Mark is just lost? You were supposed to fall from a hangman's noose back into your own house."

"Well," he said dryly, "I did fall near my house."

"Yes, but more than two centuries later."

"An amazing detour," he told her softly.

"I'm frightened, Jake. Terrified, really. We don't actually know where Mark is. We don't even know if he's lost in time and space somewhere. What if something is wrong with the black hole, or the black door, or whatever it is? Jake, you could wind up in a strange limbo. And we'll never know. My God, once you're gone, we may never know. And Mark could just be lost out there, as well."

"Shh," he said, his hands cradling her face as he looked down into her eyes. "Melody, I have no choice. I have to believe in Serena. She did save me from the hangman's noose. And I came here. Sometimes, we have to believe." He offered her a crooked grin. "It's Christmastime. Isn't that what Christmastime is all about? Faith and belief. I can't see Mark or my sister right now, but I have to believe that they're all right. Serena is the magician in the family. I have to believe that she'll know what she's doing as well, that she'll have Mark, waiting to come home. She wrote about the sunrise and sunset, so she will know. It will be all right, Melody. I swear. It will be all right."

"What if you go back in time, and wind up in a hangman's noose again?" she whispered.

"I will not," he said firmly.

He tilted her chin with one hand and very tenderly kissed her lips. "Mona?" he said.

Mona offered him a cup with trembling hands. Jake kissed her cheek and said a sincere "Thank you" to her.

He walked over to George. They started to shake hands, but then they engulfed one another in a hug.

It was Keith's turn.

"I'll always remember you, as if I had been lucky enough to have a brother," Jake told him.

Keith nodded. "You're a cool dude, Jake. Wish you could have stayed longer. I'd have liked to learn to play something…guitar, violin, flute."

"You can learn without me."

"Won't be the same. Safe journey," Keith said.

Jake nodded, stepped between the wave machines in front of the well and lifted the cup to his lips.

Melody couldn't stand it. She had to have one last goodbye.

She raced toward Jake.

"Melody!" he mother cried.

But she ran into Jake's arms. And when she kissed his lips, she could taste the strange sweet and tart herbs of her mother's potion.

There was a sizzle in the air.

A pop, and then the air itself moved, as if heat were rising off pavement in Arizona in the dead of summer.

Melody closed her eyes, trying to remember the feel of him, the warmth of the man who had held her, the scent of him, the vitality of his being and the liquid wonder of his kiss…

Suddenly, it was dark—and brilliantly white at the same time.

She blinked, looking around. The force of whatever had happened had knocked her on her rear. She was sitting in a pile of pure white snow, so clean it dazzled in the dying light like diamond stars in a midnight-velvet sky.

Something was different. It was colder.

The house was before her, but there were no lights.

Then she heard the angry female voice.

"No, no, no! Oh, no! Who, in the name of our dearest Lord, are you?"

So much for poignant goodbyes.

One minute, Jake had been holding her. He had tasted that last kiss…

Then, he was holding air.

Melody was gone.

And he was standing right where he had been all along. And George and Mona were staring at him. No. They were staring to his side.

Mark was there.

"I'm back," Mark said. He looked at Jake. "I'm back—and you're still here. What the hell?"

"Oh, no," Keith said, the words escaping him as they might a deflated balloon.

"Melody!" Mona said, and sank down to the ground as her knees buckled beneath her.

"Mom, Mom, hey, it's—it's all right!" Keith said, rushing to his mother's side.

George was standing there, staring at the place where his daughter had been.

Jake hurried over to George. "It is all right. We're going to get her back."

George shook his head. "My baby," he said. "My girl."

"George, we're going to get her back!" Jake said firmly.

"My baby. My daughter. My girl," George said.

Mona couldn't stand. Keith was trying to help her, to get her into the house. Jake gave George a little shake. "George, we have time. We're going to get her back. Do you understand? We're going to get her back. That's all there is to it."

"This was all there was to it," George said.

"She couldn't let you go," George whispered. "She couldn't let you go, and now she's gone."

Jake looked at Mark. Mark shook his head and gripped George by the shoulders. "George, it's going to be all right. Look at me. I'm back. We just have to quit messing with the lines or the waves or whatever the hell they are. Look at me. I'm fine. I'm better than fine. I've gone back. I've seen the past—"

"Serena?" Jake asked him anxiously.

"Alive and well, and back in the house. There was chaos when you disappeared from the noose. Friends got her out of the city. She's fine, I swear."

"Let's get in the house," Jake suggested.

"I'll get George's wave machines back into his lab," Mark said.

"Good thinking."

Jake led George toward the house. Keith was getting his mother inside.

In the family room, they both sat on the couch. They both just stared ahead, looking shell-shocked.

"I'll get—I'll get a couple of shots of whiskey," Keith said.

He left Jake with his parents. Jake sat down in front of Mona. "Mona. Mona, please, look at me!" he said.

Her eyes lifted to his. They began to fill with tears. She reached out and touched his face. "Jake, it's not that we don't care about you, we do. But…that's our baby. Where is she? We have to get her back, oh, dear God, we just have to get her back."

"We're going to get her back," he swore.

"We're running out of time," she said. "Sunrise, sunset. Then Christmas will be over. I read the book that your sister left. It's all that we have."

"And we'll make it work," Jake promised.

"We just botched the hell out of that transfer!" Mona said.

Keith returned, shoving a glass into his mother's hands. "Mom. Come on, Mom. You honest to God have to snap out of it, Mom. You have to make more potion again. And we didn't botch anything. We didn't count on just how much Jake meant to Melody. She had to have her one last goodbye."

"But where is she? What if she doesn't know that she has to be in a certain place, and that certain things have to happen? Oh, my God, dear God, what will we do without her?" Mona whispered.

Jake heard someone clear his throat; he turned around. Mark was back in the house. He took the seat between Mona and George on the sofa.

"Jake is right. Everyone must seriously get a grip. I know where Melody is, and she is just fine. She is in this house. Or in the backyard, just where we were. She's there, and she's safe, and she'll know everything. I was privileged to be there. Jake's sister, Serena, is wise and beautiful, and Melody is going to be fine with her for the night. First thing, we get back out there in the morning, and we do everything one more time. Jake will go back where he belongs, and Melody will be back here. And we won't regret anything of it.

Mona, George, it's fascinating. Melody will actually get to see and feel and touch the past—how many artists ever get such an opportunity?"

Mona stared at him with wide eyes. "She's kind—she's truly kind, Jake's sister?"

"Of course she's kind!" Jake said, a bit indignant.

"Kind, brilliant and beautiful," Mark said.

"We all must be strong and see this through," Jake said firmly.

"I have to make more potion," Mona said.

"I have to check my machines," George said faintly. He cleared his throat. "I have to check my machines," he said more firmly.

"Good idea, Dad," Keith said. "We are going to get her back."

George stood. He started for the back door, but he hesitated, then came back. He stopped in front of his wife, caught her hands and pulled her to her feet. He started to speak, but didn't. He just pulled her into his arms and held her.

Then George went out the back door and Mona headed to the kitchen.

Jake, Keith and Mark were left in the family room, staring glumly at one another.

"I understand," Keith said, and Jake saw that he was trembling. Keith looked at him. "I understand how you felt. My sister…my best friend. Now…now I understand how you felt."

"Look," Mark said, standing impatiently. "Melody is fine. Trust me. I was with Serena. She is fierce and bright, and has a will and an energy to make everything right. We all have to quit acting as if this is the end of the world. It's going to be a tough night, but in the morning, everything is going to be rectified."

Keith nodded. "That's what we have to believe."

"It's not just belief. It's what will be," Jake said firmly.

Mark grinned suddenly. "Great. Were you all this upset when *I* disappeared?"

Keith and Jake looked at one another. "Melody was horrified—she was determined that you had to come home."

"Melody doesn't care about me. I've faced the fact," Mark said.

Keith shook his head. "She knew you two couldn't make a marriage work. To Melody, marriage is a once-in-a-lifetime deal. But that didn't mean that she didn't care about you, Mark."

"She cares about you a great deal, Mark," Jake assured him.

Mark smiled. "Your sister cares about you, too. I thought she was going to beat me to a pulp for not being you."

"Serena is rather amazing," Jake agreed. "And she does know how to take care of herself, but…it's a hard life. There's so much work to be done. There are so many dangers out there, in the woods. A woman should never be alone out there."

"Here," Keith said.

"What?" Jake asked.

"Here, she's actually here. I think. In a different dimension, or time, or wave, or whatever," Keith said.

"Very different," Jake said. "There is no electricity, and logs have to be cut for heat. She's tough. Serena is tough. But when I left to go to war, I did so with a heavy heart. We had neighbors—but not like now. The nearest neighbor was about a mile away. In this day and age, it's easy. Or different. As far as day-to-day living goes. We were far more dependent upon one another."

"She needs someone, I see that so clearly," Mark said. "Serena, for all her strength, needs someone."

As they all sat there morosely, Brutus came click-clacking in, heading straight to Jake for some attention. "Brutus," he said. "In my time, poor Brutus might not have made it."

"But your time was better," Mark said with enthusiasm. "The house, surrounded by nothing but beautiful, pristine snow. And people, making home their lives, their real lives!"

"Actually," Jake said, "isn't life what we make it, wherever we are, whenever we may be—wherever it is that we are?"

"I miss my sister, and I want her back," Keith said.

"Oh, no. Oh, no. This is starting to get truly frightening," Serena said.

She had helped Melody out of the snow. Shivering, they had returned to the house together, and Melody had tried very hard to explain just what had happened, which was difficult, because she didn't understand it herself.

"So, your father was working his end, and I was working my end. Mark made it back to the proper time, but instead of Jake coming home—I got you," Serena said.

"Excuse me, it wasn't my plan to show up here," Melody told her.

"You just touched my brother?" Serena said. "There

is no logic to what occurred. I mean, it does make sense that the door allows for only one person, perhaps. But why you appeared here simply by touching him."

"It was a bit more than a touch," Melody said.

"Oh?"

Melody hesitated. "I care very deeply about Jake. I kissed him goodbye."

"Oh," Serena said. "Then you kissed him, and you had the potion on your lips."

"Yes, your brother drank the potion, too," answered Melody.

"I don't have the answers, but I'm assuming you were closest to the door, or the hole, or whatever it is that allows the potions to work," Serena said.

"I'm sorry. Truly sorry," Melody said.

"We'll have to rectify the situation in the morning. I'm quite certain your family must be planning the same."

"So you know about my family?"

"I had quite an interesting discussion with Mark Hathaway," Serena explained. She sighed. "He's in love with you, you know."

"He would hate me in a month, were we to marry," Melody told her. "He's extremely old-fashioned. He believes that wives should stay home, cook, clean and watch after the children."

"And that's unusual?" Serena asked, looking confused.

Melody laughed softly. "Oh, Serena! It takes a very long time, but eventually slavery ends through bloody battle. All Americans get the vote—even women. Everything didn't become one big peace rally—no government can stamp out inbred hate or that which is learned from others—but after World War II, when women had gone out to work while the men were at war—"

"World War II?" Serena interrupted.

Of course, Melody thought. Serena hadn't gotten barraged with a series of CDs. The history Jake had gotten might have been a bit fractured, but it was a decent synopsis of the years gone by.

"World War II, yes," Melody said.

"The entire world went to war—and then did it again?" Serena asked.

Melody nodded. "Most of the world, let's say. We pray now that there will never be a World War III—with the weapons we can now produce, we could blow up the globe."

Serena shivered. They both sat in silence for a few minutes.

"So, now, women work, and men stay home?" Serena asked.

"Sometimes. But most frequently now, both partners work, and both partners share responsibility for raising the children and tending the house. Choice is what we hope for—I have friends who want to stay home, and I believe that keeping a house and raising children can certainly be hard work. My mom was a nurse, though, and between her and my dad, we did very well. I adore them both. My mom usually cooks, but when she wants to go out, my dad assures her that he is capable of opening a can and using a microwave."

"A microwave?"

"It cooks things very quickly," Melody explained briefly.

"But I'm sorry, I'm still confused. Mark loves you,

wanted to marry you, and take care of you and provide for you—and that was a bad thing?" Serena asked.

"No. But I'm an artist. A good one, I believe. I love to sketch, but I also love to paint—I want to see what I can create. I want children and I want a home. But I want a husband who wants to share all those responsibilities. Do you understand? And then, too…I don't know. I cared about Mark. I do care about Mark. I was horrified by what I had done to him. Well, I didn't do it, but his association with my family made him determined to…prove that you couldn't go through time."

Serena laughed softly. "He's a very handsome man."

Melody leaned toward Serena, a slow smile curving into her features. "You and Mark must have had a very interesting day."

"He was quite wonderful," Serena told her.

"I'm glad. I'm sure that you've touched him in a way he'll never forget."

"I didn't touch him at all, not really," Serena said indignantly. "We just met."

"Of course, I'm sorry, I didn't mean anything by that," Melody said hastily. "Touch…well, I meant that knowing you probably touched his soul."

"I believe you touched much more than my brother's soul," Serena said primly.

Melody wasn't about to explain. And so she said simply, "I love your brother."

"I see," Serena said. "No, no, actually, I don't."

"You don't see how I can love him?" Melody asked.

"Well, of course. He's proud and he's strong, he's very smart and giving. He can be passionate and firm and quite charming and…"

"Yes," Melody said.

"But…he's from a different time," she reminded Melody.

"I wish that meant something. Well, it does mean something. He loves you. He's been worried sick about you. He was afraid the British would take revenge on you. He's worried about you being on your own. He meant to come back here through hell or high water, and he intended to find a way, with or without your help. Actually, without your help, we wouldn't have gotten anywhere. My mother read the journals you have in the house."

"Really?" Serena said, pleased. She sighed. "Jake has actually spent too much of his life worrying about me. My parents were killed, you know. He meant to make sure that I grew up well, that I had everything I could possibly need. His father became my father, and Jake continued with the responsibility. I've worried that he doesn't get out, that he doesn't worry about his own life, because of me. Well, of course, battle came to Gloucester, the Declaration of Independence was written, and we've been at war ever since. That, of course, changes everything. But I have worried about Jake."

"I have a brother," Melody said. "And he is very precious to me, so I understand."

"He's probably going quite mad with worry for you right now. Thank God Mark has been here. Hopefully, he'll make them all understand that you are doing well."

"He is a very good man," Melody said.

"Just not the man you love," Serena said.

"Right."

"And really—no matter what, he's not the man you love?" Serena asked. "I mean, if my brother hadn't happened along, would you be with Mark?"

Melody shook her head. "I didn't know how to tell him that we could never be."

"And you really love my brother?"

"Honestly," Melody told her.

"What a strange world it is we live in!" Serena said.

"Much stranger since I met your brother," Melody told her.

Serena laughed. "I'm going to stoke up the fire. We have a long cold night before it becomes morning."

"Christmas," Melody said.

"And I had just wished that Jake would be home for Christmas," Serena said. "Tomorrow morning, we must...well, we must just rectify this entire event."

"We all want to be home—whatever or wherever home may be—for Christmas," Melody said.

Serena nodded. She rose, saying, "I'll get the fire going and brew some tea. And I have some shortbread cookies. We'll celebrate Christmas Eve and light a candle, as well."

"That would be lovely. Thank you," Melody said.

Serena was a beautiful woman, Melody thought. Moving fluidly about in a house she loved with competence, despite the work that went with keeping such a house. And though she worked, everything about her seemed young, fresh and innocent.

"Does Jake have paper in the house? Pencils?" Melody asked.

"There's a brand-new box of Faber-Castell pencils in his desk drawer. He loved pencils. Loves pencils," Serena said.

"May I do a sketch of you?" she asked.

Serena flushed. "Of course. Yes, thank you. I would like that."

Serena brewed tea over the fire and Melody sketched, and they talked about the old days and the new, and they waited for the time when the sun would rise on Christmas morning.

Chapter 11

"Rose petals!" Mona said, the words explosive as she jumped to her feet.

"What?" George said, looking up anxiously.

"We have to get some rose petals," Mona said firmly. She looked at Jake. "I read about it in one of the references...or maybe you told me, I'm getting so confused in all this now. Rose petals, in the middle of winter. That's what your sister used when she cursed the British commander. *We* haven't had rose petals. Oh, I had rose hip in the tea in the potion, but...rose petals. I think we must have rose petals. Rose petals in the snow."

They had spent most of the evening together, in the family room. They weren't talking much. Every once in a while, Mark would make a comment to Jake about his sister, and Jake would smile and agree—Serena was an amazing woman.

And then Keith would mention how much he missed his sister, how much he feared for her, and then he would shut up because he didn't want to upset his parents.

Mark was the calmest. He was the most reassuring to the Tarletons. He had, after all, made the journey through time and back.

But now, Jake stood up and walked over to Mona, taking her hands. "Mona, you did everything right. None of us, including Melody, knew that she might wind up being the one going through the hole or door to the past. I don't think we need anything else."

"Rose petals," she said firmly. "Please. I think we need rose petals."

"Mona, it's the dead of winter," George said.

"Good heavens, George, why on earth do you think God invented florists?" Mona asked.

"If you want rose petals, Mona, we will get them for you," Jake said. He frowned. "I'm delighted to get the rose petals, but I will need help. I still don't know how to drive one of those vehicles yet."

"Gotta learn to drive," Keith said. "Unless you live in New York City. Never mind—I guess you ride well enough."

"Well, of course I ride," Jake said.

"I'll drive now," Keith told him. "Come on—we'll get the rose petals. We'll be back soon, Mom, Dad. Unless you want to come for the ride?"

"Oh, all the shops might be closed. It's night already, and on Christmas Eve," Mona said worriedly.

"We'll find a shop that's open," Keith promised.

"And red. We must have red roses."

"I'll know the roses we need," Jake promised her, before following Keith outside.

"I hope she's not right," Keith said worriedly as they got closer to town. "This is New England. Most places are closed by now."

"I see lights in some establishments," Jake said.

"Maybe a gas station," Keith suggested.

The large stores were closed. They found a convenience store open, but it was out of flowers of any kind. They tried another, and another.

No luck.

Finally, giving up, they drove home. As they passed a church—the same church Mona had mentioned she attended, where a Father Dawson had made such a positive impression on her—Jake reached out and grabbed Keith by the arm.

"Stop!"

"At church? Jake, we're far too late for the service. I mean, there's another one at midnight—"

"Roses, Keith. There may just be roses in there. And saying a prayer isn't going to hurt anything at all, will it?"

"No, it will not hurt anything at all," Keith agreed.

Folks were leaving the church as they entered. Father Dawson hadn't been giving the service; a sign noted that he would be there for the midnight service.

A young priest was kneeling before the main altar.

And there were flowers. There were flowers everywhere. Stands of flowers surrounded the giant nativity scene at the side of the main altar.

Flowers adorned the pews.

Flowers were set near the evergreen on the other side of the main altar.

"Do you see roses?" Keith whispered.

And suddenly, Jake smiled. There was a stand of red roses right next to the kneeling priest.

Jake strode down the aisle and knelt beside him. He looked up at the cross high above the altar.

A prayer.

Dear God, please, I have been granted life in this precious season. Grant, too, that come tomorrow, all will right itself with this world, and in my own.

Just then, the young priest crossed himself, looked over at Jake and smiled.

"Such an earnest prayer, sir. I think I felt it," he said.

"Indeed, an earnest prayer," Jake said, and he rose to shake the priest's hand.

"Welcome to the church."

Great. He had come to steal roses, and he was being welcomed.

"Thank you."

To Jake's surprise, the man reached to the stand and handed Jake a rose. "For a loved one. God's true gift, the beauty of the world we live in. And, remember, son, sometimes prayers are answered, and it takes a minute to realize that we have gotten just what we've asked for."

"Be careful what you wish for? You may get what you ask?" Jake suggested.

The priest laughed. "No. We just need to realize that what we want isn't always best for someone else, and what they want may not please us. Part of Christmas is giving, and that means giving when we have to sacrifice, or when we may not particularly agree. I have a feeling though, you're going to be all right."

Jake smiled and had to say, "A psychic priest?"

The priest was still grinning—either Christmas cheer, or he had a pleasant sense of humor. "Does God speak to me in dreams? No, I am just his humble servant, but I usually have a sense for those around me, and you're a good man, and you're going to come out all right."

"Thank you, Father. Merry Christmas," Jake said.

"And also to you, my son. God's blessing," the priest said, and he turned to walk away down the aisle.

"Amen, Father," Jake called after him. Keith was waiting at the rear of the church. Jake hurried down the aisle.

"We have rose petals!" Jake said.

Keith nodded gravely. "And God's blessing, so it seems. Let's get back to my mother!"

Melody felt as if she had entered a museum, and yet, it wasn't a museum at all—it was a room that still seemed alive with the spirit of the man who had used it as his office.

Jake's bedroom was actually next door, what would one day be her parents' room. His office, though, held his writing desk, his beloved collection of pencils and quills, ink pots and paper. There were a number of books and papers upon his desk, and she saw articles he had written in a number of those papers. He had written little notes to himself, one on top of a copy of Thomas Paine's *Common Sense*. There was wrapping on the side of the book, and Melody imagined that Jake had acquired it while with the army and found a courier or friend to bring it to his sister. There was a paper in his handwriting repeating words to be found in the book.

Jake had believed, she knew. Did believe, in this cause. He had been willing to die for it. Of course, she was certain, he hadn't wanted to die. But he'd been ready to give up his own life.

She felt like a sniveling child. She didn't want to give up Jake. And yet, she did love him, and it was far better to think that he was alive and well in his own time, caring for his sister, fighting for the freedom she had so taken for granted, than not at all.

She walked next door to his room, and she touched his things, and she thought of him.

At last, she took paper and pencils, and went back downstairs. She could, at least, leave him a Christmas present.

Mona was delighted with her rose. "A priest gave them to you?" she marveled.

"Yes, ma'am," Jake said. "A very pleasant young fellow."

"Well, then, let's get going," Mona demanded.

George, Keith, Mark and Jake all stared at her.

"It's midnight mass for the lot of us!" she determined.

"But, Mona, there's so much to…to…" George's tone was sadly hopeless.

"So much for us to sit here and worry about?" Mona said. "Come along, the caroling is absolutely beautiful. And we have so much to pray for!"

They all trooped back out and returned to the church. It wasn't quite time for the mass, but the church was already crowded.

The choir came in, singing "Oh Come, Oh Come, Emmanuel!"

Mona elbowed Jake on the one side and her husband on the other. "Sing!"

And so they sang. The members of the clergy entered in their robes, and it seemed that the church was alive with the beauty of lights, the sound of the singing and the ringing words of the priest. His sermon was on hope and love—that this was the season when weakness could become strength, and the greatest gift of the season was man's kindness to his fellow man. Would that it could go on all year! But Father Dawson spoke a sermon that was filled nonetheless with laughter and good cheer, and a reminder that God did help those who helped themselves—and others, as well!

They all knelt for the final prayer. Jake assumed the family was praying for Melody's safe return.

He knew that she would return.

He prayed that he would live a constructive and decent life without her.

Turning, he saw Mark's head rising; he had finished his own prayer.

"She will come back," he said.

Mark grinned. "I know that. Actually, I was praying that sometime in life, I would find a woman as fine and as beautiful as your sister!"

Jake grinned. "Thank you."

The carolers started singing again. They filed out of the church.

"I could never begin to tell you all the changes that have taken place," Melody told Serena, watching the other girl as she sat in her chair by the fire and they talked. Her sketch was coming along beautifully. "But I think that what astounded Jake so much were the lights—electric lights. We take them for granted, but they are everywhere. And my parents love Christmas, so every Christmas, there are probably hundreds and hundreds of the little suckers, in all kinds of colors, all over the house. I'll never forget Jake's expression when he first saw them," she finished, smiling.

"I remember, there was quite a thing over Ben Franklin's experiments with lightning," Serena said. "But in the end, I guess he wasn't so crazy."

"Imagine, throughout the years, many brilliant men and women, working hard in all the sciences and in technology and machinery. The inventions are amazing. But being here, now, I can see why Jake was so amazed just by the lights. To me, other inventions and events have been more extraordinary—like tiny phones that are completely computerized, robotic surgery, laser surgery…men on the moon," Melody said.

"Does he love your world?" Serena asked.

"I…I think so. It's fascinating to him, at the very least. But he loves you. And he must love the cause of freedom very much," Melody said.

"He does. And his writing is passionate and wonderful. He has a talent for explaining what he feels, and bringing that passion and enthusiasm to someone else."

"It's so funny, growing up, I thought my own little brother was the biggest horse's ass in history."

"Oh!" Serena exclaimed.

"Sorry, language has become much cruder—in the casually slash socially acceptable way," Melody said. "Anyways, we grew up—and I adore him. He's a great guy. He…he has a wonderfully open mind. I know that I have a tendency just to think that something isn't right, and then I get depressed about it instead of looking for whatever magic might be out there, and I use that term loosely, as in the magic of people or a snowflake and…well, you know. I never knew what he meant to me until I saw how Jake cared about you."

"Poor Jake," Serena said.

"Right now, I promise you, Jake is fine. Jake will be sitting with my folks, trying to assure them that they will have me back. Keith, of course, will be helping Jake, and Mark…"

"Mark is the odd man out, isn't he?" Serena asked.

"No, no, I told you—he is a friend. Someone we care deeply about," Melody told her.

"So, at least, despite the fact that my 'magic' dropped my brother onto a snow-covered road a few centuries off, he is in good stead," Serena said, smiling.

"Yes."

Melody stood, bringing the sketch she'd been doing along with her to show Serena. She was extremely proud of herself. The sketch captured Serena's beauty, and it captured something timeless about her, as well. Her lips were curled in something of a wise and secret smile while her eyes were wide and guileless.

"It's beautiful. Thank you. Have you done one of my brother?" Serena asked.

"It's at—home. I mean, this house is home, but…I did it this afternoon," she said lamely. "It exists, but in the twenty-first century."

"The twenty-first century!" Serena said, marveling. She paused. "How interesting. Your mother read my journals? And that's how she knew about the doorway…or the black hole, as you called it?"

"Yes. When this all started, she tore apart the attic, certain that she'd find something. And she did," Melody said.

Serena stood. "We should try to get some sleep," she said. She walked to the mantel and set the sketch that Melody had done reverently down upon it.

"I'm afraid to sleep. You all don't have alarm clocks," she said.

"Trust me," Serena told her. "I wake up before the dawn. I promise. I wouldn't let your parents spend the rest of their lives mourning for you."

Melody walked over to her and hugged her. "I know why Jake is so desperate to come back and take care of you," she said.

Serena drew back, smiling. "See, there's the mistake in your world. Jake is my brother. One day, I will push him into the world. Then I will seek out my own love, as well. The secret here is that I don't need anyone to take care of me. Men often need the illusion that they are taking care of you. What happens, in my world and even in yours, I suspect, in the very best unions, we're all really taking care of one another. I do love to cook, I love my own…I long for children. Pray for me in my world, as I will pray for you in yours."

"Profound—and beautiful," Melody said.

"Come upstairs and get some sleep," Serena said.

"I honestly don't think that I can," Melody told her.

"Then try to get some sleep on the sofa," Serena suggested.

"I won't sleep," Melody said.

"Rest."

"What about you?"

"I have a few things to do, and then I'll get some rest, too. I promise," Serena said.

She knew she wouldn't sleep. In a way, she didn't want to sleep. She wanted to hire a carriage and ride into town. She wanted to see other people and find out what they were thinking. She wanted to go back upstairs and explore Jake's room and his office more thoroughly. She wanted to find his clothing, and cuddle it to her, and pretend that they might have been together.

But there was no way to blame him for feeling the need to return. Serena was alone here.

It was a hard life.

She had just stretched out on the sofa when a thought occurred to her and she bolted back up.

"Serena!"

"What?"

"Won't they still be after Jake—the British. He escaped a hanging. He made a fool of the commander. Won't they be looking for him?" she asked Serena.

Serena hesitated. "I believe that it will all just lie. The action has not taken place in this area lately."

"And you think that he's going to be capable of returning—and just sitting out the Revolution?" Melody asked.

"He will have to do so," Serena said. "He can't be captured again. I know my brother—I can convince him that his writing is far more important than any physical strength he could offer as a soldier on the field again."

"A treaty is not signed until 1783," Melody said worriedly. "Lord Cornwallis does not surrender the British army at Yorktown until October 1781. There are years and years of danger ahead."

"Are any more battles fought in Gloucester?" Serena asked.

"No…not that I know of. The British come with terrible power. Let's see, I'm trying to remember my history…we lose at Brandywine and Germantown, and the British take Philadelphia…Washington does get to win some, as in when he crosses the Delaware—my God, that happens tomorrow, and though he doesn't hold the ground he takes, his surprise attack gives him supplies he desperately needs and lifts the morale of his soldiers. Wow, let's see—Gates defeats Burgoyne at Saratoga. I don't think severe action comes here again, but I have an American schoolchild's understanding of the war. Someday, though, I swear, now I am going to go back and pay more attention to history."

"Trust me," Serena said. "My brother is going to be all right. We must have faith. And, you know everything else. I'm assuming that when Jake first…arrived with you, you did what you could to find out what had happened in the past. You found journals. Surely, there were church records. You know what happened in the war—what happened with us?"

"I don't know."

"You didn't look all this up?" Serena asked with dismay.

"No, of course, you're right, we tried to find out what was said in the history books and in church records. But that was the problem. You are listed as being born. He was listed as a soldier to be hanged. But there's nothing more. It doesn't say that Jake died that day at the end of a hangman's noose—it just doesn't say anything at all. It's as if history stopped here…or on the day that Jake was supposed to die at the executioner's hand."

"How very—odd," Serena said.

"Yes, odd, but I think there's a reason for it. The books couldn't answer now—because they don't know how the story ends. So much might be fate and destiny," Melody said. "So much might be prayer—and even magic. But I think that so much in our lives is the result of free will. When the story ends, it will be written in history."

"I am down as having been born," Serena said.

"Oh, yes."

"No children though," she said sadly.

"Serena, the children would be part of how the story ends, and that's to be seen." Melody smiled encouragingly to her. "You're not listed as being deceased in those history books, either. It's as if, from that moment in New York on, you both had a clean slate."

"That's rather nice. I like that. Free will—and a future to be seen," Serena said. And she was happy.

She appeared as calm and serene as her name. Leaning back in her chair, hands folded before her, she closed her eyes.

It was not so easy for Melody. She lay awake, terrified that she would send a man back in time, and he would be hunted down, and hanged again—this time with deadly results.

Tossing and turning on the sofa, she thought about her conversations with Serena, and she thought about her home and the journals.

She bolted up again and reached for the sketch pad. She hesitated and then began to write.

She glanced over at Serena, who still seemed to be

dozing. It wasn't as if she could just leave the note on the mantel. Years would come and go.

She walked over to the stones encasing it. Touching them, she walked away and thought again, then returned to the stones, going over them again and again. At last, she found what she was seeking. There was an opening without mortar between at the bottom right-hand side. She pushed the note in, trying to make it visible and invisible at the same time. She thought about the mantel; new wood had been set over it time and again, but as far as she knew, the stone base in her house now was the stone base that had always been there.

Satisfied, she took her seat on the sofa again, and closed her eyes.

She was dimly aware of Serena rising, finding the sketchbook and writing furiously, as well.

When Serena went to follow Melody's footsteps to the hearth, Melody sat up.

"I saw you write a note. I thought I would add my own," she said.

"Well, I suppose there's a chance they will get ours—sadly, we won't get anything back from them. I don't think."

"No, we won't get anything back. But…at least we've touched them!" Serena said.

"At least," Melody agreed. She was lying on his sofa, in *his* time—his house. She could close her eyes and imagine him there, and at the desk upstairs in his office. She could see him speaking passionately to Serena about the events of the day that moved him, and she could see him at the simple things in life, whittling by the fire, playing the violin that lay so tenderly in a case upon the buffet.

This was his house, his life. She had no right to want him to change that.

They sat in the family room. No one suggested that anyone bother trying to get any sleep.

Jake tried to lighten the mood, though his own heart was heavy. "I am sorry that I never learned to drive. An automobile, I mean."

"It's easy—you just have to learn to be very careful on ice," Mark said.

"Well, there's more to it than just the mechanics," Jake said.

"What do you mean?" Keith asked him.

"Well, there seems to be a certain…a certain amount of vocal rites that go with it, as well," Jake said. "I noticed that every time you or Melody were not happy with another driver, you muttered, 'Dickhead!'"

"Keith!" Mona admonished.

"Sorry," Keith said, "I got it from Dad."

"What?" George huffed.

"I rather like it," Jake said. "Now, when a wagon or carriage cuts me off, I will shake my head and growl in my throat and say, 'Dickhead!'"

"How wonderful," Mona said, eyeing Keith sternly. "We've taught him all the right stuff."

At least it seemed that the household was smiling again. He stood and walked over to the mantel. "Of course," he teased, "I could go with your expression, Mona, for the things that don't please you."

Mona sat up very straight. "And what is that?"

"'Oh, you piss-pot!'" Jake quoted.

"I think it sounds better for a guy to say 'dickhead,' don't you, Mark?" Keith asked.

"Yeah. Stick with 'dickhead,' Jake," Mark agreed.

Jake was about to reply when he noticed the fireplace, the old stone structure that was two sided, allowing for the fire to heat the family room and the parlor.

One of the bricks, down low near the floor, seemed to have something just barely sticking out from it, like a piece of lint or fluff.

He bent down lower to look. He'd studied a great deal of the house, and done so with a keen eye—naturally. The house itself had barely changed, with only cosmetic changes being made throughout the centuries by the different owners, stamping their own personalities on the place.

Well, that and the plumbing. Modern plumbing! Ah, that he would miss.

"What is it, Jake?" George asked.

"I don't know…but it wasn't there before," Jake said.

He hunkered down. There was paper stuffed into the narrow gulf between the bricks. Paper—where the mortar or grout had worn away.

He reached for it, then hesitated, thinking that it would now be more than two hundred years old.

Fragile.

By then, Mark was standing by his side. "Tweezers," Mark said, leaning down beside him. "We'll have to be very careful."

"Here, here!" Mona cried, rummaging through her desk to find tweezers.

Jake took the tweezers from her and very carefully unwedged the papers from between the bricks. He blew at the folded sheets—trying to gently remove the mortar dust of the ages. He smiled, recognizing his own writing paper.

"Is it…from Melody?" Mona asked.

"I believe so," Jake said. But there were two. "At least one is from Melody."

"For the love of God!" George shouted. "Read it, and read it out loud!"

"Yes, yes, of course," Jake said. He set to the task of unfolding one of the sheets with tremendous care. Then he began to read, "'Dearest Mom and Dad, Keith, Jake, Mark—as Mark can assure you, I am fine and getting to know Serena, who is lovely. Mark, she has spoken very highly of you, and, of course, Jake…well, your sister believes you are one of the finest men in the world. She is amazing, and I understand your dedication. I am not at all afraid or uncomfortable, and will see you in the morning. Christmas morning, filled with Christmas magic. I love you all so much. Jake, I will probably never see you again. There will always be an emptiness in my heart, and I will never forget you. But love is about giving, and I know that you must return to your time. Not that it's really up to me at all. Know that I understand, now more than ever. All my love, Melody.'"

"Oh, my God," Mona said, her voice a whisper.

"Mom, Melody is fine, she's all right, and she found a way to tell you," Keith said. But Mona looked weak, as if her knees were going to give again, and Keith guided her to the sofa, where she sank down.

"She's really okay. My baby is really okay," Mona said.

"What's the other one say?" Keith demanded.

Once again, Jake carefully unfolded the paper.

"'Dear Brother,'" he read aloud, and he winced. The letter was from Serena. "'I am sitting here with a brave and resilient young woman from the twenty-first century, however absurd that might be. Outside, our world is white, as it always seems to be come Christmas, and just as I love it. She has told me about your concern, and naturally, Jake, I did feel an equal anxiety! There was chaos in New York and friends quickly whisked me from the city. There was no chase—I do feel that wretched man who was so determined to make an example of you was thoroughly embarrassed, and none of his men had heart for the deed. I came safely home. I waited for you…and had the sincere pleasure of meeting Mr. Mark Hathaway. Jake, I tried Aislinn's magic out of desperation. I know the spells and chants and prayers of her passages, but I don't know what works, what might be wishes, and, frankly, how any of this came to be. I have read in her passages that the doorway closes on Christmas, and there is little time left to get it all right. That I know you are alive and safe is all the sustenance I need. I am afraid for you to come home. And, oh, dear, if you have managed to find this, and are reading aloud, please do not put the Tarleton family who took you in to their home into any distress! Brother, the war is far from over, and you are dearly loved where you are. Give grave thought to your return. I will love you throughout time, wherever you may be. Tell Mark for me that he is an extremely fine young man, and he has taught me what I'm truly seeking in my own life. The greatest love to be found in the Christmas season of joy and miracles be with you all. Serena.'"

Jake felt his hands trembling.

"Jake," Keith said, excited, "she—she's warning you not to go back."

But Jake shook his head. "You don't understand. She's very brave, but—my army pay, late and small as it might be, keeps the household running. It's subsidized, of course, by the money I make writing articles for the newspapers. It's a hard time, you can't imagine…with the war going on. The fishing is down, we're ever on the lookout… I still can't desert her."

"You could be hanged again!" Keith protested.

"I've seen all your movies. Gloucester does not face danger again."

"So, you—*you*—are going to go back and hide out?" Mona asked.

"No, of course not," Jake said.

"What if the British do get their hands on you again?" George asked.

"They won't," Jake said stubbornly. "Look, pay attention to everything said between the lines. I must go back. I'm afraid for what will happen, for one, if no one returns by Christmas Day. And as brave as she may sound, I cannot leave my sister alone to weather the war and all that will come when peace and independence are finally achieved."

"They're both so clever!" Mona said, smiling as she stood. "If only we could answer them."

"Well, we can't," Keith said "But we know that Melody is fine. And that she'll be home in time for Christmas."

"Everyone where they belong," Jake said softly.

Mona suddenly jumped up. "Hot chocolate, anyone? Oh, my daughter is fine, my daughter is fine, and she's a wonderfully clever individual—she wrote to us!"

Brutus, wagging his tail, began to bay along with Mona's words.

Jimmy, not to be outdone, started barking.

Cleo mewed in annoyance, and Mona patted the dogs—and the cat—totally indifferent to the ruckus. "If we're all staying awake, hot chocolate seems like a lovely winter's idea!" Mona said.

Mark hesitated before following Mona. "You go through life, and you find some people who are truly unique and special, and you have friendships. But those really great friendships are few and far between, and hard to come by. You can know someone all your life, and never really reach that level of friendship. Then you can meet someone, know them for just a few hours, and know that you'd have been friends. Jake, that's you," Mark said, "and Serena."

Jake nodded, smiling slowly. "The pleasure, Mark, has been mine. And my sister's, so it seems."

"I was completely respectful!" Mark said quickly.

Jake laughed. "Mark, I didn't think anything but."

"All right, all right, cut the goo!" Keith said, pushing his way between them.

Mark seemed to give himself a physical and mental shake. "I'll help you, Mrs. Tarleton," he told her, as if determined he needed to move.

George silently followed the other two. Jake felt Keith watching him.

"I've got a present for you. Come on upstairs."

Keith turned, and Jake followed him. They went up to Keith's room where Keith started looking through books of photos on his shelf.

"I have a zillion pictures with Melody in them, of course. But I don't guess a digital snap will look all that good back in your day. She did a self-portrait one day when were together. Chalk. If I can find it. Aha!"

Flipping through the books, Keith came to a stop. There was a picture rendered on a fine, rich paper. It was a self-sketch of Melody. It was titled in her curving script, "A la Norman Rockwell!"

She was at a desk, sketching herself as she looked in a mirror.

"Who was Norman Rockwell?" Jake asked.

"An artist long after your time," Keith said. He pulled the picture from out of the protective clear sheaf in the book. "It's Melody. Really, Melody."

And it was. She was laughing, and a bit sheepish. Her hair was slightly askew and wildly sensual as it cascaded haphazardly around her face. The sunlight streaming through the window touched her hair, and there was a happiness, kindness and sense of humor in the rendering that was delightful. It was the woman who had plucked him from the snow, the one who had doubted him, the one who had given him her faith and her home, even without her total belief. He was afraid that his fingers would tremble.

"Merry Christmas," Keith said. "I really did want to give you a present."

There was a tap at the door. Mark was there. "Hey, your Mom is getting really agitated. She's still worried, which is natural, I imagine, since she's a mom, and Melody isn't here."

"Actually, it's odd, I feel that she is here. Somewhere, near. It's almost as if I can smell her perfume," Jake said.

Keith and Mark exchanged glances. Keith clapped him on the shoulder. "Sure."

Mark nodded, turned and walked away.

"This is killing you, isn't it?" Keith asked Jake.

"Like being sawed in two," Jake said.

"Wow. You two really did grow weirdly into being nuts about each other, huh?"

"I suppose that's one way to put it," Jake said.

"Come on, let's head down. Maybe we ought to throw a bit of whiskey into that hot chocolate."

Jake thanked Keith again for the sketch. They started out of the room, and he winced.

It was almost as if he could feel her near him.

Maybe it was something he would feel all his life. An "almost."

A life that might have been...

Chapter 12

Melody had drifted off, though she had been certain that she wouldn't do so. Serena nudged her, and she leaped up with a start.

"It's just about sunrise," Serena told her.

"Time to get ready. What do I do?" Melody asked.

She was going home. All right, so she was *home,* but she was going home. And she longed to be there because of her mother and father and Keith, and yet she hated to leave this place that had everything to do with Jake.

It was oddly like walking to an accepted execution.

Nothing like! she assured herself. It was what it was. It was what it had to be.

"You're bundled up—good. It's cold out," Serena said. She had a cup waiting on the mantel, and she handed it to Melody to drink.

"Just what is it?" Melody asked.

"Eye of newt, toe of frog," Serena said.

Melody almost spit it out.

"I'm joking, I'm just joking," Serena said. "It's herbs. Rose hip, that's one of the main ingredients. Seriously, it might help you make it through a sickness. There's nothing evil in it. I believe it's the same brew your mother is making now."

"It's—just delicious," Melody lied.

"Grab one of the lanterns. They have to be set on either side of the old well."

Melody picked up one of the lanterns. They went out into the crisp, cold winter's day. Melody looked around. Dead tree limbs seemed to drip with a ghostly appeal in the pale gray light. It was beautiful and eerie. There was no one near them, though she heard a horse neighing from the small stable next to the house.

A stable which in her time was long gone.

The lanterns were set precisely—Melody could see that Serena was very careful as she set them down. "You must be exactly between them," she told Melody.

"All right," Melody said. She felt just a bit awkward. She walked over to Serena, then decided that if the woman thought she was foolish it wouldn't matter— in only moments, they wouldn't even be living in the same window of time. She gave Serena a fierce hug.

It wasn't awkward. Serena hugged her in return.

"Now, get between the lanterns," Serena said, moving back. She looked up at the sky. "It's almost time."

They had gathered in the backyard, waiting.

George and Keith brought the wave machines back out and situated them.

Jake stood between them.

He took Mona's hands. "I'll write. I'll leave books where you can find them. I promise you, we'll finish the history of the family, and I'll see that you can find everything. Thank you, Mona. Bless you."

Mona nodded, tears stinging her eyes.

She touched his hair and his face. "I do need my baby back," she said.

"I know."

He shook George's hand solemnly. And hugged Keith.

The potion was waiting to be swallowed down, set in the snow at the spot he must stand.

Jake looked up at the sky. The winter's morning came out of a field of shadows, but the sunrise was coming, and even in winter, there would be pink and yellow and gold streaks, and then a sudden burst of pure light. There were no clouds in the sky this Christmas morning, and there was no threat of snow.

Coming…coming…coming…any second.

"Hit your switch, Keith," George told his son.

The wave machines hummed to life.

Jake walked toward the line between the wave machines and reached down for the potion. To his amazement, he was suddenly shoved.

Mark was there, reaching down for the cup.

"What the hell are you doing?" Jake demanded.

"I can go back for you," Mark said, his grip on Jake strong, his eyes intense.

"What?"

"I can go back," Mark said. "I have nothing here. You do."

"I am not letting you sacrifice your life for my commitments!" Jake said incredulously. They were fighting for the cup, but he managed to get his mouth on it and swallow some of the potion.

"You're not paying attention!" Mark said.

"Hey!" Keith called out with concern. "What's going on with you two? The sun is almost up, the door will open…what is going on?"

"Keith?" Mona cried, worried.

"Mark, give me the damn cup!" Jake insisted.

"No, don't you see, I'm the one going back. It makes no sense for you to go back. It makes all the sense in the world for me to do so. Your sister needs someone—but not you. She needs a life. If you go back, you will wind up going back to fight and with your luck, you'll probably get yourself killed—"

"Excuse me!" Jake interrupted.

"Sorry, but it's possible. If I go back to be with Serena, I'll be with her. I'll be there for her night and day. I can write, too, Jake. And with my knowledge of the future, I can write amazing articles for your time. I can even try to give some hints of what to watch out for—I can't change things such as the Revolution, nor can I stop the Civil War or any other war. But maybe my writing can save a few lives."

"This is preposterous, Mark," Jake said. "You don't belong back there. This is your world. Your world—with cars and computers and cell phones. You won't be able to make it if you try to go back in time. You saw one aspect of the past, my sister. It's a hard life in comparison. Mark!"

Mark was moving the cup, bringing it to his lips.

"Hey, Mark, get the hell away!" Keith shouted.

But Mark didn't.

The sizzle, the ripple in the area began. And a sound like thunder, as if there had been some kind of a terrible break in the door.

"Wait!" Jake heard Mona cry.

But there was no waiting.

It was as if they moved a trillion light-years in less than the blink of an eye. And he and Mark were still bursting through darkness and flashes of light together. In a split second, he saw Melody's face, seeming to speed toward them, as if from another galaxy. He saw her expression as she saw his face, the hope, the smile, the pain...

They were passing in time.

Except that they didn't. Perhaps there was some kind of corridor, and the corridor was just too small for three people.

He felt the impact as he and Mark together rammed into Melody. Then suddenly, the world was dark and they were all falling, falling, falling together.

"Melody?" Mona said hopefully. "I saw her face for a moment, I know I saw her face. But she isn't here, George, she isn't here!" she cried desperately.

"Mark!" Keith said, shaking his head.

"Mark!" George said furiously.

"Dad, Dad, he was trying to do what he saw as the right thing. But I think..."

"Melody!" Mona said as she sank down upon the back steps, burst into tears.

"Mom, we have sunset. We have sunset, it's going to be all right," Keith tried to assure her.

She looked up at her son, eyes tear-streaked, indignant. "That's what you said before!"

"How did I know—how could any of us have known that Mark wanted to be some kind of hero?" Keith demanded.

"I'm so afraid. I'm so desperately afraid…if we don't get it right this last time, the door may very well close again for hundreds of years, or whatever. Oh, my God, I can't bear this!" Mona said.

George sat on the step next to her, setting an arm around her shoulders. "Mona, we're going to bear it, we're going to get through it. Because we have no choice. Yes, things have gone pretty wrong so far. But everyone knows that this might well be the last chance. We all know it. Before sunset, we'll have it all figured out."

"She's coming home, Mom, trust me, she's coming home," Keith said, taking his mother's hands. "Melody loves her family, and she knows how much we all love her. She will come back."

Mona stared at him bleakly. "She loves Jake, too. Oh, yes, I know he just fell into her life. But I can see it in her eyes. She probably didn't want to love him, I mean, let's face it, she thought he was crazy. She's always thought I was a bit crazy, she just loved me anyway."

"Hey, Mom, we don't choose who we love, and who we love never turns out to be who it should be if you go by things on paper. No one knows what we'll feel when we're close to one another, when we get to know one another…but I do know this. We all bitch, we all whine, and sure, Melody and I complain about the two of you to each other—I mean, get serious, that's what kids are supposed to do—but she'd probably deck anyone else who wanted to mock either of you in any way. Trust me, Melody will come home," Keith said.

He smiled at his parents.

Then he mentally applauded himself for his own acting ability.

And he prayed his words were true.

Toto, I have a feeling we're not in Kansas anymore.

The quote from the *Wizard of Oz* seemed to scream through Melody's mind as she felt herself land hard in a huge pile of snow again. It had all been so surreal. Like blinking and being one place and then another, or, even, for a split second in time or in the dream of time, floating through a field of stars at warp speed.

Beam me up, Scotty.

But flying into what had appeared to be Mark and Jake engaged in some kind of wrestler's hold had been real, physical and damn hard. It had knocked the breath out of her.

They had collided.

Collided through time.

She was afraid to open her eyes. Memories of H. G. Wells and *The Time Machine* crashed into her mind along with Toto and Dorothy and Captain Kirk.

Who knew fear could manifest itself in myriad movie references?

Okay. Focus. Where was she? Had they fallen into a different century altogether? Would she open her eyes to find dinosaurs? Ridiculous, she'd never heard of dinosaurs in the snow.

Oh, God, what if they'd gone further back? Into the days of the infamous witchcraft trials. They would be snatched up and brought to trial and oh, God, that would change history and—

"Dear God! What have you all done?"

Melody dared to open her eyes at the sound of Serena's voice. She said a little prayer of thanks. Okay, she hadn't made it home, but at least she had made it back to Serena.

"Melody, Melody!"

Jake was suddenly on his knees, hunched over her where she lay in the snow, staring down at her, his eyes filled with the deepest concern.

"You know, an 'excuse me' might have worked," she said, trying to speak lightly. "I could have tried to step aside, let you guys past me."

He touched her face. His hands were cold; he wore no gloves. And still, they warmed her.

"Mel?" she heard Mark's voice.

"Oh, this is all just dreadful!" Serena said.

"You are all right?" Jake whispered.

She nodded.

He pulled her to her feet, but then he left her, walking over to his sister, looking at her a long moment, smiling, and pulling her into his arms. For a long moment, they stood that way.

Jake pulled away from her. "You saved my life."

"It was a life worth saving," she assured him. But then she stepped back and looked at the three of them, one by one.

"What on earth were you thinking?" she demanded.

"Hey, I was here with you," Melody reminded her. And the thought suddenly made her reel. "Oh, no! Mom, Dad, Keith!"

"What were you thinking?" Serena persisted, focusing the whole of her stare at the two men.

"I was coming home," Jake said, "where I belonged." He stepped back, crossing his arms over his chest. "I'll let Mark tell his story."

Mark looked at Serena, but then looked away.

"Jake could just go get himself killed. And what—you can be there with a bowlful of rose petals every time he gets himself into a scrape with the British?" Mark asked.

Serena frowned. "Jake…Jake will simply have to stay away from the war."

"That would be desertion," Jake said quietly.

"You can't desert when you're already supposedly dead!" Serena said. "Dead means that you didn't desert!"

"But, people will know that an escape was somehow miraculously managed," Jake told her.

"I rest my case!" Mark said.

But Jake spun on Mark. "Look—you don't need to be any kind of hero here. You think I'd be killed by the British? You'd probably pass out the first time you had to cut wood for the winter."

"Oh, I really resent that!" Mark said. "Three times a week, my friend, I spend two hours at the gym. They say we look alike? Well, you're puny next to me!"

Melody looked over at Serena.

Serena looked at Melody.

"I don't believe this!" Melody said.

"Neither do I. Want some tea? Something stronger, something warm? It's cold out here. And we have hours and hours to wait for sunset."

"Yes, let's go in. I am quite cold," Melody agreed.

"Puny—oh, yes, indeed, Mark. Puny. Because I'm raw muscle while you're walking around with a layer of twenty-first-century fat encasing your body."

"Fat?" Mark said. "Why—"

Melody didn't make it into the house. She stopped, turned around and raced between the two of them. She knew that neither would strike her.

She pushed one man, and then the other.

"What the hell is the matter with you two? Stop it, stop it now! Or, go ahead. Beat each other up in the snow. That will be great, and oh, so helpful!"

The men fell silent. Then Jake said, "Mark. I know what you were trying to do, and it was a noble effort. Time has been brief, but you have been a friend. We just have one chance left now, from what I understand. Sunset tonight. And so, we can have no more mishaps."

Mark let out a long breath. He grimaced to Melody and stepped around her. He offered Jake his hand. "Sorry. You're not really puny. I'll bet you made one hell of a soldier."

"And you don't have a layer of fat encasing your body," Jake said.

"All right, gentlemen, good, very good," Serena said. "You may stop now, before I'm tempted to pull out the violin and start playing. I'm freezing! May we please go in? I do have a lovely Christmas dinner planned—I'd had high hopes that someone would be with me, though I didn't exactly plan on three guests. But, for now, the more the merrier. Come in. We can all catch our breath, and then get started."

They all filed into the house.

Jake immediately decided to tend the fire, which was burning low. He added logs and stoked it to a tapering burn, then warmed his hands before it. "I'll cut more logs," he said briefly.

"I'll help—hey, honest, I can cut wood. I did grow up in Massachusetts," Mark said.

"I can even cut wood, and I'm telling the truth, too," Melody said, looking at Jake. The way that he looked back at her…her heart jumped. But they weren't alone here.

And the atmosphere was simply tense. They were waiting for sunset.

She was seeing him again—when she thought that she would never do so.

But it was just a tease.

Still, he smiled at her and smoothed back his hair, and she felt the warmth of his smile suffuse her, and it was difficult to rue the fact that she was here.

Except that she was terribly worried about her parents. And Keith, of course, who was left behind to try to keep them sane.

"Oh!" she said. "Serena, I'll be back down in a minute. I have to write my mother…." Mark hadn't made it out the back door yet. "Mark—you got our letters, right?"

"Yes," he said and looked at Serena.

Melody was too distracted to pay him much attention. She hurried up to Jake's desk and found paper and a pencil and sat down.

Mom, Dad, Keith. It's really all right, don't panic, don't cry and don't be afraid. I think we all really have it down now; only two can traverse the corridor. This is really all fine; it's wonderful to see Jake back with his sister. I think it's been remarkable for me, as well, for it's made me realize everything I have—including the most precious gift in the world, of course, my family. I mean… well, we all know that Mark and I can never be a couple, but I do want us to be very kind to him, because he doesn't have a family like ours, and I think I understand now why it's so important for him to be the dad, the husband, the provider. It's Christmas, and I will come home, I will be home in time for Christmas!

Love you, Melody.

She looked at her letter. She started out of Jake's study and down the stairs, and then paused. Serena and Mark were close together, and Mark was speaking earnestly

"I am so sorry. I do believe that it was my interference that caused the three of us to be here—which is not bad, really. It's a delight to again be in your company. But Melody must go home. She has parents."

"I know, I understand. I barely remember my own parents, but Jake's mother and father were like my own. I was never made to feel like the adopted child. They were so loving. I can only imagine that Melody's family is very much the same," Serena said. "You mustn't be sorry. I know that you meant well."

Mark touched her face. "I think that it is very fine to be here. I can chop wood, I swear it. I don't mind hard labor. Of course, I do love to write—fictional stories. But it might be a challenge and something incredible to see the people here, know about life during the war, and write about it."

"I'm sure you would be a wonderful Patriot!" Serena told him.

Mark was silent again. "My parents are gone, too. And I... I've seen the way Jake and Melody look at one another."

"You don't know my brother. He will never shirk his duty," Serena said.

"Exactly, the British will get their hands on him again!" Mark said.

He stepped away suddenly and Melody realized that the back door had opened. "Excuse me, Mark. I thought you were going to come out here and help with the wood," Jake said.

"On my way."

"Tea is brewing!" Serena said.

The door shut. Melody ran down the stairs to the fireplace. She found the crack between the bricks and added her new letter to her old letter.

"Read it, Mom, read it, please!" she whispered.

"Mother!" Keith exclaimed.

He dropped his control stick.

Desperate times had called for desperate measures. Mona didn't want to go out. She didn't want to go to church. She didn't want to eat—she wasn't putting together a Christmas meal, because Melody had to be home before they had their Christmas meal.

And so he had taken out the Wii.

Mona had roused somewhat, beating him at three games of video tennis. His father had taken them at golf, and Mona had come back in for the boxing— bringing them both down as if she had the power of Muhammad Ali.

It was one way to keep her distracted.

Every once in a while, he would see a faraway look in his mother's eyes, and then there were moments he would see a tear trickle down her cheek. Then George or Keith would hold her, and they'd start a game over again.

George was doing fairly well. Only occasionally would he sit there as if in another world. And he would say, "My baby."

Technically, I'm the baby! Keith thought. But, hey, Melody was their girl. He knew only that it was good to keep his parents distracted, because that kept him distracted.

And he was afraid.

Last chance.

Somehow, they all seemed to feel that tonight was their last chance.

That's when he noticed the letter.

And pried it carefully from the stones and handed it to his mother.

Mona cried at first.

Then she straightened her shoulders and stiffened and looked up at them both, fire in her eyes.

"Who wants me to beat the sh—sorry, the pants off of them in soccer?"

Christmas dinner in 1776 was no easy matter.

The cranberry sauce was made from preserved cranberries, and it had to be stirred and stirred and stirred as it boiled over an open fire. Potatoes had been carefully preserved in the cellar, and the bird—not a wild turkey, but a pheasant—had been a gift from the neighbor who looked after Serena.

Melody was quietly delighted that the bird had been plucked the day before. She wasn't at all sure that she'd have done well being a feather plucker. Nor did she think she would have done a decent job at the beheading part of the whole thing, either.

There were also vegetables to be boiled—greens kept in the root cellar. Amazingly, despite the hardships of war and the New England winter, Serena was able to put together an amazing feast.

They all worked to make it happen.

At about one, they came around the dining-room table. Jake said grace, thanking God for life and sustenance, and those in life who made it all worth living.

Serena, accepting a plate of meat after Jake carved, smiled. "I do know that while this is certainly distressing for your family, I must admit, it's rather nice for me."

Mark reached across the table, taking her hand. "It's rather nice for all of us."

"Jake is never here. Not since the war," Serena said.

"If I were here, I'd always be here," Mark said.

"Are there glasses? I think we forgot to put them out. And Serena has that lovely bottle of wine for all to share," Melody said, rising.

In any other circumstance, she'd be terribly tempted to yell at Mark and Serena.

Get a room, will you!

But this was 1776, and Serena was Jake's sister.

She smiled, heading into the kitchen for the glasses. Keith, now…Keith had handed her right over. But then, Keith had gotten to know Jake. He had believed in him, long before she had. Keith lived in the twenty-first century.

And Keith knew that she had fallen in love with Jake.

As she reached for the glasses, Jake joined her in the kitchen. He opened his mouth, as if he would say something light.

She did the same.

But neither of them spoke.

She rushed into his arms, and her lips met his, and she pressed against him as if she could crawl beneath his skin, and she kissed him as if she might never kiss him again.

He pulled away from her, searching her eyes, cradling the sides of her head with both hands. "Melody... your family. They love you so."

"I know."

He pulled her close to him again. He held her, and held her.

They kissed again, trembling, and then just stood holding each other tight.

"Do you need help in there?" Mark called.

Smiling ruefully, they pulled away from one another and retrieved the glasses. At the table, Mark had uncorked the bottle, and was ready to pour.

They finished dinner and cleaned up.

Around the fire in the parlor, Jake picked up his violin and handed his guitar to his sister. They played old tunes, entertaining everyone. Mark admitted that although he thought he was a pretty decent writer, he'd never learned to play an instrument.

"Too many diversions," Jake said.

"I guess."

"Come over here," Serena told him. "I'll show you."

Jake went up the stairs, mumbling something about his office.

Melody followed him. He was waiting for her. They didn't go into his office; they went into his room. They held one another, and watched the sun begin its descent.

"It's nearly…sunset," Mona said.

"It is, Mom. But it's cold outside. We have a few minutes," Keith said.

"I'm going to get the machines going," George said.

"Dad, they're not leaving from here, they're coming here," Keith reminded him.

"Doesn't matter. I want it to be optimum for those two to get back here," George said.

"The rose petals! I must have the rose petals!" Mona said. "I want them to surround the well, I want to see them fly in the air, and fall in the snow. I want everything as Serena had it—when she saved her brother's life!"

"All right," Keith said. "We'll get started then."

He and his father dragged out the wave machines, and George turned them on. Mona took the roses, the gift from the priest, and walked around the circumference of the machines and the well. She chanted as she did so.

Or she prayed.

Keith wasn't sure.

Maybe she tried a bit of both.

Then it was done. The machines hummed.

And the roses were strewn.

So beautiful against the diamond glitter of the snow.

Keith manned the one machine while his father stood by the other.

Mona waited, holding a bowl with the remaining rose petals.

"It's time!"

Serena called them softly from the foot of the stairs.

Melody couldn't stand it; she clung to Jake.

But then, it was she who released him. She had to go home. And she understood that he felt that he had to stay.

She kissed him one last time. Saying nothing, she turned and hurried down the stairs. Mark stood just behind Serena. They were both grave.

"Let's get done with the hugging and kissing now," Mark said brusquely. "Once we're out there now, we have to move, and we have to be right, and there can be no interference, none at all."

"Right," Melody said.

So she hugged Serena fiercely, and they smiled at one another.

They could have been great friends.

Then, she turned to Jake. They stared at each other. She was about to take a step toward him when she heard Mark groan.

"Not him. Hug and kiss me goodbye," he said.

"Look," Jake said. "We've been through this. It's a noble sacrifice—"

"Thank you, brother!" Serena said. "You consider a life with me—a *sacrifice?*"

"Serena! I didn't mean it that way at all!" Jake protested. "He just—he comes from a different time. He doesn't understood what led up to the war, he…he has cable television, for God's sake."

"But I'd rather have Serena," Mark said. He looked at Melody. "Hey, kid, here's looking at you—except that you never loved me, and you loved him right off the bat, and that's all right, I really understand. I understand because the minute I set eyes on Serena…oh, and don't worry, Jake, you don't have to do any kind of fatherly thing and beat me to a pulp over her. We'll take it slow. I know it's 1776, and I'd never dishonor her or you in any way, but we are going to get married."

"The sun is starting to fall," Serena said.

Jake turned to his sister. "Serena, is this a fantastic act? What if I want to stay? What if I am determined to do my part in this war?"

Serena smiled and hugged him. "I'm not a good actress at all. I've never done well with lying. I know that you are very much in love with Melody, who loves you very much in return. Why are we questioning any of this? We have it right now. And the sun is setting! This is it! Last chance."

Jake took his sister into his arms, drawing her close. "Serena…"

"You won't be deserting me. Mark needs me. And I want him. And I want you to be happy. I know that you want me to be happy, and Melody wants Mark to be happy, right?"

"Of course. Of course, Mark. But I would never want my happiness to be at any expense to you!"

"Wonderful. Now I'm an expense," Serena said.

"No, no, no, I didn't mean that!" Melody protested.

"I know you didn't," Serena assured her.

Melody smiled. "It's going to kill Jake to leave you," she whispered.

Serena looked at them both. "No, I think we will all be fine. Because what we wish for is the health and happiness of those we love, no matter where they may be. Now this is it, no changing minds, no interference, nothing. Drink those potions, you two."

Jake and Melody looked at one another. She stared into his eyes.

"Will you be all right? Will you be all right if you do this thing—for me?"

He searched her eyes in return.

"We will be all right," he assured her.

"It will be a mess. I mean, Mark will have disappeared. And you will suddenly be there. You don't have a social security number. There is no record of your existence," Melody said worriedly.

"We will work it out," Jake said.

"The sun is coming!" Mark said firmly. "We've got to get out there. I've got the lantern, the two of you, drink those potions. Now."

He was still bossy, Melody decided. But Serena, she was certain, would be able to handle him.

Mark stood back, his arm around Serena's shoulders. The lanterns burned on either side of the old well, where a strange electrical sizzle seemed to have begun.

Jake took Melody's hand, and together, they swallowed the potion.

She felt his grip, felt it so strongly. Then there was a magnificent flash of light.

Serena lifted her arms.

And rose petals flew through the sky, beautiful against the coming night and the snow.

She looked up. She thought she saw the North Star, even against the pastel sky.

Christmas. Magic could happen.

Jake knew that he would never travel such a strange path again. Feel the rush of the universe, see the stars slide by in a blink. Darkness and light, and all in the blink of an eye. He tried to hold on to it; he tried to understand it.

But it wasn't meant to be understood. There was no holding on. Whatever had really occurred since he had been dropped in a hangman's noose from the gallows, he would never fully understand.

It was over; abruptly, it was over. He tasted the cold of snow in his mouth and realized that he had landed facedown. Sunset had come with a full and sudden blanket of darkness.

For a moment, he didn't know where he was.

Rose petals littered the snow.

Had it all been a dream, a wild and desperate dream, imagined from the end of a rope?

No.

He felt her hand. Melody's hand. Her warmth against the cold; she was life against any fear of darkness. He still wasn't sure where they were, if they had made it back, or fallen face-first into the snow of a yard in 1776....

"Melody!" Mona cried.

She ran into the snow from the steps, fell into it and dragged Melody into her arms. Then George was there, and Keith.

"You made it back with Mark, too," Mona said, but then she looked at Jake.

She didn't gasp. She stared at him, and she started to laugh.

And she hugged him.

And she said, "I'll bet Mark is going to be very happy, very happy indeed. Oh, Melody! Melody, Melody! My baby."

"You know, *I* am the baby," Keith said.

"Jerk!" Melody teased.

"Ass!" Keith said. And the two of them hugged one another.

As they all embraced over and over and over again in the yard, it started to snow.

Jake looked up.

It was impossible. It was snowing rose petals.

Melody looked up, too, laughing delightedly. She flew into his arms, and she held him, and the rose petals fell all around them.

He had life, he realized, an amazing gift.

He had love, even more amazing.

He had a future. And that was what he would make of it. No, what they would make of it.

Together.

"Home. Here or there," Melody whispered. "Somehow, I think that we all came home in time for Christmas."

He kissed her.

He really had to agree.

Epilogue

Christmas
Seven years later

"A story, Uncle Keith, a story!" Serena said. He had just walked in the door, and he was lucky he hadn't keeled right over, his five-year-old niece met him with such a flurry of excitement.

"Hey," he protested. "Not 'Merry Christmas' or 'Hello,' Uncle Keith, you just throw yourself at me and demand a story?" he said.

"She's very impetuous," Mark, her twin brother said. "Merry Christmas, Uncle Keith. Please, will you tell us a story?"

"Sure. Just a minute." The dogs had come rushing in, as well. Brutus and Jimmy. And Cleo checked on him, too, looking around the corner.

The dogs didn't mind the kids. Cleo was wise to them.

Mark offered Keith a book. A picture book. Keith smiled; he hadn't seen it in print yet, but he'd known about the conception and he certainly knew the story.

"It came out for Christmas," Mark informed him. He was by far the more solemn of the two. A minute and half younger than his sister. Poor kid—Keith knew what it was like to be a younger brother. Then again, he knew that while Serena might walk all over her more-serious brother now and then, she'd fight for him with narrowed eyes and clenched fists anytime he was attacked by anyone else.

"You already know this story," he told them.

"It's a true story. It's about Daddy's great-great-great—a million greats—grandparents," Serena said. She was like her namesake, a gorgeous little creature with huge eyes and curly hair. "Please, Uncle Keith."

He looked at the book, and he was very proud of his sister and Jake. He knew that it was being touted in schools around the country. It was an illustrated book on the Revolutionary War that reached out to children, and made them enjoy history.

Written and illustrated, of course, by the team of Melody and Jake Mallory.

"All right," he said.

He sat down on the sofa and the kids crawled on either side of him.

"'Once upon a time, there was a soldier. A very brave soldier, a hero of a war that was fought so that the United States could be the United States. The soldier was captured in New York City, and an officer named Hempton wanted to make a terrible example out of him. He wanted him hanged. But it was Christmas, and the soldier had a sister who knew something about tricks and illusion and magic. Before he could be hanged, his sister arrived, and there was a burst of rose petals in the sky. And the soldier disappeared.'"

"He didn't really disappear! She just made him appear somewhere else!" Serena interrupted.

"Shh!" Mark insisted.

Keith turned the page.

"'No one knew what had happened, and the British commander was very embarrassed. Although the British held New York City throughout the war, the major who wanted to be so cruel did not last that long. He was summoned back to Britain by his commanders, and relieved of his duties.'"

"Fired! Yep, his butt was fired!" Serena said.

"Young lady, such language!" Keith chastised.

"Uncle Keith! I didn't say that his *ass* was fired, I said his *butt* was fired," Serena protested.

"Don't say either!" Keith told her, trying not to laugh as he reprimanded her. He shook his head. This one was going to be pure mischief. "Are we paying attention, or what?" he asked.

"I'm paying attention," Mark assured him.

Such precocious five-year-olds! But then again, they spent time with his mother and his father, who was managing new inventions all the time. He had taken a job with the government himself, and then again, the kids had parents who were artists and writers....

They didn't stand a chance.

"But what happened with the soldier?" Mark demanded.

He knew, of course, he just wanted more of the story.

Keith turned another page. He smiled. The sketch of Serena looked back at him.

"'Well, here's the thing. The soldier's sister wasn't really his sister. She had been raised by the family after her own parents had been killed during the French and Indian War that had been fought before the Revolutionary War.'"

"Always a war!" Serena said, shaking her head sadly with a wisdom far past her years.

"But good things, too," he said, tousling her hair.

"'So, the soldier took on a new name. He took on his grandfather's name. Hathaway. As Mark Hathaway—'"

"I'm Mark because of him!" Mark said happily.

"Right," Keith agreed.

"As Mark Hathaway, he began to write again, and sometimes, he traveled, too, because, as a writer, he had friends who were writers. And his friends often heard things from the front. The American colonies were desperate for help from the French, and Mark Hathaway wrote many stirring essays that helped involve the French. But, more important, Mark Hathaway found out about the movements of Cornwallis toward the end of the war, and he was able to get important information to him. He was also able to tell many of the soldiers that the French were coming to help, and so, the soldiers didn't desert when they might have given up. The fight for independence was very hard, and many people gave their lives for our freedom. Many people were heroes. Your great-great-great—whatever—was one of them.'"

"That's so cool, so cool!" Serena said.

"Mark was really cool. I'm named for a hero!"

"Serena was a hero, too, right, Uncle Keith?" Serena demanded.

"Of course she was."

"And it's really a true story?" Mark asked.

"You know it is. Your mom and dad wrote it straight from all the old journals your grandmother dug out of the attic."

"And so Serena—"

"Serena saved her stepbrother from the hangman's noose. Once their lives were turned around and she wound up marrying *Mark Hathaway,* she supported him at every turn. He wrote in his last journal that 'my wife has been my every strength; without her, I am nothing. My courage comes from her, as does the peace that follows my every movement, for she has given me a sanctuary, a safe haven always, a home, and the children, the beautiful children, who are everything in life.'"

Serena let out a happy sigh. "She was supercool, supercool!" She frowned suddenly. "How many children was it, Uncle Keith?"

"Eight—you can find all their names in the church register. She was a great mom, and really loved her kids. She lost her own parents when she was young, and she was still young when she lost her adopted parents. She re-created her own family, and she left the world a legacy of people."

"But Mark was a hero," Mark argued.

"Your mom and dad are kind of like heroes, too," Keith said.

Both kids looked at him and frowned. "They work at home," Serena informed him.

Most of the time, the two did work from home,

though Melody showed her work in different galleries upon occasion. Jake had continued writing.

And he was legitimate. He had a social security number and everything. They'd told his story to a friend—not the real story, but how he'd found himself in the road in the snow—to one of George's old friends who had worked for the government. He'd brought a friend from the FBI in on it all, and once he'd assured himself that Jake was not a South American mobster or dangerous psychotic, he'd arranged for the papers needed to make Jake a real human being living in the twenty-first century.

Keith knew, too, that Melody was happy Mark had persisted in being the man to stay behind in 1776. They had worried at first that someone would think they had done away with him.

But no one did.

It had been almost as if he had never existed in the twenty-first century. Since he wasn't existing there now, it was a very good thing. Melody had feared that their publisher would demand to know what had happened to the book, but the publishing company didn't have a contract on file, and they didn't seem to remember Mark's name. They did remember her, and so she was able to offer them the work now published on speculation.

Christmas. Amazing. Magic and miracles. Somehow, insanely, it had all worked out.

"Your parents work very hard, and they take care of the two of you. And they make sure that I get to spend time with you, and they're very careful to take good care of Grandma and Grandpa. By the way—has Grandpa had any explosions out there lately?"

"Just a little one!" Serena whispered.

"Little tiny," Mark agreed.

"I see. And Grandma?"

Serena giggled. "She took us to see some crazy ladies last week. But they were real cool. They gave us a bunch of incense and it smelled real good."

"How's the house in the woods coming along?" Keith asked.

They both stared at him blankly, and then, of course, he realized it was the only home they had ever known.

His parents had given it to Jake and Melody as their wedding present.

"It's cool—Dad added a playroom," Serena said.

"He chops wood real good," Mark said.

"Well. He chops wood well," his sister corrected.

"He knows how to cut it," Mark said with aggravation, rolling his eyes.

"Hey, we're home!" Keith heard his sister call out as she opened the door.

Melody and Jake came into the house, shivering and dusting snow from their coats. As they did so, a clacking sound could be heard. Poor Brutus—he was getting along in years now, but he still clicked happily to greet Melody and Jake, every time they arrived, which was often, of course, because they didn't live far from the old house, and they were frequent visitors.

Mona and George were happy to take the kids once a week so that Melody and Jake could still get in some alone time—date time, as his mom called it. And once a year, Mona and George kept the kids so that Jake and Melody could take a week and go somewhere. They invited Keith to take his vacation at the same time. Jake was in love with the world. It had been a while now, but Jake was still fascinated with everything out there. So far, they'd seen the British Isles, Paris and Rome.

Jake was dying to head out on a trip to Egypt.

Keith stood, ready to go greet his sister and brother-in-law.

Mona and George came out from the kitchen area. "Great! We're all here," Mona said, wiping her hands on her apron and going to hug her daughter and son-in-law.

Keith went to do the same. He met his sister's eyes and said, "We're almost all here."

"Oh?" She slipped an arm through her husband's and stared at him.

"I think he has a date," Jake said. He nuzzled Melody's ear and she smiled, glancing up at him.

"A date?" she teased her brother. She stepped closer to him. "Another pole dancer?"

"It's a legitimate way to make a living, if you don't get hooked on the drugs," he said. "But no—I think you'll like her. She's an arts major at Boston College."

"Ah!" Melody said. "Cool."

"Mark," Keith said, looking at his young nephew, "when your sister tortures you, deck her," he said.

"Keith!" Melody protested.

He grinned. "He didn't hear me. That was for you."

Melody and Jake laughed, still arm in arm. "Thanks for helping Mom and Dad keep an eye on the kids while we set up their presents at the house."

"I'd say you're welcome, but I just walked in on the little munchkins. Hey," he added seriously, "the book really came out beautifully."

"Thank you," Jake and Melody said in unison.

The doorbell rang.

"Wonderful, wonderful!" George said. "We're all in time for Christmas!"

Keith started to walk past his sister to answer the doorbell.

"Uncle Keith, Uncle Keith! You didn't really finish the story!" Serena said.

He stopped and glanced at Jake and Melody.

He looked to the kids.

"Why, they all lived happily ever after!" he said.

Even me! I think my Christmas magic is now here.

Magic and miracles, he'd determined, we're all created by man's greatest asset—the ability to love.

He answered the door.

It was great to be home for Christmas.

* * * * *

AN ANGEL FOR CHRISTMAS

To Eric Curtis

Certainly one of the world's finest photographers

Prologue

Gabe Lange's quarry was right in front of him.

The chase had begun in vehicles, his a police cruiser. The perp had quickly taken the lead in a stolen Maserati. Still, Gabe had discovered that the police car was well equipped to handle such a race, and he'd been right behind him all the way. In fact, while the con had eventually crashed into a snowbank, he'd managed to swerve to a stop, without even spinning in the snow and ice as he might have done.

Luke had surely faced some injury in the crash; sore muscles, if nothing else. Gabe had come out unscathed. But Luke appeared to be good at disappearing, even amidst a crash, and for a moment—when Gabe had followed him up the first steep hill that led to the road up the mountain—he'd lost him.

He could not lose him; it was Christmas Eve. He

couldn't let Luke loose on some unsuspecting family about to settle down to a Christmas Eve dinner. He could already picture the kind of home where Luke might try to find entry; a couple placing the last of the presents under the tree, perhaps. There might be a crèche set up on a coffee table, a tree with brilliant lights facing the parlor or living room with a multi-paned window allowing the lights to shine upon the snow. Little ones would be put to bed; the father might be doing the last work, scratching his head as he tried to follow the "simple" instructions for finishing a bike or a video system that would be there, big and beautiful, beneath the tree. Here, especially here, in the mountains of Virginia, people had a habit of being welcoming. The houses and old cabins were few and far between, and the neighbors, even those who only came for the summer and holidays, learned to be welcoming and giving. Usually, of course.

Maybe Luke would happen upon the one family who was more than wary of strangers, and ready with a shotgun.

But Gabe hadn't lost Luke; when he came around a copse of trees, he saw him again, limping, but continuing upward once again. The roads here were poorly plowed, but even with snowdrifts swirling through the air and the few feet of accumulation, the path that led to the sparse population here was apparent; it was an indentation in the banks of snow.

And Luke was heading toward it.

Gabe quickened his pace, grateful that he had the kind of body that had been kept in shape; powerful arms and legs, and good lungs. That seemed especially important now. Breathing was good one minute—the air being so crisp, smogless, empty of diesel fuel, the fumes of buses and trucks—and then hard the next; the snow was still coming.

He heard his own breathing as he surged on upward. Luke had a body that was honed as well; young, muscled and lithe. Had he been a gymnast or a sprinter at some time? He was moving just like—just like a bat out of hell.

Huffing and puffing, Gabe kept climbing. When he reached the road, Luke had once again disappeared.

He held very still, trying to listen.

But the snow kept the dried branches of the naked, skeletal trees snapping and the wind that hurried the snow flurries along seemed to whistle and moan; he couldn't hear any other sound.

He turned, searching out the trees, and then he looked to his feet, hoping that the flurries weren't falling fast enough to erase all signs of footprints.

He could barely make them out. Luke had escaped across the road into the trees to the northwest, but it seemed that he'd somehow doubled back....

That realization dawned just in time for Gabe to turn around halfway and almost ward off the blow that came his way when the perp, Luke, cracked him hard over the head with a massive oak branch. The wood was dry and brittle, and he could almost hear it cry out at the abuse as his own head began to spin, and the jarring pain took hold.

Gabe fell to his knees. Luke let out the sound of delighted laughter. "Gotcha!" he said.

No. It wasn't ending here. Gabe wasn't dying in a pile of snow while Luke went on to torment a family on Christmas Eve.

Or worse.

He reached out, glad of his strength as he snaked a firm grip around his opponent's ankle, jerking him off his feet. Luke crashed down beside him. He tried to seize the advantage and jump on his quarry, but Luke rolled, and Gabe was left to stagger to his feet. There was something trickling down his forehead, blinding him.

Blood.

He let out a cry of determination and flew at Luke, tackling him down into the snow. Luke fell once again. Gabe landed a good hook to Luke's left cheek, but he had no time for satisfaction. Luke, bellowing in pain, still managed to catch hold of something in the snow.

A rock.

"Oh, my old friend! The night is mine now. I'm ahead of you at every step!" Luke said with pleasure.

Go figure. Luke found a rock on the road beneath the snow. As proud as a crow, he held it for a fraction of a second above Gabe.

"The challenge is on—and you've lost already!" he said.

He brought the rock down hard against Gabe's skull, and Gabe went down....

He saw the flurries in the sky, and couldn't help but think, *How beautiful. So much on God's earth, even in winter, was stunningly beautiful...*

He slumped down, stars spinning before his eyes, and then fading away to the blackness of a moonless night...

Gabe came to; he didn't know how much later. He blinked away the pain, and pressed cold snow against his face, hoping that would help clear his head. It did.

He tried to stagger to his feet. His first attempt failed; he tried again.

When he stood, he realized that his vision was fine. The world seemed to be a strange shade of gray because dusk was falling. Somewhere, people were watching the extraordinary show of the sun sinking in the west; here, the day was just going from opaque and overcast to the murky gray that promised a very dark night very soon.

Which way had Luke gone?

He brought his gloved fingers to his face, and noted that something was off. He stretched out his arms and looked down at his legs, and groaned.

Luke had stolen his clothing—his Virginia Department of Law Enforcement uniform.

God help him. The challenge was really on now.

Chapter 1

The landscape was crystal, dusted in a fresh fall of snow that seemed to make tree branches shimmer, as if they were dotted with jewels.

Of course, the same new snow that made everything so beautiful could also become treacherous, Morwenna thought, trying to adjust her defroster as the car climbed up the mountainside.

With her initial reaction of, "How beautiful," barely out of her mind, she wondered why her parents hadn't decided to buy a retreat in the Bahamas, Arizona or Florida instead of forever maintaining the centuries-old, difficult-to-heat rustic old cabin in the Blue Ridge Mountains. If the snow started up again—which forecasters were predicting—the beauty would definitely become dangerous.

"Other people opt for warmth," she muttered aloud.

"Birds do it—they fly south for the winter!" If the snow had started up a bit earlier, she might have had a great excuse not to come.

That thought immediately made her feel guilty. She loved her parents. She even loved her siblings—with whom she'd been fighting all her life. But this was going to be a rough Christmas. She winced; Shayne was going to be miserable. *His own fault.* She'd tried to tell her brother many times that he needed to start working harder at communicating if he was going to save his marriage. Shayne always thought that he was doing the right thing, and, of course, if it was the *right* thing in his head, everyone knew it was the wrong thing. Then, of course, there was Bobby. Baby brother Bobby, hardly a baby anymore; he was on his third college, having come home midsemester twice. Bobby was brilliant, which made her all the more angry with him, but so far, he'd majored in political science, education and biology. Now, he was once again searching for himself.

She was about to stop the car; the flurries were growing stronger, and even in her nice little Audi, the defrosting system was beginning to wear out in the woods on the mountaintop. Her mother had grown up there, but Morwenna and her siblings had not. When Stacy Byrne had met the rising young attorney from Philadelphia, Michael MacDougal, she had fallen head over heels in love, and had left home behind to follow him, wherever he might lead. But she'd lost her parents at a young age, and the house had become hers. By then, of course, it had needed extensive repairs and just about a new everything to remain standing. Her father might have joined a zillion private firms as a criminal defense attorney and made oodles of money, but he liked working in the D.A.'s office, and that was where he had stayed. They had never wanted for anything, but she often felt sorry for her dad—maintaining the cottage in the mountains had precluded any possibility of him buying one of those nice little time-shares in the islands or a warmer climate.

They were all grown up now—well, more or less. Bobby *was* twenty-one. But every time Morwenna thought about a brilliant excuse *not* to join her family for Christmas and accept one of the invitations she so often received to head to Jamaica or Grand Cayman for the holiday, she always chickened out at the last minute. Was that actually *chickening out?* No! Honestly, it was doing the right thing. Maybe she was feeling an edge—even an edge of bitterness—because Alex Hampton had urged her to join him for a jaunt to Cancún for an eight-day hiatus, a lovely bout of warmth from Christmas Eve until January 2. Of course, she'd asked Alex to join her in the mountains, but others from their office were going to Cancún, and, he'd explained, he had to go since he was the one who had instigated the trip.

Sure, he'd had to go. Why? He couldn't have just explained that the two of them were dating—no, more than dating. They were together. They should have been together at Christmas.

Well, he hadn't. And—perhaps because he'd been so stubborn, she'd been stubborn as well. And maybe she had hoped until the last minute that Alex would realize he was in love with her, and he had to come with her on a family holiday.

But he hadn't.

So Alex was on his way to Cancún, and she was... nearly blinded in the snow on top of a frigid mountain in Virginia.

She should have given in, she thought.

But he should have wanted to be with her; Christmas was a time for family!

For a moment, the cabin looked like a shack in the wilderness. Then it seemed that the snow miraculously cleared. She saw the porches, and the extensions of the wings. And from inside, the lights from a Christmas tree. Red and blue, green and yellow, festive and glittering out onto the snow. Her mother's home was reputed to have once been the property of Thomas Jefferson, or at least the property of a Jefferson-family relative. It had been a tavern way back when, and had eighteenth-century pocket doors that slid across the parlor; at night, when the family had finished with the business of the day, children had been sent upstairs to bed while the doors had been opened, and all in the vicinity came to drink—and, she'd heard, plot against the British. During the Civil War, the MacDougals had been what would have been referred to today as "closet" Abolitionists, which had made the place part of the Underground Railroad. It did have history, she thought. She was amused to think as well that, since the area was known a bit for the Hatfield-and-McCoy kind of feuding, it had even survived the aftermath of the war, when grown men had dressed up in sheets as the Klan and come around burning down those who had aided the North in any way.

"So, it's still ours!" she murmured.

She had arrived.

Morwenna wasn't sure if her other siblings had arrived yet, or how they had come, but the garage door was open despite the snow. Her mother wouldn't have wanted them to have to stop to open the doors, and the kids no longer had automatic openers for the door.

She wished that, in all their great wisdom, they'd managed a garage that connected directly to the house. But they hadn't.

She grabbed her bag and, huffing and grunting, dislodged it from her small car. She slipped out the side door and headed for the house.

Once again, she stared at it.

"You're a white elephant!" she said aloud to the structure.

Naturally, it didn't reply.

She began the trudge to the porch. "Home, yep. Oh, yeah, home for the holidays."

Bobby MacDougal added another ornament to the tree, wincing as he heard what had been the low murmur of his parents' voices grow to a pitch that was far louder.

They were fighting about him, of course. They'd fought about him many times in his twenty-one years of life; he was the misfit of the family.

He didn't want them fighting about him. Then again, while his mother had a tendency to view the world through Pollyanna eyes, his father was more on the doom-and-gloom side and was always practical. But, then, of course, he worked with the worst of humanity at times, and Bobby had to figure that swayed his thinking now and then. On the other side, his mother liked to believe that everything was going to be all right when there wasn't a snowball's chance in hell that it would be.

Still, he didn't want to be the cause of their argument.

He'd tried—good God, he'd tried, really—but he hated the law. His father always thought it would be great if he got a degree in anything that was academic, and he had always understood facts and figures, and he honestly loved the different sciences. But he only loved exploration as a hobby, he didn't want to dissect frogs or other cold-blooded creatures that the powers that be had decided were fine to take apart. He now knew what he wanted; he just knew that his parents would be horrified, and so, since he had arrived at the mountaintop a few days ago, he'd tried to keep silent and listen to the lectures.

And those lectures were endless.

He understood that his father was a superachiever, but his father of all people should have understood. Mike MacDougal made a decent living; he might have swept the world away. He had chosen not to, which would make people think that he'd be understanding of the fact that his son wasn't looking to dominate the stock market, just something to do for a living that would suffice—as long as he was happy. Bobby had tried once to explain that he didn't need to make a fortune; he wanted to get along fine. He'd made the argument that when the economy went down, even computer scientists were struggling for a living, and that nurses might be in high demand, but hospitals couldn't pay them. His father always just stared at him blankly.

Bobby looked at the little ornament he held. He

hadn't realized that he'd picked it up, or what it was—one of his mom's cherished antiques. It was a little angel with a trumpet. He assumed that the angel was trumpeting the birth of Christ.

"Ah, but maybe you're just a naked little cherub—advertising!" he told the ornament.

He could really hear the voices from the kitchen now. His father's voice was growing aggravated. "Look, Stacy, you're missing the point. He's going to wind up being a bum on the streets of New York, drinking out of a paper bag and asking for handouts. And for what? Because he 'can't find himself'?"

"Shh! He'll hear you," his mother whispered.

"He should hear me—he knows how I feel. You've got Morwenna, working more than sixty hours a week at that ad firm, and you've got Shayne, who works all day *as a doctor,* and comes home to take care of the kids."

"Shayne only takes care of the kids on his day," Stacy MacDougal reminded her husband.

Mike was silent for a minute. "The point is," he said. "He works hard."

"Too hard," Stacy said more quietly.

"If that bitch of a wife of his had just appreciated the time he was putting in for her and the kids, she'd still be with him—and she and the kids would have been here, too," Mike said.

"I am going to miss the children terribly!" Stacy said.

At least they'd stopped talking about him! Bobby thought. *Still, he was sad. He'd cared about his sister-in-law. She had her eccentricities like everyone alive;*

she had probably just been fed up. Shayne was so sel-dom home; she had little help and no social life.

"The thing is this—no matter what, Shayne and Morwenna are going to be all right," Mike said. "They know how to *work*. They'll survive. You know, Stacy, life isn't one big Christmas holiday. It's reality. You have to work to make a living. You have to make a liv-ing to have food and shelter!"

Back to him!

He set the angel or cherub or antique-whatever on the tree. As he did so, he heard the purr of an engine and hurried over to the window—the Audi. Morwenna had arrived.

Morwenna would jump right into the lectures with their father. Great. At least Shayne was just depressed beyond all measure, so tangled up in his own misery over his divorce that he wasn't about to pick on any-one else. He'd be able to let Shayne bemoan the loss of his wife as soon as he arrived. Better than listening to the same lecture over and over again.

"Hey!" he cried loudly. "Morwenna's here!"

Bobby hurried to the door, rushing out to help his sister with her bag. He grinned as he saw her; Mor-wenna was always the height of fashion. She'd grown into a stunning woman, tall and leggy, with eyes so deep a blue they were the kind referred to as violet. Her hair was their dad's pitch-black, although now, Mike MacDougal's hair was definitely showing more than minor touches of distinguished gray. Morwenna's hair, however, was the old MacDougal hair, as lustrous as a raven's wing. And stylish, of course. Perfectly coiffed. She was in advertising and marketing, and he knew that in her mind, people trusted you to make them look good when *you* looked good.

"Baby bro!" she said, dropping the suitcase to give him a fierce hug.

That's the way it always started out; hugs and kisses and warmth and happiness.

Then...drumroll...the sniping began!

"Hey, big sis," he said. He frowned, looking around. "Where's the boy toy?"

She looked at him with irritation. "*Alex* is in Cancún. He couldn't get out of it. I guess he planned it before he knew that I had to come home. He kept trying to get me to go, but..."

"Ah, poor girl! Cancún. Hmm. And he went without you," Bobby said.

"It's business, Bobby. He had others in the firm going with him."

"Sure," Bobby said.

"Let's get this inside. I can do the carrying. Was it bad getting up?"

"Horrible."

"I hope that Shayne is close behind," Bobby said.

"Hey, I'm just glad that Shayne is coming! I've talked to him, and he is just about the most depressed man in the world right now," Morwenna said, her voice troubled. "I hope he doesn't back out and work hundred-hour emergency shifts just to have something to do."

"Shayne is coming. He said he might not have the ex or his kids, but we'd be the best place a depressed lonely guy could be for Christmas," Bobby assured her.

"*Our* family is the best group to be with when you're depressed?" She laughed.

He grinned. "Family—the only people you can rip to shreds in the name of love! Naw, we'll make him feel better."

"Good. At least, I think so!" Morwenna said. She glanced at him. "Well, how's it going for you?"

"Fine."

She looked at him skeptically. "Honestly, though, Bobby, you dropped out again?"

He sighed. "I didn't drop out, Morwenna. I finished the semester."

"But you're not going back?"

Lord, save me! Maybe God heard; before Bobby could answer, he heard the crunch of a car's tires on the snow. "Hey, it's Shayne!"

He should feel guilty; his manically depressed brother had arrived. Now, they could all worry about Shayne's problems!

"Yeah, it's Shayne," Morwenna said. She shaded her eyes against the glare on the snow. "He's not alone. Who is that?"

"Think he picked up a hot babe for Christmas?" Bobby asked.

Morwenna elbowed him. "Shayne…with someone he met in the last few days?"

"No, no, too small. It's the kids," Bobby said. "Looks like Connor is in the front, and that's Genevieve in the back."

Shayne stopped the car in the driveway. Bobby thought that the kids were so excited that they had to get out. Connor had just turned nine, and Bobby was sure that the divorce was hard on him. Though Genevieve was just six, it seemed that she actually comprehended the change with the flexibility young children seemed to have.

She jumped out of the car. "Uncle Bobby!" And rushed him like a guard about to tackle. For a moment he caught his sister's expression. She seemed a little hurt, and a little jealous.

But, then, he'd taken a lot more trouble to make sure that he'd seen his nephew and niece over the years; he knew that Morwenna always meant to.

She was just busy.

"Hey, little one!" Bobby said. He hiked her up on his hip. "Give Aunt Wenna a nice smooch right on the cheek there!"

Genevieve did; and she reached out with a cherubic smile. Morwenna took her, giving her a good hug and a kiss back. She looked at Bobby. Was there even a bit of gratitude in that glance?

Then Connor came flying out of the front, racing to them. He just gave Bobby a hug; Bobby opted not to pick him up. It might be against the boy's dignity. Besides, at nine, Connor was tall and solid.

The car moved on into the garage.

"Didn't know you were coming, munchkins," Bobby said.

"We weren't—then Mommy said we might have a better time with Daddy. And she said that we might really hurt Gram and Gramps if we didn't come," Connor said.

"Yep, she said that Connor and I were lucky to be loved by so many people," Genevieve said.

Yes, Bobby thought, *his sister-in-law—or ex-sister-in-law—would have said just such a thing, and meant it. She'd never known her own grandparents, and her parents had died the year before she'd met Shayne.*

Shayne had emerged from the car by then and was walking toward them. "Hey, family," he said. He was trying to smile.

"You got the kids!" Morwenna said.

"Yeah. Yeah," Shayne said reflectively. Shayne, Bobby thought, was just as pretty as Morwenna—in a manly sort of way, of course. His brother was a good six foot three with the same dark hair and deep blue eyes. He was fit, and his posture was as straight as an iron girder. He had embraced being a physician, and lived well. Bobby had smoked on and off, over the years; he'd given it up last time because his brother had tortured him so much that the withdrawal was easier than listening to Shayne's speeches.

"That's great," Morwenna said. "That was kind of Cindy."

Shayne sniffed. "Yeah. Kind. She's heading to Europe with the new love of her life. She decided that the kids might be a hindrance."

"Hey!" Morwenna said, frowning. Shayne had the grace to wince, realizing that both his children were there, listening.

Shayne hunkered down by Genevieve. "Hey, guys, remember the rules at Gram's house—you don't come outside without someone here. What's the other rule— do you remember, Connor?"

Connor nodded gravely. "Never take the side path out to the garage or shed in winter. Never. Never, never, never. The snow hides the slope and we could fall and get hurt."

"Good," Shayne said. "Now, Genevieve?"

Genevieve giggled. "Oh, Daddy! We know where the path is!"

"Genevieve, don't come outside without an adult ever," Shayne said. His voice had taken on an angry tone. "I'm serious."

Connor came closer to his sister. "She knows, Dad. She just likes to argue lately. It's a kid thing."

Shayne nodded, looking at his son with gratitude.

Genevieve hugged him. "I'm sorry, Daddy. I wish Mommy was here, too. She makes good snowmen."

Shayne nodded. "Yes, she makes good snowmen, but she is off on a trip, so we'll have to make do with whatever Uncle Bobby and the rest of us can come up with. Now, run in and give big smooches and hugs to Gram and Gramps, okay? You're going to be the best surprise for them!" Shayne said.

"Shayne," Bobby said quietly. "You've got to be careful."

"I know, I know. Sometimes I can't help it," Shayne said.

"Shayne, damn it. Bobby is right!" Morwenna said firmly. "Cindy is *not* a bad human being, and she was never a bad mother. I told you, she needed more time from you. She held down the fort when the kids were babies—I doubt if you ever changed a diaper—and—"

"Stop it, Morwenna! I changed plenty of diapers," Shayne said. "You weren't around much, so how the hell are you going to tell me what I did and didn't do! I was working—"

"Come on, Wenna," Bobby said. "Shayne was a good dad—you really do work a lot—"

"Better than you, who can't even get the hell through school?" Morwenna interrupted angrily.

Before he could answer, they all froze in silence. They'd heard…*something.*

"What was that?" Morwenna asked. She frowned, turning around. "We're the only shack up here!"

"House," Bobby said.

"Whatever. You have to head down to the lower peak just to get to the tavern," Morwenna said.

"Maybe it was nothing," Shayne said. "Or," he added, giving her a rueful smile, "the voice of God, warning us not to go inside like squabbling children."

"And lay off each other," Bobby added softly. "We are supposed to be adults."

"No…toward the trees," Morwenna said, frowning.

The sound came again. It was definitely a groan.

"There is someone up here," Shayne said. He started walking.

Morwenna ran after him, leaping like a rabbit through the snow. "Shayne, stop. Let me get Dad, and his gun."

"Morwenna, let's see what it is," Bobby said.

"It's a man—I can hear human groans," Shayne said.

Bobby rushed past Morwenna and grabbed her hand. "Come on—he wouldn't be groaning if he was dangerous!"

"It could be a criminal," Morwenna warned.

"Up here? A criminal came all the way up here to groan by our shack? Please!" Bobby said.

Shayne was in the lead, striding through the snow, with Bobby—dragging Morwenna along—following.

Right at the copse that bordered the snow-driven path, there was a man half buried in the drifts. As

Shayne hunkered down by him, reaching for a pulse, Bobby studied him.

He appeared to be about thirty, with tawny blood-matted hair and a face with aesthetic contours, although they were half concealed, since he was on his side in the snow.

"He's alive," Shayne said. "Steady enough pulse, though it's slow."

"We've got to get him in," Bobby said.

"In! He *could* be a criminal," Morwenna insisted.

"Wenna!" Shayne looked across the fallen body at his sister. "What should I do? Leave him out here to freeze to death? I'm a *doctor*. I can't do that."

"Well, of course, we can't let him freeze to death," Morwenna said. "It's just that…he's a total stranger."

"So what other choice do we have?" Shayne asked.

"Morwenna, it will be okay," Bobby assured her. "Hey, there's a pack of us, and one of him. It's going to be all right. And Dad does have his shotgun."

"Can he actually shoot?" Morwenna asked.

"Well, I've seen him go skeet shooting," Bobby said, grinning. "I think he hit a few plates."

"What? When?" Morwenna asked.

"When we were kids, remember? We were in Memphis. The parental units brought us all on a canoeing vacation, and we went to see Graceland. It was great, if I recall."

"Yeah," Morwenna said, lowering her eyes. "It was great, wasn't it?" she said softly.

"Doesn't matter right now whether Dad can hit the eye of a needle or miss the side of a barn, it's freezing out here," Shayne said. He had deftly run his hands over the stranger, checking for broken bones or other injuries. "Seems like just his head is bleeding. Maybe he got stranded, got out of his car and fell. God knows, this place has lots of rocks, for certain. Wenna, back up. Bobby, get around over there."

"I'm not puny—I can help," Morwenna said.

"I know that you're the queen of Pilates, Morwenna, but let Bobby help me right now," Shayne said.

"All right, all right, I'll get the door. Be careful, you two. Maybe he's faking it."

"One, two, three…lift beneath the shoulders," Shayne said.

"Your children are inside that house," Morwenna said worriedly.

"You know he could sue you if we injure him more, Shayne," Bobby said, still not having moved.

"That can't be helped—he'll freeze. He might be in shock…he might well be on the way to hypothermia," Shayne said. "Look, we have to move him, or he'll die."

"I guess that we really have no choice. We can't—"

"No, but…we can't let him just stay here. I guess we can't ask questions or get to know him," Morwenna said.

"I just hope we don't hurt him worse," Bobby said.

Bobby did as his brother instructed, dipping low, and sliding his arm beneath the stranger's back while Shayne carefully did the same from his angle. The stranger groaned again as they managed to get him to his feet.

"It's all right, it's all right!" Shayne said quickly. "We're bringing you in. We're trying to help you."

The man had green eyes, Bobby noted. Strange green eyes. They were actually a greener color than he'd *ever* seen before, and also weirdly translucent.

He noted that Morwenna was staring at the man, looking into his eyes.

And the man was staring back at her.

He managed a single whisper. "Thank you."

She turned and hurried to the house while they followed more slowly with the injured man.

Morwenna opened the door and stood back. Shayne and Bobby staggered toward it, and paused in the doorway, catching their balance.

She looked at Bobby. "Well, this will be different," she said softly. "I can't help but wonder just *who* in the hell we've invited in for Christmas?"

Chapter 2

"What in the name of—" Mike MacDougal began, hurrying into the parlor as his sons stumbled in with the bleeding stranger.

Morwenna looked at her father; she was worried about what they were doing, herself, but to avoid a family argument over Shayne's absolute determination to be a physician at all times, she waved a hand in the air.

"This guy was out there hurt, Dad," she said. "We have to help him."

Stacy, drying her hands on a dish towel, came hurrying into the parlor as well.

"Oh, no! The poor man. Get him onto the sofa, Shayne. Oh, he's bleeding! I'll get a clean washcloth and warm water. I'll—" Stacy began.

"Hey!" Mike protested. "Bleeding, in the snow, in the middle of nowhere? How the hell did he get here?

How do we know he's not an escaped convict or mass murderer?"

"That's what I said, Dad," Morwenna replied, setting a hand firmly on his chest. "But your son, the physician, refused to allow anyone to bleed to death. Now, Dad—move, please!"

Mike groaned, staring at the man on the sofa. "If you saw everything that I saw, you'd be more careful," he said.

"Dad?" Shayne said.

Genevieve and Connor appeared in the kitchen doorway—just their little heads popping out.

Morwenna hurried toward them. "Hey, little ones. Want to do me a favor? Run upstairs to my bedroom and bring me one of the pillows off my bed. And a blanket, huh? Can you do that?"

They both nodded at her gravely. "Don't worry," Connor told her. "My father will help that man."

"Of course he will," Morwenna said.

She went into the kitchen. Her mother was already filling a basin with warm water; she walked to the pantry and found a stack of fresh linens. "Mom, can I take these?"

Her mother glanced at her. "Of course! You can take anything. The guy's bleeding!"

Stacy was ready with the basin. Morwenna grabbed the towels and they returned to the parlor. Shayne nodded his gratitude and took the basin and the towels. "Looks like he took a good wallop to the side of his head…and there, on his temple. I'm going to need my bag. It's still in the car."

"I'm on it," Bobby said. He turned and exited by the front door.

"Don't just hover!" Shayne said, looking up at Morwenna and his parents as he began to dab carefully at the stranger's wounds. "I think he needs to breathe, too, you know?"

They all stared blankly at him for a minute, and then took a step back.

The kids came clunking down the stairway, bearing a blanket and pillow.

"Good, good, let's get his head propped up," Shayne said. He glanced at his sister, perhaps surprised she'd asked that one of *her* pillows be used for the cause.

She shrugged and watched her older brother as he moved the stranger's head carefully. "His vital signs are growing stronger. I think the blow weakened him and the cold did the rest," he told them. "Of course, I can't make sure he hasn't suffered any serious head trauma until we get him to a hospital."

The stranger stirred. By now, Shayne had washed away the little trails of blood that had streaked down his face.

It was a good face, Morwenna thought. *Nicely chiseled, a bit like the statues she'd seen of Greek and Roman gods. Except, of course, he had a slightly more rugged appeal. Actually, he was a very nice-looking stranger.*

And still a stranger! she warned herself.

They needed him out of their house.

His eyes flew open as she entertained that thought. He was looking straight at her.

She was surprised when she knelt down and touched his cheek. "Hey, it's all right. *You're* all right. We're the MacDougal family. We found you outside in the snow. Do you know who you are? Do you know what you're doing up here? You're hurt."

"Morwenna," Shayne said. "One question at a time for the poor man."

The stranger struggled to sit up and winced. Shayne pressed him back down by the shoulders. "Don't try to get up yet. Let's see how you do. Someone hit you good."

He eased back for a minute, closing his eyes again. "Yeah, someone hit me good. Um…my name is Gabe."

They all looked around at one another. "I'm Gabe," he repeated. "Gabe Lange." He winced, and opened his eyes again. "Could I possibly have some water, please?"

"Water, of course," Stacy said, and turned toward the kitchen.

"Move slowly, and when the water comes, take your first drink slowly," Shayne instructed.

Stacy returned quickly with the water. Morwenna thought that actually, it must have been pretty scary for him to open his eyes, to find all of them looking down at him as if he were an unknown wounded creature they had dragged in.

But, then again, he was.

She glanced at Bobby, who seemed to be a step ahead of her. "Hey, urchins!" he said to Connor and Genevieve. "Let's give your dad the doc some space. I need some help upstairs with presents."

"But…is that guy going to be okay?" Connor asked.

Genevieve's little lips were trembling. Morwenna turned toward her niece. "Yes, of course, my darling. Go on up with Uncle Bobby. The nice man just needs some rest." She glanced at Shayne. Was that all he needed?

"Come on, Lady Niece, Lord Nephew!" Bobby said.

The kids followed him up the stairs.

Morwenna suddenly found herself thinking all kinds of horrible thoughts. He wasn't all right; he was bleeding internally, and he was going to die on her mother's sofa on Christmas.

She lowered her head quickly. What a horrible concept! A man's life could be in the balance, and she was thinking that his death might affect their Christmas!

The stranger's gaze was on her when she raised her head again. A small smile tugged at his lips as if he had read her thoughts. "I'm strong, really. I'm feeling better already."

"Well, lie still until I've gotten that wound cleaned up," Shayne said firmly.

Gabe winced when Shayne laced the wound with disinfectant, but he didn't let out a sound. "The thing is, you probably do have a concussion," Shayne told him. "You'll need to be careful."

"One of us can stay with him and keep an eye on him," Stacy said.

"I'm going to call an ambulance," Mike told her, speaking up. "Any objections?" he asked. He wasn't speaking to the stranger; he was looking at his wife, daughter and son.

"Not to an ambulance," Shayne assured his father. "What the heck happened to you?"

"Obviously, he got into a fight!" Mike jumped in, his voice harsh.

"I'm with the Virginia State Police," Gabe said. "I was after a man. He eluded me."

"Gabe Lange, with the Virginia State Police?" Mike demanded. Her father sounded as if he was interrogating a prisoner of war. Maybe, in his mind, he was.

"There's nothing to worry about," Gabe assured them. He looked at Morwenna and grimaced. "I was an idiot. I let him get away. But I crawled up here before I passed out. I'm afraid he's long gone."

"I'll call that ambulance," Mike said, reaching into his pocket for his cell phone. He stared at Gabe while he dialed. Nothing happened, and he frowned at his phone: "3G, 4G—10G! I don't care how many *Gs* you have, the damned things never work in some places. They're all full of it. Wenna, you're on a different carrier—try your phone."

"Okay, Dad, let me just see where I dropped my purse," she said. She had dropped it inside, hadn't she? Maybe not.

"I think it's outside," she said.

"Morwenna Alysse MacDougal!" her father said. "What have I taught you about—"

"Hurt guy on the sofa, Dad," Morwenna said. "You always told me that human life was worth more than anything I could possibly own, remember?"

He scowled at her. She hurried outside. She had dropped her purse somewhere out there. It took her a few minutes, but she found it and walked back in the house, pulling her cell phone from it as she did so.

"What number do you want me calling?" she asked.

Mike MacDougal looked at their uninvited guest. "Nine-one-one, of course."

She dialed. She looked at the phone—it, too, said that she was out of range. "Sorry," she told him.

"Well, what the hell is going on?" Mike demanded. "We always have decent satellite coverage up here."

"Dad, calm down—it might be the storm," Shayne told his father.

"Try your phone, Shayne," Mike insisted.

Shayne sighed. He was standing again; he'd patched up Gabe Lange's head nicely, and there was color returning to the man's cheeks. He did look well enough to sit up. He might be entrenched on the couch with her blanket warming him, but she did think then that he must be wet and freezing beneath the covers.

"No bars, Dad. No coverage. It's one hell of a storm brewing up," Shayne said.

Mike snapped his fingers. "Let me see if I can get them out here online!"

He headed for the computer in his office, just down the hall from the stairway.

"Thank you," Gabe told Shayne. "Thank you for patching me up—a stranger on your doorstep."

"Hippocratic oath," Shayne said, grinning. "We're not supposed to trip over the injured and ignore them."

"If I hadn't fallen where I had...if you all hadn't seen me..." Gabe said.

Mike came storming back in from the office. "The goddamn cable is down!" he said irritably.

"Mike! It's Christmas. For the love of *God*—watch your language!" Stacy said.

"Mom, Dad, *please,* both of you!" Morwenna murmured.

"Dad, you don't need the cops anyway—he *is* a cop," Shayne said.

"Likely story!" Mike said.

"Mike!" Stacy gasped.

"Dad!" Shayne and Morwenna said in unison.

They didn't deter their father at all. He turned on Gabe Lange. "I have a shotgun in this house, and I know how to use it. I'm a district attorney in Philadelphia, young man, and I know my way around crooks. And if you're a cop, where's your gun? Eh? Where's your uniform?"

"My gun was lost quickly—I try never to use firearms. Innocent people get hurt as often as the bad guys, so it seems. But, yeah, I carry a weapon. Now it's gone, somewhere in a bush halfway up the mountainside," Gabe said. "Look, sir, I'm not here to hurt anyone, I swear it!"

"And so the devil swears!" Mike muttered, and walked away.

"Sorry, the lawyer side of my husband is always angry. But he's a really good man," Stacy told Gabe. Then, she suddenly thrust her hand forward. "I'm Stacy, my husband is Mike. Your real live doctor is Shayne, and this is our daughter, Morwenna. She's an artist and advertising exec. She took business as well as art. Don't you think that was incredibly smart? She is able to use her talent *and* keep a job, and—"

"Mom!" Morwenna said, interrupting her quickly. She glared at her mother, meaning, *Let's not just air the family laundry.*

"He doesn't need a dossier on all of us!" she added and laughed to soften the statement. "To finish the introductions in the family, my little brother is Bobby, and Shayne's kids are named Connor and Genevieve. Welcome to our home for Christmas. I'm so sorry about what happened to you. Won't your family be worried?"

Gabe looked away from her for a moment. "I have a

huge extended family, but my immediate family wasn't expecting me. They'll be fine without me—there's a lot of work that goes on tonight. I'm grateful that you've taken me in."

Shayne squeezed his shoulder. "I would be happier if you were in a hospital," he said.

Gabe pushed back the blanket and sat up, despite Shayne's protests. "I'm not even dizzy anymore. I swear," he said. "I'm not sure I'd want to hit the ring for a few bouts or anything, but I'm doing fine."

"Then sit."

"I'm sitting," Gabe said.

His teeth began to chatter.

Shayne brought out his little light, and told Gabe to follow the beam. He inspected their guest's eyes with a serious expression, then let out a sigh and shrugged. "Your pupils are showing no signs of a possible problem."

"He's fine, but he's freezing," Morwenna said. "He must be soaked."

"Oh, how very rude of us," Stacy said. She looked at her oldest son. "Shayne, there must still be jeans and T's and flannel shirts up in your room. Can you loan something to Mr. Lange?"

"Gabe, please," their visitor insisted. "I *am* on your sofa."

"Of course." Shayne seemed troubled, but he shook his head. "We'll head up to my old room. You can get out of those wet clothes, take a shower and then put on something dry and warm."

"That would be great. My most sincere gratitude to you all," Gabe said.

"I'll give you a hand getting up," Shayne said. "Use the banister—I'll support you on the other side."

Morwenna hovered, watching as they started up the stairs. "Great kids," Gabe told Shayne.

He didn't ask about their mother; somehow, Shayne volunteered information.

"Yes, they're great kids. They've stayed that way through the divorce," Shayne said.

"Most important thing to remember in a divorce— your children still have you both as parents, the people they love most in the world. I'm glad to hear that you and your ex are respecting one another. You should be proud."

Morwenna didn't get to hear her brother's answer; they were already up the stairs.

Her father emerged from the kitchen, a glass in his hand.

"What the hell is going on?" he demanded.

"Honestly, Mike, it's Christmas!" Stacy said.

"Shayne is giving him something to wear that isn't soaked with snow," Morwenna said.

"I'm getting the shotgun," Mike said. "I just don't trust that guy. I'm going to have it on hand at all times."

Genevieve, unsurprisingly for her age, was not an ace at wrapping packages. In a few instances when he didn't cut the paper quickly enough, she cut pieces that were too small. Small items, stocking stuffers, were wrapped in enough paper to conceal a small elephant.

"Wow, there's a lot of stuff here!" Connor told Bobby, his eyes wide. Then they clouded. "I guess we won't get much here," he added.

"We won't get presents?" Genevieve asked.

"Of course you'll get presents," Bobby told him.

But Connor shook his head knowingly. "We did get presents, Genevieve. Remember? Daddy and Gram and all sent them before, and we opened them at home." He looked at his uncle apologetically. "We got good presents, Uncle Bobby. Gram likes to give presents, huh—is that why there are so many here?"

"Gram has always loved to make everyone a stocking," Bobby said, "including Gramps. But I wouldn't worry—you'll get presents."

"Yes!" Genevieve said. She had a little lisp. Her front tooth was loose. "Santa Claus will come here, right?"

Shayne knew that Connor didn't believe in Santa Claus, so he brought a finger to his lips and winked.

"That's right. And Santa Claus can find any house," he assured Genevieve.

Connor rolled his eyes. "Yeah, sure."

Shayne poked his head in the doorway. "Hey, Bobby, thanks. Want to take over in my room for a minute?"

"Sure. Take over what?"

"Watching our—guest. The guy we picked up—Gabe—is freezing. The snow soaked through his clothing. I've got him in my room, but I need you to stand by the door while I dig in my closet for something for him to wear."

"I can find him something—" Bobby said.

"No, that's cool, I still have you by an inch or so in the shoulder and chest region, and the guy looks like he's about my size. I just don't want to leave him standing there. Connor, you can watch your sister for a minute, huh?"

"Yeah, sure, Dad," Connor said. He made a face.

"Bobby still has scissors from when he was in grade school. Can you believe that Gram keeps stuff that long?" he asked with a laugh. "I'll watch her, but I don't think Genevieve can hurt herself."

"I can cut paper!" Genevieve announced proudly.

Shayne walked over to ruffle his son's hair. "Thanks," he said. "And, of course you know how to cut paper, Genevieve. You're a very bright little girl."

"Mommy taught me," she said.

"Yell if you need me," Bobby said, rising quickly to follow his brother out to the hall and to Shayne's room. *Shayne's room. None of them lived there anymore; actually, they'd never lived there. Well, Mom had, and they had often spent summer months and spring and Christmas breaks there. This place evoked a lot of good memories. His parents were in Philadelphia, Shayne was in Pittsburgh and Morwenna was in New York. Not that far, as the world went. But this was where they had always gathered.*

Where it seemed their mother had created a memorial to the past, when they'd actually been a family.

Bobby was suddenly ashamed of his thoughts. They *were* a family.

The bathroom door was ajar.

"He took a serious crack on the head," Shayne said when Bobby crooked a brow at him. "He could fall— he could need help. Look, none of us are in high school football anymore. Just hang around outside the door and be ready to rush in if you hear him slip or scream or rip out the shower curtain, huh?"

"Fine, I'll be ready," Bobby said. He leaned against the wall by the door that was an inch or so open. The water started to spray.

He heard his brother fumbling around in the closet. Shayne emerged. "I'm just going down to toss this stuff in the dryer—freshen it up. I'll be right back."

"Big bro, you're the M.D. Don't be gone long," Bobby said.

"Two minutes. Just going to toss the stuff around because it's been in a closet," Shayne said. Two minutes? Hell! What if something happened? What if the guy did fall? Shayne was right—they weren't accustomed to showering in a mass steam room of sweat anymore.

Awkward.

He could hear the shower spray, and nothing else.

He tapped lightly on the door. "You all right in there?" he asked.

"Yep, fine, thanks."

"Yell, if—"

"Thanks!"

Bobby was startled when the shower stopped. He backed into the foot of his brother's bed and sat with a plop.

Gabe Lange came out from the bathroom, one towel tied around his waist as he used a second to dry his hair.

"I can't tell you how good it feels to be warm," Gabe said.

"Ah, great. Yeah. I can imagine."

"Are you from here? Winter can be pretty brutal, huh?"

"My mom is actually from here. I was born in Philadelphia. We were all born in Philadelphia. I mean, Shayne, Morwenna and I," Bobby said. "What about you?"

"Down in the city," Gabe said. "Richmond."

"Nice. So—how did you come to be out here in the mountains?" Bobby asked.

"State police—we go wherever. Within the state, of course. So, are you a college student?" Gabe asked him.

Bobby couldn't help but roll his eyes. "Yes, and no. I've just applied again. I've been to Columbia and Northwestern."

"Those are good schools. Where are you trying to go now?"

The question was entirely innocent, and a natural get-to-know-you question. Bobby looked at the door; he didn't want Shayne to hear him.

"They don't know it—none of them know it—I applied to Juilliard."

"Ah. For—"

"I'm a guitarist, and I want to write my own music," Bobby said, warmth entering his voice; he was speaking quickly. "My family—they're all superachievers. My dad could write his ticket anywhere, though he's stayed with the D.A.'s office. Maybe he'll run for something someday, who knows? My brother is, as you know, an M.D., and my sister, bless her heart, is an executive with one of Manhattan's finest ad agencies. All respectable moneymakers."

"And are they happy?" Gabe asked him.

"Well, yeah, I think. Shayne loves medicine. I know—through the years—that my folks have talked about his work every time he got an offer to go into private practice. And Morwenna…"

"Yeah?"

"She was an artist once. A really good artist."

"Doesn't she get to use that talent at the ad agency?"

"I think that was the idea. But I think it got lost in

one of the executive meetings," Bobby said wryly. "I loved it when I was a kid. She was always drawing fantasy creatures for me. Being snowed in up here isn't really anything all that new. It's happened before. God forbid they sell this place and head south!"

"Would you want them to?" Gabe asked him.

Bobby thought about that for a minute. "Palm Springs, Daytona Beach…snowbound mountains!" He laughed. "No, I don't suppose I would want them to sell. The house is historic—really historic. You can tell by the horrible plumbing and the really bad electricity. But the place really means something to my mom. And, in all honesty, I guess it means something to me, too."

"That's nice to hear. But, what's the story with your music?" Gabe asked.

"According to my father, music is a hobby. Not a career. You go to school for a career." Bobby looked at the door again. "I'm an adult. If I really want it, I can just stop taking parental financial aid and go it on my own. It will be much harder, but I'm willing to give it a go. The thing is…" Bobby trailed off.

"Yeah?" Gabe pressed.

He laughed suddenly. "I guess it's a good thing. We fight like cats and dogs, and it's hard to plan a family dinner with a pack of overachievers…but, still, my parents always loved us. It's the way that they look at me that kills me. It's the disappointment." Bobby shut up, wondering why the hell he had just kind of spilled out so much to a stranger. Maybe, he thought, because he'd needed to tell someone, but he didn't want to tell them until he knew what might happen. He knew the odds were against him; getting into Juilliard was a numbers game, and there could only be so many people who got into the school. There were other music schools—if he didn't make it, he'd try again.

But he didn't want to tell anyone in the house that he'd auditioned. He didn't want them to see his hope, or, his disappointment if he didn't make it. Even though it meant they were sure to lecture him through the holiday, he was sticking with the story that he'd gotten a job working in New York City for the coming semester, until he figured out just what he did want. It wasn't a lie; he did have a job offer working with a group of musical waiters at a place called Napoli. They waited on tables, stopped, picked up their instruments and did quick numbers in between.

Even if he made it into Juilliard, Mario, the head of the group and a great vocalist, had assured him they'd be happy to work with his schedule.

It was all okay, really. But he could just hear his father's voice: "A singing waiter? What kind of life is that, Bobby? What if you want a family, kids? There's no advancement, Bobby. Nowhere to go."

"Sounds to me like you know how to get where you want to go—just have to hang in and take those first steps. So," Gabe said loudly, "Christmas here every year, huh?"

Bobby realized that Shayne was coming back with clothing for their guest.

He'd told a stranger, and not his brother, what he was hoping to do with his life.

"Yep, every year," he said.

As Shayne walked in, Bobby walked out. "Patient seems to be fine," he said.

Back in his own room, he found Genevieve and Connor sitting in the midst of a massive pile of wrapping-paper scraps. Rudolph was dancing here and there, and little blue snowflakes lay in strips across the floor.

"Nice job," he said cheerfully. He looked around at the mess. "I think I hear Gram calling you from the kitchen!"

He led them back past his brother's door, and could hear the drone of Shayne's voice. No surprise. Shayne was willing to talk about the difficulty of the divorce at the drop of a hat.

Except that Shayne didn't seem to be doing all the talking. He stopped speaking now and then, and Bobby could hear the stranger's voice.

That he was speaking wasn't odd at all.

That Shayne apparently stopped speaking to actually listen was odd indeed.

Chapter 3

"Dinner's ready!" Morwenna called up the stairs.

Her father had been in his study and he emerged, slipping an arm around her shoulders. "So, kid, what happened? I thought we were going to get to meet Mr. Perfect this year."

"He couldn't come, Dad, and he isn't Mr. Perfect."

"But he's a major presence in your life, right?" her father asked her.

"Dad, we've been seeing each other about six months. He still has his apartment, I still have mine. I—"

"I should hope so!" Mike said, disgruntled.

Morwenna chuckled softly. "Dad! You'd be surprised at the mismatched couples that jump in together in New York. The cost of living is staggering. But we're both doing well, and he's really a nice guy."

"So nice that he isn't here with you at Christmas," her father said. He shook his head, crossing his arms over his chest. She had seen him in the courtroom, standing in just that position, when he was arguing the guilt of an accused.

He was good at the stance.

"Dad, an entire group from our agency was going to Cancún. Alex put the trip together before he knew that I was coming home."

"And a bunch of adults couldn't go to Cancún without him?"

"Hey! I'm an adult, too. I could have gone with them."

Mike MacDougal shook his head sadly and sagely.

"No, because you know that you would break your mother's heart if you did something like that."

"When people are together—married, cohabiting, etcetera—they often go to one family one year, and another family the next. And children of divorced parents sometimes wind up so confused they don't know where to go anymore—so they head to Cancún."

Mike was silent, shaking his head for a minute, and then said, "Here's the only truth I know—we're all going to die. You can even get out of the 'taxes' part of death and taxes. And when we die, there's only one thing we take with us."

"What's that?"

"Love," Mike said, tapping his heart. "You and your siblings will talk about your mother and me when we're gone, and that way, we'll still be alive. Love lives on— not trips to Cancún, fruity drinks imbibed on a beach, or expensive clothing, or even a hotshot job. Your family loves you…you deserve a guy who knows about family, and love."

Morwenna stared at her father, stunned. She'd never heard such a speech from him before.

"You were the one who pushed me through school," she reminded him. "Then it was, 'We all have to be independent, make our mark in life! There's no one you can depend on but yourself.' I went to school. I learned how to negotiate, engage a client, play all the business games. I even own stock, for God's sake."

She was surprised when he didn't laugh, or at least crack a smile.

"Christmas," he said softly, "always makes me kind of sentimental."

He walked past her. Bobby came down the stairs, followed by Shayne, the kids and their strange guest, Gabe Lange.

"What's up? What's with that look?" Bobby asked her.

"Dad. Our father has gotten all weird," she whispered, looking past him with a careful smile. "Christmas Eve dinner is on, Mr. Lange."

He looked even better. Despite looking a bit worse for wear, the guy really did have a great face, all the right bone structure in place, but a face that wasn't too pretty, and the structure didn't take away from the strength of his jawline. In Shayne's flannel shirt and old jeans, he looked like a sandy-haired woodsman. He could have done a commercial for some kind of rugged men's cologne.

She reminded herself that many a serial killer had offered the world a pleasant face. She still didn't trust him. He was a stranger in their midst.

"Thank you," he told her. "Thank you for having me in your home like this. Christmas is a special time. I didn't really mean to intrude," he told her.

"Well, I guess you didn't collapse by our house on purpose," Morwenna said dryly. "Come along."

She led the way from the parlor along the hall to the dining room, attached to the kitchen. Her mom was directing their extra guests to take their seats.

They hadn't expected Shayne's kids, and they certainly hadn't expected Gabe Lange, but her mother could always manage to make a meal stretch. Turkey would be the main course tomorrow. For Christmas Eve, Stacy always cooked a strange conglomeration of food—linguini with clam sauce, and potatoes and rice, a roast, broccoli with hollandaise sauce, green beans with slivered almonds, a massive "kitchen sink" salad and bread pudding. Perhaps the meal stretched so well because there were so many items to be had.

Morwenna looked at her mother. "What else? What can I get? What can I do?"

"Drinks," her mother said, setting the bowl with the linguini on the table. "Take a tally. Kids, are you having juice? What would you like?"

They were all startled when Genevieve answered with a little sniff. "I would like Mommy to be here," she said.

The adults froze. Connor placed his arm around his sister. "She's on a trip. We'll see her again soon," he said.

Morwenna dived in quickly, not wanting Shayne to say anything. She knew he couldn't understand what had happened to his marriage, and that he didn't intend to hurt the kids. He also couldn't help but be bitter.

"I'll bet she'll come back with great and wonderful gifts!" Morwenna said, walking around to hug Genévieve. "So, until then, what will you have to drink?"

"Can we have soda, Dad?" Connor asked.

"It's Christmas Eve, why not?" Shayne told his son. Morwenna caught her brother's eyes. He smiled at her; he was not going to make a disparaging remark about his ex-wife. Something about him seemed to have changed, just since he'd gotten to the house. Maybe he'd had a long talk with Bobby upstairs.

"Two sodas... Bobby? Soda, beer, wine?"

"Hey, it's my first 'legal' Christmas. Please serve me a lovely glass of Cabernet," Bobby said. "And Dad can't even get arrested because I'm legal these days!"

"I'd have myself arrested?" Mike asked.

"Yeah, you would, Dad. In the name of justice for all!" He laughed. "My dad may be the best assistant D.A. in the country. I think he'd have himself arrested under the innkeeper law," he told Gabe.

Mike groaned. "You were underage—you and your friends. It's illegal for an adult to aid a young person in securing alcoholic beverages. Now you are twenty-one. Go for it."

"Tough to grow up in such a household," Shayne told Gabe.

"Not so bad. We just decided to smoke pot, since everything was illegal for us," Bobby said cheerfully.

Mike looked as if he would explode.

"Chill, Dad, chill, just kidding!" Bobby said.

"An honest man. Rare to find," Gabe said. He had a curious expression. "I think I'd like a beer, if I may. Sounds intriguing—um, good, sorry. Sounds good."

The seeds of mistrust settled more deeply into Morwenna's soul. *Intriguing? Beer? Where the hell had this guy been? Locked up somewhere?*

"Mom, Dad, Shayne?" Morwenna asked.

In the end, she had two caffeine-free sodas, four glasses of wine and two bottles of beer. She moved into the kitchen to get the drinks, and found herself pausing to look around.

And feel guilty.

Stacy even cleaned while she cooked. With all that she had prepared, her mother had kept up with pots and other utensils as well. She had done so much; every year she did so much. She'd always been an at-home mom. Morwenna wondered if she had ever had her own set of dreams, and if their father's career had changed Stacy's life. She'd always cooked breakfast, made lunches, driven the children to Girl Scouts, Boy Scouts and Little League, sewn costumes, bought the candy, gone trick-or-treating and done everything imaginable.

Stacy followed her into the kitchen. "I'll get the sodas," she said. "If you pour the wine."

"Mom, why don't you just sit, and let me do this."

"Are you kidding? I'm in my element, sweetheart. And we don't get days like these often anymore—you know, when I have all of you!"

Morwenna walked to the counter where her mother was pouring the sodas. She slipped her arms around her waist. "Mom, did you ever want to really do anything? I mean, you know, have a career—do something else besides wait on Dad and all of us?"

Stacy turned to stare at her, her eyes wide. "Morwenna, *this* is my career, my life."

"But, did Dad stop you from having any other

dreams? Now would be the time to fulfill a dream. It's never too late, you know."

She was surprised; she was trying to stand up for her mother, and her mother was angry. "You get it out of your head that your father stopped me from doing anything. Because of your father, I could live my dream, I could have *this* career."

"But we're gone now, Mom. We're all gone, out of the house, grown up."

"And that means you're not my children anymore?"

"But Dad pushed me so hard to make sure that I had a career—" Morwenna began.

Stacy quickly cut her off. "Your father pushed *you,* yes, because you needed more. And because the world is changing. Now two people have to work sometimes in order to afford to raise a family. I guess you don't understand. You have all your sleek, chic clothing, designer briefcases and all-important meetings. And I concentrate on making sure a roast is edible. But, Morwenna, don't try to fix me. I like what I am, and I like what I do, and there are ups and downs in life all the time, but I'm *happy.* Maybe your ex-sister-in-law is the only one who really knows that, since she made sure that the kids came here for Christmas. The only one who appreciates family, it seems, is the one no longer in the family!"

Morwenna didn't have a chance to respond; Stacy expertly balanced the four wineglasses and seemed to sail out of the kitchen, her head held regally high.

"I wanted to draw!" she said, aware that her mother couldn't hear her. "I wanted to draw, and paint, and create things!"

She hesitated, aware that, supposedly, the job she

had taken would allow her to do just that. But she had become a stereotype of corporate America instead.

"I like my clothes!" she told the swinging door.

She tucked two bottles of beer under her arm, picked up the sodas and followed Stacy back to the dinner table.

"Ah, Morwenna is here now. We can say grace," Stacy said.

Mike stood and looked around the table. "Thank you, Lord, for the food we are about to eat. Thank you for the safety and lives of our family. Amen."

"Nice," Gabe commented.

"Better than the old joke, eh, of just saying *'Grace'*!" Bobby teased.

"We know better than to give the task to you, son," Mike said, but he was grinning.

"Wait!" Genevieve said. "Wait, Gram, please! Can we do that thing that Mommy's family does?"

They all looked at her. Genevieve grinned and stood up. She took Bobby's hand and reached for her brother's.

"Ah, Genevieve, what are you doing?" Connor demanded.

"Give me your hand, Connor. I don't have any cooties!" Genevieve said.

Connor shrugged and gave her his hand. "This is just silly. Mom isn't here."

"Hey, your sister wants to have your mom here— in spirit," Shayne said. "And let's all try to make each other happy, huh?"

Genevieve grinned happily. "Okay, everybody, now, *shake a lot of love!*

Around the table, they held hands, and on Genevieve's command, they all shook their hands up and down.

"Now," Genevieve said complacently, "it's almost kind of Christmas!"

"They don't even really know what day Christmas Day is supposed to be," Connor said. "Some popes or priests somewhere got together to pick a day."

"That's right, Connor," Gabe said. "But it doesn't take away from the fact that the day was chosen, and it's the day when Christians celebrate the birth of Jesus. So, it's the chosen day, and your sister is right—it's almost here."

"So it might have been any day," Morwenna murmured. Except that she was heard. She looked at Gabe, who was staring at her with amusement.

"What? It's a day for miracles or the like?" she asked him softly.

"Miracles are what we make ourselves," he said. He looked upward. "Maybe the Lord can lend a hand, but we have to create magic ourselves."

She groaned softly. "A do-gooder cop. Great."

He just grinned. She did, too.

And, somehow, the meal went along with the conversation pleasant instead of strained, with the family asking questions instead of throwing out accusations, and her father actually asked Bobby to bring out his guitar when they got to the bread pudding.

He played Christmas carols and the family chimed in, except for Morwenna.

Gabe looked at her. "Are you really that 'bah, humbug'?" he asked her.

"No. I sound like a wounded hyena when I sing," she told him.

"But these are Christmas carols. Everyone sings Christmas carols." He looked upward again. "He doesn't care what you sound like."

Morwenna laughed. "I think I'll pick up the plates."

She was surprised when he caught her hand. "'O Little Town of Bethlehem,'" he said. "I know you know it. I'll help with the plates. One song, huh?"

With an exaggerated sigh, she sat again. She sang along with the family, watching Gabe. "See?"

"I thought you were great."

She drew back, looking at him suspiciously. "Do you actually have a family?" she asked him.

"I do. I have a wonderful family," he assured her.

"Why aren't you going crazy, trying to find a working phone?" she demanded. "You're not with them."

"Because I'm not the kind to beat my head against the wall when something can't work," he told her.

She wanted to argue the point, but she really couldn't. The storm had done nothing but grow stronger in the hours since she had arrived, and it did seem that they had lost all phone connections. Were the satellites all snowbound as well?

"No television for the kiddies," she murmured. "No computer games."

"Bobby, play 'Silent Night' for me, please?" Stacy asked.

Bobby looked over at his mother. "Sure, Mom. I thought you didn't care for the song on a guitar that much. You always like it on piano."

"And one of these days, I'm going to get one here," she assured him. "But, please, play it for me."

"Nothing like a rock version of 'Silent Night,'" Mike said.

Of course, Bobby heard him.

"I'd love to hear it, too," Morwenna said. "Scrooge can go into the kitchen!"

They all managed to laugh at that, even Mike. And Bobby played. Gabe sang the song alone this time with a clear, smooth, fluid tenor voice that was absolutely beautiful. When the song was over, everyone at the table just stared at him.

"Wow," Bobby said.

"That was all you. You can really play," Gabe said.

Fearful that a fight would begin over Bobby's music versus his college education, Morwenna quickly rose. "Let's get the plates into the kitchen," she said.

"Really, kids, I'm fine," Stacy said.

Morwenna looked at her mother. "Mom, please let us help. Remember, you don't get all of us that often and we want to be with you—if we help, we're with you."

Stacy nodded, but looked at Connor and Genevieve. "Shayne, maybe you could read the kids a story. I'm afraid that we have no internet and we're not getting television reception, either."

"No cable?" Connor asked, horrified.

"Yes, but that's okay. We can do other things to have fun!" Stacy said.

Shayne looked blankly back at his mother. Morwenna felt her heart contract. Shayne was too much like her; they both worked so much they didn't really know how to have fun.

Just as that thought struck her, Bobby piped up. "I know what we'll do! Auntie Morwenna will draw up a Christmas creature, and we'll make up a story about it as we go along."

"Doesn't anyone have an iPad?" Connor asked hopefully.

Yes, actually, she did, Morwenna thought.

But Bobby was looking at her hopefully. She smiled. She really loved her little brother. He might be the ne'er-do-well of the group, but he had heart. She winced inwardly. *And he did have talent. But Dad was overprotective and mistrustful of everyone. He'd worked with too many crooks. In his mind, too, he'd let too many go free. So had they fallen back on their father's words too many times because they were afraid of taking chances? Afraid of having faith in their own abilities?*

"Plates in the kitchen!" Morwenna said. "We all help Mom, and then we'll do a whole Christmas story of our own in the parlor!"

As she passed Shayne with plates, he caught her arm. "You really don't have your iPad?" he asked hopefully.

"Shayne MacDougal, believe it or not, the artist in me loves a pencil and paper, and we're going to play," she said. "Difficult, I know. But your kids will love it, and you don't have to be embarrassed. Hey, you can play a monster."

She hurried by her brother. *Shayne loved his job. He just needed to realize that his loved ones needed healing as much as his patients.*

With everyone helping, it was quick work getting the table cleared. Luckily, the dishwasher and electricity were still functioning, so within twenty minutes, food was stowed, plates and glasses and serving pieces rinsed and set to wash and the kitchen squeaky clean.

Mike asked his sons for help with the logs; they rebuilt the fire in the parlor. They managed to do so, only jokingly taunting one another as they shared the labor.

But, before they could start, Stacy turned back to the kitchen. "We have to have hot cocoa for the performance."

Bobby groaned. "You'd think we were starving, Ma."

"She likes to have the fire—and her kids drinking cocoa," Morwenna said.

"Spike mine, Ma," Bobby called.

When cocoa was finished—spiked for the adults, plain old cocoa for the kids—Bobby ushered his mother back to the sofa. He hiked Genevieve over his head, and then set her on his mother's lap.

Morwenna hurried to her room and found one of her old sketchbooks and quickly looked up something she had created years before—Magala, the Christmas elf. She ran back downstairs with the sketchbook. "Bobby, you get to be Wager, the traveling troubadour." She frowned, and then looked at Gabe, who was waiting expectantly. "Gabe, you can play Magala, the Christmas elf," she said, and showed him the picture. "And, Shayne, you get to be Mr. Mean, the Abominable Snowman who lives by the workshop at the North Pole."

"Great!" Shayne said.

But Connor giggled, and Shayne flashed his son a smile. He lifted his arms in a huge Abominable Snowman pose.

"Who are you, Aunt Morwenna?" Genevieve asked, cuddling her teddy bear as she sat on her grandmother's lap.

"The narrator," Morwenna said. "Hang on just one

minute." Glancing at her pictures, she scurried first to the kitchen. She found a new mop head and came back to put it on Shayne's head, which delighted the kids further. But Shayne wasn't complete until she had whitened his face with cold cream. The more Shayne groaned, the more his kids laughed, and she was happy when she saw him smile—despite the goop on his face.

Bobby had secured one of his old Robin Hood hats from a long-gone Renaissance festival, and for Gabe, Morwenna found an old pair of Halloween ears. They were ready.

"Intro!" Morwenna told Bobby. He strummed a light tune that grew dark.

"Once upon a time, up at the North Pole, there lived a good elf named Magala," Morwenna said.

Gabe got into the action, leaping up, smiling and bowing. It was good; he didn't seem to have suffered any real damage from his fight in the snow.

"He worked all day at creating toys for children," Morwenna continued.

Gabe pantomimed the creation of a bicycle, and everyone laughed as he kept turning the invisible instruction sheet around and around.

"But, nearby, in the darkest, dankest cave, lived Mr. Mean, the Abominable Snowman," Morwenna said.

Bobby played a few dark and threatening chords as Shayne stood up, lifted his arms and shoulders in a huge display of strength.

"I'm mean!" Shayne said. He looked at Morwenna. "How am I mean? What do I do?"

"While Magala works day and night, trying to make a wonderful Christmas for children everywhere, Mr. Mean plans to destroy all the toys!" Morwenna said.

Bobby played even darker music.

Shayne walked over to Gabe, stared at him and picked up the imaginary bike. He threw it to the ground and then hopped up and down on it.

"That's what I always felt like doing with those instruction sheets," Mike said softly, drawing laughter from all of them.

"Daddy, you're so mean!" Genevieve said, delighted.

"And I just stare at him while he ruins Christmas?" Gabe asked.

"No! Here's the thing—Mr. Mean goes away all proud of himself for having taken care of Christmas. But, you see, Magala is a magic elf, and as soon as Mr. Mean is gone, he just puts the bicycle back together again, and he does it double time," Morwenna said.

The children were delighted as Gabe tried to perform all his actions again in double time.

"So, all the toys were ready to go, to be placed in Santa's sleigh," Morwenna said.

Gabe put his hands on his hips and nodded proudly.

"But!" Morwenna said, and Bobby strummed out a dire musical warning.

"Mr. Mean came in and stomped on the toys again!"

Big-armed and growling, Shayne grabbed the imaginary bike, tossed it to the floor and hopped up and down, his dramatic antics growing with each jump.

"And then what happened?" Connor demanded, clearly drawn in.

"Magala didn't have any presents for Santa's sleigh!" Genevieve said.

"Ah, but you see, he did," Gabe told her.

"But the bike is smashed to bits," Connor protested.

"Smashed, yeah, broken. But all the pieces were there," Gabe said, flashing Morwenna a quick smile.

"So," Morwenna said, "Magala the elf picked up all the pieces, and when the children awoke in the morning, they realized that they hadn't just gotten a present—they'd gotten a puzzle, too. They just had to work together and connect the pieces."

Genevieve, with wide and innocent eyes, leaped up and ran over to stand by the imaginary bike.

"My dad could put it back together. Especially when he's not being Mr. Mean!" Genevieve said.

"Ah, yes. And there's the magic to the Christmas story," Morwenna said. "When Mr. Mean realized that he couldn't break something that can't be seen or touched—like the love shared at Christmas—he gave up being Mr. Mean, and he became Mr. Nice, and he went about the country, finding children who didn't have fathers, and helping them put all their toys back together again!"

Bobby strummed the guitar. "The end!" he announced.

"The end, and time for little people to go to bed," Shayne said. "Morwenna—"

"Absolutely, my beautiful little niece is in with me," Morwenna said.

"And I'll take Connor, and—"

"Gabe can have the lower bunk in my room," Bobby said.

"But for now…young'uns, to bed! Santa can't come if you don't go to bed," Shayne said firmly.

"I'm not that young," Connor protested, standing tall to prove his point.

"Hey—Uncle Bobby worked hard on that tree. And

your grandmother baked cookies for Santa. You're going to go to bed, and Santa is going to come," Morwenna said. She was surprised when Connor looked at her, blushed, lowered his head and smiled.

"Alrighty, Auntie Wenna," Connor said. "I like playing your games. I'll think of it that way."

"That's wonderfully mature, Connor," she told him.

"Kiss Gramps and Gram, and let's go on up," Morwenna suggested.

Connor kissed his family, and Genevieve followed him around. When he reached Gabe, Connor somberly shook his hand.

"And a good night to you, young man," Gabe said.

Genevieve impulsively gave Gabe a kiss on the cheek. He smiled. "Thank you. And good night, Genevieve. I have a feeling you'll go through life fixing the things that need to be fixed, young lady. You have a good night's sleep."

"It works when we all fix stuff, huh?" Genevieve asked.

Gabe grinned. "Just like magic," he agreed.

"Come on, come on up," Morwenna urged the two. Shayne probably had the kids' presents out in the car, in the garage, and the storm was still pounding them. It was going to be a trick to get everything in. She was worried, too, about what they'd find in the house to give the children so that they had something to wake up to; they'd sent the family presents on ahead to Cindy a few weeks ago, since she was going to have the children for Christmas and Shayne would have them for the New Year's weekend.

"I'm good, Auntie Wenna," Connor said at the door to Bobby's room. "I'm cool. I can put myself to bed."

She hesitated. He reminded her of a brave little warrior standing there.

"Both your parents love you very much, Connor," she told him.

He nodded. "Yeah, well, I just need to learn to handle things on my own. I've got Genevieve to think about."

Morwenna smiled and ruffled his hair. "Good night, Connor. Love you."

"Love you, too, Auntie Wenna," he said.

She brought Genevieve into her room, stood with her while she washed her face and brushed her teeth, helped her into an old flannel gown of her own that was far too big, but which Genevieve wanted to wear, and sat at the foot of the bed.

"Say prayers with me, Auntie Wenna?" she asked.

"Um, sure," Morwenna said a little awkwardly. She smiled; as a child, she had gotten down on her knees at night and told God all her problems. As an adult, she'd figured out that he was busy with more serious issues, such as war, starvation and disease.

When had she gotten to a point where she believed that she had to fight alone against the world? When she'd figured out hers was just a little life, a grain in the sands of time.

She knelt down next to her niece and folded her hands prayer fashion.

"Dear God. Happy birthday to baby Jesus—whatever his birthday might be. We love him, no matter when it is. Please keep my mommy and daddy safe, and Auntie Wenna, Uncle Bobby, Gram and Gramps. And don't worry about toys for me this Christmas. Honest." She opened her eyes for a moment to take a sideways glance at Morwenna. "Auntie Morwenna will let me play with some of her stuff, so I'm really good. Oh, thank you for the bread pudding. It was especially yummy. Amen."

"Nice prayer, young lady. Good night."

"Aren't you going to say your prayers?" Genevieve asked her.

She looked at her niece for a moment. In her head, thoughts she couldn't say out loud in front of the child—or anyone—swirled into a prayer. *Dear God, please don't make it that I am an idiot; that Alex really wants to be with me 'cause he believes I'm on the top rungs of the professional ladder, and that he isn't in Cancún, chasing after Double-D Debbie from Accounting on the beach....*

She gave herself a mental shake and folded her hands again. "Dear God, thank you for my brothers, my mom and dad, and especially my nephew, Connor, and my niece, Genevieve. Guard them for me, please, through whatever life offers." She hesitated a minute. "Help me be a better, more understanding me."

Genevieve nudged her. "And happy birthday to baby Jesus."

"Yes, of course. Happy birthday to baby Jesus."

"And may we all get back together again. My mom and dad," Genevieve said, looking upward again.

Morwenna rose and lifted Genevieve, hugging her. "Sometimes, honey, that just can't happen. What you need to know is how much they both love you and Connor."

"How can they love anybody when they hate each other so much?" Genevieve asked her.

"They don't hate each other."

"They sure act like it sometimes," Genevieve said.

"They—they're just angry because they...they..."

"They didn't know how to fix things," Genevieve said. "That's why I really prayed that we could learn to fix things."

"Praying for miracles," Morwenna murmured.

Genevieve smiled sadly at her. "Well, fixing things is like a miracle."

"Yes, it is, sweetie, yes, it is," Morwenna agreed. She tucked Genevieve into her bed, pulling the covers close. "I'll leave the bathroom light on, okay, kid? And the door ajar."

"Good night," Genevieve said. "Don't let the bedbugs bite."

"Let's hope not. We'll have the same bedbugs," Morwenna said. Genevieve giggled. Morwenna kissed her once again and left her, cuddling her teddy bear.

She hesitated and looked out the window from the upstairs hallway. She could see that Shayne had bundled up and was headed to the garage. About ten feet behind him, someone else was walking. Too broad shouldered to be Bobby; it was Gabe. Gabe Lange was going out to help him.

Something stirred inside her.

Distrust. Sadly, she had a lot of her father inside her. She didn't naturally trust anyone. And they found him in the snow. He claimed to be a cop, but he hadn't been wearing any kind of uniform, and they'd found him with no identification. Was he who he said he was?

All she knew at that moment was that the guy was following her brother. On a dark, snow-swept night. They were heading into the garage.

She tore down the stairs, pausing at the hooks by

the door for her coat and scarf. Her brother was likely lost in his own thoughts as he always was, unable to feel the first hint of danger.

Luke DeFeo shivered, staring at a cottage that sat on the side of the mountain. It was dark, but everything was dark. Still, he had the feeling that there was no one there.

He swore aloud in the night. The air was bitterly cold, and he could feel it. He wanted to be off the damn frigid mountains, but there seemed to be no traffic anywhere in the area, and he had yet to stumble onto any signs that life actually existed in the frozen wasteland. He cursed Gabe in his mind; this was one hell of a way to spend the night.

He'd thought he'd killed him; he'd thought that he'd killed Gabe, but he hadn't. The deadly game between them was still on. Luke could somehow sense that Gabe was still out there.

Well, he didn't have to sense it, not really. Stumbling around in the snow and ice-covered wilderness, he had come upon the place where they had fought—and Gabe had been gone. So he was still out there, somewhere in the night.

Luke made his way to the little wooden cottage on the mountain. It was dark and he couldn't hear any signs of life. He rapped at the door and received no answer. After a moment, he threw his shoulder against the door, and then kicked it in. He stepped into the house, but as he did so, he knew that it was empty. The inhabitants were apparently smart—they'd gone somewhere for the holiday.

He looked around, and wondered if he wanted something from the cottage. But there wasn't anything there; it was empty and it was cold. It was a shelter against the cold and the snow and the wretchedness of the night, of course.

But he couldn't stay.

He hadn't killed Gabe.

He left the door to the cottage swinging and started out, feeling the bitter cold again. He could take it.

He was going to find Gabe, and end the game between them.

Chapter 4

"I'm going to head out and help Shayne," Bobby told his mother. He'd come from the kitchen, having insisted he clean up the hot-cocoa cups. Stacy had been straightening out the apron around the Christmas tree to ready it for Shayne's packages.

"You don't need to help, Bobby—Gabe went out behind him, and Morwenna went running out after him." She was staring at the tree as she spoke, but turned to smile at him. "You did a beautiful job with the ornaments, Bobby."

"It was easy. Dad did the lights. That's the pain in the ass, Mom."

She rolled her eyes. "Butt, Bobby. Pain in the butt. It's a nicer word." She stepped closer to the tree, studying one of the ornaments. It was the little angel or cherub he had pondered himself earlier.

He walked over to his mother, setting a hand on her shoulder. "That's pretty," he told her.

She smiled. "I think I told you the story that goes with this ornament, years ago."

"Did you?"

"It belonged to my great-great-grandmother."

"Mom, the house is almost two hundred years old. And half the stuff in it belonged to your great-great-grandmother."

"Ah, but this one was special! During the winter of 1864, a wounded Union soldier found himself running through the mountains, terrified, of course, about what might happen to him if he was captured by a Confederate guerrilla band. The commanders of the armies, both sides, were fairly honorable men, but sometimes the militiamen and the guerrillas combing the mountains were fanatics—not so much on the eastern front, but in the west the men were often little more than common murderers. Anyway, my great-great-grandmother found him trying to seek shelter in the barn—the garage now. And she couldn't let any wounded man suffer, and took him in to nurse him. When the menfolk in the family wanted to turn him in, she said she just didn't give a damn about the war, she cared about people. He got a fever, and he was delirious, and when he woke up, he said that she was his angel. His angel of mercy. He had this little ornament to bring home as a gift for his mother, but when he left, he said that his mother would want the angel who had saved his life to have the figure. He said that he prayed the angel would look after her all her days. She lived to be ninety-nine, so I guess the angel was looking after her."

"Great story, Mom," Bobby said. She smiled. And for that minute, Stacy looked almost like a young girl again. She was his mother, but it seemed that he could take a step back for a moment and take a look at her as a human being. He smiled inwardly, thinking she must have really been something at one time. He'd always known that his big sister was beautiful. And now he could recognize the fact that Morwenna had gotten her looks from their mother.

Kids seldom saw such things, but it was nice to realize—Stacy was still a pretty woman.

"The story gets better," she told him. "The Union soldier she saved went on to become a congressman from Massachusetts—and he helped fight to stop the punitive measures toward the postwar South." She touched the ornament tenderly. "When I was little, her daughter, my great-grandmother, used to tell me that angels did influence our lives, and that they helped us sometimes, when we didn't even know they were there. I like to believe that, Bobby."

"Sure, Mom." He gave her a hug. He marveled at his mother, and he had to wonder if people did come together for a reason. His mom was the ray of hope and light. His father was the doomsayer. They could both be right; Mike MacDougal had seen all the worst that man had to offer his fellow man. Stacy believed in the goodness that she felt prevailed among most people.

"They've been out there a while," Bobby said. "I think I'll help. Maybe there's a bicycle out there and those misfits are dropping all the pieces!" With a quick kiss on the cheek, he left her, striding to the door for his heavy coat.

* * *

The snow kept falling in huge, wet flakes and the wind blew hard. Morwenna felt as if she was battling a storm in the Antarctic as she made her way to the garage. When she reached the side door, it was a fight against the wind to open it. But she suddenly felt desperate; she could see through the four-paned little window that Gabe was standing close to her brother by the trunk of his car.

The door flew open, slamming against the wooden wall of the garage.

Both men looked toward her; Gabe hurried over, drawing her in and closing the door.

"Hey!" Shayne said. "What are you doing out here? It's freezing!"

"I, um, you were taking some time. I thought you might need help," Morwenna said. She felt a little ridiculous, and then not. They didn't know Gabe Lange.

"Oh, we were just talking," Shayne told her. "I was showing Gabe some of the things for the kids."

"And we were discussing the merits of live action versus video games," Gabe said. "Shayne's right—this one electronic thingy he got for Connor is great—it's a word game, teaches you how to spell, and what the definitions for the words are once they're found. And you win funny little cars with each correct answer—virtual cars."

"Will it work—does it have to be downloaded?" Morwenna asked. "I'm surprised we still have electricity. The cable is down, and none of the phones work."

"It's battery operated, and doesn't need any downloads, so Connor will be able to play with it no matter, tomorrow," Shayne said. "I have to admit, I think the kids had a great time tonight—without electronic devices."

"Who knew you'd make such a great Mr. Mean?" Morwenna said lightly.

Shayne half smiled. "It was fun. I really had fun."

"Do you write children's books?" Gabe asked her.

"No! Oh, Lord, no," Morwenna said. "I'm an executive at an ad agency in Manhattan."

"Yeah, I heard that. But, people may do one thing for a living, and another on the side. I thought that maybe you wrote for children on the side. And I take it that you draw a lot?" Gabe asked.

"Sure. Sometimes. I always loved to draw."

"Once upon a time you spent a lot more time just doodling," Shayne said.

"I can't. I mean, I don't really have the time. Not anymore. Now I spend a lot of time in meetings," Morwenna said.

"You should illustrate," Gabe said.

She hesitated. She could have explained that she had intended to, things hadn't quite gone in the direction she had intended. "I don't really have the time," she said simply. "I can come up with the creatures, but I'm not sure what they should be doing. A story needs a beginning, a middle and an end."

"But you could work with someone else, right?" Gabe asked her.

"Sure," she murmured. "Maybe in my retirement."

"I guess we all do what we need to do in life," Gabe said. "You're good. And it's obvious that you love it. Maybe take a sketch pad on your next vacation."

"This *is* my vacation," she said.

"Morwenna is mourning the fact that she's not in Cancún," Shayne told him.

"I am not! I chose to be here," Morwenna said.

Shayne laughed and brushed her cheek with his knuckles, teasing her as he had when they'd been in high school. "Sense of duty, right, sis? Her lover boy is off in Cancún, and she must be dying to know what he's up to."

"Shayne, please, it's a mature relationship," Morwenna said.

"Ah," Gabe said knowingly. "Like an open relationship?"

"No! Oh, for God's sake, please. It's possible to have a relationship in which people remain monogamous when they're apart," Morwenna said.

"Sure," Shayne said, turning away.

"It is!" Morwenna insisted.

"I was agreeing with you, Morwenna. I'm sorry— I didn't mean to hurt you. I was just teasing, really," Shayne said.

"You didn't hurt me," she protested. *A lie! She was worried; if it had been a really good relationship, wouldn't he have told the others just to be adults and have a good time on their own because he wanted to be with the woman he loved at Christmas?*

Or were their values simply different? she wondered. It was hard to admit; she had come because of a sense of duty. But she had also wanted to come— Christmas to her had always been this house on top of the mountain. New Year's might be right for a wild jaunt, but Christmas meant being with the ones she loved. That didn't negate other values, she assured herself. It was just what it meant to her.

"I'm not a family member, but I'm glad that you're here," Gabe told her. "It's been nice to meet you."

She gave him a weak smile. *Really? I'd have thought about leaving you in the snow; I'm my father's daughter, braving the trenches of Manhattan in a state of continual suspicion.*

She wasn't sure what to reply.

"Well, you made a great Christmas elf," she told him.

"I'm going to haul in the first bag of stuff," Shayne said. He grimaced. "We were talking about putting the bicycle together out here…keep all the packing and stuff out of the house," he said.

"We were just about to start, and I'm afraid the reality may be as hard as the imagery we were playing with before," Gabe said.

"I'm good with directions. I'll help," Morwenna said.

"Okay, you two get started. I'll be right back. Or as soon as the wind will let me," Shayne told them.

Gabe got the door so Shayne could head out with a large canvas bag. She saw that the box with the bike parts was already on the floor, opened. "Where are the directions?" she asked Gabe.

"Right here," he said, handing her a sheet from the top of the box.

"Easy. A1 goes to A2, as soon as you have B1 connected to C1, and then, somehow, D2 has been thrown into the lot. Ah, there's E3!"

Gabe groaned, and started pulling all the pieces out of the box. They knelt down together to study the diagram.

Morwenna couldn't help but be aware of him as a

man, and she found herself wondering how she would have felt about him if they'd met under different circumstances. But, of course, this *was* a strange circumstance, and she was committed.

She had never been able to date casually. Of course, she'd dated Alex before they'd become a couple, and she'd found it awkward and difficult. Her friends in Manhattan had tried hard to teach her that every dinner didn't have to lead to sex, and that she wasn't obligated to have sex, but then again, didn't she want it now and then? In college, she'd had one relationship, and they had both been honest and committed, and then, at graduation, they had realized the bond wasn't strong enough for either of them to change their goals in life, and they had parted as friends. And eventually, of course, their calls had grown infrequent, and time had gone by.

Then, Alex had come into the firm, and the first time they'd gone out, she'd been smitten. She'd still held back until they'd been seeing each other for a few months, and the time had been right, and she'd believed that they both really cared about each other. She had to admit to herself, though, that they hadn't used the all-important four-letter word yet—love.

"Hand over A1 there, will you?" Gabe asked. "The body of the beast!"

She did so.

"Your brothers are really good guys," he told her.

"Love them to pieces," she said. "I just wish that…"

He looked up at her. "What?"

She laughed suddenly. "You're reminding me of how it was when we were kids. I could be ready to throttle

Shayne or Bobby, but if anyone else said something about them, I'd be ready to throttle that person."

Gabe grinned. "I guess that's the way it should be."

"I think that Shayne's current situation is just terribly painful. He really loved Cindy. I don't think he was a great husband. I mean, he's so dedicated to his patients. Oh, he adores his kids, but Cindy was the one who was with them most, and I think he's as happy as can be that he does have them for Christmas, but without Mom and Dad or Cindy, I don't think he remembers how to do Christmas."

Gabe found the "screwdriver included!" bag and nodded as he divided his attention between her and his task. "The most intelligent people in the world can usually look around and figure out what would fix things for someone else, and yet struggle with their own situation," he said.

"Genevieve broke my heart tonight. In her prayers, she basically asked God to put her parents back together."

"That's natural."

"And probably impossible. Cindy, I'm sure, thought long and hard before she left my brother."

"Nothing is impossible while we're drawing breath, kid," he said lightly.

"Then you believe in miracles, huh?" Morwenna asked him.

"If you think about it, life itself is a miracle. Sure, I believe in miracles." He grinned at her, pausing for a moment. "Just like your little play—miracles are out there. We have to make them happen."

"Well, you're just like Little Miss Sunshine, Pollyanna and a ray of light, all rolled into one," Morwenna said. "Life isn't like that. It's all messy, and complicated, and I'm sure that Shayne tried to fix things. Sometimes, when things are broken, they're shattered, and that's that."

He laughed and sat back for a moment, staring at her. "Wow! From what I can see, you all have a really good life going here. The three of you grew up with parents who really love you. They have their personalities and their opinions, but they love you, and it's obvious that every move they've ever made was with your best interests at heart. Shayne is doing what he loves for a living. You have a good job, even if it's not what you planned, and if you had any balls, you would do what you really wanted. Your problem with the fellow your brother referred to as lover boy or boy toy is probably the fact that you decided you needed *someone,* even if he wasn't the right one, and you're really not happy with yourself, so you're playing the game of trying to assemble the right pieces. Bobby—"

"Yeah, go on, pick on Bobby, the dropout!" Morwenna said, angry and about to get to her feet and leave.

"I was about to say that Bobby is the one on the right track. He knows what he wants—and he's going to go after it. His biggest fear is hurting those who love him while he's on the way. All that he needs is a little faith."

Morwenna frowned. "What are you talking about?"

"Your brother really is a brilliant musician. Have you ever really listened to him play? He's amazing. He wants to pursue it. But in your family music is a hobby. Bobby can make more out of it, he just feels he has to prove to all of you that he can do it before he really gives it his whole heart. But he's moving in the right direction."

"Well, thank you, Mr. Cop-without-a-badge-or-uniform!" Morwenna said. "And how do I fix my life?"

"Oh, Morwenna, that's so easy. Quit playing the game. Stop trying to fix other people, and support them, in whatever they need. Don't try to play any roles in life, and stop and think about what you really want," he told her.

"So simple!" she told him with heat. "So simple—and maybe you might want to think about life that way yourself! You're just great at pointing out problems. Surely you have something in your life that you're not dealing with. Maybe you should worry about yourself."

"I didn't mean to be intrusive," he said. "You're just good people—you should be happy."

"What is happy? I mean, who is happy every single minute?"

"Content, then. Happiness is going through life with problems, and yet knowing where you're going, and enjoying the moments that are filled with laughter and love."

I am happy! she thought defensively.

Was she?

She turned away from him. This time of year, getting together—it *could* be one of those times when they were just happy, and appreciating one another.

"Hey," he said softly, and she looked up at him. For a moment, she felt as if the fleeting seconds of time they shared, on the floor in the cold of the garage, were some of the most intimate she had ever known. His eyes were a green like the grass in summer. They seemed to speak in a whisper to her soul. She wanted to touch his face, and marvel that anything with such rugged appeal could be so tender and knowing.

She almost moved back. She liked him. And she was in a relationship, and she wasn't going to have any dreams about a stranger suddenly cast on their doorstep.

"I'm sorry," he said. "I can see that you all wind up in tangles because you do love one another so much. But here's the good—whether or not there is a miracle and Cindy and Shayne wind up back together or not, they're on their way to being the best they can possibly be. Cindy sent those kids here, right? Likely because she decided that they should have a real family Christmas, even if that meant it was one without her."

Morwenna sighed. "Shayne thinks she wanted quality time with the new love of her life."

"Well, of course he does. Someday he'll step back and rethink that."

"What's this about Bobby? He's my brother—what do you think you know about him that I don't?" Morwenna demanded.

"You should ask Bobby," he told her. "Hand me part D3a, will you, please?"

She did so. For a moment, she didn't really see him. She rose awkwardly, thinking about the things Gabe had told her. It was true; Shayne was hurting. And Bobby…

She wanted to talk to her brother. Alone.

"There we go!" Gabe said.

Startled, she looked back to him. He had risen as well; the bike was completely assembled.

"Wow," she said.

He grinned. "Not bad, eh?"

"Not bad at all. Now, all we have to do is get it to the house in this storm."

As she spoke, the garage door opened with a thud. Bobby, bracing himself, stood in the doorway.

"Thank the Lord! It's done, and I don't have to help," he said, eyeing the bike.

"That's the ticket," Morwenna said. She smiled at her younger brother. "Get here as soon as it's done. But you can help. We have to get the bike up to the house. Where is Shayne? I thought he was coming right back?"

"Connor called him from upstairs—he wanted a glass of water. And maybe he still believes in Santa, just a little, because he didn't want to come down the stairs—maybe jinx the possibility," Bobby said. "Shayne's with him now."

"Good for them both," Morwenna said, her voice a little husky. She realized that she was fighting the desire to cry. They did have their health. They had each other. People, good people, were out of work, starving in America and around the world.

She walked over to her brother and gave him a fierce hug. "I love you, Bobby." Then she hurried out of the garage and headed for the house.

Despite the cold and the wind, she paused. The bright lights of the Christmas tree shone out on the crystal-white glitter of the snow. It was beautiful. The warmth inside beckoned to her.

Life itself was a miracle.

And the beauty of the night, even in the wind and snow, was astounding. She smiled to herself, thoughts swirling in a real prayer.

Happy birthday, Jesus. And thank you.

* * *

"Easier said than done!" Bobby laughed. He had the back half of the bike; Gabe had the front. It wasn't even that big a bike; it was just awkward making their way through the snowdrifts to the house. When they reached the door, though, Morwenna was waiting, and they were able to walk right in, shedding snowflakes as they did so. Bobby stared at Morwenna, feeling awkward for a moment. He smiled at her.

She smiled back.

Shayne came down the stairs just as they entered.

"Hey! Great. That's amazing! It's already together!"

"Your sister reads directions well," Gabe said.

"Let's put that right here, to the left of the tree," Stacy suggested. "Shayne, you did a great job getting stuff here at the last minute for the children."

"Thanks," he said huskily. "Too bad I can't give them the one thing they really want."

"No, not Cindy," Morwenna said, walking over to Shayne. She stood on her toes and gave him a kiss on the cheek. "But they've got their dad, and you're a great dad, Shayne."

"I suck," Shayne admitted.

"But you're already working on not sucking," Bobby said. "So all is good! Mom, the tree looks great. Absolutely great."

"I just have to sneak up to my room when I'm sure Genevieve is deep asleep to get a few more things," Morwenna said. "I have a little dress-up set I'd bought for Alex's niece and a comic-book creature one of our clients gave me. My real gifts for the kids went through Cindy, of course, but they'll have something from me."

"I scrounged together a few old pieces, too," Stacy said. "They'll be good."

"Well, I didn't scrounge anything, but I have a Christmas-morning present for them, too," Bobby told them. He grimaced. "I wrote them a song."

"Their own song. Cool, really cool," Gabe said.

Mike MacDougal studied his son. "That will be great, Bobby. We'll all look forward to hearing it."

Bobby thought that his father sounded a little awkward; words of praise had always been hard for him. He smiled.

Stacy stretched and yawned. "Well, I'm to bed," she said. "It's been a wonderful Christmas Eve. Thank you all. Thank you all for being here with us."

Stacy walked over and kissed Morwenna, then Shayne, and then came to Bobby. There was something glittering in his mother's eyes.

Happiness, he thought.

He hugged her warmly in return. "Good night, Mom," he told her. "Thank you. It was a great Christmas Eve dinner."

"Glad you liked it," she told him. She turned, and paused, seeing Gabe. Stacy smiled warmly and gave him a hug as well. "Welcome to our home for Christmas. You're all set, right?"

"Your family has been great. I have more than I would have had anywhere," he assured her.

"Well, good night, kids," Mike said. He repeated Stacy's actions, giving each of his children a hug, and pausing in front of Gabe. He offered him a handshake. "Merry almost Christmas, Mr. Lange."

"And to you, sir," Gabe said.

Mike stared at him. "Aren't you worried? Your, uh, your prisoner is still out there—at large nearby."

"I will be vigilant," Gabe said. "I won't let any harm come to your family."

Mike wagged a finger at Gabe. "Trust me. *I* won't let any harm come to my family."

As his parents walked up the stairs, Bobby heard his father whispering to his mother. "What do we know? The guy could be a crook! We could wake up to find out that he's robbed the entire place. Or worse, we could *not* get to wake up at all!"

"Hush!" Stacy said.

But Mike raised his voice, intending to be heard.

"You know I always sleep with that shotgun by my bed. You never know when a starving bear is going to wake up."

"Bears hibernate, Mike, you know that," Stacy said.

Then they were upstairs and out of earshot. The three MacDougal children looked awkwardly at Gabe.

"Dad's been a prosecutor for a really long time," Bobby said.

Gabe laughed. "Hey, he's a bright man, and he's seen the worst. That's okay. It's not a bad thing to be prepared for—bad things."

"Yes, despite all the miracles in the world," Morwenna said, "they do happen!"

"So do good things," Gabe countered. As he spoke, the old grandfather clock in the parlor chimed midnight.

They all stood still, listening.

"Merry Christmas, bros!" Morwenna said then, and kissed Shayne and Bobby. She studied her brothers' expressions. "Merry Christmas," she said again softly.

"And I hope that your present is the future, and that it brings you all that you want—and deserve," she said. She moved quickly away, and walked over to Gabe.

She hesitated a minute, and then gave him a hug. "And you'd better not prove to be a lowlife thief or anything of the like," she told him.

She turned around to look at them all. "I'm going to grab those little gifts for the kids. And, then, I'm cuddling up with my niece to get some sleep. See you all in the morning."

She ran up the stairs. Shayne, Gabe and Bobby called after her, "Merry Christmas!"

They looked at one another. "I'm going to go on up and cuddle with my son, myself," Shayne said. "Guess I need to grab those chances when I get them," he said.

"'Night, Shayne," Bobby said.

Shayne paused in front of Gabe. "Merry Christmas. And thanks."

"Hey, I need to thank you all," Gabe told him.

Shayne nodded and headed on up.

"Top bunk or bottom?" Bobby asked Gabe.

"Whichever one you don't sleep in," Gabe said. "I could be dying of hypothermia right now. Or resting on a slab at the morgue. I'm delighted just to be indoors."

"Actually, we're lucky we found you. It's been a helluva good Christmas Eve with you around, stranger. Glad to have you," Bobby told him.

And it was true. What might have been tedious had been fun; what could have been arguments had turned to camaraderie and laughter.

He found himself turning to the tree. One of the golden glowing lights was touching the face of the little angel ornament.

An injured cop had turned out to be their Christmas angel, in his way.

"Want some water or anything before I turn out the lights down here? It won't be completely dark. We leave the tree lights on through the night. My mom used to say they were a beacon for Santa. And, of course, since we burned logs in the fireplace, she convinced us that Santa had a key."

Gabe laughed. "Nope, I'm good. Thanks. I'll head on up. Which did you prefer? The upper bunk, or the lower?"

"Top—but I really don't care."

"I'll crawl into the lower," Gabe said.

Bobby started around the house to check the doors and turn off the lights. When he returned to the parlor, he saw that Morwenna had set her extra gifts under the tree for the kids.

She was just walking back up the stairs.

"'Night, sis!"

"'Night!" she called back.

As she reached the upper landing, Gabe was just coming out of Shayne's room. Shayne must have supplied him with the flannel night trousers he was wearing.

Gabe and Morwenna almost ran into each other. Gabe was still shirtless, carrying the pajama top in his hands.

Morwenna seemed to have frozen there.

As had Gabe.

Bobby grinned.

Two such beautiful people; Morwenna in a long white flannel gown, raven hair flowing down her back; Gabe, appearing to have such strength.

"'Night!" Morwenna said, the sound almost desperate. She turned and fled into her own room.

"Good night," Gabe called after her.

Bobby grinned as he walked up the stairs. He thought that Morwenna had a bit of a crush on their visitor—and that the feelings were returned.

Gabe had already turned into the room. When Bobby entered, their visitor was in the lower bunk.

"Merry Christmas," Bobby said, crawling up.

"Yes," Gabe said thoughtfully. "Merry Christmas."

Bobby yawned. For a moment, he thought that if their visitor was a maniacal killer, he'd be the first to go.

But the guy wasn't a killer of any kind. He was certain. He didn't know how he was certain.

But, as the stranger seemed to be teaching them, sometimes, you just had to have faith.

Chapter 5

Morwenna woke up with a start. She could actually hear bells; church bells coming from the little village that was around the bend and down the mountain about a mile.

She started to move and realized that something warm was next to her, and she raised her arms quickly, hoping that she hadn't batted her niece in the head. She looked down at Genevieve, still sleeping soundly, little cheeks rosy and flushed.

She looked like an angel.

It had been nice sleeping with her; nice to wake up with a trusting little bundle of a child next to her. She rose carefully, trying not to awaken Genevieve, moved to gather fresh clothing as silently as she could and then headed into her bathroom to shower. As she turned on the water, she thought back to early yesterday morning, when she and Alex had stood in the shower together. They had teased and played, and it had been nice, and of course, he'd reminded her that she could still get on the plane with him—no matter what it cost, they could buy a ticket. She'd reminded him that he could forget Cancún and come with her.

But they'd parted anyway. He hadn't let her drive him to the airport; they were all going on one plane out of Kennedy, he told her, and Kennedy would be in the opposite direction. He wished her a wonderful Christmas, and sounded sincere when he said that she should enjoy her family.

She hoped she had sounded equally sincere when she had told him to enjoy Cancún.

Just a little more than twenty-four hours ago now and yet it seemed like forever.

As she stood under the warm spray of the shower, she wondered how her life in Manhattan could seem so far away. There had actually been moments when she hadn't really thought about Alex in Cancún, or really worried half as much as she might have. Well, that was probably thanks to the stranger, too; he seemed to be keeping them all on their good behavior.

And, apparently, he *wasn't* a maniacal serial killer, since she was pretty sure they'd all wakened that morning in their beds.

Dressed and ready for the day, she stepped back into her room. Genevieve was still sleeping.

Morwenna hesitated, and then quietly opened her bag. There was a wrapped gift there in her luggage, one she had forgotten to give Alex. She'd planned it as part of his Christmas stocking if he'd come home with her, since at the MacDougal house, everyone got a stocking.

It was a little box of her favorite men's cologne. She studied the prettily wrapped little package. She honestly didn't even know if Alex liked it or not. He'd said he did when they'd started dating. But then, at that time, if she liked something, he liked it.

It was cologne, she could replace it easily. She found a new tag and put Gabe's name on it, and the words *From Santa.*

Morwenna left the room and hurried downstairs.

There was no one in the parlor as she dropped the little gift under the tree, or in the dining room. Her mother, she knew, was up. But as she headed for the kitchen, she paused. She could hear her mother speaking to Gabe.

"It's my favorite day. My favorite day of the year. It always has been. I like my birthday just fine, mind you. Thanksgiving is wonderful, and so is Easter. But Christmas…I don't know. I always believe just a little in magic when it's Christmas Day," Stacy said.

"It's a lovely day," Gabe replied.

She started to move on in, but then hesitated; her mother spoke again, bringing up her name.

"I wish I could give that magic to my children," she said. "Morwenna…"

Morwenna tensed.

Eavesdropping was not at all nice! she reminded herself.

But she felt frozen in place.

"My daughter," Stacy continued, "I love her so much. And I don't know what happened. I think she forgot how to be happy. I think she even thinks she *is* happy most of the time, but…take a look at my husband. He's a rather suspicious fellow. Well, his father wanted him to be an attorney. I don't think he even liked the law at first—he went into the law because that's what the sons in the family did. Then, along the way, he discovered that he did have a passion for seeing that *victims* received what was right, and that those who hurt others must be put away. He did what people thought he should, but somehow he made it work on his terms. He seems gruff and hard sometimes, but when he wins a case and comes home having put away the bad guy, he's so happy! You're in law enforcement— you must understand some of the feelings he has, and how he can be up and down and frustrated. And when he doesn't win, I'm there to help him through the struggle. But with Morwenna…I fear sometimes that we hurt her. She's like a little hamster on a wheel, running and running. I worry that she's not going where she wants to be. Last night really brought it home to me. She's forgotten—and I think that most of the world forgets—that it's nice sometimes just to wake up and be happy for what we do have, and remember that *happy* isn't a constant state for anyone"

"Well, Mrs. MacDougal, I think you are wise beyond measure," Gabe told her. "And, to be truthful, I think that your daughter is very smart, and a very good person, and that she will find her way."

"Wenna!"

She turned, her cheeks reddening as she heard the whisper from the dining room doorway.

Bobby was there. He had pure mischief in his eyes and he shook his finger in a "no-no" gesture. He tiptoed up to her. "Eavesdropping? On your mother?"

She elbowed him in the ribs. "I wasn't eavesdropping!" she protested. "I just got here."

"Yeah, and you always walk around with your ear glued to the wall," Bobby said.

She elbowed him again. "Hey! Lay off the ribs, will you? There could be a hot girl in my future somewhere," he told her.

"Your future here? In this house?" she asked skeptically.

"No. But, my dear, just because the weather *was* so wretched we couldn't get out of the house and our little area, things always change! If the weather holds, we'll go down to the village. Gabe can get ahold of his headquarters and tell them that a con is running around somewhere, and we'll have a wassail drink at the old tavern later on. I think Mom wants to go to the cemetery and do her prayer thing there, and, of course, there's church tonight," Bobby reminded her.

"Ah, yes! Drive-in Mass."

"Gotta love Father Donaldson. He says that if he can get his parishioners into the church for twenty minutes and a quickie mass, it's better than no mass at all."

"Which works for Dad," Morwenna agreed. "I think Mom would like a service with more singing, and a sermon that's longer than 'Please, Lord, help team X win the Super Bowl!'"

"I think that Mom is just glad Dad goes to church, and agrees to her little MacDougal prayer service at the cemetery," Bobby said.

"You're probably right," Morwenna said.

Stacy came through the swinging door, smiling. "I thought I heard you two out here. Good morning. Good—beautiful—Christmas morning!"

Gabe followed her out of the kitchen, smiling to see them. Morwenna caught his smile—Lord, but it was a good smile. But he wasn't just a stranger, she reminded herself, there was something about him that made the odd little sensual twinges she was feeling seem just not right somehow.

Didn't matter! Soon she'd be back in Manhattan, running the rat race and spending time with Alex.

"Merry Christmas," he said.

"And likewise!" she returned. "You slept well?"

"Like a baby."

As Gabe replied, Morwenna's father came into the dining room. "Merry Christmas, all. The little ones up yet?"

"Genevieve was still sleeping when I got up," Morwenna said.

"Well," Mike said, "I imagine they'll be up soon enough. Is coffee on in the kitchen?"

"Yes, dear, I'll get you a cup," Stacy said.

But Mike MacDougal set his hands on his wife's shoulders and kissed the top of her head. "Thank you, Stacy. I can get coffee. You spoil us all."

"I'll take some, too, Dad," Bobby said.

"You can come in and fix your own coffee. I don't know what you take with it these days," Mike said.

As Mike disappeared into the kitchen, they heard a loud screech of delight from the parlor.

"Kids are up!" Stacy said happily, hurrying out.

Morwenna followed her mother. She paused though, in the doorway, her smile deepening, something tugging at her heart.

Connor and little Genevieve were in front of the tree, hand in hand, staring at the ornaments and the packages beneath. Connor had let out the whoop, having seen his new bicycle.

"Santa came—I told you he would come," Genevieve said.

Shayne had followed his children down the stairs and stood behind them, silent. Connor turned around and hurried over to him, throwing his arms around his father. "Thanks, Dad," he said huskily. "It was the only…like, *thing* that I wanted and kind of needed."

Morwenna felt her heart would break as she watched her brother put his hand gently on his son's head. "I'm afraid you won't be able to use it much for a while. I'm pretty sure the snow is piled high in Pittsburgh, too. And don't worry—you don't have to keep it at my apartment. You can keep it at your mom's house. You go back and forth from school there most of the time."

Connor nodded. "Thanks," he said again.

"Daddy, can I open something, please?" Genevieve asked. "Connor can see his bike! My stuff is all wrapped," she said.

"Ask your grandmother. She's our mistress of ceremonies," Shayne said.

Genevieve looked hopefully to her grandmother. "Go for it, Genevieve. In fact, why don't you and Connor hand out the presents. Hand them all to everyone first, and then we'll open in order of our ages, youngest to oldest."

Genevieve giggled. "That means me first!"

"And Connor second."

"Anyone else for coffee or cocoa?" Morwenna asked. "I can make it while Genevieve is handing out the gifts."

"I'll help you," Gabe said. He shrugged. "I'm not a family member—I can give out coffee and keep the kitchen going, and I'll enjoy watching all of you in between."

"You may be surprised," she told him. "But sure, help me hand out coffee."

Genevieve and Connor were already out by the tree, looking for names on tags.

Morwenna smiled as Gabe followed her into the kitchen. As she poured coffee into mugs, Gabe got the milk from the refrigerator and found a copper-bottomed pan hanging from the wooden overhead above the workstation in the center of the kitchen.

"Why don't I heat up the milk for the cocoa?" he said.

Morwenna went for the sugar, and looked over at Gabe. "This fellow that you were chasing—what had he done?" she asked.

"Luke DeFeo? He's been sentenced before—petty larceny. This time he stole the funds for the homeless from a church just outside Richmond."

"A thief, but not a murderer?" Morwenna asked. "Well, that's good to know, if this guy is running around the mountain somewhere."

"Not a murderer; but still a very dangerous man," Gabe said. He hesitated, adding the chocolate squares Morwenna provided to the heating milk. "Sometime this evening, thanks to your brother's kind medical care, I'll be able to head out and try to track him again. I really need to find him before the day is done."

"Why? What difference will it make when you catch him?" Morwenna asked.

Gabe looked at the milk and chocolate he was stirring. "Because he's especially dangerous on a day like today, that's why." He looked at her.

There was something about his words that seemed strange.

"Yes, I guess, what with all the presents. But I'm not sure you should head back out into the snow today," she said. "You seem to be absolutely fine, but you did take a nasty beating yesterday."

"I'll be fine," he assured her.

She realized that she didn't want their uninvited guest to leave.

"Gabe, we are the citizens you're supposed to be protecting, no matter the actual jurisdiction. If you're looking for someone who might be interested in stealing, you should hang with us most of the day."

"I will protect you from him," Gabe said, his tone almost fierce.

"I believe you will," Morwenna said. She felt awkward for a moment. "Mom likes to do a little service at the cemetery, and then we're heading down to the village tavern for a drink. And hey, we need some outside company, to divert us from ripping on each other," she said. "Kind of sad, isn't it? Most of us really love our families so much, and yet, we're cruel to one another in a way we wouldn't be with others. I guess that's because others would just walk away."

"That's one way to look at it," he told her. "Maybe, sometimes, we're mean to our families because they're the people who see what we don't want to admit to ourselves, and will love us no matter what."

"I think I'm just going to call you Mr. Sunshine from now on," Morwenna told him.

He laughed, stirring the hot chocolate mixture a last time. "Doesn't that have to do with the fact that you can see the glass as half-empty—or half-full?"

"Come along, Mr. Sunshine. The gifts are surely divided by now," Morwenna said.

They made two trips with the cups of hot chocolate and coffee, and then took seats on the sofa where their presents had been left. Morwenna quickly saw that she wasn't the only one who had found something for Gabe; he had a stack of four gifts.

He looked around the room. "You didn't need to do this! You gave me everything—by taking me in," he said.

Genevieve came to him and with her little hands pushed him down into his chair. "Santa knew you were here, Gabe. But I get to go first!"

Morwenna noted that her mother had done a good job whipping up stockings for the children at the last minute. Genevieve received Fruit Roll-ups, quarters for the games at the tavern and a pretty little set of silver earrings—probably something her mom had bought for herself, since she was always losing one earring. She was delighted. Her present from her father was a real working kids' stove and an electronic game. Stacy had wrapped up one of her collectible Cabbage Patch dolls, and the little girl was in awe of it, playing with it as Connor opened the rest of his gifts.

Then Bobby told them that his gift was a song, and he pulled out his guitar and sang to them:

Christmas morning, what a thrill, for Gen and Connor are here,
Pretty girl, handsome lad,
Giving us the best Christmas ever had!
Christmas Day, what a thrill, for Gen and Connor here!

Clever girl, brilliant lad,
When they're around, nothing can be bad,
Oh, it's a Gen and Connor Christmas,
How we love it, ever so dear,
Connor and Genevieve,
Ring the bells!
Light the lights!
When Gen smiles, all the world is bright!
Ring the bells!
Light the lights!
When Connor is with us,
The world is all right!
Oh, it's a Gen and Connor Christmas,
A Gen and Connor Christmas,
And Christmas Day
Burns so bright!

The kids, giggling all the while, pounced on Bobby, hugging him.

"Hey," Bobby cried. "Munchkins! Watch the guitar."

"Come on, Uncle Bobby. You're up next!" Genevieve told him.

"Okay, okay. Pummel the flesh, but not the guitar, eh?" Bobby teased. "Gen, you help me with that one. I don't wrap well, and I open even worse."

"You can't open a present badly," Genevieve told him, but she began tearing at the wrapping paper for him.

Bobby was also delighted with his gifts. His stocking had been filled with Pez animals, beef jerky, turkey jerky and more. His parents had gotten him a new, down-lined coat. Shayne had gotten him an electronic reader with a special music application, and Morwenna had gone out of her way wrapping up a gift certificate to a national-chain music store, nestled in a bed of guitar picks, strings and a tuner.

"Now you, Auntie Wenna!" Genevieve said. "Are you really bad at unwrapping, too?"

"Well, of course I am," Morwenna said, sitting her niece on her lap. "Go for it, girl."

First, the stocking. Morwenna's had sugar substitute, lip gloss guaranteed to prevent chapping in cold weather, nail polish and emery boards. Genevieve happily tore apart Morwenna's gifts for her. Morwenna oohed and aahed over her presents—a computer bag with just the right number of pockets, a beautiful black cocktail dress, a snow hat with matching gloves and a tiny little box.

"What's this?" Genevieve asked.

"I don't know. Open it."

Genevieve opened the little box. It held a delicate gold chain that held an angel or cherub, almost like the one on her mother's tree. It was a beautiful piece.

Morwenna looked around the room; there was no signature on the box.

"Mom, where did you find this?" Morwenna asked.

"I didn't. Mike?" Stacy asked.

"No, I didn't buy it, I'm sorry to say," Mike said.

"Not me—I'm the hat and gloves," Bobby said.

"I'm the computer bag," Shayne said.

"Santa Claus!" Genevieve announced.

"How curious," Morwenna said. She took out the chain and little medallion, and Bobby offered to fasten it around her neck. She felt it as it lay against her flesh, and touched it gently. "I'll figure out my secret Santa, guys. But thank you one and all."

"So who is next—Shayne or Gabe?" Connor asked.

"Gabe—I believe I'm older," Shayne said.

Gabe seemed humbled and appreciative as he opened his gifts. When he got to Morwenna's present, he smiled at her. "Uncanny! It's my favorite. But—"

"Hey!" Stacy said. "You're our guest. Please enjoy what little we have to offer. And, now, Shayne, it's to you!"

Shayne feigned excitement over his gifts and Morwenna wanted to make it all better for her older brother.

It was his first Christmas as a divorced man.

The kids went on to help Mike and Stacy open their presents, and then Stacy announced that it was time for a quick breakfast.

"But not too many people in the kitchen, please, or I can't get anything done," Stacy said. "Morwenna, you and Gabe can come with me. Bobby, you and Dad set the table. Shayne, gather up all the wrappings and get them into the garbage—all right, everyone?"

It was agreed. Stacy had her crowd well in hand; she turned on a Christmas CD, and everyone went about their tasks.

On egg duty with Gabe in the kitchen, Morwenna realized that he had put on a spray of the men's cologne she had given him.

She smiled. "Nice," she told him. She hesitated, staring at him. "Was the angel from you?"

"Angels are from above," he teased in return.

"But, seriously, was it? Was it meant for someone else in your life?" she asked.

"Was the cologne?"

"Cologne is easy—it's in every department store," she said.

He laughed. "Maybe angels are easy, too, if you just look."

She turned away, humming to the song on the CD, "O Little Town of Bethlehem."

"You don't sound at all like a sick hyena," Gabe told her.

"Anyone can hum," she assured him.

"Watch the eggs!" Stacy commanded.

They both laughed. Once Stacy pulled the toast out and Morwenna's father and brothers wound up in the kitchen and they all bumped into each other as they brought the food out to the table.

In a few minutes breakfast was all set up, and they gathered around the table, and there were several minutes of "Pass the toast, please," or "Can you hand me that plate of hash browns?" until all their plates were filled. Coffee and drinks were poured and passed, and everyone praised Stacy for a delicious breakfast, and then Bobby told the kids to go up and get their snowsuits on, threatening them with a snowball fight.

When the kids had gone with Shayne to get dressed for the snow, Stacy sat back with her coffee and said, "Bobby, play us something. Something Christmasy and magical."

When Bobby returned with his guitar, he perched on a kitchen stool and strummed a few notes.

"'O Holy Night,'" Gabe suggested.

Bobby nodded and played and sang. When he finished, Stacy stood and came over and kissed him on the cheek, tears brimming in her eyes. "That was really beautiful," she said.

"I've applied to Juilliard," Bobby said, wincing slightly as he looked at his father. "I may well not make it. I don't know how many incredibly talented people apply every year. But I know how you feel, Dad, and you won't be responsible for helping me. I've found a way to work through school."

"Juilliard!" Stacy said.

"Juilliard," Mike repeated, frowning slightly, clearly taken off guard.

"Juilliard is one of the most prestigious schools in the country, Bobby. I hope you make it!" Morwenna said, surprising herself with her readiness to step in for her brother.

"I'll know in the next few days," Bobby said, sounding amazed by her enthusiasm. "I missed the usual auditions, and had to get a special audience with the music school, but somehow, believe it or not, they were chock-full of pianists and violinists, and a little light on those auditioning for guitar this year. So…I'll know right after New Year's."

"Juilliard," Mike said again. He blinked. "Bobby, do you know how hard it is to make a living with a guitar? Every kid out there has one. Every kid dreams of being a rock star."

"Might as well dream big," Bobby said. He glanced at his sister, silently thanking her for the support she had offered him.

"It's not just a 'rock star' thing, Dad," Morwenna said. "You just heard him play a Christmas carol that was so beautiful, it made tears spring to the eyes."

"It's a hard, hard living, son," Mike said.

"I don't mind working hard," Bobby said.

Morwenna glanced at Gabe; of course, he wasn't a member of their family, and he hadn't said a word.

As she looked at him, though, she realized that he had known. Bobby had told him.

Mike stood. "We can talk about this later," he said.

Bobby stood as well. "We can talk all you want, Dad, but my mind is made up. I know you want the best for me, and I respect that. But if I don't make it into Juilliard, I'll find another music academy or institute. I'm going for what I want. I'm not going to be Morwenna, brilliant—and languishing in business meetings!"

"What?" Morwenna gasped. "Bobby, I have a great job—"

"Yes, you have a great job, and it should have given you a wonderful outlet for your work. But it didn't. It turned you into corporate America, which would be just fine, if what you really wanted was corporate America. You're not that old, Morwenna. Actually, that wouldn't even matter. You can start over at any time in life—you can start over and start drawing again. Anyway, sorry. I didn't want to ruin Christmas for anyone. I'm going to head out and have a snowball fight with the kids like I promised."

Indignant, Morwenna watched him go. She blinked hard; she had a great job. She might know herself that corporate America hadn't been her dream, but to the outside world, she had an enviable job. She had a great guy, Alex. This—this being home for the holidays— this was out of context.

She looked at her parents. They still seemed to be in shock.

Gabe stood up. "I think I'll join in the snowball fight," he said. He looked down at Morwenna and offered her a hand. "Are you coming?"

"Yes, I'm going to whack the sh—the stuffing out of Bobby," she said. She headed out quickly, and Gabe followed her. At the door she slipped into her heavy parka and gloves, and burst outside, gathering up a handful of snow before she reached the yard. Connor and Genevieve had been using one of the high-growing pines as shelter against Bobby's attacks. Morwenna headed straight for her brother with a big, wet, sloppy snowball.

She creamed him.

The kids, laughing delightedly, came from around the pines. Bobby was down in the snow, howling in protest and laughter, when Shayne came running out and pelted Morwenna. She stood, aimed back at him and hit Gabe in the chest.

In a few minutes, they were rolling in the snow, all soaked and still tossing snow and laughing.

Morwenna was vaguely aware of the crunch of footsteps on the snow; she was still startled when a deep, loud angry voice called out.

"Hey!"

They all paused, rolled and looked down the slope. A tall man in a Virginia State Police uniform and parka was heading up toward them.

"Hey!" he shouted again. "Stop right there, all of you. Don't move. You're harboring a *murderer!*"

Chapter 6

Stunned, half-frozen in the snow, Morwenna stared at the newcomer.

He was a tall, well-muscled man of about thirty, or thirty-five, dark-haired, with fierce dark eyes and a rugged-looking face.

He could have been a cop...

He was in uniform...

"Get up, Gabe!" he said, striding over to stand above Gabe, Morwenna and the kids where they were tangled together in their snow brawl.

Gabe stood, staring at the newcomer. "He isn't a cop," he said evenly. "He has the clothes because he stole them off me. He isn't a cop, and I'm not a murderer, and *he* isn't even a murderer."

Morwenna was vaguely aware that the door to their house had opened and closed.

Genevieve was clinging to her pants. Connor was just staring wide-eyed.

Shayne walked the few feet to the men. "All right, let's sort this out here," he said. "May I see your credentials? Are you armed?"

The man's eyes flickered for a minute, and then seemed to gleam with an angry fire. "My sidearm was lost when I grappled with this escaped convict. Trust me, he's dangerous. I need to take custody of him now."

"He's lying," Gabe said. "He's the convict. The thief."

The door to the house burst open and Mike, followed by Bobby, came bursting out of the house.

Mike had his shotgun, and it was aimed at the two strangers in their midst.

"All right, what the hell is going on here?" Mike demanded.

"I'm Officer Luke DeFeo of the Virginia State Police," the newcomer said, his voice filled with authority. "You've been deceived by a criminal, a convicted killer."

"That's a lie. He's the con. You found me half dead in the snow because we wrestled when I was trying to bring him back to justice. He stole my clothing, and gave me his," Gabe said. "You have to believe me. This man isn't a murderer, but he could prove to be the most dangerous man who ever walked into your lives."

"Don't be ridiculous! Put that gun down. You can see that I'm the cop!" Luke DeFeo said. He started walking toward Mike angrily.

But Assistant District Attorney Michael MacDougal was no man's fool. Morwenna was proud when her father cocked the shotgun and said, "I have damn good aim. You stay right where you are. Now, can either of you prove what you're saying? Let's see some ID."

"Look at what I'm wearing!" DeFeo snapped.

"I can see what you're wearing," Mike said. "And you may well be a cop, but this fellow has been with us for a lot of hours now, and we're all alive and well, and it seems that things are appearing in our house rather than disappearing."

Morwenna felt the little angel against her neck. It wasn't studded with gems, but it was still a nice piece. He had given it to her.

Suspicion crept into her mind. Had he taken it off someone else? Maybe someone now lying dead in the snow.

"You leave him alone!" Genevieve said, leaping up with the agility of a child and running to DeFeo. She gave him a hard kick in the shin.

DeFeo let out an angry yell, and almost reached for Genevieve.

"My sister!" Connor cried.

"You touch my daughter, and I'll kill you, cop or no!" Shayne announced. "Genevieve, get over here."

Genevieve obeyed without a murmur.

"Connor, you, too," Shayne said.

Gabe and Morwenna stood, dusting snow from their bodies, staring, and watching and waiting.

"You're going to find yourself under arrest for aiding and abetting a criminal," DeFeo said.

"Let's see your credentials," Mike said firmly.

"Hey, you can see I have a badge."

"And I'll see some ID, too," Mike said firmly.

DeFeo scowled. "I don't have my wallet—I lost it in the tussle with the con you're protecting!"

"If you have no real ID, I have no real proof. No one is going to intimidate me," Mike announced. "If I know one thing, I know the law. And I know that we don't have any way of knowing which of you is telling the truth. So—you. Yeah, you, Virginia State policeman. Raise your arms. Bobby, see if he has cuffs. And if he does, put them on him."

"Yes, sir! Yes, sir, Dad!" Bobby said, and sprang into action.

Morwenna had never seen her brother Bobby as the tough-guy type, and then again, she'd never seen lifesaving Shayne threaten someone's life. But then, his children had been threatened, and now Bobby was ready to spring to the fore.

"If your son touches me, I'll see that he does jail time, too," DeFeo warned.

"And if you touch my son, I'll blow your head off," Mike promised.

Bobby walked straight for DeFeo. "Listen, buddy, if you're legit, and we all wind up at a police station looking like fools, we'll take our chances in court," he said.

"You're risking your lives!" DeFeo said, standing still as Bobby found the cuffs he did have hooked to his belt and slipped them around DeFeo's wrists. "I'm telling you, he's the criminal. If you hold me against my will, he'll find a way to kill me, and slaughter you and your whole family in your beds!"

"We're not taking any chances," Mike said. "We're not taking chances—with anyone. I'm going to disbelieve both of you—until we learn the truth. Morwenna, get in the house. I have good nylon rope in the pantry. I want Gabe tied up, too."

Morwenna stared back at her father, blinking.

"Morwenna!"

She looked down at Gabe, stunned to realize that they really didn't know. If Gabe was a crook, he could be damn good at deceiving people. It felt as if the cold suddenly swept through her. *Why wouldn't he have killed them last night?*

Because he'd wanted his turkey, that's why.

Gabe looked up and said calmly, "Get the rope, like your father says. Keep us both tied up, and away from the house. Keep your family safe."

"But, Daddy," Genevieve began.

"Hush," Shayne said softly.

"Connor, Genevieve, come with me, please," Morwenna said, and hurried into the house. Stacy was standing in the parlor, looking out the window, her face knit in a worried frown.

"Morwenna?"

"That guy showed up, saying Gabe is a crook, and that he himself is a cop," Morwenna explained briefly.

"I was so worried when I saw your father get the shotgun. I tried the phone again, but that and the computer are still down, too. We've got electricity, but the television is all static. Morwenna, what are we going to do?"

"Keep them both tied up until we can get help," Morwenna said.

"We're on a mountaintop!" Stacy said.

"Mom, Dad has it covered. Besides, we have cars," Morwenna assured her.

Morwenna hurried back out, disturbed to see that her mother had come out to the front without even bothering to put on her coat. Though she had locked the door behind her, with the children inside.

She rushed by her, though. Gabe was standing a distance from Luke DeFeo. He offered his hands to her as she approached him.

"Behind his back!" DeFeo said. "Like you did me!"

"Wait!" Stacy said. She walked forward into the group. "One of these men is a criminal, and we really don't know what kind of criminal. But one of them isn't. And we're not breaking any arms or starving either of them. Tie their hands in front. We have the shotgun, and there are five of us adults here—we can watch them."

Shayne walked over to their mother. "Mom, we can't know how long until the phone and computer are back up, and it looks like we might have more bad weather coming in. We have to make sure that these guys are secure."

He pointed to the sky; it had been so blue.

Now, gray clouds were hovering. Strange gray clouds. Morwenna couldn't tell if they were coming from east or west, north or south. But they seemed to be converging over their house.

"We'll take turns watching them," Stacy insisted.

Gabe lifted his hands.

"Secure, Morwenna!" her father called.

"Yes, sir."

Gabe didn't move. She was close to him. The subtle scent of the cologne she had given him seemed to sweep around her. She looked at him. His eyes remained steady, green and open.

She looked down and tied his hand securely in a clove hitch. Her father, still keeping an eye on Luke DeFeo as Bobby recinched the metal cuffs, walked over to see that she had tied the knot correctly. He nodded his approval.

"Now what?" DeFeo asked. He let out a sigh. His voice changed to something that was just weary. "This is ridiculous, honestly. You all need to help me. You seem like a nice family. I don't want you running into trouble. If you don't see what's going on here soon, you will face jail time, and you've just afforded yourselves a miserable day. You're going to spend your Christmas staring at the two of us. I would have taken this wretch back to justice!"

"And how were you going to do that?" Mike Mac-Dougal asked him, his words barking. Morwenna imagined him in a courtroom. Her father, she knew, often managed to get people to say things they had surely never intended to say. "You came by foot."

"I'd have walked the bastard down the mountain," DeFeo said, his tone angry again. Then he seemed to gain control. "Look, you've all been fooled. You don't know what you're dealing with here."

"That's right," Shayne said quietly. "We don't know what we're dealing with here."

"And there's no way in hell anyone is walking any-one down the mountain," Stacy said. "It's a hard trip at best—hours walking in spring. There is weather coming in again."

"That's right, and you should let me handle it. We'll be out of your way in a moment," DeFeo pleaded.

"So…what now?" Morwenna asked.

Mike looked at the sky. "It may clear up soon enough," he said. "I can't tell right now exactly what the weather is going to do, but I think it would be foolhardy to try to reach even the village right now. Looks like we'll have to hold tight for a while."

"The garage and the shed," Stacy said. "You've got to keep them separated, and out of the wind. As soon as the weather clears, we'll get them both down to the tavern. They must have a way to reach some kind of help there."

"Bobby, you're on watch with Gabe. Shayne, you take DeFeo. The toolshed is empty. I brought the shovel and anything else anyone could use as a weapon into the house once we had a guest in the house," Mike said, glancing toward Gabe. "Shayne, you keep the shotgun. God knows what someone could find in the garage. I'll spell you in thirty minutes. Morwenna, you'll take over for Bobby."

Morwenna nodded. Neither of the men offered resistance as they were brought, handcuffed, to their respective places, Mike behind them both.

Morwenna looked up. The sky was darkening, and it couldn't have been later than ten in the morning.

As her father walked back to the house, he said, "I guess we'll have turkey later, Stacy. As soon as we can, we'll head down to Scott's Tavern with these two men."

Stacy started to walk into the house, and then she paused, looking at her husband. "The cemetery is on the way," she said.

"Stacy, we've got a criminal on our hands, and—depending on which man you believe—one of them might be a murderer."

Stacy straightened her shoulders. "The weather is going to be iffy all day. The cemetery is on the way to the village. It will only take a minute or two."

"Stacy," Mike said, "we could walk all the way and get rid of these two guys—"

"Mike! There's no guarantee that we'll have any communication when we reach the village, and no guarantee that there will be someone there who can watch them. This may remain our burden until we can get help up the mountain. The cemetery is on the way—we're going to stop briefly. We can keep the shotgun on them for one minute while we say a prayer. I'm still saying my Christmas prayers over my family's graves!"

With that, Stacy walked firmly into the house. Mike followed, but the door slammed in his face. He turned and looked at Morwenna and the kids. "All right, so the cemetery is on the way. How ridiculous is all this? One of us will stand with the shotgun trained on the two of them, and we'll say a prayer—in a graveyard. Christmas!"

He didn't say it, but Morwenna could almost imagine that he did.

Christmas! Bah, humbug!

"Look, I'm really sorry about this," Bobby said. And then, a little edge of doubt crept in. How often had he seen his father exhausted when a judge had ruled out key evidence and the jury was being swayed because the con could speak so persuasively?

Did he want to believe in this guy because this guy wanted him to believe in him?

"At least, I think I'm sorry," he muttered.

"It's all right. Man is a creature who must see something, hold it, find it tangible, before he really believes," Gabe said.

"He is wearing the uniform," Bobby pointed out.

"So he is."

Gabe walked ahead of Bobby into the shed.

There were two little windows in the small building, so light could come in. When there was light. Right now, the sky was darkening. Bobby ushered Gabe in; even out of the growing wind, though, the shed was cold. The garage, he figured, was just as cold. But there were lights in the garage; several of them. The shed had one overhanging bulb. Bobby turned it on. It provided some light. A concrete floor had been poured years before, but the concrete emanated cold.

Bobby sat down against the back wall. There were wooden shelves and brackets, but, as his dad had said, the few tools they usually kept there had been brought into the house. His father, he realized, was a smart man.

"Bobby, there's nothing in this shed I could use to hurt anyone, if I had that in mind," Gabe said. "You don't have to stay out here—it's freezing."

"Yeah, it's cold," Bobby said briefly. "When Morwenna comes, I'll see to it that you get some blankets out here. And, hopefully, this won't last long. We'll get you both down to the tavern, or we'll get law enforcement up here one way or the other."

Gabe nodded. "Hard to tell. If a bad storm comes in…" He grinned. "Too bad you didn't bring your guitar. I'd be entertained. Honored, actually. And, at least you've said what you needed to say to your family now. You've got it in you."

Bobby laughed. "You want to know the funniest thing? I had confidence, and I had hope. But now that I've spit it all out, I'm suddenly afraid."

Gabe thought about that for a minute. "Well, before, if you failed, you were just failing yourself. Now, in your mind, if you were to fail, you'd be failing them instead."

"Failing everyone," Bobby murmured.

"Personally, I think the only way you fail is if you never try," Gabe said lightly.

Gabe seemed comfortable enough—he was shivering a little—but he seemed relaxed. *Resigned,* maybe. They might have been having a conversation in a warm kitchen over a cup of coffee.

But, Bobby thought, if he'd wanted to, Gabe could suddenly...

Head butt him?

"I'm telling you the truth," Gabe said, as if reading his mind. "I'm the cop—he's the bad guy."

"And I want to believe you," Bobby said.

"I'm glad."

"But I can't let you go."

"I know that. I understand."

"My mother, my sister...my niece and nephew... they are all vulnerable here," Bobby said.

"I know. I told you...I understand."

Bobby walked away from the door, looking up at the sky.

It seemed the darkness was closing in all around them, but in the center of it all, there was light. Maybe the weather would break.

He prayed heartily that it would do so...and soon.

Shayne leaned against his car, the shotgun in his hand as he stared at the man in the Virginia State Police uniform.

The guy wasn't fighting with him. He was just leaning against the garage, staring at him with a hard look that made his features severe.

"I wish you'd listen to me," DeFeo said at last. "You look like an intelligent guy. You can *see* that I'm a cop, no matter what kind of story that guy gave you. Look, he's got that green-eyed thing going for him. He knows how to say all the right things. That's how he managed to break out. He was being transferred from one facility to another, talked the guard into letting him have a cigarette—then bashed the poor fellow's head halfway in. You should be worried—that's your sister, I take it—and your mom. And your children. You've got a lot at stake here. Think about it. He's been using you."

"He could have killed us in our sleep last night or robbed the place blind," Shayne said. "He didn't."

DeFeo sighed. "Ted Bundy."

"What?"

"Ted Bundy. The serial killer. You know he actually babysat for his neighbor, right? John Wayne Gacy—he was a clown. Hey, kids love clowns. Don't you get it—the good-guy thing is an act."

"He's been acting well enough to win an Oscar," Shayne said. His voice was even. His pulse was racing. What if they were wrong? This guy did look and sound like a cop. And he had a badge—but he didn't have an ID.

Shayne felt a cold sweat break out.

His children... What if they had entertained some kind of real crook, a killer? What if Gabe Lange was just what this guy said he was, and DeFeo had come upon them just in time to save them?

"Officer DeFeo," he said, "you may be all that you

say you are, but we don't know that any more than we know that he *isn't* who he claims to be. Just wait it out. When we can, we'll get to the authorities, and if we've wronged you, I'll apologize a thousand times over."

DeFeo shook his head, disgusted. "And what if he breaks out? Who is watching him next? Your sister, right? What if she falls for his act?"

"My sister isn't stupid."

"Not unless he talks her into being stupid. I'm sure he's given her all kinds of speeches on how wonderful she is at something, at how she needs to trust her instincts and have belief in herself and all that. That's his game. I know this guy—trust me," DeFeo said.

"She's not going to fall for any lines. She's in a relationship."

DeFeo laughed. "Sure. And he's making her doubt that relationship."

"This conversation is going nowhere," Shayne said. "I'm not letting you go."

"Just because your father is a fo—just because your father is misguided is no reason for you to wind up caught in the trap. You're taking a chance with your children. That's damn dangerous, my friend. I'm telling you, he's been using you. When he was done playing his game, when your mother had cooked everything up for a great turkey dinner, your family would have been done for. You really want to thank your lucky stars that I found this old house when I did."

"My father isn't a fool, DeFeo. He's done the one really smart thing—he's refused to take either of you at face value."

"Sure, that would be smart. If it weren't possible that Gabe would escape—and bring us all down, be-

cause I'm handcuffed and can't help you. Let's pray
he doesn't get his hands on that shotgun, that's all I
have to say."

Shayne didn't answer him. He couldn't help but listen to him, and he couldn't help but wonder if he was
right.

DeFeo was silent for a while. "Cute kids," he said
finally, as if he felt the need to talk about something.

"Yep."

"You here with them alone? Where's the wife? Oh,
sorry, you're divorced, I take it."

"Yep."

"I've been down that path," DeFeo said. "I guess she
was good to let you have them for Christmas. Usually,
after a divorce, the mother has the power. Fathers are
screwed. They pay all the bills, and the wives either
hound them for more support, or play games, not even
letting the dads see the kids."

"You're divorced?"

DeFeo nodded. "I spent hours working. She spent
them at a gym. Took off with a personal trainer, and
still got the kids. And I still pay the bills."

"I'm sorry to hear that. Hope you get them for a
while around the holidays."

"She claimed she wanted the holiday, and then,
turns out the trainer dude she was seeing didn't want
kids at the holidays. But, this year, I had to work, so
it was too bad." He smiled. "Sorry, I guess I shouldn't
be happy, but he took off for San Diego without her.
So, she has the kids for Christmas."

"How many?"

"I have the same thing as you—my boy is ten, and
my little girl is five."

"Mine are nine and six."

"Just about the same."

Shayne shifted, pulling his scarf higher around his face; it was really cold in the garage.

"What's the weather doing? Can you see from there?"

"It's still dark and gray, but no snow."

"I'm just saying, I hope your dad can carry through his plan to get us somewhere before Gabe Lange makes his break. Because, if not, well, it's going to be one hell of a Christmas."

"This is just ridiculous," Morwenna said.

Her father was pacing in the parlor; Stacy was trying to distract Connor and Genevieve with their new toys, but the children had picked up on the tension in the air.

Mike walked to the window. "The snow is deep. If it starts up again and we're walking down to the tavern, someone could really get hurt. I wish it would just do something, one way or the other."

"Well, it's like an ice age out there," Morwenna said. "I'm going to get blankets, and we'll go and spell Bobby and Shayne. They have to be half-frozen, and we've got to do something for both those men, since we've no idea which man is the good one."

"Gabe is really nice," Genevieve said. "How could he be a bad man?"

Mike looked at his granddaughter. He walked over to her, hunkered down and pulled her to him, hugging her tenderly. "Sometimes, it's just hard to tell. And sometimes, we have to really listen and weigh everything that's going on. Sometimes, wolves wear sheep's clothing," he said.

"I'll get the blankets, Dad," Morwenna said.

"There are plenty extra in the hall closet," Stacy said. "And there are some of those little hot packets that you all use when you go out sometimes. They're in a box in the closet, too. Hang on. I'll fix a couple of thermoses with coffee," Stacy said.

"We don't have to baby either of them, Stacy," Mike said.

"Keeping someone alive is hardly babying them!" she said indignantly.

"We're not killing anyone," Mike said wearily.

"I just have a bad time myself not believing Gabe," Stacy said.

Mike stood and looked at his wife. "We're not disbelieving him, Stacy. We're being safe."

He indicated the children. Stacy nodded. "But coffee won't be a bad thing."

"No, Stacy," Mike said. "You fix those thermoses."

Ten minutes later, Morwenna and her father started out of the house, each holding a thermos, a blanket and a handful of heat packs.

As they neared the garage, Mike warned, "Morwenna, take care. Please. I don't think that guy could possibly find anything in the storage shed to hurt anyone with, but…remember, words can be a dangerous weapon. *Kind* words can be dangerous. That man was a guest in our house…he made us all laugh. But it could have all been a lie. Don't fall for anything, please?"

"I'm not going to fall for a man I don't know. Come on—you know that I'm involved with someone else."

He was silent as they walked for a minute; she could hear the loud crunching sound their feet made in the snow.

"And I know that even while you've cheerfully explained to us why this 'someone else' isn't here, you're trying to sell yourself on the same explanation. Just be careful. I can see that Gabe Lange could be a very attractive man."

"Dad! I was raised by a prosecutor, and I live in Manhattan. I'm nearly as suspicious of all humanity as you." She kissed his cheek, and turned, heading for the shed.

Bobby hadn't closed the door; he was standing in the door frame, hugging himself, and looking as if he was nearly shriveled with cold.

"Go back to the house," she told him. "My turn to take over."

He nodded to her gratefully. "That blanket for me?"

"No, you're heading to the house. It's for Gabe."

"Oh, yeah, makes sense. You going to be okay? You're sure?"

"Fine. Go," she said.

She gave him a little shove and looked into the shed. Gabe was seated on the floor against the wall, and like Bobby, he was curled in on himself as much as was humanly possible.

"Here," she said, tossing down the blanket. He tried to catch it awkwardly with his tied hands. She came close enough to drape it over him, and then carefully stretched out her arm to give him the heat packs. "I have coffee for you, too, but you can put those down your shirt. They'll warm you up for a good hour or so, maybe even two hours."

He nodded, apparently familiar with the little beanbaglike sacks. Morwenna could appreciate her mother's wisdom in seeing that the men were handcuffed with their hands at the front of their bodies rather than be-hind; she wasn't sure she would have wanted the task of trying to slip the heat packs down into his clothing. It was disconcerting to come even this close.

He managed to get the packs beneath his clothing. Keeping her distance, she handed him the thermos.

"Thanks," he told her. He opened the thermos and took a long swallow of coffee.

"Makes a man feel like he might thaw out again one day," he told her.

"Sure," she said.

"That's better. May be the best coffee I've ever had," he said.

"I'm sure my mother would be glad."

"How's she doing?" he asked.

"My mother? She's fine, of course. We're all going to be fine. We'll watch both of you until we can get you down to the tavern," Morwenna said.

"Thank God," he murmured.

She stared at him.

"I've been telling you the truth. And when we reach the tavern, you'll know that. Is the weather clearing?"

Morwenna hesitated. It had grown quite dark earlier, but it did seem now that it was beginning to lighten.

"I think so," she said.

"Then we'll be able to leave soon… How about you?" he asked. "How are you holding up?"

"I'm fine."

"And I'm sorry. This is a tough Christmas for you."

"No, it's not."

"Sorry, I just meant—"

"You meant the fact that 'boy toy,' as my brothers

call him, didn't bother to come with me," Morwenna said irritably.

"Look, I'm sorry."

"I know, sure. And maybe he's just not the right one for me. And maybe he's enjoying beach bunnies in Cancún."

Gabe grinned. "If he is, he's a fool."

"Your lips to God's ear!" she said.

He laughed. "Something like that. Honestly, I'm just anxious that we move before...well, he's a tricky devil, that one. DeFeo. I'm grateful that your family didn't just believe him. I'm afraid that he'll pull something, and everyone will be in danger."

"I thought he was just a thief."

"You can never trust a cornered thief."

Morwenna stepped away from the door for a moment, studying the sky again. It did seem to be clearing, but not in the ordinary way. It appeared almost as if the light was breaking right above the house, like a giant golden ball, and rays of darkness ebbed into it, and then curled back, ebbing away again.

"We should be able to go soon," she said curtly.

She frowned. The front door to the house had opened. Genevieve, cradling her precious teddy bear, was stepping out of the house alone.

"What the heck is she doing?" Morwenna wondered.

Gabe stumbled to his feet, coming to the doorway.

"No!" Morwenna called suddenly.

Genevieve was trying to come out, to see for herself what they were doing. Whatever distraction her mother had been employing with them, it wasn't working.

The little girl was sneaking out—and trying to make sure that she wasn't being seen.

Morwenna could see that her niece meant to approach the shed from the cliff side. Since she was trying not to be seen, she was running around in a wide fashion; she knew that she wasn't allowed to go too far around the house, and yet it suddenly seemed as if she didn't remember. She was a child—a curious child. Morwenna wasn't half as angry as she was afraid.

If she went too far, which she could easily do in the snow, she'd be on uneven ground, and could tumble down a hundred feet or so.

"No!" Morwenna cried.

Too late.

Genevieve let out a shrill scream as she stepped into the snow…and hit nothing beneath it. As Morwenna bolted across the yard, Genevieve began to fall.

Chapter 7

"We can go out soon," Shayne heard his mother say. She'd been sitting beneath the tree with Genevieve, polishing her nails with a pink color from the package Morwenna had given her, when Shayne had first come in. He thanked God for his mother; she loved his children and she was good with them.

But now, coming back to the parlor from the kitchen, Shayne saw that Stacy was looking out the window. He knew that she was anxious. The kids were growing increasingly restless. Of course, if it was storming, they knew they had to stay in. But they'd been anxious to help with the turkey dinner, and now, Stacy wasn't cooking, and Christmas Day had taken a drastic turn.

"The clouds—or whatever!—are just sitting up there," Stacy said, staring out at the sky. "It's just gray and…actually clearing, maybe."

She turned around suddenly.

"Genevieve?"

Connor was playing with the electronic game he'd gotten. He didn't look up.

"Connor, where did Genevieve go?" Stacy asked.

Connor looked up. "She was right here," he said, frowning.

Stacy looked back to the window and gasped.

"Oh, my God! She's on the side path!" Stacy cried.

Shayne bolted for the door and threw it open, unaware of the blast of frigid air that hit him. Genevieve had disappeared beyond the snow.

"My God!" he cried, and raced to the side path that was so pretty in summer, so treacherous in winter.

"Genevieve!" His daughter's name tore from his throat.

In an instant, a fraction of a second in time, he realized that he'd been a bitter fool; that even with the pain of the divorce, he'd been the luckiest man in the world. He had two beautiful, healthy children, and they were worth everything in the world.

And now...

As he ran, he could see his sister coming from the opposite direction. And someone was behind her, and then, overtaking her.

Gabe Lange.

Hands still tied, he was moving like cannon shot, a blur in the snow and the gray. Then, he cleanly disappeared.

He had pitched himself down the ledge, toward Genevieve. Morwenna screamed and followed him.

Shayne heard his heart thundering, heard the gasp

of his breath as he reached the path and beyond; the ledge. And he stopped himself in time.

Gabe had managed to get himself down the slope and wedged next to some kind of brush; he'd prevented Genevieve from tumbling farther with the length of his body. He was struggling to keep his grasp on whatever bush or outcrop of rock was beneath the snow. And Morwenna was just above the two; he could see the branch she held—naked and thin, stripped bare of green, as if it were a skeletal hand reaching for her instead of the other way around.

"Hold still! I'll get rope!" Shayne shouted.

He turned to head back to the house; his mother was behind him, terror in her eyes. She was ready to pitch herself down the mountain, but Shayne grabbed her shoulders.

"Mom! The rope, the cord of nylon rope in the kitchen—go get the whole thing, quickly, please!"

"Oh, Shayne!" she cried.

"Mom, go!"

She turned and fled back to the house; he'd never seen her move so fast.

"Hang on!" he called down the slope.

"Hanging on!" Gabe called up.

Bobby and Connor came running out behind Stacy, who now had the rope. Shayne looked around; there was nothing close enough that was steady and stable to work the rope. Bobby hurried to him, seeing the problem. "You and me, bro. You and me!" he said.

He nodded. "I'm bigger. I'll be the anchor, you the control."

Bobby didn't argue with him; they had perhaps seconds before something down the slope began to give.

He expertly knotted the nylon around himself while Bobby made a loop with the other end.

Bobby stood at the precipice, testing his footing. He called down to Gabe. "I've got a loop—coming your way."

Shayne angled himself down on the ground, using his weight as an anchor as Bobby tossed the rope down. It fell almost to Genevieve on the first try, and Bobby cursed beneath his breath. Shayne lowered his head, praying. He heard his sister cry up. "Bobby, I've got it. It's good. I'm getting it to Gabe and Genevieve."

"Got it!" Gabe called.

Shayne heard Genevieve's terrified tears then, and he winced, gritting his teeth, digging in farther. The ground was so slick, with patches of ice beneath the snow. He felt something on his legs; his mother had thrown herself down into the snow, too. They looked at one another, and despite his terror, he offered her a weak smile. "Thanks, Mom. We're going to do this."

She nodded grimly.

"I can't! I can't!" Genevieve cried. "Auntie Wenna, I'm so scared."

"Let Gabe get the rope around you. Your daddy is up there. He's going to get you."

"Bobby?" Shayne asked.

His brother was hunkered down, trying to guide the rope, but Bobby glanced at him. "Gabe is getting the loop around her. Morwenna is talking to her, assuring her."

Shayne was aware of the soft sound of sniffles near him. He looked around. Connor was just standing there, frozen as he watched, too little to help, too big not to know what was going on.

And he was surely blaming himself that his sister had slipped out.

"Okay!" Morwenna called up. "She's secure!"

Bobby started to pull on the rope. Shayne heard Genevieve sniffling and crying again. As Bobby secured the rope, Shayne began to inch backward.

Bobby swore suddenly; Shayne saw Connor make a dive.

"What?" he cried hoarsely.

"It was stuck—Connor slipped it. We're good. Keep moving."

His daughter wasn't even heavy; she was a little thing. And yet he felt as if he strained as he never had before, as if each millisecond was years in the making.

"I've got her!" Bobby cried, and Shayne dared look up again. Bobby was falling back from the ledge, Genevieve in his arms. Shayne lowered his head, trying to stop the shaking that had seized hold of his body.

Thank God, thank God, thank God, thank God...

His instinct was to rise and grab his daughter; he knew he couldn't do so. He called out to his mother. "Mom, get Gen. Get her inside, please. Connor, get Gramps. Get him out of the garage—now, please, Connor."

He heard the footsteps in the snow. Morwenna wasn't heavy—maybe a hundred and twenty pounds. But the snow was slick, and the hauling was hard. "Bobby?"

"I've got it back down. Morwenna has the rope... it's around her. Now, Shayne, now, I'm hauling it up."

Again, Shayne began his backward crawl in the snow. He kept fit; being a physician had made him do so, but he felt every muscle, and it seemed every speck of blood and bone in him, ache with the effort.

As he thought he might not make it, his father came running across the snow; he reached Bobby's side and took on some of the weight, and Shayne inched backward again.

He heard his sister cry out. "I'm here—I've caught the ledge. Just…your hand, Dad."

Shayne looked up again. Mike MacDougal had Morwenna in his arms. The two of them fell backward in the snow, Morwenna half laughing and half crying in their father's arms.

"We've still got Gabe down there!" Bobby reminded them all.

"If you were smart, you'd leave him there."

Shayne twisted to see who was talking. Of course, Mike had left his post at the garage door; Luke DeFeo had followed him out.

"If you're really law enforcement," Mike said, "you'll remember that you catch the criminals, and the justice system sees to punishment."

"And if you're an ADA," DeFeo countered, "you know that half the scum of the earth winds up in court—and then walking."

"Shayne, you ready?" Bobby asked. "Rope is going down again. Can you handle it?"

"Yes," Shayne said.

And yes, he would.

"Go! You've got Dad to help you lever the weight."

This time, it was going to be really hard; Gabe Lange was at least six-two, and had to weigh a well-muscled two hundred–plus pounds.

"Damn!" Bobby swore. He'd not gotten the rope down far enough.

As he pulled it up to toss it down again, they all heard the cracking of a branch, as loud as thunder in the crisp and silent air of the tension-filled winter morning.

"Hurry!" Morwenna breathed.

"Got it, got it," Bobby assured her.

He tossed the rope again.

They heard Gabe shouting from below. "I have it!"

Just as the echo of his words died, they heard a crack like a gunshot; it was the end of the bush that had broken Gabe's fall down the slope.

Shayne felt himself jerked forward as Gabe's weight fell fully on the rope.

Morwenna screamed, throwing herself on Shayne to further anchor him; Mike lunged forward, catching the rope with Bobby, and they both leaned back, trying to brace their boots against the slick white snow.

"Wenna, back…inch back little by little," Shayne said.

She obeyed him; she wasn't much on size, but the fact that she was there with him, clinging to him as if he were salvation itself, gave him strength. She braced his legs, moving as slowly as a snail, adding weight to his anchor as he painfully wormed his way back, feeling as if his shoulders would break and his spine would snap if they didn't make it soon.

But then, just when he thought he wouldn't make it, the pressure eased up. He and Morwenna had been trying so hard to keep moving that they actually slid backward a foot when the tension on the rope eased.

Again, he dared to look up. Mike had dragged Gabe up the last few feet. And now he, Bobby and Gabe were lying halfway entangled with one another by the slope, gasping for breath, laughing with relief and congratulating one another.

Shayne rolled to his back and looked up at the sky. It had cleared; the dark clouds were gone.

He glanced to the side. Still handcuffed, Luke DeFeo was looking on.

"He's a damn good actor," he said quietly to Shayne.

"I don't give a damn if it was an act or not," Shayne said. "My daughter and my sister are alive."

Morwenna, showered, changed and headed downstairs. She could hear her father speaking to her brother Bobby, and she stopped before reaching the parlor.

"He showered, got into dry warm clothes and let me put the ropes right back on him," Bobby said. "Dad, I just can't see how the man could be any kind of killer."

"I have to admit, Bobby, I just don't see it either. But the thing is, we still don't *know*. What if DeFeo is right?"

"Dad, Gabe pitched himself over a cliff to save Genevieve," Bobby said.

"So did your sister," Mike said huskily.

"Morwenna is my hero, Dad. But she's Genevieve's aunt. Gabe was ready to give his life for a little girl he just met."

She heard her father sigh deeply. "I know that, Bobby. But the sky has cleared. We're getting these guys down to the tavern. Someone there will have some way to communicate with the rest of the world. And if we're right, and Gabe is a good guy, we'll know it then."

Morwenna hurried down the stairs.

"Where are our—prisoners now?" she asked.

"In the kitchen," her father told her.

"With Shayne?"

"Shayne is trying to make Genevieve and Connor understand that they still have to learn to listen to what they're told," Bobby said.

"Then who is watching the prisoners?" she asked.

"Your mother," Mike said.

"Mom?"

Mike grinned. "Don't underestimate the power of a mother and grandmother, Morwenna," he told her. "She's grateful to Gabe, but she's hard as nails when she wants to be. She knows we're all going to start down to the tavern."

Morwenna stared at her father and Bobby with surprise, and then hurried into the kitchen.

Both men were seated on stools by the island workstation with steaming cups in front of them. It wasn't coffee; Morwenna smelled the aroma of chicken soup.

Stacy was seated away from them at the far end, the shotgun in her hand.

She glanced at Morwenna as she entered. "Make sure you're dressed good and warm," she told her daughter. "We're going to leave as soon as everyone is ready."

"We're walking down, I take it?" she asked her mother, eyeing the two men. They were at opposite sides of the table, but Stacy had seen to it that neither could possibly reach out and grab her—or the shotgun.

"We have to. There isn't a plausible path a car could make anywhere on the mountain right now," her mother said. "Yesterday was dangerous, and there's been more snow since then. Last night, late in the night, I woke up, and I saw that it was snowing again."

Morwenna couldn't help but look across the table at Gabe. He looked at her with a grin and a shrug.

"On this walk, you'd better keep a close eye on Gabe Lange," DeFeo warned. "Don't you people see? He figured that once he'd saved the little girl, you'd be so grateful, you'd untie him."

"He could have died," Morwenna pointed out.

"Yes, but he's facing life in prison or a death sentence if you get him down the mountain," DeFeo said. "The Commonwealth of Virginia still carries out the death penalty when the judge determines that it's appropriate. And you people still don't know the half of what he's capable of."

"We've established that," Morwenna said.

"Fine—take your chances walking down to the tavern," DeFeo said.

"That's what we're doing," Stacy said firmly.

"Stacy!"

Mike's voice sounded from the parlor.

"Yes, Mike?"

"We're ready. Head them on out," he called.

"You heard my husband," Stacy said. "Rise slowly and carefully, gentlemen, one at a time, please, and keep your distance from each other as we head out."

The men rose. Gabe stared at Luke. "After you."

"No, no. I wouldn't be so rude. After you," DeFeo said.

"DeFeo, you first!" Morwenna said. "And I'll be behind you with a frying pan, and trust me, I actually know how to use one on someone's head!"

"Careful not to get in my line of fire," Stacy said lightly.

DeFeo started out. For a moment, Morwenna thought he was going to make a lunge for the knives in the wooden holder on the counter; she quickly made good on her threat and reached for the copper-bottomed frying pan above her head, but it appeared he had just stumbled; he righted himself, balancing against the counter as he headed out.

In the parlor, Stacy handed the shotgun over to Mike. Shayne had brought the children down, dressed in dry snowsuits for the walk down to the tavern. Genevieve was clinging to Connor; Connor had an arm around his sister. She was still white-faced and silent.

Morwenna knew that Shayne had to have done something to discipline her, no matter how grateful he was that she was alive. What she had done was against what she'd been told, and she had certainly been terrified by her misdeed.

Still, she offered her niece a smile. Genevieve looked up at her brother, and then ran to Morwenna, burying her face against Morwenna's thigh.

"Sweetie, we're all right," Morwenna said gently. She lifted the little girl, and looked at Shayne. She didn't think that her brother had been too hard on his daughter.

"Head on out," Mike said grimly.

Bobby led the way; Morwenna followed, Genevieve in her arms, Connor close behind. Ahead of the others a little, Morwenna asked Genevieve, "What made you run out like that? Daddy told you never to go near the path in winter."

Genevieve didn't answer. She laid her head against Morwenna's neck.

"Sweetie?"

"I had to make sure you didn't hurt him."

"Hurt—Gabe?"

Genevieve nodded.

"What made you think someone was hurting him?" Morwenna asked.

Genevieve looked up at her without speaking.

"She decided to look at the angel, and she dropped it, and she was all freaked out for some reason," Connor said, shaking his head with the wisdom of his older-brother years.

"Honey, the angel on the tree is just an ornament," Morwenna said. "And no ornament in the world is worth risking one pretty little hair on your head."

"It didn't break," Genevieve whispered.

"Well, that's good. But it doesn't matter."

"It did matter. I almost broke it," Genevieve said. "We should never hurt our angels. Angels are there to protect us."

"She's just not going to make any sense," Connor said sagely.

"I understand," Morwenna said, smiling. "But the ornament didn't break, and it is an ornament, Genevieve, a pretty ornament that makes us think of angels. But it's all really all right."

"Follow me—I know the road best," Bobby said. He looked back at her and grinned. "I am the baby, you know. Adult baby now, of course, but I've spent the most time with the folks around here lately. I'll keep you from sinking into the snow." He frowned, arching a brow to Morwenna. "How long do you think you can carry her?"

Morwenna wondered that herself. The snow was deep, at least two feet, and every step they took was something of an effort.

"I think the snow may be taller than she is," Morwenna said.

"We can trade off," Bobby assured her.

Morwenna turned back. Shayne had positioned himself between DeFeo and Morwenna and his children; Gabe followed DeFeo, and her mother walked by her father's side at the rear.

She shifted Genevieve's weight. It was true; Genevieve might be a little bit of a girl, but she got heavy quickly as they floundered in the snow. The path, even with Bobby leading, was rough; there were patches of ice, and he warned her about them as he slipped and slid his way in the lead. They were going downward, and though, beneath the snow, the road was decent, it was bound to be difficult going.

Her arms began to ache, but she was determined to make it another ten minutes; Bobby was the lead, testing the ground. She was afraid that Shayne would wind up with muscle spasms, after all that he'd been through, dragging everyone back up the slope. Her father had the shotgun, and she was afraid that her mother would snap somewhere along the line. Stacy could be so strong—but how strong?

"We are idiots, you know," Bobby said.

She looked at him, smiling. "I'm certain we often are—on many levels. But why are you saying that?"

"We have little sleds! Why didn't we bring one of the sleds—we could have pulled the children."

"Because we weren't thinking. Because we don't know who is a convict and who is a good guy."

"All right…but we should have thought of the sled," Bobby said.

Morwenna hugged Genevieve more tightly.

She winced, thinking of the horrible minutes she'd been caught on the ledge. First, trying to get Genevieve up. She'd never imagined what it could be like to be so terrified for her own life, and even more afraid for the life of the little girl. Terrified, and frozen.

Gabe can't be bad! she told herself. *She could recall his words; she could almost hear his voice aloud as she remembered the way he had assured her: "It's all right. I've got a hold here that's solid enough for a few minutes. I've got Genevieve. Just get the rope… there, you can do it. Have faith in yourself, Morwenna, you can do it."*

And still, when DeFeo spoke, warning them that people could appear to be so many things that they weren't, doubt crept in.

He could have let Genevieve go; he could have even reached for her, and killed her on the ledge.

Ah, but then what would he have done? As DeFeo said, he was securely "handcuffed" by the rope. He would have died himself on the ledge, with no one to haul him back up.

He'd never *had* to go over the ledge; he'd risked his life to do it.

But if there was the possibility he was facing a death sentence…

Doubt!

Why was doubt so much easier than faith? Or, could doubt and care be associated with simple intelligence.

And where the hell did instinct fit into it all? Her instinct was to trust Gabe, but could it be that people were too easily led?

"The cemetery is ahead on the left!" she heard her mother call out to Bobby.

"The cemetery?" she asked incredulously.

Bobby turned to her.

"Mom still intends to say her Christmas prayers at the family grave site and tomb, come heaven or hell!" Bobby told her.

"There's too much snow! We won't even see the graves," Morwenna protested.

"You try to tell her that!"

The old stone wall of the little cemetery in the mountains was, at least, still above the snow. They reached it in about a minute, and Morwenna realized that Bobby had kept them on a straight-and-narrow path, following the line of the road. There was a curve in the wall ahead—the entry, which could be accessed by cars when cars could get on the road.

With any luck, she thought, *the gate would be locked!*

But the gate wasn't locked.

Bobby looked at her. "Not our lucky day," he said lightly.

Despite the fact that the gray clouds that had hovered earlier had moved on, the cemetery seemed shadowed and eerie. It lay beneath the naked and fragmented branches of trees, with only an evergreen here and there to remind the living that spring would come again.

The snow lay heavy over many of the graves, and they were clearly the first ones to brave the road into the graveyard that day. The tips of a few stones just peeked over the snow in some areas.

Bobby was careful to keep them on the roadway through the graveyard—that way, at least, no one would trip over any of the stones, markers or memorials that lay beneath the blanket of white.

"Just ahead," Connor murmured.

Morwenna was glad; she was going to have to trade off with someone. The world was icy cold; she could see her breath coming from her in a fog, but her arm burned like a fiery rod, the muscles giving in after the long walk.

She paused for a minute, staring ahead. Her mother's maiden name was Byrne; the name, she had been told, meant raven, and a large raven stood guard on the wrought-iron fence that led to the little vault and the graves that surrounded it.

High atop the vault, there was a beautiful marble angel. The angel wasn't lowered upon one knee in sorrow, but rather seemed to stand tall against the wind, robes and wings flying behind it as it proudly faced the world. She'd always liked the angel. She wished, in fact, that she'd at least draw something so beautiful at some time in her life.

Bobby pushed hard at the wrought-iron gate; it creaked and squealed, fighting against the snow as it scraped open. Morwenna entered the enclosed area, and set Genevieve up on one of the steps to the vault that was still higher than the snow.

She heard the others pile in behind her, and she thought of the incongruity of their group there; the kids, her mom, determined to say her Christmas prayers at the family grave site, and her father, ready to pray with her mother while still keeping a sharp eye on their prisoners, his shotgun at the ready.

"Mom?" Morwenna said.

Stacy moved forward to the steps, hugging Genevieve to her side, and looking out at them. "Christmas Day, again, and we're all together, and I'm so grateful. I want to thank God for the family that came before me. I want to tell my folks that I loved them very much. And I want, most of all, to say thank-you for the family that I have now. Guide us, be with us. Keep us safe."

"You're definitely not safe yet," DeFeo said quietly.

"Will you stop—this is a sacred time for my mother!" Shayne snapped angrily.

As he spoke, they were startled as a large black bird suddenly shot through the trees, letting out an eerie shriek. Morwenna ducked as it flew by them.

Stacy watched the bird without flinching. "It's a raven!" she said, and laughed. "Mike, I think that the family is grateful that we're here."

"All right, all right, it's a great and wonderful family day," Luke DeFeo said. "Let me help. Bow your heads in prayer!"

Startled, Morwenna watched him, but slowly, one by one, the other members of her family did so.

"Praise be to the God and Father of our Lord Jesus Christ," DeFeo said, his voice ringing clearly, "who has blessed us in the heavenly realms with every spiritual blessing in Christ. For He chose us in him before the creation of the world to be holy and blameless in His sight. In love He predestined us to be adopted as His sons through Jesus Christ, in accordance with his pleasure and will to the praise of His glorious grace, which He has freely given us in the One He loves. In Him we have redemption through His blood, the forgiveness of sins, in accordance with the riches of God's grace that He lavished on us with all wisdom and understanding. And He made known to us the mystery of His will according to His good pleasure, which He purposed in Christ, to be put into effect when the times will have reached their fulfillment to bring all things in heaven and on earth together under one head, even Christ."

He finished speaking.

"Very nice," Gabe said. "Ephesians, I:3-10."

DeFeo arched a brow to him, a look of satisfaction on his face.

Stacy didn't notice either of them. "Amen!" she said happily.

Morwenna found that she was studying the two men; Gabe didn't seem disturbed, but he was watching DeFeo curiously. DeFeo looked very proud of himself, as if he had proven a point.

"Thank you, Father," Gabe said then, smiling as he looked up at the angel. "Thank you for this family, for the pride and courage and love to be found among them, even here, among those who have passed over to your realm. May you bless the lives of those who have proven to be so kind, and who value human life, even among those they know not as friends or enemies."

"Amen," Stacy said again, and this time, her family followed suit. "Anyone else?" she asked.

"Dear God and Jesus," Genevieve said. "Happy birthday again. Also, could you please make it just a little bit warmer?"

"Amen!" Bobby said, laughing. And he added, "This was lovely, Mom. But maybe we should move on."

Morwenna heard a slight rumbling. She looked up.

It seemed that the clouds were coming back again. And again, strangely, light remained among them. The angel on the tomb stood proud in a fierce ray of light, the sun, somehow, shooting down upon it through all the turbulence in the atmosphere.

Shayne came to her side. "I'll take Gen," he said quietly. "I can't believe you made it this far."

She smiled at him, and touched his cheek. She found herself thinking of the way they had fought like cats and dogs as children, and she was suddenly aware that he would have killed himself, not just to get his daughter back, but her, too.

"She's not so heavy. Okay, I'm lying. My arms are killing me. But you must still be feeling some muscle pain of your own, huh?"

"Yeah, but it's all over," he said, grinning. "My arms can take a little more."

He bent down to pick up his daughter.

"It's cold, Daddy," Genevieve said.

"Actually, sweetheart," Stacy said, "I think you prayed it a tiny bit warmer."

"We're almost down to the tavern, baby," Shayne said. "We'll get some nice hot cocoa there—hey, and I'll bet they have turkey on the menu, too."

"It won't be as good as Gram's turkey," Genevieve said.

"No, it won't be, but it will be warm."

"Move 'em out!" Bobby said, taking the lead again.

Morwenna paused, looking up at the angel that rode so beautifully over the tomb.

She smiled suddenly. She barely remembered her mother's parents now, but they had been good people. Hardy mountain stock, very independent—and very loving at the same time. They hadn't built the tomb, of course. The tomb dated back to the early eighteen hundreds.

And yet, someone, way back in her family, had known what a tomb should offer; not sorrow and pain, but pride and hope.

"Morwenna!"

She started; her father was waiting for her, and nervously watching the procession that had gone ahead of him at the same time.

"Coming, Dad!" she said.

But as he started away, she said her own prayer.

"Thanks," she murmured huskily, adding quickly, "Thank you for Genevieve, and thank you for me, and for us all…and help us! Please help us do what's right."

She almost expected the angel to move.

It didn't.

She turned and hurried out after her family. It was still another twenty to thirty minutes down the slippery road until they reached the little tavern nestled in the mountains among the pines.

Chapter 8

Breaking onto the last stretch, Bobby was glad to see that the lights were on at Scott's Tavern, or, as a neon subtitle below the main sign stated, Scott's Ye Olde Tavern and Grill.

There were even two cars parked in the lot, but Bobby didn't think they'd be going anywhere soon; there would have to be some major digging done before the roads were navigable. He wondered if people from the tavern had held off on the digging because, like his family, they'd expected snow to begin falling in earnest again at any point.

He turned back. Now, DeFeo was heading along behind him, Gabe behind Defeo, and behind Gabe, Shayne was walking with Connor's hand in his. His father had Genevieve and walked alongside his mother, and following behind, ever aware she was carrying a loaded shotgun, came Morwenna.

"Yes, we've made it," Gabe said, coming up so that he stood next to Luke DeFeo, and giving him a smile.

"Not really, not yet," DeFeo said.

Then Bobby wasn't really sure what happened. He didn't know if DeFeo went after Gabe, or if Gabe went after DeFeo, or even if one of them had slipped on a patch of black ice, which knocked them over the embankment together.

Either way, they were sliding away fast.

"Hey!" he shouted to the others.

Shayne, of course, had seen what had happened and was already racing up to Bobby; Bobby started down through the snow and brush for the men. They were still rolling, snapping branches and twigs off dead brush as they sped along. He began to run, leaping over obstacles, aware that Shayne was right behind him.

"Hey, stop!" he yelled at the two men.

They were fighting in desperate, awkward moves, since they both had their hands cuffed or tied. DeFeo got his arms around Gabe's neck, and Bobby shouted again, seeing the man's face begin to turn red. But Gabe was surprisingly agile and strong, throwing himself forward so that DeFeo was thrown over his head and sent into the brush again. When DeFeo would have risen and charged, he was stopped by the loud sound of a bullet blasting into the air.

"Stop it! Now!" Morwenna, as fierce as a lioness, was standing up on the embankment, the shotgun in her hand. But even as she spoke, Gabe was at DeFeo's side; he wasn't attacking him. He was giving him a hand to get to his feet.

As he neared the two of them, he heard them talking.

"Great! Give me a hand, huh? Oh, how *saintly* of you," DeFeo said.

"You've got on borrowed togs," Gabe said. "You want to be careful with them."

That sounded odd. Maybe he'd heard him wrong. Maybe he was just speaking lightly. But why get into a fight with a guy that might have killed one of them and worry about *togs. Clothing?*

"Come on, you two," Bobby said, determined to sound as fierce as his sister looked, standing on the embankment. "Let's go. The tavern is just ahead."

To his amazement, they both listened to him. Gabe led the way. Luke DeFeo followed.

"Still need the cops," DeFeo murmured.

Gabe ignored him. Bobby waited, following as the two men headed back up to the road.

"What the hell was that?" Morwenna demanded when everyone reached the road.

"Hey, we fell," DeFeo said. He looked at Gabe.

"But you, you…"

"That's the tavern, right in front of us?" he said.

Morwenna looked at him. "That's the tavern."

"They still have electricity. Maybe they'll have internet service, or working phones," Gabe said.

"Maybe they will, and maybe they won't," DeFeo said. "You haven't won anything yet, you know."

"Ah," Gabe said, "but my glass is always half-full."

Morwenna could have kissed the ground when they finally walked into the tavern. Whether she was right or not, she didn't know—but the responsibility for deciding which man was telling the truth had, at the least, been expanded. Once they walked through the door, she saw her parents' old friend, Mac Scott, behind the bar.

As long as she could remember, Mac had been behind the bar. He owned Scott's, which was a small legend, in a way. To anyone who lived in the area, or visited the remote mountain area with any frequency, Mac Scott's place was *the* place.

It was the *only* place.

Nestled in a little valley in the heights, it lay on the outskirts of what might optimistically be called a village. It was next to a shop that sold cold-weather gear and hiking and climbing equipment, and down and across the single street from the church, and across from the gas station–slash–convenience store that accommodated the area. A rangers' station was down another level, and the little area served all those who kept homes, part-time or year-round, in the mid area of the Virginia Blue Ridge peaks.

"Morwenna! Morwenna MacDougal!" Mac called from behind the bar. He was a big, tall man, a mountain man whose ancestors had been in the region for years.

He still looked like a massive highlander.

"Mac, hey," she said.

"Is the family with you?" Mac asked.

"Right behind me."

"You're early. What, did Stacy cook turkey for breakfast?" Mac asked.

Stacy shook her head, hurrying over to the bar as the others filed in behind her. "Mac, we have a problem. Do you have a working phone, or internet—or any way to contact anyone? We had a stranger hurt out by us—"

"Wow. Was Shayne there then? Thank God that boy is a doctor," Mac said. He frowned, and she realized that he was looking over her shoulder and seeing Gabe and Luke DeFeo being ushered in—the one with his hands tied, and the other in cuffs.

He looked back at Stacy, arching a black shaggy brow. "Shayne's got some bedside manner," he said quietly.

"Very funny. The first guy, Gabe, the lighter-haired one, said that he was a cop, and he'd gone down in a skirmish with a con. The second guy came and said that *he* was the cop, and the first guy was the con, and we have no way of knowing who is telling the truth," Morwenna explained. "Neither has ID."

"Well, hell," Mac said.

"You—that booth," her father told Gabe. "And you, DeFeo—you in that booth over there."

Mac looked at Morwenna again. "You've got to be kidding me."

"Mac, does it look like I'm joking?" Morwenna asked.

Genevieve ran over to join her at the bar, crawling up on a stood to smile at Mac and reach out for him. In Genevieve's six-year-old world, she realized, nothing precluded a hug from an old friend.

Mac reached over the bar, and Genevieve hugged him. Mac was her "big bear," she always said.

"Hey, there, little missy," Mac said. "Merry Christmas."

Frowning, he looked at Morwenna.

"So, can you help?" she asked.

"Morwenna, I'm sorry—my cable has been out forever. I've still got electricity, and I was counting my blessings for that! But I can't get anything on television except for the local channels. And I haven't been able to call out on the bar phone or on my cell since yesterday morning. Once that snow started coming in yesterday, everything went wacko."

Morwenna frowned, looking toward the back booth. "Who else is here?" She craned her neck, trying to see who might be sitting in the high-backed booths.

"The Williamsons and their two boys—do you know them? Brian Williamson's folks owned his house, just like your mom's folks owned your house on up the mountain," Mac said. He was talking to Morwenna again, but looking over at the booths—and Mike MacDougal, with his shotgun.

"Have they been stuck here?" Morwenna asked. "Snowbound, I mean?"

"No," Mac said. "They walked up, the same way you all came down."

As they spoke, of course, the Williamson family noted that there were newcomers at the tavern; Brian Williamson, plumber by day, banjo player upon occasion, rose and walked across the tavern to the booths, frowning as he saw Mike MacDougal with a shotgun.

"Mike, Merry Christmas, and what the hell?" he demanded.

Morwenna watched as her father went through the explanation. "You don't happen to have a working phone on you, do you?" Mike asked Brian.

"No, Mary and I were just talking about that— phones and internet, kaput! The boys were playing pool until a few minutes ago." He looked from one stranger to the next as he spoke. He added firmly, "But you've done well to bring them down here. Now you've got

Mac and me and the boys—they're fifteen and seventeen—to make sure that neither of these fellows causes any mischief."

"I'm an officer," Luke said, "an officer of the law, and if anyone in this place had any sense, you'd all realize it. If you help these people keep me incarcerated and that con gets away, I promise you that you'll have hell to pay as well!"

Gabe lowered his head, shaking it, and then looked up at Brian Williamson, and across the pool table and the bar at Mac. "He's a liar. And the MacDougal family knows that I'm not out to hurt any of them."

Mac leaned across the bar. "Who the hell knows which one of you is a liar? Mike, what can I get you to drink? Don't you worry none. You have help around you now to keep an eye on those men."

Morwenna frowned, realizing that the TV was running.

"Mac—you have television. So…how?"

"Yeah, the cable is down, but I jimmied the old antenna. We're getting some local stuff," Mac said. "It comes and goes. Some static, some show. Well, now, you had a long walk down here in the cold. What can I get everyone?"

"Hot chocolate!" Genevieve said, not in the least shy about asking her "big bear" for anything.

"Yeah, sure, thanks," Connor said.

"I'd love a beer," Mike said, still watching both men as he approached the bar.

"Yeah," Shayne said huskily.

"Not me. I'll have a nice Irish coffee," Stacy said, approaching the bar as well.

"Mac, do you have any turkey? My tummy is rumbling," Genevieve said.

"Mac, you're getting a lot of orders here. If I may, I'll come on back and help," Morwenna told him.

He was well equipped for the clientele he got during the winter season; he had a steamer that made hot chocolate, and it was easy to use. Morwenna figured all the kids were going to want hot chocolate, so she went ahead and made cups for the Williamson boys, too. When she set them on the counter, Bobby was there to take them out for her. Mac was pouring draft beers, and her father was seated on a bar stool then, watching the two men in the booths. Stacy sat by her husband, pulling her granddaughter onto her lap.

"Think Mac does have turkey?" she asked hopefully.

"Mac, got turkey?" Morwenna asked.

"Yes, I got turkey," Mac said. "And I'll just get you situated with drinks, and go on back and get you some food, too," he assured her.

"What about them?" Morwenna asked, looking at her father and indicating the men in the booths. Brian Williamson and his wife, Mary, were watching the two strangers.

"I could go for a beer," Gabe said.

"Give them both a beer. What the hell. Looks like we're all in a fix here," Mike said.

Morwenna poured the drafts for their prisoners, and then walked around to the tables. She set one down in front of Luke DeFeo first, and then one in front of Gabe. As she did so, DeFeo said, "Look! The picture's back on the television. Turn it up, please, someone.

Maybe the news will come on and show that Gabe Lange is a wanted man."

He was right; the TV set suddenly went from static to a picture.

They had just missed a news report, but the picture was suddenly clear, and an attractive young anchorwoman was seated at a desk with a similarly attractive young man.

"Happy holidays to our viewers across the world," the woman said.

Morwenna found herself slipping in to sit at the booth across from Gabe, staring up at the screen.

She was startled when Gabe's hand fell on hers. "Remember what I told you before," he said quietly.

"What? Told me about what?"

"About *you*," he said. "You should never just settle. You should never spend your life living out someone else's love, career or goals. The best is out there—the best of everything that will really make you happy. And you will find the way, and the right people in the world. Don't become a hamster on a wheel."

She shook her head, irritated. There was actually something on the television, and she wanted to see the familiar sight of people far away moving across a big flat-screen television. It was sad to realize, but TV was a *norm* in the average life, even when one wasn't exactly watching it.

And maybe the powers that be would break in with a news bulletin!

"People of all faiths and creeds now partake in our American holiday season, which, to everyone, becomes a time of spending their days in either family bonding—"

"Or not!" the man at her side interrupted jokingly. His co-anchor laughed as she looked at him.

"Yes, and some take off for exotic locations," the woman said. "With that in mind, we've had our reporters around the globe bring us a short video on Christmas—around the globe!" she said.

The screen flashed to a scene at the Vatican where throngs, in their Christmas best, stood in Saint Peter's Square as the pope spoke. The anchorman narrated over the visual clips.

"Isn't it beautiful at the Vatican? For some, it's the holiest of holy days! The scene is familiar at Westminster Abbey in London." The scene switched to England; there was snow on the ground outside the abbey, and it looked like a postcard. Christmas lights fell upon gargoyles and angels, and Morwenna could almost hear Big Ben chiming in the background.

"In areas of the South, we have a different kind of music going on," the young anchorwoman said, and the television screen portrayed a church with far more simple decor; plain pews and a minister directing a choir; for a moment, the music was beautiful and a chorus sang gospel renditions of very old carols.

"Now, it's fun time, too," the anchorwoman said, and they switched to a scene of a couple at a ski resort, the man laughing as the woman nearly fell, uneasy on her skis; she grabbed on to him, and they exchanged a long kiss.

"And, if cold isn't your thing, there are the beaches of Mexico!"

Morwenna looked over at Gabe. His head was down, as if he knew what she was going to see before she saw it.

He seemed to be concentrating.

She frowned, and glanced back at the television.

For a moment, static broke up the picture.

Then the screen straightened.

What was the size and population of Mexico? Morwenna wondered. *The country was certainly fairly large, and the population was well over a hundred million. There must have been hundreds of thousands of tourists besides, and yet...*

There he was on the screen. Alex. Tall, handsome, perfect corporate-America Alex, tanned and well-muscled, looking like a cover model. He was running down the beach in bathing trunks, chasing after...

Yes. Yes, it was Double-D Debbie Richards from Accounting.

And the camera stayed focused on the pair as the sparkling water of the Gulf of Mexico flew up around them in a crystal spray, as Alex caught up with a laughing Debbie, encircled her waist with his arms and crashed with her into the surf.

The screen changed as the newscasters brought their audience to Australia, and then onward to Jerusalem.

Morwenna didn't really see any more of the pictures dancing before her eyes.

She felt Gabe's hand on hers again. She met his eyes.

"You're not surprised," he told her quietly. "And more than that, you're not brokenhearted. You've known that you've been playing a role, and it came to you fairly easily. Morwenna, don't let what you saw eat at you. You're due to have much more in life. Much more that is *real*."

She heard his words; they were nice words. She still

felt frozen, as she hadn't once in all the fierce cold that had surrounded them in winter's white chill.

She was barely aware of Gabe's hand on hers.

No matter what he said, it hurt. Seeing Alex up there... She had just said goodbye to him yesterday morning.

Bobby slid into the booth next to her. She was suddenly aware of the world around her again. She could see her mother, still entertaining Genevieve at the bar. Her father was sitting at the bar having a conversation with Brian and Mary Williamson while keeping an eagle eye on the two booths. Shayne had walked back to where Sam and Adam Williamson were playing an electronic game with Connor.

"What's the matter?" he asked her.

"What?" she asked, looking at him.

"You've turned white." He stared at Gabe, his eyes narrowing, as if he suspected that Gabe had said something that had disturbed his sister.

Yes, that's exactly what he thought.

"What did you do?" he demanded of Gabe.

Somehow, those fierce, protective words from her cheerful, guitar-playing baby brother brought a flush of warmth into her system again.

"He didn't do or say anything," Morwenna said.

"Then…are you sick? Are you all right?" He set the back of his hand on her forehead.

"I'm fine," she assured him.

He glanced at the television.

"Oh!" he said softly. "You're wishing you were in Mexico." He squeezed her arm. "I'm sorry, sis. I guess it's hard to think that you could be lying out on the beach, or splashing in the water—instead of trying to figure out if we have a cop and thief or a cop and a homicidal murderer on our hands."

"I wasn't after a murderer," Gabe said quietly.

"And I wasn't wishing that I was anywhere else," Morwenna said. She looked at her brother, and a smile came to her lips. "Really," she said, and she realized it was the truth. In their day-to-day lives, her brothers were so far away. And they were busy. And it was easy to forget that while she worried about her brothers and their lives, she forgot sometimes just what they meant to her.

And what she meant to them.

"It's okay. *I'm* okay, really. It was just the TV."

Bobby's eyes widened suddenly as he stared at her. "Oh!" he said.

"What?"

"Mexico, oh, my God! We haven't had a television, and we have it for two minutes...was that *Alex* on the screen? With that girl?"

Double-D Debbie from Accounting.

She didn't say it out loud.

"Oh, Wenna, I'm so sorry," Bobby said.

"It's okay, really. It's okay," she said.

He looked at Gabe. "You *knew*. How the hell did you know?"

Before Gabe could answer, they were all startled by a different voice coming through the speakers. "We are interrupting your local programming for a news bulletin. Be on the lookout for—"

The screen suddenly turned back to snow; no words issued through the speakers, only a fizzing sound that went with the snow.

"Lost it again!" Mac said, walking back from the

kitchen area into the bar. "It's been like that all day, on one minute, and gone the next. Little Miss MacDougal, I will have your turkey out in just a matter of minutes."

"Turkey," Mike echoed, staring at the snow-covered television screen, and then lowering his head as he shook it.

"Can you believe the TV went out right when it did?" Bobby asked rhetorically.

"Yes, I can," Gabe said. His eyes were downcast. He was talking to himself, really, Morwenna thought, and he sounded a little bitter, and somewhat resigned.

"Bobby, dear baby brother, let me out," Morwenna said. "I'm going to go and help Mac with the dinner plates. He's all alone here, and nine of us just plopped into his bar. He definitely needs a hand."

"Sure. I can help, too," Bobby said.

"No, no—two can handle it. You stay here—and keep an eye on him," she said, looking at Gabe.

His eyes met hers. Still that clear green, and so seemingly without guile.

He didn't smile; he didn't say a word. He just looked at her, and when she turned to walk away, she knew that his eyes were following her.

He may not be the con, she thought. But there was something odd going on. It was as if he knew far more about them and their situations than they did.

She turned and stared at Luke DeFeo. He was looking back at her. "We'd love turkey, too, you know. Please," he said politely.

She nodded. "We don't intend to starve anyone."

He smiled.

And it was strange; she thought that he, too, knew something that she didn't.

A chilling thought struck her: What if they were both cons, just playing a game with the family? And what if...?

What if they were both just depending on the decency of the family, waiting for a chance to rob them all blind or—or worse?

She squared her shoulders. There was nothing she could do that they weren't already doing.

Waiting.

Hoping.

Praying.

Shayne finally left his position at the bar and walked over to the booths; Bobby was across from Gabe, keeping an eye on him.

He slid in across from Luke DeFeo.

"You would have seen it. You would have seen that he was the homicidal escaped con if the television hadn't gone out."

"Maybe," Shayne said, reminding himself to maintain a poker face, no matter what the man had to say to him. "And maybe we would have seen that you're a lying scumbag."

DeFeo took a swallow of his beer. His handcuffs clinked together as he did so.

Despite the hindrance, he seemed to really enjoy the beer.

He lifted his glass. "I'm grateful...grateful to your family. At least, you're not treating us like animals. At least, not too much so."

"You're not animals. And, frankly, around my family, animals are treated like people. My mother is a sucker for any lost puppy or kitten that comes her way."

"And what about you—and yours?" DeFeo asked.

"What do you mean?"

"Oh, yeah, I forgot—you're divorced. I guess it would be the wife who wanted to take in every stray."

Shayne blinked, not speaking for a minute. Yes, of course, over the years, they'd had many a visitor. When a dog or cat made it into their yard without a tag, they kept it, and Cindy spent endless hours walking the streets, putting up flyers and heading to every animal shelter in the area to see that a flyer went up. She raged against those who didn't neuter or spay their pets; she cried over the fate of ill-treated creatures. And, to her credit, any time Cindy hadn't found the rightful owner, she had found someone in need of a stray.

"Sorry, didn't mean to cause you any pain. I know what it can be like. I've gone the route," DeFeo said.

"We're all doing all right," Shayne said.

"Sure, sure, of course."

"Turkey!"

Shayne heard the excited cry come from the bar; it was Genevieve, of course. Mac had decided to bring the first plates out to Shayne's mom and daughter.

But Genevieve squirmed off her grandmother's lap and reached for the plate. "I think they're hungry," she told Stacy, inclining her head toward the booths. "They looked like they were fighting before. Maybe 'cause they were hungry. Daddy told me that people do bad things sometimes 'cause they don't have anything, and they're hungry. So I'll give that man my plate, and maybe he won't look like he's snarling all the time."

Shayne smiled, and he reminded himself that whatever agony and loss he felt over his marriage, Cindy was a good person, and a good mother, and between them, they'd created a couple of really good children.

Genevieve, the plate wobbling a little precariously in her hands, walked over and set it in front of Luke DeFeo.

He studied her for a long moment.

"Thanks, kid," he said.

The television screen flashed back into working order; local news was on.

"We expect snow at this time of year," a weatherman was saying, "but the intensity of the drifts that reached the mountains was higher than predicted. Plows are busy, and police and rescue agencies are out on the roads searching for those who started out for homes in the Blue Ridge area and didn't quite make it home for Christmas."

A cameraman was focused on a car that had slid into an embankment, precariously near the guardrail. From that area, if a car had gone over...

Shayne leaned forward, feeling as if his heart were caught in his throat.

It couldn't be. It couldn't be Cindy's Subaru! Cindy was on her way to Paris; she'd started seeing a travel agent when the divorce had been final and he'd been offered a freebie at a chalet in France. She'd been due to leave on Christmas Eve.

Of course, it couldn't be Cindy's car. There were thousands of Subaru Foresters in the area. They were good cars for harsh winters.

It was a moss-green Forester, just like his wife's car. Ex-wife's car! he reminded himself.

Shayne glanced around quickly, wondering if the children were watching the screen; they weren't. Genevieve was still staring at Luke DeFeo, smiling, as if she admired him a great deal, and Connor was involved in his game.

He stared back at the television screen.

If there was a cameraman there, the driver and passengers, assuming there were any, had to be all right.

"It's an overhead shot," DeFeo said.

"What?"

"Look, it's an overhead shot. Must be a helicopter... Look how the shot shakes, zooming in and out."

He was right.

Shayne felt every muscle in his body tighten; he studied everything he could for the seconds that the waving shot remained on the screen. He searched for a sign of some kind that would tell him exactly where in the mountains the car was stranded.

He found it, right before the screen switched to a traffic pileup in Charlottesburg.

Dead Man's Curve.

It wasn't an official designation, and he wasn't sure just what mile marker it was in the Blue Ridge. It was about five miles down from them. He knew it from the overlook at the apron of the curve and the flat-face rock just to the side of it.

He stood, heedless of DeFeo. He walked over to the bar. Mac had paused to exchange a few words with his father.

"I don't know, and I don't know why, but I think that Cindy is stranded on the mountain, maybe freezing to death. Dad, I'm going down there."

Chapter 9

There would be no arguing with Shayne; Morwenna knew that.

Stacy, of course, was upset. Shayne might be a working physician in his mid-thirties and a father himself; he was still *her* child. Stacy was disturbed already—of course they all were—and now this new danger to her family seemed to be making her even more anxious. "But, Shayne, really—Cindy is supposed to be in Europe by now," Stacy said.

"There's no way you could know that you saw *Cindy's* car," Mike said.

"Look, I know exactly where the car was stuck," Shayne said. "You don't understand. I have a feeling. A gut feeling. And I know Cindy, and I know that she never knew these mountains like we do. She's probably in that car—maybe even injured. I have to go. I have to."

"I'll go with you," Morwenna said.

Both her parents gasped.

"No, Morwenna, let me go with Shayne," Bobby said.

She turned to look at her brother. "Look, Wenna, I'm not saying you're out of shape or anything. You're in great shape. But I do way more in the snow than you do. I'm a far better skier, I am much better with a snowboard and I'm even a better hiker."

"You can't take skis out there," Stacy said. "The snow is covering too many ruts…you won't always see the ledges—with the sun out, the snow can be blinding."

"And if you walked again, it could take forever," Mike said.

"I've got a snowmobile out back," Mac said. "She's not the newest model, but she's a workhorse. If you follow close to the road, you'll be safe enough in it."

"You have any survival kits?" Shayne asked him. "Bobby, don't make Mom and Dad worry for two. If Mac can lend me the snowmobile, I'll be there and back in no time."

"Hell, no," Bobby said. "I know the roads better than any of you. I'm the one who still spends the most time here."

"Kid!" Luke DeFeo called from the booth. "Your brother doesn't know that his wife is in any car stuck anywhere. She's in Europe. That car could belong to anyone. I understand how you feel, but you need to be sensible."

Morwenna looked at him. Could the man really be worried about her family?

Genevieve had been standing there, looking from adult to adult. She suddenly cried out and ran to her father. "Daddy, is Mommy out in the snow?"

Shayne shot Luke DeFeo a murderous stare. "No, darling, probably not. I'm just kind of a worrywart, you know that. I saw a car stuck that looks kind of like Mommy's."

Morwenna hadn't even seen Connor come over to stand behind his grandfather.

"It could be Mommy," he said. "She was crying before you came to get us yesterday morning, Dad. She wanted us to be with you, but she didn't want to be away from us."

Morwenna felt something behind her back and she turned around, startled. Gabe Lange had left his booth, and stood just behind her.

They were getting too lax! They needed to be watching him.

"Connor, I don't think that you have to worry. Your dad is a doctor, and I think he would have thought about getting to that car whether it's actually your mom in it or not. Whoever is stranded probably needs help," he said.

"I have to go," Shayne said quietly.

Stacy looked at her son for a long moment. "Yes, of course you do," she said.

"You realize," Luke DeFeo called from his booth. "Gabe wants two of the able-bodied men out of here because he's planning something. This could be a fool's errand; that car could have been stranded since last night, and whoever is in it is probably dead."

Genevieve started to sob. Stacy picked her up. "Honey, it could be someone else's car, and your mommy may be safe in a nice warm chalet somewhere," she said.

"And there are two able-bodied men and a few strong boys here as well," Mac protested in a growl. "Shayne, there's a rescue kit on the back wall of the kitchen—take that. The snowmobile keys are right by it. You and Bobby get going. You'll be back here in no time, and you're going to want to be back before dark."

"We'll be here—Mac and my family and I," Brian Williamson said firmly. "Everything will be status quo."

"We'll be fine, won't we, Mom?" Morwenna said, setting an arm around her mother's shoulders.

"At least grab a piece of turkey before you leave," Stacy said, forcing a smile.

"All right, we're going," Shayne said. Genevieve came running over to hug his legs; Shayne picked her up and gave her a kiss on the cheek. "Don't you worry, munchkin. And Connor, you watch out for your sister for me, right?"

Connor nodded gravely.

The two grabbed their coats and headed around the bar to go out through the kitchen. Mike was staring worriedly after his sons; he held the shotgun in a lax position.

Morwenna turned to Gabe. "You! Back to the table," she told him.

"This worries me sick!" DeFeo said from his position in his booth. "They're on a fool's errand. The snow is blanketing all kinds of hazards. And," he said, looking directly at Morwenna, "your brother hates his ex-wife."

Genevieve gasped.

"You shut up, and shut up right now," Morwenna said, approaching the table. "One more word, and you may be the ghost of J. Edgar Hoover, but I'll knock you out flat with my rifle butt and not feel a twitch of guilt as I do it!" she warned.

There was an uncomfortable silence.

And they all heard the motor of the snowmobile start up and rev.

Morwenna looked from DeFeo to Gabe Lange, who had taken his seat again. He was watching her. He smiled when their eyes met. "They're going to be fine," he told her with assurance.

"Maybe," DeFeo said, sounding weary. He groaned. "I really wish you could see what's happening here. This man is being as nice as he can be. He's trying to make you all like him. He's pretending to be good and kind, and worried about you rather than himself. That's his act. He's seducing you all with his gentle personality. And then he'll strike."

They were all silent for a minute.

"Eat your turkey!" Stacy told him. "Before we lock you in the outhouse!"

DeFeo smiled. "There's an outhouse?"

"We can arrange for one," Mike assured him.

"I wish you'd let me help you," DeFeo said. "You're good people. I wish I could make you see what you're doing, and that you're being used, which puts you into a greater realm of danger."

Bobby was glad that Mac Scott was a real mountain man; his survival kit contained rope, carabiners, pulleys, water, bandages, water and medical supplies.

His snowmobile had three compartments, and one held a heavy windbreaker and blanket, while another held flashlights and emergency flares.

He convinced his brother to sit behind him and let him do the steering; Shayne was feeling desperate, he knew, but his brother was never stupid. Bobby did know the mountain best.

Still, it was rough going. The snow was deep, and all discernible lines between the road itself, the embankment on the right and the guardrails on the left had all but disappeared.

Bobby kept the speed in check. At the best of times, in a car with the world's finest tires, mountain roads could be treacherous. No one in their right mind would have been on the roads late yesterday; only those who really knew the mountain could have foreseen just how bad it was going to be.

Were they crazy? Was Cindy in Europe? Were they really on a fool's errand, whose only possible end would be to come across a corpse frozen in place behind the wheel?

And yet it was true; Shayne had panicked because of his ex-wife. But, if he had realized that he could reach the car and that it might be occupied, he would have come out anyway. No physician had ever taken his oath more seriously.

He was jarred from his thoughts as the snowmobile suddenly bounced high and slammed back down—he'd hit a rock or obstruction on the road. He heard Shayne swear, and felt his brother's arms tighten around him. When they landed, he cut his speed, slowing almost to a stop and shouting back at Shayne, "You okay?"

"Yeah, yeah, slow her down more, I guess," Shayne said.

"Can't save anyone if we're dead or broken," Bobby agreed.

He'd almost come to a stop; he revved the motor again, making sure to keep it alive as well. The snowy air hit his face with a fierce blast—stinging. He hugged the mountain as closely as he dared. They were on a road, damn it, but they might as well have been on a field of snow. Only the towering heights of the pines and evergreens on the mountainside gave him any sense of direction.

He should have grabbed a ski mask. He felt as if his nose was so cold, it was burning off.

He rounded bend after bend, and slowed as the slope became greater.

He blinked hard as his eyes watered at the cold air. He didn't dare look too far to the left; they could see the towns in the valley below, so far down that they looked like little houses in a Christmas display.

He focused on driving, and again, they curved down another bend.

And there they saw the moss-green Subaru, slammed against the overhead, and the embankment, and far too close to the ledge.

If Morwenna had been feeling fraught with tension before, it was nothing compared to the way she was feeling now. Shayne and Bobby were gone, and from the time they left, she discovered that she was looking up at the big, carved bear-framed clock over the bar.

Seconds ticked by so slowly.

Brian and Mary Williamson and their boys had been

a godsend; Brian had gotten it into his head to teach Conner how to play pool, and so he and Mary—an excellent player herself—were distracting him to the best of their ability. Stacy was keeping Genevieve as busy as possible, having her help out, putting down and picking up plates and refilling beverage glasses.

Mac and Morwenna had gotten the rest of the turkey dinners out, only everyone had seemed to have lost their appetite. The boys ate a few bites between shots; Morwenna played with her fork, herself, pushing her food around on her plate.

Only their two prisoners seemed to clean up their turkey and stuffing, mashed potatoes and gravy, green beans and cranberry sauce.

They, too, seemed to be watching the clock.

It had seemed like forever before the day had begun—it was only four in the afternoon. Morwenna prayed that her brothers would return before the sun fell in earnest.

The TV had given nothing but static since it had last gone out.

"Hey!" Gabe called to her softly.

She narrowed her eyes, looking at him. It was best, she'd decided, to keep away from both the men. Gabe had thought immediately that Shayne and Bobby should risk their own lives. DeFeo had openly voiced the thought that if it was Cindy in the stranded car, she might well be dead.

"Is that a jukebox? A working one?" he asked her.

She looked down past the pool tables.

"Yes, it still works."

"Maybe it has some Christmas carols," he said. "May I go look?"

Morwenna looked at her father. Mike now maintained an iron grasp around the shotgun.

Her father shrugged. Stacy looked up; Genevieve was on her lap and they were drawing pictures on a cocktail napkin.

"Go ahead. And, remember, Dad *will* shoot you if you make a wrong move," Morwenna said.

Gabe eased himself out of the booth and headed down past the pool players. For a moment, Morwenna feared that she had been an idiot; Gabe could have stopped by one of the boys, slipped his bound wrists over the head of one of them and threatened to strangle him. He could have then threatened a life…using a child as a hostage to escape.

She pictured the scene in her mind's eye, and she almost cried out in fear and warning. But she saw that her father had no intention of risking the children. He had risen, and though Gabe couldn't see him, Mike had kept himself in a position to shoot if Gabe had made so much as a move in the wrong direction.

Gabe walked right by the pool players and down to the jukebox.

He looked back at her with a rueful smile. "It works off of quarters."

"Here!" Mac spoke up from behind the bar and opened the cash register to find a handful of coins; he handed them to Morwenna. She met his eyes, and he nodded. "Lord knows, we could use something in here beyond the sound of that TV static," he said.

Morwenna walked down to the jukebox with the coins in her hand. When she reached it, she began to feed them into the machine.

"You all have to be careful," DeFeo said.

"I am careful—always," Mike told him.

Gabe was able to hit the button that changed the pages.

"A17. Nice, Bing Crosby and David Bowie singing together, 'Little Drummer Boy' and 'Peace on Earth,'" he said.

"You're letting him run the show!" DeFeo warned.

"He's choosing a few Christmas tunes. A nice idea, really," Morwenna said.

"So, I'm stuck here in cuffs with a group that is going to be in big trouble when the real law arrives. But we all get to play Christmas tunes. Great!"

She opted to ignore DeFeo.

"Play what you choose," Morwenna said.

Gabe hit A17 without answering DeFeo. He flipped more pages. Morwenna was startled when Genevieve called out "Do they have 'Rudolph the Red-Nosed Reindeer'?"

"Well, I'll just bet they do," Gabe told her. "And there it is! D22!"

"I'd like 'Do You Hear What I Hear?'" Stacy called.

"And there's the ever-popular 'Rockin' Around the Christmas Tree'!" Mike called from the bar.

He was still clutching the shotgun. What a contrast to Genevieve, who wasn't questioning what she believed in any way. She simply liked Gabe.

The faith of a child...

Gabe began to push buttons. As he did so, Morwenna stepped back to join the boys gathered around the pool table. Connor grinned up at her; she realized that although he was still worried about his parents and aware of the tense situation in which the family found itself, he was doing all right.

Friends had made that so—learning pool tricks from the Williamson family was easing the day for him.

She smiled back at him. "A budding pool shark, eh?" she teased affectionately.

He smiled back at her. "My dad…my dad is going to be okay, right, Auntie Wenna?" he asked.

She saw that Gabe was still listening and obeying as the group in the tavern vied for selections on the old jukebox. His eyes were alight.

She had been suspicious of the man from the beginning. Then she had begun to believe in him. Then she had found her way back to mistrust. And why? Because someone else spoke against him.

She winced. Well, that hadn't stood history very well. Proof was needed. Well, proof was what they awaited.

"You dad is going to be just fine, Connor," Morwenna said. "And so are we."

But just as the words left her mouth, the electricity went.

And the tavern was pitched into shadow.

Bobby braked the snowmobile just off the point where he *thought* the road made way for the lookout point. Shayne dismounted and instantly started for the car.

"Bro! We have to be careful. That car is right on the ledge," Bobby told him.

Shayne froze in his tracks, as if at his statement, and Bobby saw that his face was white. And then he knew why. He couldn't see that it was indeed Cindy in the car, but he could see the driver.

And the driver was in a hooded parka, head down

on the steering wheel. Frost and snow covered most of the windshield.

There was no way to tell, until they touched the driver, whether the person was alive or dead.

"All right, come on, Shayne, I want to bring you both—and me!—back alive. Let's take it slow." He reached into the side compartments on the snowmobile. He got out the rope and the pulley chair, and followed Shayne as his brother more cautiously approached the car. He saw one of the huge light poles by the side of the road. It wouldn't carry the weight of a car if something happened, but it would carry the weight of a man—and a woman.

"Approach the car, and carefully open that front door just in case the ground by the back tires is—is gone. Grab the person out of the car, and screw whatever the hell else is in it, okay?" Bobby said. "I'll tie us together with the rope."

Shayne nodded. "Let's hurry," he said.

Bobby took the rope to the massive light stand and quickly tied it around, securing it with double loops. He hurried back to where his brother stood, already securing himself. He looked at Bobby. "Thanks," he told him.

"I'll be right here, but not coming close. Until she's out of the car, and you need me," Bobby said.

His brother moved toward the car then, taking every step carefully.

Bobby looked back at the rope attached to the giant light pole, and then frowned as he looked up at the light. Dusk was settling on them more heavily now with each minute that passed.

And the streetlight hadn't kicked on.

Strange, the lights usually came on automatically as dusk moved in.

Unless, of course, the electricity had finally gone in the mountaintops here.

And, if so, back at the tavern, his family was locked in darkness.

Bobby forced himself to remain still, to watch his brother, and to wait. He couldn't go screaming like a terrified child, and rush back to the snowmobile and leave Shayne and the driver.

What if the woman was Cindy, and she had skidded and lost control last night, and she had frozen to death already?

He didn't dare think it.

What about his family, back in the tavern, suddenly pitched into darkness?

His father was a smart man; he'd have his shotgun at the ready.

But could he aim in the dark?

"Almost there," Shayne called to him. "And the ground feels steady thus far...don't know about the back, and I'm not going to test it."

Shayne stood then by the driver's-side door. He reached for it slowly, and opened it more slowly. He let out a cry as the driver slumped to the side, and into his arms. He fell to his knees, cradling the woman in his arms.

Bobby heard a strange sound; it was like a rumble, but it was a quiet rumbling. He looked at the Subaru, and the back end of it seemed to be sinking.

"Shayne, get her out of there!" Bobby shouted. He went for the rope, ready to drag his brother if it went taut against the pole.

But Shayne stood, cradling his ex-wife to his chest, and he started a stumbling run through the snow toward Bobby. And as he did, Bobby heard a creaking sound, once and again, and then growing louder, and he saw that the Subaru was slipping, slipping...

There was a loud smashing sound as it hit the guardrail, and then a rumble as it burst through the railing and went tumbling down the mountain.

"Brace yourself!" Bobby said, hunkering down.

And Shayne dropped to a knee, covering Cindy's body with his own. They both waited for an explosion.

None came.

Bobby stood slowly and walked as close as he dared to the ledge. He looked over, and he was glad to see that the Subaru had not exploded, or hurt anything other than a number of scraggly, half-dead winter trees and brush. It had landed—right side up—on a narrow ledge about fifty feet down.

He looked at Shayne. His brother had gotten Cindy to the snowmobile; he had her wrapped in the blanket, and he was trying to urge some brandy through her lips. Bobby hurried over to them, falling to his knees in the snow, and looking down at his sister-in-law's face. She was such a beautiful woman, but right now, he felt a burst of cold fear sweep through him. She was so white; her eyes were closed, and her lips appeared to be a strange shade of blue.

"She's—she's—" Bobby began.

Shayne smiled grimly at him. "She's alive," he assured her. "She's...she's a fighter. She's going to make it. Her pulse is weak, but steady. She's going to come around. We just have to get her back as soon as possible, and get her warm...and I can find out if any damage was done. She should get to a hospital, but the tavern will do. I need her to come around...to sip some of this."

Bobby felt words coming in a repetitious prayer.

Let her live, let her live, please, God, let her live.

"Come on, come on, come on...please, God!" Shayne breathed.

Cindy suddenly choked, coughed and stuttered.

Her eyes flew open in panic, and she strained at the arms that held her: Shayne's.

A weak scream escaped her lips, and then died as her eyes focused on Shayne's face.

"Shayne!" she said.

"Hey," Shayne said, his voice tremulous. "You're all right. You're all right."

Was she? Bobby wondered. God knew, she might be suffering from some kind of frostbite.

She saw Bobby then. "Bobby!" she whispered. "My God, you two found me...how on earth did you find me? You couldn't have known that I was coming. I didn't know that I was coming until it was time to leave for the airport, and then I knew I—I knew I couldn't leave for the whole week, and I tried to call you all, but no one was answering and I just took a chance, and, oh, Lord, please forgive me, Shayne... I meant to get here and beg that you all forgive me for show- ing up so rudely, and let me spend the holidays with the kids, too, and—"

"Cindy, you may be suffering some real effects from this," Shayne said gently. "Drink a bit more of this, and let me get you some water, too. We'll wrap you up really tightly in the parka, because it's even colder when we're on the snowmobile. It will be slow going...

the thing is only meant for two, but I know that we'll manage. The tavern is warm, and once we're there, we'll talk."

"But, Shayne, I asked you to take the children, and I came here, and then…I thought I was going to die. I was terrified to move in the car." She stopped speaking and stared at Bobby. "The car, I was in the car…"

Shayne looked at him. "Um, well, it's standing. But I have a feeling the insurance company might consider it to be totaled," Bobby said.

"Oh! Oh, God! It did go over! I was terrified when the car spun out and stalled, and then when the wheels wouldn't catch. There was nothing for them to catch on!"

"It's okay, Cindy, you're safe," Shayne said.

"Shayne, you risked your life for me," Cindy said, her eyes filled with wonder as she looked at him. "After everything…but, it's what you do, isn't it?" Her eyes filled with tears.

Shayne drew her to him.

"Cindy, don't cry. Please, don't cry."

"But you forgive me?" she whispered.

"Forgive you? For loving our children? Don't be silly, Cindy, there is nothing to forgive. And you will always be a part of the family, and always welcome," Shayne said.

"And we'll all freeze if we don't get back," Bobby interjected.

He glanced at the light pole, and far up—at the light that wasn't lit.

Cindy was alive.

And now, the worry that something had gone wrong at the tavern began to eat into him again.

"We need to hurry, as much as we safely can," Shayne said.

Screw safely!

Bobby's urge to get back to the tavern was almost overwhelming. He began hurriedly gathering the equipment they had used, stuffing it into the compartments. He crawled back onto the snowmobile and felt Shayne doing his best to get on with his ex-wife in his arms.

"What is it? What's wrong?" Cindy asked.

Where in the hell did they begin to explain?

He'd leave that to Shayne, Bobby decided.

He turned on the snowmobile's lights—a contrast to the darkness now settling heavy on the mountains.

The cold hit Bobby's face as he revved the snowmobile into gear; going back would be even more treacherous.

He kept seeing the pool of light before him.

And all he could think was *dark, dark, dark.*

His family was trapped in the dark, with strangers whose intentions were still unknown.

Chapter 10

The sudden darkness seemed complete at first; the sun was almost down outside the tavern walls, and the shadowy world of the outside was now inside, compounded by the walls surrounding them.

But it wasn't completely dark.

There was that moment when it was just suddenly dead silent, smoke gray, and dead still, and yet shapes and shadows seemed to run amok.

They were frightened, of course; man's fear of the dark was an instinct left over from prehistory when darkness meant the coming of fearsome beasts of prey.

Morwenna wasn't sure at all why such stark terror came to her. It wasn't unusual that they should lose the electricity. Mac had a generator, and it would kick in soon. But she had the strangest feeling that *this* sudden darkness was worse than any other, and that something evil was moving about the room. Light couldn't come back to them fast enough.

Something almost touched her, and for a moment, she felt as if her skin was literally crawling, as if a horrible scent of death, decay and sulfur filled the air.

She reached for Genevieve, terrified that the little girl was in some kind of danger. She groped blindly, watching shadows move.

"Hey, folks, it's okay, everything's all right now. We've got an emergency generator," Mac said.

As if on cue, low light returned to the tavern, and the jukebox spun into action. Bing Crosby and David Bowie came on together.

Morwenna looked instantly for her niece; she was standing beside and slightly behind Gabe, almost wedged against the jukebox. She had a wide-eyed look of fear on her face.

"Baby, it's okay," Morwenna said. "It's all right, see, the light is back on."

"Auntie Wenna, I was scared!" Genevieve said.

Morwenna quickly hunkered down by her side.

"It's all right. It was just dark," Morwenna said.

But Genevieve shook her head. "No, didn't you feel it...someone was here, someone very, very bad!"

"Genevieve, no one else is here. It was just a matter of moments before the lights came back on."

Genevieve looked up at her. "No! No, Gabe saved me. He saved me from the bad thing, the evil thing that was here."

"Hey!" Mike said suddenly.

Morwenna quickly glanced to her father. He had jumped up first, apparently to look for his family members, and to assure himself that they were all right.

"What?" Mac asked.

"He's gone!" Mike said.

Morwenna looked to the booth where Luke DeFeo had been sitting.

It was empty.

She quickly looked around the room. DeFeo wasn't anywhere to be seen.

She had the uneasy feeling that he had been near; that he had nearly touched her.

And Genevieve.

"Well, hell, maybe that's just good riddance!" Mac said.

"I didn't hear or see the door open," Connor noted, frowning.

"Well, he is gone," Stacy said. "Maybe—maybe it is just as well."

Gabe spoke up suddenly. "No, no, it's not just as well. He's still out there somewhere. And he's dangerous."

"Dangerous? But," Morwenna said, turning to him, "*you* said that he was a white-collar criminal. He said that *you* were the dangerous one."

He shook his head. "You don't understand…you can't understand. He's—all right, he's on the run. And he may want to bring a few down with him. You have to let me go after him."

He walked around the pool table, toward Mike. As he did so, Morwenna noticed the distance from the booths and around the pool table to where she was standing.

Luke DeFeo couldn't have come around the whole place so quickly. Could he? And yet she had the uncomfortable, uncanny feeling that he had.

"But—he's out there, alone in the snow. He won't be coming back here," Mac said.

"He's out there, and he's thinking of something, and he will come back," Gabe said firmly.

"My sons are out there," Stacy said. "My sons are out there, somewhere on the mountain."

"I can find him. I can stop him," Gabe said. "Look, please. I was with you for a long time, and no harm came to you. Trust me. Let me go after him, before he finds a way to hurt anyone. Please."

A silence followed his words. Thoughts raced through Morwenna's mind.

There was simply no way to know the truth; maybe Luke DeFeo had escaped because he was desperate to find a way to communicate with the law. Maybe he had escaped because he was a cop, and he was going to come back.

And maybe every word that Gabe was saying was the truth. He'd done nothing but show them gratitude and kindness since he'd been with him.

She stepped forward, coming to stand behind him. "I think we need to believe in Gabe. He's been nothing but level and kind—he risked his life for Genevieve, and I don't care what DeFeo said—Gabe risked his life, and you don't do that unless there is something really decent in you. He wants to set out to find Luke DeFeo. I say we let him go, and I say that I go with him."

"What?" Stacy said incredulously, sliding off her bar stool to stare at her daughter.

"Mom, I'm well over twenty-one," she said quietly.

"No, I should go," Mike said.

Morwenna shook her head. "No, Dad. You and Mom need to stay. You need to be here, because you're really great parents." She paused, looking at Genevieve and Connor, not wanting to scare the children, but hoping her parents would understand.

If something had happened to Shayne, Bobby or Cindy—and something was to happen to her, God forbid!—the kids would need stable, loving parents.

And that, she realized, *they were.*

She smiled suddenly. "Gabe will never hurt me. I know it. I know it just as I know the sun will rise in the morning. And I'm going to untie his hands, and we're going to go out together. When we reach Shayne and Bobby, I'll come back with them. But they have to know that DeFeo is out there, and he could be very dangerous. We can't accomplish that with one person—I'll need to come back, and Gabe will need to find DeFeo."

"Now, wait, I can go out with this man," Brian Williamson said.

"Or me," Mac volunteered.

"I'll be able to find my brothers. I *know* I'll be able to find my brothers," Morwenna said.

"This is crazy!" Mike said, still studying her.

"It's what we need to do, Dad. Mr. Williamson, you need to stay with your kids. And Mac, well, you just need to watch out for everyone here. And I need to find my brothers, and Gabe needs to stop DeFeo," Morwenna said firmly.

"And my mommy!" Genevieve said. "You need to find my mommy!"

"If she's with them," Morwenna said.

"She is," Connor said. "She is. My father went to find her. He *knew* that she was out there, and he went to find her. And I know that he did."

"Morwenna!" Her father lowered his head. "Morwenna, we just don't *know!*"

But Genevieve came to stand next to Morwenna and Connor. "I know!" she said. "I know that Gabe is good, and that he can find my daddy. Gramps, please, let him go, and let Auntie Morwenna go with him to bring my mommy and daddy and Uncle Bobby back."

Her father stared at her. She didn't know if he was thinking that he couldn't really stop her, or if he was feeling the same way; *they had to be right about Gabe Lange.* He nodded slowly. "You're taking my only daughter out there," he said to Gabe.

"I'll be careful with her," Gabe promised. "I swear to you, I would lay down my life for her."

Genevieve tugged on Morwenna's shirt, and Morwenna hunkered down to her. Genevieve looked at her with a child's wide eyes and then reached out to touch the little gold angel she was wearing around her neck.

"You'll be protected. You have your angel."

Morwenna smiled.

Faith, again.

Children could be so amazing. And it could be argued that faith could lead to stupidity, and that fanatical faith could lead to horrible things, but this wasn't that kind of faith. There was something in Gabe Lange's eyes unlike anything she had ever known before.

He made her believe.

She walked across the tavern, collecting her coat and gloves and scarf.

"We'll be back before you know it!" she assured the room cheerfully.

"Wait!" Mike protested. "You're just walking out with nothing—"

"We'll find Bobby and Shayne and the equipment. Dad, I know this mountain, and the valleys. We'll find them soon—I know it. I'm good, I'm fine. Have faith in me!"

Mike looked into her eyes. He smiled slowly and painfully. "I do have faith in you," he said.

Gabe followed her, and turned back. "You are going to be all right, and so are the others. I will find DeFeo. And I will stop him."

Bobby drove the snowmobile slowly and carefully; even so, the air was biting, and bits and chips of snow and ice flew before them and around them. Shayne's face was numb.

And yet, he felt a sense of wonder as they moved through the snow.

He had never been a violent man in any way, and certainly not with his wife or children. But when he looked back, he could see the danger signs that had led to his divorce. He had been oblivious to the amount of time he was gone—he felt that his days had been full from beginning to end. He *had* changed diapers. In fact, when trying to explain why she was leaving, Cindy had told him that he'd been a wonderful father when the kids had been babies. He was still a wonderful father.

He had tried to understand when she'd told him that she'd rather be alone on her own than always alone with him. That hadn't made sense. Not then. He'd been perplexed; he didn't go to strip bars, he didn't head out on wild nights looking for something new, hoping to get lucky with an exotic stranger.

But she hadn't thought that, apparently.

And he hadn't seen it coming, and when he did, it had been too late. She hadn't been angry; she had told him that she just didn't know him anymore, and he certainly didn't know her. And it was better to be alone, going about life on her own schedule than wondering what his might be, or if and when they were going to see him. Maybe if she wasn't always on the spot, he'd show up for his son's baseball games, or realize that Connor was falling in love with music, much like his uncle Bobby, who would really stop and listen to him at times.

Now, of course, it was all so clear.

He still loved his wife.

He was certain that even if she had fallen out of love with him, she still cared about him.

And his hold on her was firm; he realized at that moment, as long as he had breath in his body there was hope, and if they never made it back together again, he was desperately glad that she was alive. She was a wonderful person, and an exceptional mother, and thank God, no matter what they chose to do themselves in the future, they were lucky—they knew how to be family.

Cindy moved slightly in his arms, wedged between him and Bobby on the snowmobile. She looked up at him, and she smiled.

She didn't try to speak, the snowmobile was making far too much noise.

He wished he could try to explain; he had been indignant, so certain that he had done nothing wrong.

And he hadn't. He just hadn't been there.

But the way that she looked at him then…

He brought his lips as close to her as possible, and whispered against the roar of the motor, "Cindy, I…

don't ever feel that you have to…to look at me that way or be too grateful… I mean, I know I wronged you, and I'm just so grateful that you're alive!"

"I *feel* alive right now," she told him. "And I feel that I'm *with* you as I haven't been in forever, Shayne."

He started to lean his head against hers. Then he heard his brother shout over the loud *whir* of the snow-mobile. "Almost there! Just one more bend!"

Shayne nodded. He moved his head enough to smile at Cindy.

"The kids will think that you're the best Christmas present ever," he told her.

She smiled.

Then Shayne heard Bobby shout, "What the hell?"

He slowed the snowmobile, but too late.

They hit something again, something buried beneath the white drifts.

And the snowmobile veered to the side—thankfully inward, toward the mountain—but then it careened into the pines, cracked against a tree and overturned.

"You know where you're going, right?" Gabe asked Morwenna.

She looked at him; it was bitterly cold. They'd already made the walk down, and made it through the snow. But it seemed that the going was rougher now. It was difficult to make sure that she was staying on the road, and it seemed that here, even more so than higher, the snow had collected in deeper piles.

She shrugged with a sheepish smile. "Down," she told him. She added anxiously, "They should be getting back up toward us, but I keep thinking we should hear the motor of that snowmobile—it's old, and it's loud."

"We'll catch up with them soon," he said.

"And how do you know that? And aren't you looking for DeFeo—not my family?" she asked him.

He looked ahead, and there was something grim in his expression.

Morwenna gasped. "You think that DeFeo is after my brothers! But, why? Why would he be after my brothers? Why wouldn't he just want to escape?"

"He wants to use them," Gabe said after a minute.

"Use them? As hostages? Gabe, he's unarmed, and my brothers aren't exactly puny!"

"He has his ways." Gabe looked at her then and sighed. "There are many things that you can steal from someone that aren't really tangible."

"That made no sense! What could he steal from my brothers?" she asked.

"Sorry," he said. "He might be after something extremely tangible—like the snowmobile."

She kept looking at him; he had changed his mind—regarding what he might have said to her.

"Gabe, what are you really trying to say?" she asked, and her concentration was so hard on his face as she tried to read what was behind his passive expression that she stumbled and fell into him, bringing them both down into the snow.

"I'm sorry," she breathed, pressing her gloved hands into the biting snow to rise above him, blushing.

He shook his head. "It's fine," he said. He stared up at her for a long moment, and there was something of wonder in his eyes, and then he sighed. "We need to move," he told her.

He laughed, getting his footing, and helping her to find hers once again.

"We've got to keep walking," he told her.

"We'll freeze," she agreed. "And we have to find them."

"We will find them."

"You're so sure!"

"Ah, well, you see," he said lightly, "I believe in Christmas, for all that it means."

"You're not talking about a lit tree and ornaments, are you?" Morwenna said, smiling at him. "You are sunshine and light," she added dryly.

"Ah, well, I know that it's sometimes hard to see, and often impossible to understand, but I do believe in a greater power, and I may be a cop, but I do believe that *most* people are inherently good. We have basic needs, and then we have wants…and then we have desires. We're easily hurt, and when we're hurt, we're defensive, and we lash out. There really are seven sins, you know," he said lightly.

"And we all, in some way or another, fall into them all?" she asked.

"Not all of us into *all* of them," he said, grinning. "And," he added, "Christmas Day is special in many ways. You know—if you're a kid, you wait for Santa. If you're Christian, you believe in celebrating the birth of the man who taught us that we could be saved from all the bad we can fall into because we are human. No matter how people see their faith, the world is really one big family, and they say, too, that it's a family above and below the world as well."

"Heaven and hell?" Morwenna asked him.

He grinned. "Think of it all as one big family. Except there was one child who was very, very bad in his behavior. He envied his sisters and his brothers, and he envied every other creature, certain that everyone and everything was loved more than he was. And so let's say his parent sent him to stand in the corner, and while he was standing in the corner, he plotted a zillion other ways to get into trouble—and to get others to get into trouble with him. Now, as badly as he might be behaving, like any child, he's still loved. But his brothers and sisters have to look after him all the time, and make sure that he doesn't hurt others or get them into trouble with him."

Morwenna stared at him incredulously. She laughed softly. "Okay, so we're all one big family. God and man and—"

"All the angels," he told her. "Those who are well behaved, and, of course, the brother who just can't seem to behave. But, you see, here's the good thing—as bad as things look, and as bad as they are at times, we do have Christmas, when we celebrate the fact that good will outweigh what's bad. Belief is the hardest thing in the world…belief in what's intangible, and belief in ourselves."

Morwenna looked ahead, and she didn't know why, but she was suddenly reminded of the scene she had seen on television. Mexico. Over a hundred million strong—and a country with tons of tourist cities. But Alex had managed to get himself captured—with Double-D Debbie—for a few seconds on camera. She had been hurt, yes. Hurt—or had she felt humiliated? Or was it both? Of course she felt hurt. *But had she known? Had she realized, when they couldn't come to an agreement over the holiday, that there was something that…that just wasn't there?*

And if she was so hurt, why didn't she feel it now?

Because she loved her brothers; her brothers loved her. And they were out there somewhere.

She turned and looked at Gabe and laughed. "You are one crazy policeman, you know?"

He shrugged. "Maybe. But I'm also a very lucky one today."

"Why is that?"

"I happened upon people who prove the point that decency and goodness can so often win out. Miss Mac-Dougal, I do indeed rest my point!"

She shook her head, smiling.

"If we find them," she whispered then.

"We will," he assured her.

"How can you be so certain that everything will be all right?" she demanded.

"Because of you, right now. Because I know that you won't stop until you find them."

She laughed again, with a dry note in her voice. "No, you don't know the mountains. Terrible things happen so easily. There are high ridges that fall straight down a thousand feet. When there's weather, there are horrible potholes that can wreck almost any kind of vehicle. And there's treacherous ice. And the weather is so cold—we can all freeze on the mountain."

He smiled at her again. "Well, then, I will have been privileged to have known you all."

She met his eyes, and she felt oddly warm and certain despite the cold. "No," she said softly. "I think we have been privileged to have known you."

He looked back at her for a long moment.

"Look!" Gabe pointed out. "Look—there are some tracks, and something…"

"Something what?" Morwenna demanded.

"Something heavy was dragged through the snow," Gabe said.

And it had been. There was a flattened path of ground ahead of them.

"Hurry!" Gabe said, and he started ahead of her, somehow making tremendous speed across the slick ground.

And then it seemed that the world around them groaned, as if there was a crack of thunder that had split the sky. The sound echoed and ricocheted through the trees.

"What…?" Morwenna began.

"He's found them," Gabe said grimly. "DeFeo has found your brothers."

Bobby had felt himself lose control; it had been like spinning on black ice…no, he had been spinning, but it's because they had hit something beneath the snow that shouldn't have been there.

The impact of the vehicle had shuddered down the length of him.

And then he'd landed in the snow, and for a moment, he was aware only of the cold, the feel of the air and the pain in his body. There was something on top of him. The world was white…

He was pinned beneath the snowmobile.

"Shayne!" He cried his brother's name. "Cindy!"

"Yeah, yeah…" Shayne said. "Cindy, Cindy…"

He felt his brother trying to scramble around him, pulling his ex-wife from the wreckage.

"Is she all right?" Bobby asked.

"I'm—I'm okay!" Cindy said.

"Bobby?" Shayne asked, rushing to his side.

"I can't—I can't get out," Bobby said.

"Can you feel your legs, can you move them?" Shayne demanded.

His brother was there, down on his knees in the snow, next to him. Bobby tried to wiggle his toes and move his ankles. He didn't think that anything was broken; he was just stuck.

"Yes, yes, I can move everything," Bobby said.

Shayne nodded. "All right, I'm going to try to move the snowmobile. And when I do, you have to wriggle out quickly."

"Gotcha."

"Shayne, what do I do?" Cindy asked.

"You can try to add your weight when I lift," Shayne told her. "Ready?"

Cindy stood by him, ready to lift.

But though Shayne was strong, and had Cindy's help, the weight of the snowmobile was just too much.

"Listen, you two just get back to the tavern," Bobby said, forcing cheerfulness into his voice. "Get help, and get back here."

"I'm not leaving you like this," Shayne told him.

"Hey, Shayne!" Bobby protested. "We can't all just stay here—where will that get us?"

"I'm going to get a pulley system going...we've still got the rope. Cindy, you should probably be in a hospital, but can you take the rope—you remember how to do the knots, right?"

"Of course," Cindy said. "Hey, I didn't spend time with Dad for nothing! I mean, your father," she amended quickly. "I've got it. I'm really all right, Shayne, I can help. Give me the rope."

"All right," Shayne said, pausing and looking

around. "There...walk over there. That tree looks good and sturdy and it's at the right angle...take that end of the rope, Cindy, and make sure it's a good knot."

Bobby heard the snow crunching as Cindy hurried off to do as she had been instructed. He watched as Shayne studied the snowmobile and the way it had fallen and then started to loop the heavy nylon rope around the snowmobile. "With the tree helping to create a lever system, we will get this thing up in no time," Shayne promised him.

Bobby was able to grab his brother's ankle. Shayne looked down at him.

"If you don't get this up now," Bobby said sternly, "you're going to take Cindy to the tavern, get Dad and Mac and come back for me."

"I'm going to get it up. What, are you kidding me? Can you imagine Mom if I come back without you? Don't worry—I'm going to manage this!" Shayne told him. "Cindy—"

Shayne went dead still, and quiet. Bobby tried to twist around and see what was going on; he couldn't.

He could only see his brother's face, and his features were knotted in a look of wary dread.

"What?" Bobby whispered.

But Shayne didn't look down at him.

Bobby heard someone else speaking, and he knew the voice.

Luke DeFeo.

"That's right, I have the pretty little ex-missus!" DeFeo said. "And nothing is going to happen to her. As long as you all play it right. I want that snowmobile. You're going to get it up and running, and then everything will be fine."

Bobby strained and twisted, trying to see around the snowmobile. He managed to wriggle enough to look around the front; Luke DeFeo had Cindy in a choke hold against his body.

"I know what I'm doing," he said quietly. "One wrong move and her neck snaps. And I still get the snowmobile. Are we clear?"

"Perfectly," Shayne said, ice in his words.

Bobby saw DeFeo smile. "Don't worry. I let her get a good knot on that rope before I nabbed her. Dr. MacDougal, now it's all up to you and your brother there. I want the snowmobile up, and I want it running, and when it is, I'll take your ex with me just down the road a hair, and I'll leave her for you gentlemen to find again."

Cindy was staring at Shayne, tears in her eyes. Bobby knew why she hadn't screamed; she was flat against DeFeo's back, and his arm was in a hold that prevented her from uttering so much as a squeak. She looked at Shayne with apology in her eyes, and fear that she couldn't quite hide.

Cindy hadn't even known about DeFeo! She hadn't known anything about the strange night that had passed, or about the stranger day that had followed...

The darkness was beginning to settle around them in earnest.

And with the darkness would come a greater cold.

"I have to get to the tree with the lever," Shayne said. "I'm moving, and I'm going to need to be there. I'm going to get the snowmobile off my brother, and we'll get it up together. Don't do anything. I'll get you the damn snowmobile."

"Fine. Do it," DeFeo said.

Something of a little squeak did escape Cindy as DeFeo jerked her back and away from the tree.

Bobby cursed himself for getting stuck beneath the snowmobile. If he had just realized what could have happened, if he'd have tried to jump clear...

Bobby saw as Shayne moved, delving first into the storage compartment for the lever. He then heard his brother's footsteps crunching through the snow as he headed for the tree.

He could barely see Shayne anymore, and DeFeo was caught in the crazy light that emanated from the headlight of the snowmobile. There was something not quite right about the man.

He could hear Shayne, struggling with the pulley system he was trying to assemble and work with the tree and the rope. His brother, he thought, had it rigged, and he was using all his strength to pull. The snowmobile seemed to ease up on Bobby; he tried to slip out.

His brother let out a grunt, having to stop for a minute.

"Or," DeFeo said quietly, "you could leave me to deal with this. Take the little lady up to the tavern— and leave me here with your brother. What a fix! Desert your baby brother. What should you do, Shayne? You've got about two more minutes to move that snowmobile, or I'll take charge in the way that I see fit."

"I'm not leaving anyone!" Shayne snapped.

"Then you'd better get going, right?" DeFeo warned.

Shayne faced him. "Really? Aren't you a bit of a fool? The minute you release Cindy, we'll all be right on top of you, you lying bastard!"

Bobby winced. He wasn't sure that threatening the man was the way to go. But Shayne wasn't going to leave him, and he wasn't going to let the man hurt Cindy. He was testing Shayne, trying to make him decide between the mother of his children and his brother.

"What do you care about the woman?" DeFeo asked him. "Didn't she leave you? Didn't she walk out on you, screw around with some other man using the money you worked for? The bitch is only here now because she couldn't stand you having her children."

"If you hurt her," Shayne said, "you will be a dead man."

DeFeo started to laugh. Bobby blinked. He looked so strange in the glow that was cast by the headlight. He seemed bigger than he had been. He seemed to radiate a strange smell so powerful that it even reached Bobby where he lay, caught beneath the heavy snowmobile.

It was something like the scent of...brimstone!

"Boy, where's the Hippocratic oath now?" DeFeo said. "Well, Mr. Moralist, you'll have to figure out something here, won't you? Your brother or your ex-wife, the precious mother of your precocious little brats!"

"I'll get you the snowmobile!" Shayne said.

"Oh, I don't know," DeFeo said. "Maybe I'll just take her with me all the way..."

His hold on Cindy must have eased a fraction.

She cried out, "Shayne, don't let him hurt Bobby, don't—"

The sound strangled as he clenched his arm more tightly around her.

Dear God, Bobby prayed. *What do we do, what can I say, how—*

He was suddenly aware of a rush of sound. And suddenly, Cindy was almost flying toward him in the snow.

DeFeo cried out in surprise.

And Bobby realized that someone had come up behind DeFeo; they had all been so intent on the interaction between them that none of them had heard a thing.

They hadn't seen a thing...

But someone had come.

Gabe Lange.

Morwenna ran as fast behind Gabe as she could. Following him, she had first gone dead still in horror. The snowmobile was on its side...on top of someone!

And then, of course, she had seen DeFeo's back. And she had realized that he was holding someone in a death grip. And she hadn't even had time to think.

Gabe had taken off.

And then he was on DeFeo's back.

She heard a scream, and it came from Cindy, who had been thrust forward, falling into a massive drift. While Gabe attacked DeFeo from behind, DeFeo reached around, shouting out in rage, grabbing at Gabe.

Morwenna raced toward the trees, finding a stick. She ran around in front of the grappling men and began thrashing hard at DeFeo with her haphazard weapon. He lashed out with a fist, and he struck her in the chest. She was stunned at the blow; it sent her flying back hard into the trees. She was aware of Shayne rushing by her, ready to join the attack, and then she was aware of Shayne again, flying by her as if he weighed no more than an Easter bunny.

She heard Bobby, roaring in frustration, unable to help. She saw that Cindy was up, crawling over toward

Bobby, and that Shayne was trying to rise, shaking his head, as if he could clear it.

She scrambled to her feet and looked around for a weapon. There was a huge tree branch by her feet and she went for it, and then charged in again, whacking at DeFeo—trying to make sure that she missed Gabe.

Except that she didn't miss him; she caught him in the arm. He bellowed, but he didn't even seem to notice her, so intent was he on DeFeo.

"Give it up! Give it up!" Gabe raged to DeFeo. "I've won. You're done here, you're done here! Give it up!"

Shayne charged in again, going for DeFeo's legs. He toppled the man, but Gabe went down, too. Morwenna grabbed her branch, trying again to get a good crack in on DeFeo's head.

She aimed well, and this time, she hit him.

She *knew* that she hit him.

But he didn't even notice. Even though the sound seemed like a shot in the cold air, *it didn't even faze him.*

She went to strike again, but to her amazement, both men were up.

"You've lost!" Gabe shouted again. "You've lost!"

But DeFeo didn't want to give up the fight. His face contorted in a hideous mask of rage, and he stared at Gabe, as if he *knew* somewhere he had been defeated, but he just couldn't accept that it might be so. He was going to lunge at Gabe again, but then another sound seemed to rip apart the crisp air and the icy mountaintop.

A roll of thunder. There was no lightning, there was no sign of a coming storm…

But the sky suddenly lit up as if the earth had spun

crazily toward the sun for one bizarre moment; then the sound of thunder roared again.

The night returned to darkness.

DeFeo turned, and started to run. Gabe tore after him.

"No, Gabe!" Morwenna shouted. "Let him go!"

Gabe looked at her briefly. "I can't," he said quietly.

He turned and ran after DeFeo. She saw Gabe catch hold of DeFeo again.

"Stay still—give in and stay still, please!" Gabe begged the other man.

It wasn't to be. DeFeo let out with a punch that landed hard on Gabe's jaw.

"No," DeFeo cried. "You have to win, and you know it. And I just have to escape you."

The man sounded almost gleeful.

Gabe twisted to secure the other man's arms, but DeFeo wasn't willing to give in. In the struggle, they began to roll. They rolled hard and fast, and she shrieked again in horror; they were rolling toward the ledge. She could barely see in the darkness of the night, but she could still hear the two and they kept rolling…

"Gabe!" she cried.

But she couldn't see the two men any longer; she couldn't hear them. There was no crunch of snow. There was no grunting, no sound of blows falling… nothing.

She felt Shayne behind her, setting his hands on her shoulders.

"Oh, my God!" she breathed. "We've got to find him."

"We'll go after him," Shayne promised. "We'll go after him. But we've got to work here first. And fast."

"Shayne—"

"Bobby is caught," Shayne said, and he looked into her eyes. "And…I'm sorry, Morwenna, so sorry, but if Gabe does lose…DeFeo could come back."

"Just get me out!" Bobby cried.

"Come on. Cindy—" Shayne began, spinning around.

Cindy was already waiting at the tree. "I don't even know what just happened. But we've got to get Bobby out from under there. And we're going to be all right. Come on!"

Morwenna looked at Shayne, and together they hurried to the tree. Shayne took the front position. Morwenna strained. Her muscles ached to the core. They strained and pulled, and slowly, with Shayne shouting instructions, they brought the snowmobile back to rest on its tracks.

She fell back in the snow, exhausted and amazed that Shayne's system had worked. Her brother walked to the snowmobile, hunkering down to help Bobby up. Bobby winced, trying to stand.

"Nothing broken," he said.

"The tavern is just up ahead. Take Cindy. Get her back to the tavern," Shayne said.

Bobby nodded, realizing that he couldn't help.

"Can you make it without the snowmobile?" he asked Bobby and Cindy.

"We will make it without the snowmobile," Bobby assured them. "You two need it."

Cindy nodded, hurrying to Bobby to lend support to help him limp along.

But, as Morwenna watched, Cindy paused, staring at Shayne with anguish in her eyes. She rushed to him, caught hold of his jacket, rose to her toes and kissed his lips.

And, if only quickly, Shayne kissed her back.

"We've all got to move!" he commanded.

Cindy nodded and ran back to Bobby.

Shayne mounted the snowmobile. The headlight was still on; he turned the key in the ignition and nothing happened. He turned it again.

And the motor sprang back to life. Shayne carefully eased it into Reverse, and the mangled machinery moved.

"Go!" he said to Bobby and Cindy. He looked at Morwenna. "Climb on!" he told her.

She did so quickly, and they moved on into the darkness of the night.

Chapter 11

Bobby's leg was killing him. He was sure that he hadn't broken any bones, but he had done some mean damage to himself.

He leaned hard on Cindy for support, and they moved through the night. He could hear the strain of his breathing; even in the dim light of the moon that shone down upon them, he could see the massive mist of each breath he took.

Cindy labored at his side.

"I'm sorry!" he said.

"Oh, Bobby," she returned. "I'm all right, really. I'm tougher than I look, and I was never really hurt badly. I was frozen…blacked out a bit, but I'm all right. You can lean on me."

"Maybe you should run ahead," he suggested.

"Never," she told him. "Bobby, I don't understand anything about tonight."

"I'm not sure *we* even know what happened," he said.

"That light…" she murmured.

"Strange, huh?"

"Very!" she said. Then she stopped in her tracks. "Bobby!"

"What?"

"I can see it!"

"See what?"

"A star!"

"What?"

She laughed. "I see a star, and it's actually the tavern! The electricity must have just gone back on. Look! It's all lit up, and it seems like a zillion colors are shining out—oh, it's the lights on the tree, Bobby. I can see the tree with the star on top! Look through the pines, and you can see the tree right through the window!"

He paused, and he peered through the trees.

And he smiled, unaware of the pain in his leg.

The star at the top of Mac's tavern tree seemed brilliant. It was a guide, and it was a sign.

They were almost there.

"Cindy, come on. Hot chocolate is so close I can almost taste it!"

They took the beat-up snowmobile around bend after bend.

And there was no sign of either Gabe Lange or Luke DeFeo.

Shayne drew to a stop, revving the motor as he tried to look around.

"Morwenna," he murmured. "We're not going to find them."

"No, no, no!" she said. "They've gone over the ledge. Oh, Shayne…"

"Maybe not, Morwenna. Gabe is a resourceful fellow."

"We can't give up! We can't give up."

"Morwenna, you can't go over the ledge. It's a far drop down."

"We can't give up."

"We have to. It's dark—the light isn't showing us much. They might be down over the ledge, but safe on some kind of outcrop. They might have wound up taking the fight up one of the slopes. They could have wound up in the trees anywhere."

He was right; she felt ill.

"Oh, Shayne!"

He turned and touched her cheek. "We could be heading for frostbite now, Morwenna. We have to go back. We need a helicopter, and we need light. We'll get Dad and Mac, we'll see if anyone has been able to get hold of someone who can really help," he said gently.

She nodded and leaned her head against his back. "Shayne, we tied him up!"

He nodded. "Yep."

"Genevieve never stopped believing in him."

"No," Shayne agreed. He cleared his throat. "DeFeo arrived in a cop's uniform, Morwenna. We had no choice."

"But he saved Genevieve's life. And then…he might have saved all of us."

"He did save all of us," Shayne said.

She nodded against his back. Her heart ached.

This hurt. This hurt in a way that was far worse than anything she had ever felt. It seemed silly and irrelevant that she had cared at all that Alex had been on a beach—chasing Double-D Debbie.

Shayne revved the motor and carefully turned the snowmobile.

When they finally reached the place where the fight had begun, Morwenna begged him to stop for a minute.

She crawled off the snowmobile and carefully moved toward the ledge.

"Wait! Be careful. I'll get a light."

She heard her brother swearing softly as he struggled to open the bent-up storage compartment on the side of the snowmobile that had hit the ground. She heard a wrenching sound as it gave, and then she was aware that Shayne followed her to where she stood with a high-powered flashlight.

Silently, they searched the terrain below them. The moon was casting a decent glow, and they looked and looked.

"Anything?" she whispered.

"No," he said.

"Try farther down, Shayne. Cast the light down."

He did.

But no one was there.

Shayne set his arm around her shoulders and led her back to the snowmobile. "It's good that we didn't find them, you know that, right?" Shayne asked her.

She imagined Gabe at the bottom of the mountain, crushed, mangled and bleeding.

"Yes," she said huskily. Silently, she crawled on the snowmobile behind him.

"Hey!" he said.

"Yeah?"

"The lights are back on at the tavern," he said.

"So they are."

Bobby wasn't sure he'd ever seen anything as beautiful as his mother's look of joy when he and Cindy stumbled into the tavern.

Ah, but maybe there was. It was Genevieve's face as she saw her mother.

"Mommy!" she cried. Delight in her voice. "Oh, Mommy!"

Genevieve threw herself against Cindy, who nearly fell over.

"Careful!" Connor cried. And then he was sobbing, too.

"I knew that Daddy would find you," Genevieve said. "I knew that he would!"

"I don't know how he even knew that I was out there!" Cindy said, accepting hugs from all around.

Bobby found himself crushed in a ferocious bear hug by his mother, and then his father. And he wondered if the way that his father looked at him with such pride and love wasn't one of the best gifts he'd ever received at Christmas.

Then his mother cried out, "Bobby, you're hurt!"

"Just a sore leg. My brother will fix it."

Stacy drew back, concern in her eyes again. "They're not here. Shayne and Morwenna. Where are they?"

Then he and Cindy tried to explain, each interrupting one another to add a detail.

"But—but they went to try to help Gabe. Against DeFeo!" his mother said, fear in her voice.

"They're on the snowmobile. They're fine. It's still working. And, Mom, honestly, I think that Gabe is going to rearrest DeFeo. I don't think there's any question," Bobby said.

Brian Williamson came over to them. "Bobby, get that wet coat off. Come on, everybody. These two need to be warmed up."

Mary jumped to at her husband's words, smiling as she hurried to put her coat on Cindy until she could warm up. Bobby felt himself divested of his wet snow gear and bundled into an oversize coat.

"My God," Stacy said, hurrying to the window. "Where are they? Where are they?"

Cindy walked over to Stacy, touching her gently on the shoulder. "Mom...I mean, Stacy, I'm so sorry. Shayne should never have been out. I don't know how he knew to come looking. I just can't believe that he did..."

Stacy turned to look at her. She reached out and drew her into a big hug.

"It's not your fault! It's not your fault at all for wanting to be with your family at Christmas. And you call me Mom forever, no matter what you two do in the future, do you hear me?" Stacy demanded.

Cindy nodded, tears in her eyes.

Mike walked up behind her, pulling her from his wife and into his arms.

"We are always happy to see you, Cindy," he told her. "Listen to your old dad."

Cindy started to cry.

Bobby felt tears welling in his own eyes.

"Now is the time for Irish coffee!" Mac boomed

out. "Stacy MacDougal, come back here and help me. Those children need something warm in their bodies!"

"Yes, yes, of course," Stacy said. "And we'll need to make two extra, because Shayne and Morwenna will be back any minute."

She walked around the bar to busy herself helping Mac.

The Williamson family stood near the window, watching, offering silent support.

Genevieve and Connor clung to their mother.

Bobby sat back in a booth, his leg up. His mother brought him the first steaming Irish coffee. He smiled at her. He sipped it. "They'll be here," he said firmly. He pointed at the star at the top of the Christmas tree. "It will lead them home, you'll see. The electricity miraculously came back on at the right time to see to it that the star leads them back. It brought Cindy and me in."

Stacy nodded. "Yes, yes, it did."

Bobby perked up suddenly. "Listen! Listen, I can hear the motor," he said.

"They're coming!" Adam Williamson said from the window. "They're coming!"

Stacy stood by Bobby, closing her eyes in gratitude. She looked at Bobby. "It's a beautiful sound right now."

Shayne slipped his arm around Morwenna as she crawled off the back of the snowmobile. She hadn't realized it, but her cheeks frozen on her face—and her "cheeks" were frozen elsewhere, as well. Without Shayne's arm around her, she might have stumbled.

The door to the tavern burst open.

Her mother and father came running out, heedless

of the cold, hugging them both and urging them into the warmth.

Morwenna felt like a star, friends and family everywhere, helping her off with the wet and on with dry, a sweater and a scarf someone had once left behind, and held in the tavern's back room in hopes the owner would return for it. Her mother held her hands in her own, rubbing them and warming them. Hot, stiff coffee was set before her, and her father listened while Shayne explained where they had searched, and that they hadn't found anything.

She tried not to cry.

She couldn't believe that Gabe Lange had been in their lives so briefly, and that she felt as bereft as she did. She wanted to pray that he was alive and was so afraid he couldn't possibly be.

She was vaguely aware of everyone talking as she sipped her laced coffee.

"DeFeo could still be out there," Mike said.

"You enjoy your family," Brian Williamson told him. "I've got the shotgun, and I'll be watching the front."

"And no one is coming in the back," Mac assured him. "Windows and doors are bolted."

"He's not coming back," Morwenna said. "Not unless…not unless Gabe is dead," she whispered.

"Gabe isn't dead!" Genevieve announced fiercely.

"Of course not," Morwenna said. She tried to smile at her niece. But Genevieve wasn't worried.

She was trying to reassure her aunt.

"Gabe isn't dead," she repeated. "He's going to find us all again." She pointed at the star. "He'll see it, too!"

"You're absolutely right," she told Genevieve.

She wished she believed it.

She leaned back again, taking a long swallow of the coffee brew. It was good. The alcohol warmed her to the core. It seemed impossible, but she was warm again. She closed her eyes, and she listened to those around her.

She could hear Bobby and her father talking.

"I'm hoping for Juilliard, Dad," Bobby said. "I'm really hoping. And I will work my way through it. I wouldn't drop out, I swear."

"Son, not that I don't have faith in you—I do," Mike said. "But—here's the thing. If it isn't Juilliard, we'll search. We'll search until we find the right school. There's Ball State University of Music. There's Harvard. And, son, you will get into one of them," he said firmly.

"Thanks, Dad," Bobby said softly.

She opened one eye, and was glad to see them at the next booth, heads together, close.

She turned her head around a little, and there was Shayne.

With his family.

He was seated next to Cindy. They were close. The kids were on top of both of them; Shayne held his son in his lap while Cindy held her daughter. It was such a perfect picture.

She didn't know if they actually would get back together. But whether they did or not, they would always share a very special bond now, she thought. And the fighting would all be over.

She closed her eyes again. She smiled. It was good. And yet...

Her heart ached.

Morwenna looked at the TV to distract herself. The television was still snowy, but a picture was starting to show.

A newscaster stood on a roadway. Morwenna could see the buildings around her and she recognized the little town just at the base of the mountain. The reporter was standing just outside the police station.

"Police have recaptured escaped white-collar criminal Luke DeFeo," she said, her voice cheerful. "DeFeo managed to escape during a prisoner transfer yesterday, midday. It's Christmas for the cops, too! The con walked right into the police station, half-delirious, and gave himself up. One of the state's finest, Detective Gabriel Lange, had been in hot pursuit—we have no information as to Lange's whereabouts, but rescue crews are out now, searching for him. In other news, despite the snowstorm, electricity is being restored to about five thousand homes, and in all, it looks like a white and merry Christmas. Over to you, now, Walter!"

"How the heck did the man get down the mountain so fast?" Mac asked incredulously.

"Really, that's just about impossible," Mike said.

"You think they got the right man?" Bobby asked.

"Yeah, they flashed his picture up there in the corner, didn't you see it?" Mac asked.

"Maybe he fell down half of it," Stacy suggested.

"Well, they have him, and that's that," Bobby said. He limped over to Morwenna and slid into the booth next to her. "Gabe is going to be all right, too, then."

"Sounds odd, doesn't it, Bobby?" she asked.

"What's that?"

"DeFeo handed himself in," Morwenna said. "He

handed himself in. That really doesn't sound like the guy who was fighting Gabe on the mountain."

"But it was him, Morwenna. And," he said, offering her a smile, "they will find Gabe. And he'll be all right."

She smiled, squeezed his hand and leaned her head back again. She fingered the little angel on her chain.

But it was bitterly cold out. He was on a mountain. He could have fallen. He could be somewhere with his leg broken, or worse.

"Morwenna," Bobby said gently.

She opened her eyes.

"They have helicopters, they have search dogs, they know what they're doing," he said.

She nodded again.

Something seemed to flash before her eyes. She turned. The star on the top of the tavern tree seemed to be glowing more brightly.

Electrical surge! she thought.

"Bobby, let's see that leg. Mac will have something. You've got bruised muscles or torn ligaments, baby bro. I need to get you wrapped up," Shayne said, coming over to assist Bobby.

"Yes, sir," Bobby said.

He kissed his sister's forehead, and went to Shayne to have the damage assessed.

Genevieve came over to her. She looked at Morwenna solemnly. "Gabe is going to be okay. I know it, Auntie Wenna."

She put her arm around the little girl, pulling her closer.

"I'm sure he is. He was telling me a little story about

the angels getting feisty at Christmas. And there's a fallen angel, you know."

"Lucifer," Connor said.

Morwenna smiled. Her nephew had come over to try to give her comfort, too.

"Right," Genevieve said. She was very grave. "Except that God loves everyone, even those who are bad."

"Fallen," Connor said, sighing with great patience.

Morwenna smiled. "When you get in trouble, you know your folks still love you, right?"

Genevieve nodded gravely.

Morwenna reached for one of the big white napkins in the holder at the end of the booth and found a pencil. She started to sketch for the children. "So, here, you see, here's Lucifer, who is like a bad child, trying to instigate trouble. Now, as you said, God loves everyone, no matter what, just like a parent loves a child, even when that child's behavior is not so good. But a parent knows when he or she has a kid who can cause trouble…" She paused, sketching an angel. "So he sends out a friend, or maybe even a sibling or a cousin, an angel who does behave, to try to make the mischief-making angel behave, and not hurt other people. Is that the story, Genevieve?"

"Yes!" Genevieve said. "Gabe was saying that God sometimes has to send out one of his good angels to make sure that trouble doesn't happen." She looked at her aunt in wonder.

"That's a nice thought, Genevieve," Morwenna said.

"It's a nice story! I really like that story!" Genevieve said. She touched the paper Morwenna had been drawing on. "You can draw in people," she said. "You and my dad and Uncle Bobby, Gram and Gramps, Connor and me. And maybe even my mom."

"Definitely, your mom, too," Morwenna agreed, and sketched.

When she finished, Genevieve reached up and touched the little gold angel that hung around Morwenna's neck. "We have angels," she said. "Good angels. Like Gram's little angel on her tree. I held it, and I dropped it, but I never broke it," she said.

"No," Morwenna assured her, hugging her again as she smiled at Connor. "You didn't break it—none of us broke what was really important today," she said. Looking over Genevieve's head, she noted the star on the tree again. It was odd how it seemed to be burning more and more brightly.

"As if it is leading someone home," she murmured.

"What?" Genevieve asked.

"Sweetie, let me get up," Morwenna said. Genevieve obliged, and Morwenna hurried toward the door, heedless of a coat or the cold.

The moon was out, and the glow from the tavern seemed to be lighting up the mountaintop as she burst out into the night. She saw nothing at first, and she felt the cold, and wondered if she was an idiot.

Then she heard a groan. She might have imagined it. But she hadn't.

She raced out into the snow, listening. "Gabe!" She cried his name, and ran along the edge of the trees. "Gabe!"

She heard something…a rustling. And then she saw the heap of a man in the snow.

She raced over to him, falling to her knees.

It was Gabe!

He lay as if he had been walking to the door, and then collapsed.

"Gabe! Gabe! Oh, my God, you're hurt, you're…"

She touched his face, searched for a pulse.

His eyes opened, and he stared at her. He stared at her without a single sign of recognition.

"Gabe, it's Morwenna. You're hurt. We're going to get you in. Oh, thank God, you're alive!" She couldn't help herself. She leaned in and kissed his lips, quickly. She moved away, just an inch, looking into his eyes.

She saw confusion…and yet, a strange sense of recognition. And she wasn't sure if she moved, or if he moved, but she found that she was kissing him again.

Or he was kissing her. And the kiss was good, and sweet, and natural. And if it weren't for the circumstances, she would want it to be much deeper, and far more…

Passionate.

But he had been hurt, and they were out in the snow, and others would be there. She broke away, touching his cheek tenderly. "I…" he began, but fell silent.

"It's all right. Don't try to talk. We're going to get you in, get you warm. Oh, Gabe!" she said. Tears stung her eyes. They were instantly like ice. She didn't care.

"I can't remember," he said. He winced. "My head…"

"May be a concussion," Morwenna said. "But it's all right. Shayne will know what to do. You're going to be all right. And I don't know how you did it, Gabe, but Luke DeFeo is in custody and—"

"DeFeo," he said. "Yes, I was chasing him and then…I don't remember."

"You were wonderful," she assured him, worried.

He almost smiled. He touched her cheek. "I know that I have been saved by an angel!" he told her.

She shook her head, clutching his hand. "No, *we* have!" she told him. She thought that she'd never really understand what had happened that Christmas on the mountain, and she couldn't help but wonder just what had been at play. Had she and her family been caught in a strange battle? A battle in which they had actually been given a choice between a fallen angel and a strange force for good that gave them back something special they had been missing as a family, and in life.

And now…

She smiled.

Was it possible? Had the angels taken on the flesh and blood of the men they had known in the last hours? And was the man she now faced in essence the same— but not the same at all?

She heard Shayne shouting to his father and Mac; her mother was out on the steps. They were all calling out with concern and joy that he'd been found. The church bells began to peal, and she remembered that it was still Christmas night, and the one service for the few people in the little mountaintop area would begin at eight.

It was still Christmas.

She stared down at Gabe, into the green of his eyes, and she realized that something about him was just a little bit different, and yet…

He was Gabe. And so much about him was going to be exactly like the man she had come to know.

Her family rushed around her. She was aware that her mother was scolding her for being out without a coat. Genevieve was hopping up and down, saying she had known that Gabe would come back to them.

Her father and Shayne got him to his feet. They started moving toward the tavern.

Morwenna followed, and paused, looking at the star on top of the Christmas tree through the tavern windows.

She smiled. "Thank you! Thank you so much!" she said, her voice a whisper in the night air. "And as Genevieve would say, happy birthday."

* * * * *

New York Times Bestselling Author

HEATHER GRAHAM

Enter a place of history, secrets...
and witchcraft, with the next chapter in the
Krewe of Hunters series.

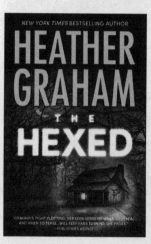

Devin Lyle has returned to the Salem area, but her timing couldn't be worse. Soon after moving into the eighteenth-century cabin she inherited from her "crazy" great-aunt Mina—who spoke to the dead—a woman was murdered nearby.

Craig "Rocky" Rockwell is new to the Krewe of Hunters, the FBI's team of paranormal investigators. He never got over finding a friend dead in the woods. Now another body's been found there, not far from Devin's home. And she's been led to a third body—by...a ghost?

Devin's discovery draws them both into Salem's rich and disturbing history. And as the danger mounts, she and Rocky begin to fall for each other. But the two of them need to learn the truth, and quickly—or Devin's might be the next body in the woods....

Available now, wherever books are sold!

Be sure to connect with us at:

Harlequin.com/Newsletters

Facebook.com/HarlequinBooks

Twitter.com/HarlequinBooks

HARLEQUIN® MIRA®
www.Harlequin.com

MHG1637R

SPECIAL EXCERPT FROM

H HARLEQUIN®

ROMANTIC suspense

Returning to Dead River is anything but welcoming
for Dr. Rafe Granger, who lands himself in the middle
of an epidemic…and discovers a connection to the
powerful Colton family he never anticipates.

Read on for a sneak peek of

COLTON HOLIDAY LOCKDOWN
by C.J. Miller

Dr. Rafe Granger would never escape this rotting purgatory.
His return had brought with it a terrible series of events:
an unidentified virus was claiming victims by the dozens,
the virus research lab had been trashed and a murderer had
escaped the local prison and was adding to the terror and
paranoia of every person in town.

Rafe entered the clinic through the single metal entry
door. The smell of smoke hung in the air. Behind the reception area, the clinic's patient files had been pulled from the
shelves and littered the floor. The culprit had done much
worse to Rafe's office and the lab.

Dread pooled low in his stomach. What had been taken?
The most critical work had been stored in the lab.

Rafe checked over his protective gear, pulled it on and
entered the lab, noting the lock was broken on the door.
Anger and frustration shook Rafe to his core. The inside
of the lab was a disaster—tables overturned, equipment

thrown to the floor and petri dishes and beakers smashed on the ground. But the most alarming thing was what had been done to the samples. The small refrigerator they'd been using to store the carefully labeled Vacutainer tubes was open and emptied.

Rafe let loose a curse he almost never used. This situation was beyond all repair.

He felt a hand on his back and whirled around, coming face-to-face with Gemma Colton, one of the clinic's registered nurses.

"Where are our samples?" Gemma asked, sounding shocked and panicked. Her green eyes were filled with concern. As many times as he had looked into those green eyes, the vibrancy and beauty of them struck him every time. "Who would do this?"

"Not sure. But that virus is deadly on the street," Rafe said.

"We already have an epidemic and now we have to worry about someone running around with vials containing the virus," Gemma said, her voice shaking.

Rafe heard shouts and banging from the clinic. He and Gemma exchanged looks. What else could go wrong?

Don't miss COLTON HOLIDAY LOCKDOWN by C.J. Miller, available December 2014 wherever Harlequin® Romantic Suspense books and ebooks are sold.

INTRIGUE®

THE NEW SHERIFF IN TROUBLE, TEXAS HAD A LOT TO PROVE. THE LAST THING HE NEEDED WAS A GORGEOUS CIA ANALYST GETTING IN HIS WAY—AT CHRISTMASTIME NO LESS!

Trouble's newly minted sheriff, Garrett Galloway, is determined to move on from his traumatic past. But when Laurel McCallister tracks him down and begs for help, he can't say no to the smart, beautiful CIA analyst. She's desperate to find the assailant who killed her niece's family—and now wants her dead.

On the run, Garrett, Laurel and her young niece escape to a Texas ranch, but danger follows. Garrett's courage lessens Laurel's initial distrust of the mysterious lawman, and sparks fly in the remote cabin. Now he must succeed for more reasons than avenging Laurel's family.

CHRISTMAS JUSTICE

BY ROBIN PERINI

Available December 2014,
wherever Harlequin® Intrigue® books and ebooks are sold.